Praise for *The Hollow Ground*

"Harnett's deeply atmospheric historical novel of the harsh old mining life captures the despair of a family at the mercy of the earth's elements and their own worst impulses."   —*Booklist*

"Brigid is no ordinary hard-luck heroine; her voice rings true, offering a matter-of-fact telling that never falls into self-pity or melodrama. Set against the 1960s Pennsylvania coal mine fires, this debut novel is a dark and rewarding read."   —*Library Journal*

"In 1960s Pennsylvania mining country, a young woman experiences the curse that's plagued her Irish-American family for decades. A murder mystery, coming-of-age novel, and family saga all in one."   —*San Diego Magazine*
(5 Books to Read This Month)

"The best novel so far this year . . . Harnett's pitch-perfect rendition of the coming-of-age voice . . . is achingly real, endlessly sympathetic, with just the right touch of childlike perception of adult truths. The 1960s setting is rendered with fine, original details. . . . a finely wrought novel with an original voice, a compelling story and an unforgettable heroine."   —*Providence Journal*

"In Natalie S. Harnett's accomplished debut novel there's more than a hint of Eugene O'Neill in this atmospheric meditation on the legacy of a generational curse once pronounced by an Irish priest on a Pennsylvania mining community. . . . In *The Hollow Ground* Harnett has written an impressively nimble debut novel."
—IrishCentral

"[*The Hollow Ground*] is being compared to *A Tree Grows in Brooklyn* and *To Kill a Mockingbird* so the story woven by Harnett . . . is not lacking for scope or ambition." —*The Irish Echo*

"Complicated family relationships mixed with the emotional aftermath of disaster and death are all shown through the eyes of the Irish-American preteen."

—*United Mine Workers Journal*

"A story of resilience well told. In Brigid Howley, the desperation is consuming." —*The Free Lance-Star*

"This cursed Irish-American clan will grab you by the brisket and not let go. Delicious reading!" —Gary Shteyngart,
New York Times bestselling
author of *Super Sad True Love Story*

"*The Hollow Ground* recalls nothing so much as the dark and powerful dramas of Eugene O'Neill. Cast in the surreal glow of mine fires burning out of control, its characters are both accursed and quirkily alive, with secrets from the past seeping into their lives like the gases that poison their homes. The voice of the innocent who tells the story is deeply affecting, making for a richly observed and moving novel." —Rebecca Newberger Goldstein,
Whiting Writer's Award winner and author of
36 Arguments for the Existence of God

"Natalie S. Harnett's *The Hollow Ground* is a coming-of-age novel, a murder mystery, a family saga, and an American tragedy of an environmentally and economically devastated region. But most of all, it's a painful and powerful story of love and survival."

—David Gates, Pulitzer Prize finalist and author of *The Wonders of the Invisible World*

"A grand achievement, a story fierce in its honesty about family love and betrayal."

—Maureen Howard, National Book Critics Circle Award winner

"Natalie S. Harnett in *The Hollow Ground* has captured the essence of the people, history, and culture of Pennsylvania's Anthracite Region, and how too often the small towns here, most notably the real-life Centralia, faced existential threats from coal mine fires that seemed to burn forever."

—David DeKok, author of *Fire Underground: The Ongoing Tragedy of the Centralia Mine Fire*

THE
HOLLOW
GROUND

NATALIE S. HARNETT

Thomas Dunne Books
St. Martin's Griffin 🕮 New York

THOMAS DUNNE BOOKS.

An imprint of St. Martin's Press.

THE HOLLOW GROUND. Copyright © 2014 by Natalie S. Harnett. All rights reserved. Printed in the United States of America. For information, address St. Martin's Press, 175 Fifth Avenue, New York, N.Y. 10010.

www.thomasdunnebooks.com

www.stmartins.com

The Library of Congress has cataloged the hardcover edition as follows:

Harnett, Natalie S.
    The hollow ground : a novel / Natalie S. Harnett.—First Edition.
       p. cm.
    ISBN 978-1-250-04198-2 (hardcover)
    ISBN 978-1-4668-3919-9 (e-book)
    1. Young women—Fiction. 2. Irish Americans—Fiction. 3. Coal mine accidents—Fiction. I. Title.
    PS3608.A7495H27 2014
    813'.6—dc23

2013046181

ISBN 978-1-250-06775-3 (trade paperback)

St. Martin's Griffin books may be purchased for educational, business, or promotional use. For information on bulk purchases, please contact the Macmillan Corporate and Premium Sales Department at 1-800-221-7945, extension 5442, or write to specialmarkets@macmillan.com.

First St. Martin's Griffin Edition: August 2015

10 9 8 7 6 5 4 3 2 1

For Mom, Dad,
and Chris,
with all my love

ACKNOWLEDGMENTS

My family went above and beyond to make this book happen. From endless support, to back rubs and babysitting—Mom, Dad, Erik, Chris—you never faltered.

For your generosity and faith, thank you, David Gates. Rebecca Goldstein, your encouragement over the years brightened them. Tad Friend, you've been so kind.

So many people at St. Martin's have been great: Joan Higgins, Laura Flavin, Jennifer Letwack, Erin Cox, Richard Tuschman, and Young Lim. Also great: Ann-Marie Nieves!

A thousand thank-yous to Toni Kirkpatrick for loving it!!! And for making this such a wonderful experience. Giant hug to Kent D. Wolf—awesome reader, dream maker—you *believed*.

So many friends helped to get me here: Ezra Cappell, Grace Cantwell, Val Matheson, Anne Foley, and, of course, my reading lab ladies. I'm forever grateful to Jerry Hughes's countless and careful readings. I'm also grateful to the Carbondale Historical

Society and Museum, the Lackawanna Historical Society, and the Lackawanna Coal Mine Tour. I could not have done this without Chris's and my mother's research, readings, edits, and love.

Come away, O human child!
To the waters and the wild
With a faery, hand in hand,
For the world's more full of weeping than you can understand.

—WILLIAM BUTLER YEATS

PROLOGUE

We walk on fire or air, so Daddy liked to say. Basement floors too hot to touch. Steaming green lawns in the dead of winter. Sinkholes, quick and sudden, plunging open at your feet. Where the hollowed out ground didn't burn, it collapsed or sank. Here is what's known as the Anthracite Coal Region of Pennsylvania, fed by the largest vein of anthracite coal in the world. That coal was blasted, hauled, breathed, and swallowed by our daddies' daddies and by theirs before them. And when those mines shut down, those snaking, black tunnels were left to flood—to shift. They were left to burn.

Burning more than coal, I'd tell you. When I was still curled and wet in my ma's belly, those mines burned my memory. Burned me with the want to see them for myself. To enter their long, sloping darkness and know what my daddy went through before whatever it was got broke inside him.

I'm not saying I knew what I'd uncover when I crawled and scraped my way into that narrow monkey shaft. I'm not saying

I knew the secrets I freed from there would change us permanently for worse or better. I'm just saying that sometimes what we seek is something we hope, with all our blood and bone, we'll never find.

PART I

1961

One

When Ma was seven years old her heart turned sour. She said it never turned sweet again, but I remember a time, long before the mine fires burned beneath our towns, when Ma's eyes glowed like sunlit honey, when her voice rose and fell as pleasantly as a trickling creek. While Brother was swelling up Ma's belly, or flailing around in the crib, or crawling on the brown linoleum of the trailer over by Mercher's Dump, we were happy. The thing that changed Ma wasn't there. But I remember the moment it arrived. Me and Ma were playing tiddlywinks at the kitchen table. Daddy was still in bed, watching us from his cot in the living room and telling a story about the tiddlywinks queen and princess. Back then I was so young and stupid I thought all daddies slept that way, separate from the rest of us, dozing till noon. Brother scribbled chalk on the kitchen floor, trying his best to make that cruddy linoleum look pretty.

Through the kitchen window came this light, the color of swallowtail or goldfinch wings. I've never seen a light like that again. It felt like it shot through the slats of my ribs, searing me with a kind of happiness maybe all kids feel 'cause they don't know any better. But then deep in Brother's plump little throat formed this squeal of delight. Within seconds he was up, standing all on his own, and charging toward us with his first steps.

Ma turned, spreading her arms, cooing like a mourning dove. But when he fell into her, sobs shot from her mouth like the fire itself had flamed up through the floor and singed the skin from her bones. I lunged from my chair and pulled the baby from her arms, thinking he'd hurt her. Which I guess he did. Because right then her eyes went from liquidy amber to the scratchy dull color of sassafras bark. Her voice ever afterward bobbed with nettles.

Whenever I reminded Ma of this moment, she said her heart forgot it was broken but then remembered. How can you make it forget again? I'd ask. Over and over, I'd ask. But her mouth merely pressed into that tight squiggle that made me think of the worms I dug up for fishing. The worms still lived after you cut a piece of them off. I guess that's how it was for Ma. A piece of her was gone and for a little while she forgot about it.

When I woke that February morning, the morning that changed our lives, the pinkish air pushing in the opened window told of snow. I snuggled closer underneath the covers toward Auntie and pictured the mine fire flaming along the veins of coal beneath our town, veins as numerous and intricate as the blue ones on Auntie's legs. The fire lived by sucking air through the ground and burping up gases through our walls. I sucked in and blew out to see my breath form a cloud, which made me think of the Holy Ghost. A white blob was how I pictured Him, a white blob hovering over the apostles' heads before burning them all with tongues of flame.

Auntie used to say the flames gave the apostles more than the gift of language, the flames gave them understanding. I thought if that was true, perhaps the fire eating the underground mine shafts of Centrereach was trying to tell me something—to give me its own kind of wisdom. I'm Brigid, named after Saint Brigid, who was named, some say, after the pagan goddess of fire. A saint who made the sores of a leper disappear. Smoothed the cracks in a madman's mind. A healer, like Auntie, though Auntie never allowed anyone to call her a healer. Something healed *through* her, she said, explaining that she was something like a messenger.

Groaning, Auntie sat up. She reached for a mug of water on the nightstand and with a spoon tapped at the film of ice that had formed during the night.

"Auntie," I asked, "how can you make a heart forget?"

Auntie took a sip from her mug, wincing at the sting of the cold water on her teeth. Slowly she shuffled to the closet where she stretched to unhook the shaggy bathrobe that hung on the door. As she slipped into the robe, a hidden smile tugged at the sides of her mouth. The story of "The Great Forgetting" was one of my favorites and Auntie savored the retelling of a town in the Carpathian Mountains where the people had been pillaged for so many centuries that they knew no joy.

Tugging the belt snug on her robe, Auntie spoke and as she did the white hairs on her chin glistened in the dresser lamp's light: "They prayed for years to forget the past until they no longer believed God listened. Then one day the youngest child in the village awoke to find a perfectly round egg in his crib. Word spread of this marvel. Within hours, the villagers forgot everything—not only their grief, but the curves of their beloved's face, their children's names. They stumbled through the streets, meeting neighbors, childhood friends, their very own father or mother, as if meeting that person for the first time. Their only memory was of the babe finding the oddly shaped egg. 'Don't hurt the child,' a big fat shiny black crow squawked."

Auntie bent her arms like wings and flapped them. We both smiled in pleasure. Auntie loved telling the story and the way she spoke I loved to listen. When Auntie came to America as a little girl, her grammar school trained the Ukrainian accent out of her, a different kind of forgetting. But if you listened carefully you could still hear the sounds of her first language lilting her words.

Auntie dropped her arms and continued: "But as soon as the snows melted, the healthiest of the young men carried the tot to a mountain crag. There, they left him to die and by the following dawn marauders conquered the village, slaying every person, young or old. Now only the story of what happened to the town remains."

Auntie touched one of the colorful wooden icons on her dresser top and made the sign of the cross backwards. Auntie was Great-uncle's wife and we loved her, but she wasn't raised Catholic. Daddy said that wasn't her fault because the place she was born was so horrible even God left it. But Auntie said her hometown in the Ukraine was a Garden of Eden until an iron curtain closed around it, making it impossible to go back. "They say home is where the heart is," Auntie often said. "That means I'll never see my heart again."

While Auntie rummaged in her top drawer for the heavy woolens she wore under her housedress, I charged out from the covers, reaching for my red woolen coat on the chair. Slipping into it, I waited for the magic of its heat as I stood by the window watching the early morning twilight give way to dawn. In the distance, hovering above the fields, was a mist that I imagined was the ghost of the family curse coming to get us, even though I knew the mist was caused by the fire burning beneath the ground. Thinking of ghosts made me think again of the Holy Ghost with its tongues of flame and I quivered with excitement at the thought that something important might happen that day.

Once the chill was off my skin, I crossed the hall to Brother's room. Brother's little body nestled cocoonlike under Auntie's brown and lime green granny-square afghan. With his back to the wall, his pink mouth sucking the cold air, Brother's slender face had a kind of sweetness to it that only little kids get.

"Come on," I said, kicking at the mattress. "Take off your pajamas and put on clean underwear. Then put on your clothes." If you didn't tell him exactly what to do, it was your own fault when he screwed it up. We'd all learned that lesson.

I handed him fresh clothes, then shuffled to the opposite end of the hall to peer into Ma and Daddy's room. Ma and Daddy slept with their backs to each other, aimed for escape, exactly the way all Howleys sleep. This, I thought, was Auntie's magic. Before we moved in with her, Ma and Daddy never slept together. But as soon as Auntie invited us to move in, she started brewing a remedy to sneak into Ma's and Daddy's morning coffee. Within weeks they started not only sleeping together, but eating together too.

Head cocked, I listened until I was certain I heard Ma's breezy sighs in between Daddy's rasps. Then I rushed down the hall to pound on Brother's door. "It's Saturday, stupid," I growled. "My favorite day. If you mess with me, I'll let you-know-who into your bedroom tonight."

I waited. He had a morbid fear of the boogeyman. Being a little kid, Brother believed the family curse made him more susceptible to monsters and ghosts coming into his room at night. I was five years older and knew the curse usually came from somewhere you'd never expect.

"Breakfast, Auntie," I called as I pounded down the stairs. I set the oatmeal to boil and by the time Auntie came down, I had her apple sliced and her hot water with lemon ready.

Auntie squeezed my shoulder. "What a good girl," she said, bending near enough so that her wiry hair brushed my cheek, the closest she ever came to a hug or cuddle. As much as I craved to be near her, Auntie's love didn't come by way of touch.

I poured Brother and me two glasses of milk and as we settled down to eat, Auntie told stories, real ones about gruesome farming accidents, starving winters, rivers that made towns into lakes. Stories from before she came to this country and after. Long ago, before World War I, Auntie married Gramp's brother. She married *into* the curse, yet you wouldn't know it to hear her tales of woe. Still, her stories usually ended with the town paying some cripple's doctor's bills or repairing some widow's house. "It was a time," she'd say, always with a whistle of regret, "when everyone helped everyone. When things were getting better, not worse."

After finishing her stories, Auntie left to deliver a remedy to the Clarks—our neighbors who'd nearly died from carbon monoxide poisoning while watching TV with the windows shut—and minutes later, Ma and Daddy made their way downstairs. Barely awake, Ma didn't even nod at me as she passed through the kitchen to step out onto the sun porch for her first smoke of the day. Through the glass door I watched her, the pom-pom on top of her striped knit hat bobbing, her long stringy light brown hair snagging the watery February sunlight and shimmering golden. Golden was the color Ma said her hair used to be when she was little, the color I always wished mine was. Mine was a color neither blond, red, or brown. Mouse color, Ma said. But I would have done anything to have hair the rich brown of the field mice who darted through our cupboards.

Daddy sat on one of the wooden kitchen chairs with his bad arm resting on the table. When Daddy was young his arm got smashed in the Devil Jaw mining disaster and it ached him ever since. When I pictured Daddy in that disaster I thought of the tunnel as a gaping mouth and the chunks of coal jutting like teeth closing down on him. Daddy's brother was killed that day and Ma said a part of Daddy died with him. I used to like to think about that dead part of Daddy and what Daddy would be like if all of him was whole and alive the way he must have been before the disaster. Daddy rarely talked about dead Uncle Frank or the disaster but when he did his eyes darkened over like dusk fell inside them.

That morning Daddy complained about the cold, wondering when the government would give us the gauge meters they'd promised so we could monitor the gas levels in the house and not need to leave the windows open. Then he nodded toward the porch and said, "Time to get moving, princess." It was in everyone's best interest for me to get Ma's breakfast ready fast. Ma was a heavy smoker and could barely function till she had her first smoke, but she was already coming out of her haze, sharpening her tongue on the icy air.

"Don't go giving her no swelled head, Adrian!" Ma shouted.

"She ain't no princess and the world won't treat her like one. You just make things harder on her thinking it will."

"Ah, what a bite on that Irish tongue," Daddy said, kidding because that tongue was nothing like it usually was, dulled by the nicotine coating her mouth and the exhaustion she always felt by the week's end.

Ma swung open the door and tramped to the table. Dutifully I heated up the pan, thinking how the way people liked their eggs matched their personalities. Ma all folded with the center golden part cooked and flattened. Daddy, raw and drippy, running all over with just a flick of a fork's tine.

"Goddamn it, Brigid," Ma shouted, pointing at where I'd glopped egg onto the stove. "That's what happens when you don't pay attention. When I was your age, they wouldn't give me nothing to eat for the whole day if I'd wasted good food like that. Accident or not!"

"Lores," Daddy said as if he'd swallowed the "Do" of Ma's name. Dolores means sorrow and Daddy always tried to take some of that sorrow from her and hold it inside him. As he sat across from her at the table, you could see it in him—the sadness with Ma's name on it. Brother probably saw the sadness too because he came over from where he was playing with his cars on the kitchen floor and nestled his head to Ma's chest, her breasts just as pointy as all the features of her face, and it struck me that this was all Brother probably remembered—Ma and Daddy joking and eating together. He was only six years old so he probably didn't remember the trailer over by Mercher's Dump or home being anything but Auntie's house.

I flipped two eggs and served Ma. Then I did Daddy's breakfast. The two yolks on the plate looked up at him like gleaming eyes in a ghost's face. Daddy slopped with his toast at the yolks, letting the yellow ick drip down his chin—a family joke. We always pointed and gagged, watching him perform this disgusting feat like he was a circus performer. This time he played it up special and my stomach clenched like so many fists. He was supposed to take Brother to Katz's Department Store for their end-of-winter coat sale, but afterwards he must have been planning to go to Pete's Pub. Ma must have been able to tell too because she said, "Take your time today, Adrian. I'm thinking of having some of the girls over to play cards."

I knew Ma didn't want Daddy around when her girlfriends came over because she was ashamed that he had no job, which was crazy because most of the daddies around had no job. I guess Daddy knew too because he said, "I'll take all the time I want." And then he looked her dead in the eye so she knew not to start with him. For me, I didn't mind if Ma had some of her friends over, even though it meant I'd have to clean up and serve coffee and cake. I didn't mind because while she was at work and while Daddy and Brother were shopping, me and Auntie would have the house all to ourselves. And whenever me and Auntie were alone together we'd sit on the couch, sucking on candies, Auntie reading her mysteries and me reading whatever historical romance I was into at the time.

When Brother and Daddy were finally ready to go, Brother swung open the front door and rushed out into a choke of cloud caused by the fire heating the wet ground. Daddy shrugged into his peacoat, grimacing with pain. When he got back home, I told him, Auntie would make him a remedy to get the damp out of his bones. "Okay, Daddy?" I said.

But Daddy said nothing. His eyes were that icy blue they got when they were looking off to that other place, the place that turned him empty inside. The place he thought he could fill with dice and whisky.

When he stepped out onto the porch, he turned first one direction, then another, squinting into the gathering fog like something was out there to get him. Brother beckoned from where he stood near one of the boreholes in the street, the long pipe smoking as it vented out of the ground. Brother waved his little knit hat that he'd crushed in his hand, but Daddy jogged down the steps, hands thrust deep into his coat pockets, and walked away from him.

Ma thrust her head over my shoulder and yelled, "And pick up some milk for god's sake," but her words sunk in the heavy air. Sighing the way she always did before heading off to the mill, she tilted her head. Gleaming in her eyes was something as timid as a baby deer. Every now and then the shy, tender part of her surfaced. "I know you want to go reading with Auntie," Ma said to me. "But don't forget your chores. Don't go having no fun first."

"Yes, Ma," I said, but as soon as the door closed behind her, I headed to the kitchen and brewed a pot of tea. When me and Auntie were alone together, before we settled down to reading, we always sipped a cup of tea and Auntie told me things she'd never told anyone else.

That morning me and Auntie sat on the sofa and sipped a peppermint tea that we'd picked and dried ourselves. "Listen now," Auntie said. "Remember our family picnics at Culver Lake? And the afternoons we all spent ice-skating on Adam's pond? Weren't they fun?"

I nodded. Auntie knew I loved it when Ma and Brother and

me hunted crayfish along the lakeshore or when Daddy and I skated backwards across the pond with Ma doing figure eights around us.

Auntie put a finger to her chin and looked off toward the window. From the way she opened and shut her mouth several times I could tell she was searching for the right words. "And then there were all the times when something good happened out of the blue. Like when your ma found fifty dollars just lying on the ground or when your poem was chosen best in class. You know what I mean? If you only think about what's bad, well then, life's bad. You see what I'm saying?"

I smiled and stirred my tea, tapping the spoon dry on the edge of the cup. I had no idea what Auntie was getting at, but I always wished to please her. I lifted the cup to my mouth.

Auntie continued, "I guess what I'm trying to say is that even though both my boys were killed, one on Okinawa, the other in the mines, I don't believe in the family curse."

Shocked by her words, I gulped the tea, burning my tongue. The curse was as real and basic as sunlight or water. I couldn't imagine our lives without it. Scalded, my tongue felt puffy as I said, "How can you say that, Auntie?"

"There isn't a family curse," Auntie explained. "Or that's not exactly what I mean. There is one. But it's not out there," she said, pointing out the window. "It's in here." She aimed a thick, slightly crooked finger at me and prodded my chest.

"Inside *me*?" I said, pulling at the cable knit of my sweater as if the curse was hiding somewhere underneath my clothes.

Auntie sighed. "Not just you. Inside each one of us. You see we make—" But Auntie was cut off by an explosion deep in the ground and she completed her thought by saying something in Ukrainian that I knew was a bad word because she'd said it before and would never tell me what it meant. The explosions were something we'd gotten used to because they happened sometimes in winter when the outlets the fire used for air froze over, but Auntie was clearly thinking about the damage the explosion might have caused. She stood and said she'd check on the shed that, with each explosion since Christmas, had started tilting farther toward the left, slowly sinking like an absurd shed-ship into the ground. I didn't see what the bother was. It was an ugly shed and we didn't even store anything worthwhile in it, but I'd learned not to stop Auntie from checking on it. That crumpling old shack meant something to her.

Not bothering with a coat, Auntie tramped through the kitchen and banged open the porch door. Through the little window over the sink I watched her walk the gravel path. Flakes of snow so small they resembled ash wafted down around her. I spread some of Auntie's elderberry jam on a heel of bread and stood at the counter working my jaw hard to chew it. When I next glanced out the window, the snow had so thickened the fog that I couldn't see a thing. Absently I began peeling the potatoes Auntie and I had planned to boil for supper. I'd been reading a book about Anne Boleyn, the second wife of King Henry VIII, who was said to have had an extra finger. I wondered if she'd used that extra finger for a special purpose, like playing the harp or picking locks, and I tried to picture the various ways it might have grown out of her hand—directly out the side or stuck like a twin to her pinky. I reasoned that if I were a king an extra finger would interest me since I'd probably be bored by everything ordinary. It wasn't until I'd nearly finished peeling the potatoes that I realized Auntie hadn't returned.

"Auntie?" I shouted through the sliver of screen visible where the window was open. There was no answer. The flecks of snow had thickened to flakes that had a tinge of yellow to them. The color was odd and pretty all at once and I couldn't decide if it reminded me of something sick or of something lit up just barely by sun. Dying light, I decided, remembering a poem Auntie had read to me. And then I got afraid.

Slowly I made my way onto the sunporch. With just a push on the back door, it opened wide and I gagged on the sulfur smell the fire sometimes caused. I stared toward the corner of the yard where the shed stood, but the air was so steamy I could only see a few feet in front of me. Fear cracked my voice as I called, "Auntie? I can't see you. Auntie?"

Cautiously I took first one step, then another, the fog growing hotter. "Auntie?" I called again, my voice now a squeak. I took a few more steps and then just stood there gawking at the gaping hole where the corner of the yard used to be. For what seemed like forever I stood there silent, when I could have been shouting for help, when I could have been saving Auntie.

It wasn't until flames burst up from the pit that the first scream escaped my throat. I screamed to Auntie, I screamed to the fire. I screamed so that God would have to hear, would have to listen.

I don't know for how long I stood there, but by the time a fireman picked me up, my mouth was as dry as dust and hardly any sound came out. "She's gone," he said. "The ground gave way." He carried me out the alley to the front yard, my skin singed from the smoke, my eyes stinging.

"My fault," I whimpered.

"No," he said. "There was nothing you could do. Hush now."

But I knew it was my fault. Already I knew. It was my fault because Auntie had told me the curse's secret—that it lived inside each one of us—and for that the curse had taken her away.

Two

Our lives were empty with Auntie gone. We felt the loss of her in everything and the whole world seemed more fragile and tender because of it. We rarely spoke of her though, which Daddy said was the Irish way. "If you talk about what's sad, all you do is make yourself sadder," he explained and so we didn't talk. We took what we could carry out of the house when the firemen let us inside to get what we needed (they wouldn't let us live there anymore because the ground was too unstable), and I think in a way it was worse having the house still standing there, filled with the memories and familiar musty smells that had made it our home. I guess we felt that we were as boarded up and condemned as it was.

"We walk on fire or air," Daddy would say when he saw the sadness dragging on us. This was something he told us whenever fate or the curse struck a blow. He meant it to prove that the hollowed out ground that either burned with flames or sagged into nothingness had given us a kind of magic—had made us able to survive what would kill anyone else.

"Tall tale-telling," Ma would call it, but she always said it with a smile and telling tall tales was another part of the Irish way. Though none of us had ever stepped foot in Ireland. But as Ma said, "Time sharpens some stuff." And I guess over the years of us living in America time had honed the bits still left Irish. I hoped time would do the same to my memories of Auntie until every detail about her was as clear and sharp as cut glass.

In the weeks after losing Auntie we lived in a hotel that the Red Cross paid for. We weren't the only family there who'd been displaced by the fire but we were the only ones who still slept with the window open, even though we were far on the other side of town, away from Auntie's house and the fire burning beneath the fields.

Ma and Daddy slept in the bed, and me and Brother slept in sleeping bags on the floor. Sometimes Daddy switched with me or Brother and he took the sleeping bag and one of us would sleep with Ma. My nights with Ma were the ones I liked least of all. Ma slept like a wild cat, clawing at the sheets, breathing in ferocious huffs. Sometimes I'd wake with scratches.

From time to time, me, Ma and Brother would go look at the house. Though it wasn't yet spring, all the daffodils and tulips Auntie had planted years before had sprung up from the heat in the ground and had colored the yard red and yellow. I remember the afternoon when we found two kittens playing on the front lawn. The kittens were mangy gray matted things, but they romped around, enjoying a rain puddle like there was nothing better in the world. I think it was right then, watching those kittens play, that Ma decided to accept Gram and Gramp's offer for us to go live with them. Something in Ma just kind of gave way and she leaned against the fence like she'd fall down without it. The usual tightness around her mouth softened and I guessed that was probably the closest Ma ever got to surrender. She didn't say anything but Brother and I both understood what had happened. We'd soon live in a house again and not a hotel room with a shared bathroom. We'd soon live in a town far, far away from the place that held our loss of Auntie.

That night after dinner at the Y, Daddy made his usual plea to go live with his parents and Ma acted like she was still dead set against it, once again referring to the fight she and Gram had had five years ago when they both declared they'd never speak to each other for the rest of their lives.

All I knew about that fight was that it concerned Gram's grandma's ring, a ring Gram had promised to give Ma on Ma and Daddy's wedding day but when the day of the wedding came, Gram said she couldn't find it. Ma wound up with a plain old silver ring as a wedding band and whenever she could, she'd wiggle that ring at Daddy saying she'd never be respectable till she had a proper wedding band. "Fancy, Adrian, with diamond chips. You know the type I mean."

As we sat at one of those long cafeteria tables at the Y chowing on franks and beans, Ma said, "I swore I'd never go in that woman's house again. Now what kind of fool would I look going back on my word?"

Ma turned to straddle the bench so Brother could sit between her legs. I sat next to Daddy. He had his good arm around my shoulder so I could lean against his chest. He didn't answer Ma. Sometimes your best offense against her was saying nothing at all.

"Even if I did forgive that old bat," Ma said, eyes narrowing, "why go to them? They got their own fire, don't they?"

Brother and I met eyes and smothered smiles. For Ma to even mention going meant she'd already made up her mind and was just making Daddy work for it.

"Who around here doesn't have a fire?" Daddy said and Ma couldn't answer. There were coal mine fires burning all across the state. The town of Laurelton had to just pick up and move with nothing left of the old town but some paved streets and stone foundations. Daddy added, "The Red Cross can't take care of us forever."

"No," Ma quipped. "That's my job, ain't it?"

Daddy flinched at her cruel tongue and talked about how we couldn't wait for the government to give us money for Auntie's house. "That could take months, maybe even years. You know that. And it won't be what the house is worth. Hell, how much could it be worth with a fire pit as a backyard?"

Ma talked a blue streak about the factories she'd heard were hiring in places like Stroudsburg and Mechanicsville. "We got options. That's alls I'm saying. Heck, I still got my job at the mill. Eventually we could save enough to rent somewheres."

"Children need a home, Lores," Daddy said and Ma squinted the way she did whenever something hurt her. She stroked Brother's hair, which was usually a wispy strawberry, but it hadn't been washed in so long that it just sort of stuck a greasy brown to his head.

"Don't worry, Adrian," she said. "I'll go and I won't say another thing about it, but don't try and pretend we're going 'cause we got to. We both know you been dying to go back there ever since we left. To the place where it all happened, where it all went wrong."

"Nah," Daddy said, his expression settling into the one he used when Ma said something too crazy to bother with. "You just watch, Lores," he said. "I'll give Mother a talking-to. Everyone will be nice." He took his arm from around me to reach across the table and touch Ma. "Everyone," he added and clamped his jaw to remind us of what he could be like.

By the following day Daddy had called Gram and the plan was set for us to leave Centrereach by the start of the upcoming week. Brother and I didn't mind leaving so much because the fire had already forced a dozen of our classmates to move and it made us feel better to be the leavers for a change rather than the ones left behind. Sometimes, though, when I'd recall the words Ma said about Daddy wanting to return to the place where it all went wrong, I'd get the kind of edginess I felt whenever the curse was near. It was then I'd occupy myself telling tall tales about Gramp and Gram to Brother.

I'd tell him how Gramp had been mining since he was a boy and that the black chunks he coughed up were the coal bits he'd held inside him for all those years. "Which just proves you can't escape your past," I'd say, repeating something Auntie used to say, "it chooses when to escape you."

I'd tell him that during World War I Gramp had been a sniper sneaking up on Germans and shooting them in the eye. That he'd slashed tires and people's faces and been locked up in the county jail, all in revenge for wrongs against fellow miners or himself. Then with my own hands I'd pretend-snap a chicken's neck and describe what Gram could do to various fowl. The more I spoke the more I scared Brother and the more comforted I felt.

"Come on," I said, tickling him while Ma and Daddy tried to pack all we owned into the car's trunk. "We want to go, remember? We won't have to share the bathroom with strangers and we'll have our own beds to sleep in."

Brother's eyes clouded with doubt. He folded his arms. "Want home," was all he said, seeing straight through to what each of us felt.

Barrendale, Pennsylvania, where Gram and Gramp lived, was nearly seventy miles northeast of Centrereach and as far as Ma was concerned, was a place as horrible as it sounded. The last time we'd been there Brother had been so young he didn't have any memory of it. I don't know if that made it easier on him or harder. As it was, I didn't remember much but a street in the town that was as steep as a mountain and a hutch in Gram and Gramp's living room that was filled with sparkling things I wasn't allowed to touch. Gram and Gramp were merely shadowy figures who said hardly any words to me at all.

As Daddy took Brother to the bathroom one last time, Ma told me, "Your daddy could stand on his head and juggle and Gramp wouldn't even notice or care. And that mother of his! You know what she said when Daddy's brother died?" Ma had repeated Gram's words numerous times but I knew she wanted me to listen fresh, so I said, "What, Ma?"

"'Shame the good one died.' That's what she said. Can you believe it? His own mother! And still your daddy wants to go back there. Worse, I think that's why he *wants* to go back. Because they don't care. Somehow he likes that." Ma pressed her lips together and bounced her head as if she'd just proved Daddy was nuts.

On the way out of town we stopped by Auntie's house and Ma said, "Just don't even think about it." And we knew she was referring not only to Auntie, but our move to Barrendale and everything we'd had to leave behind. "Auntie would want us to keep our spirits up. Both you kids know that. So don't go worrying about the fire they got in Barrendale." Ma turned to shake her finger at us. "Ever hear how lightning don't strike twice? Well fire don't neither."

But I knew lightning could strike twice; it could strike hundreds of times in the same place. It struck the water tower in Centrereach over and over.

"Off we go into the wild blue yonder," Daddy sang. "Come on," he said, catching my eye in the rearview mirror, pleading with me to help lift everyone's spirits. I joined in with "Climbing high into the sun." Daddy's next glance in the mirror was grateful and approving and we smiled at each other in our private, special way. Then we all sang "Go, Tell It on the Mountain" and "I've Been Working on the Railroad" as we watched the Pennsylvania countryside go from factories and stores to roly-poly countryside that went on for as far as the eye could see. As we got closer to Barrendale the road cut through high jagged walls of rock that were layered and raw and stuck all over with icicles, telling you just how ancient this countryside really was.

Daddy slowed for a turn and pointed at the lowest layer of rock. "Look at that," he said with a kind of genuine excitement we'd all learned to ignore. "Sedimentary rock. Formed hundreds of millions of years ago. We're seeing right back into time!"

When we neared the outer limits of Barrendale the road looped along the edge of a mountain and we looked down into a valley dotted with clusters of small towns. On impulse I belted out, "Mine eyes have seen the glory of the coming of the Lord," but no one joined in and we entered the city in silence.

Ma sucked her breath. "Place looks worse than I remembered."

Daddy didn't say anything, but he slowed the car and in the rearview mirror I watched his eyes shift suspiciously from side to side as if he thought he was being duped and this wasn't really his hometown.

Tree roots had pushed up the bluestone sidewalks on the narrow hilly streets and there wasn't an even space of ground anywhere to be seen. Steps slumped or tilted. Orangey brown bricks showed beneath the pockmarked, worn-out asphalt and heaps of slag were piled in abandoned lots. There were blocks of empty stores with their names faded from the brick and a grimness to the buildings that made the whole town feel deserted, which in a way it was. Back when the mines and canal and gravity railroad had been thriving, Barrendale had been one of the biggest cities around and the loss of what the town had once been was reflected in every alley and blank storefront.

"You just remember what we agreed on," Ma said to Daddy. "What you promised. We both get jobs and save every last penny. We ain't staying here a minute longer than we have to."

"Promises shmomises," Daddy said, beaming a guilty smile to show he'd been joking.

I was sitting behind Daddy so I could see Ma's profile in the passenger seat. She opened her mouth and from the way she held her jaw I could tell she was eager to say some sharp thing. But Gramp had said he was sure to get Daddy a job, so Ma was on her best behavior. Whenever Daddy had any prospects of work she had to at least give the appearance of listening to him.

We crossed a small bridge over a dinky creek that miles from there grew into the great Lackawaxen River. The bridge divided the main part of the city from the working-class neighborhoods. Many of the houses were narrow and wooden with their faces sitting smack up against the sidewalk. "Miners' homes," Daddy explained. "The ones the company owned." And you could just feel the oldness and all the living that had gone on in those buildings as if the wooden beams and shingles had stories to tell. Other homes had wraparound porches and picture windows and yards bushy with forsythia eager to bloom. Some of the lawns were already a spring green but others were the spiky brown of cut hay. Most of those dead lawns sported holes drilled, we knew, to flush out the fire, a treatment they'd already tried in Centrereach. Here and there between houses we could see West Mountain smoking.

"The fire is only on the west side of town," Daddy said to reassure us. "Mostly beneath the mountain. Far from Gram and Gramp's. And they've got it contained. Not like Centrereach." At Daddy's mention of Centrereach we all gazed longingly out the window as if Auntie's house might rise up out of the cool Barrendale air.

We turned up a long hill and entered a neighborhood where the houses were spaced farther apart. Some houses had gray-and-red-speckled shingles that were supposed to look like red brick. Others were painted white with dark green or black trim. They were all set back from the road with spacious front yards and graveled paths leading up to their front doors. There was something relaxed and well cared for in the tree-lined streets that made us all breathe easier. You could just feel that the fire hadn't touched here.

Gram and Gramp's house was at the top of the hill behind two enormous ash trees. Its shingles were painted yolk yellow and the wide windows of its closed-in side porch glinted in the sun. As Daddy parked in the driveway, he hummed, "Off we go into the wild blue yonder." Slowly we all got out of the car and then for I don't know how long just stood there, staring down at the trunk, which had been packed so full it had needed to be tied closed.

Eventually we heard, "Well, what are you gonna do? Just stand there all day?"

Startled, we turned toward the porch where we saw Gram hunched. The hump at the top of her spine pushed her head forward like a turtle from its shell. She swung open the door and gazed down at us from the top of the steps. Tightly permed pinkish blond curls haloed her face, which looked as dried up and crinkled as a peach left out in the sun. Coral-colored lipstick was caked into the seams of her thin lips and the whites of her eyes were webbed red. She had on a beige housedress with a pin in the shape of a peacock up by the collar.

"Good to see you, Mother," Daddy said.

Ma pointed at me and accused, "She's *your* grandmother. Say something."

"Hi, Gram," I said. I took Brother's hand. "Brother," I said, "this is Gram." Brother looked at Gram as if he expected snakes to slither out her ears.

Gram held a cigarette to her mouth and inhaled deeply, looking with distaste over first me, then Brother. "Who on earth else would I be?" She briskly turned, craning her head back over her hump, to say, "Come on and keep your voices down. Gramp's napping."

Up the stairs we went, Daddy and Ma pushing me and Brother in first. Inside the porch was a sofa and a bunch of wicker furniture that we walked quickly past to reach the living room where we found an orange plaid couch smothered in plastic and a variety of ceramic statues and doilies perched on the bureau and end tables.

Gram smashed out her cigarette in an ashtray shaped like a swan. "And don't you let me catch anyone smoking inside," she warned. "Gramp's lungs can't handle it." With her finger she swiped at the dresser top and then held her blackened finger up with disdain. "Just so you know, this filth ain't my fault. Blame all that flushin' and drillin', that's who to blame. Not a woman this side of town can keep her house clean." Gram clomped into the kitchen and washed her finger in the sink, leaving us to stand huddled in the entry between the two rooms, not certain where to settle.

"Well, Dolores," Gram said to the pink and purple violets lining the little shelf above the sink. "I'm lettin' you come stay in my house. You think you'd be the first to say somethin'. To thank me at least. Not to mention 'pologize for not speakin' to me all these years."

"Apologize?" Ma said, snorting a laugh.

"Now, now," Daddy said. "Past's past, right, Mother?"

"Can't argue with that!" Gram exclaimed.

Daddy looked at Ma, his brow creased in that firm look that often worked on her.

"Past sure as heck is past," Ma agreed as if the words were meaningless.

Daddy clapped his hands. "Now that's taken care of, let's get unpacked."

Gram pointed at me from where I stood in the entrance to the hall. "Girl, how old are you?" I hesitated and Gram said, "My Lord, are you a nincompoop?"

"Eleven," I said.

"Right on the verge," Gram said, as if I were about to hurl myself into a pit of evil. "Ain't fittin' for a girl that age to share a room with her brother."

"She'll share with me," Ma said and grabbed my arm, hustling me through the living room and down the hall. When we reached Daddy's old room that he'd shared with dead Uncle Frank, she pushed me in ahead of her and then loudly shut the door. As soon as we met eyes, we burst out in giggles. Then fingers to mouths, we shushed each other.

The room was fairly small, the walls painted the pale blue of a winter sky. Beneath a window was a dresser and to the right of that a desk. Up against the opposite wall were bunk beds. Ma sat down on a little wooden chair, lit a cigarette and inhaled deeply. From the proud glint in her eye as she exhaled, she was probably imagining she blew the smoke right into Gram's face.

On a shelf above the desk were sports trophies and photos of Uncle Frank as the county fair king, the dairy king, and of him holding the trophies that sat dusty on the shelves. I looked over the photos, having never seen a photo of Uncle Frank before. He didn't look like Daddy at all. Daddy had shiny black hair, but Uncle Frank was blond with a half smile that made him look like he had something on you, like he knew something you didn't. A devil-may-care smile, Ma called it. He was taller and broader than Daddy even though he was two years younger.

"People said he should have been a movie star," Ma said, "but I never thought he was *that* good-looking."

I'd often imagined Uncle Frank growing up with Daddy, going to work with Daddy in the mine, but he'd looked different from how he did in these photos. But as soon as I tried to remember how I used to picture him, I couldn't anymore.

Craning her head around, Ma took in the shelf of photos and awards. "Jesus Christ. Like a shrine to him," she muttered. "This is where they had us sleep after we was married. Can you believe that? Newlyweds in bunk beds! I still can't believe it."

Ma put out her cigarette by smashing it against the bottom of a paperweight and we unpacked what clothes we had into the dresser and closet. "Don't go making this out worse than it already is," Ma said, pointing at my mouth, which had slumped into a permanent frown. "We couldn't fit Lady Maribel in the car," she repeated yet again, referring to my porcelain-headed doll with the chipped nose that I'd had forever and that Ma had made me dump in a donation box. "And they got a library right here in town. I bet they got all the books Auntie bought you anyways. Don't you think I miss what I had to leave too?"

Ma twirled some of her hair around her finger and then nibbled on the end like a little girl. She talked about the favorite quilt and tablecloths she'd had to leave behind. "You might not see it now but we're lucky. We didn't have much to begin with. Imagine if you had a dozen dolls and a dollhouse and a doll carriage. You'd be missing *all* them, not just one busted-up doll and some books." Ma stuck her tongue out at me to get a laugh. She always had a backwards way of looking at things that made you think different.

Daddy and Brother moved their boxes into the basement

where they'd be sleeping on an old fold-out couch. "It won't be that bad down there," Daddy said to Brother about the basement. "It'll be like we're camping out or something. We'll make a game of it, you'll see."

We were all seated on the plastic-covered furniture in the living room and Brother started pounding at his head with his fist.

"What's wrong with this child?" Gram said.

"Nothing!" Ma said with a twitter at her mouth. Brother was going to be left back this year and his teacher wanted him to go see a psychotherapist, something we weren't supposed to tell anybody in Barrendale. Ma thought another year of kindergarten was just plain stupid and we all thought head shrinks were for sissies.

Daddy stood up and brushed at his pants as if they had a bunch of invisible crumbs stuck to them. "Want to say hi to Gramp?" he asked in such a way that we knew we'd better lie or not answer.

"Don't you be botherin' Dad," Gram said. "He's 'cuperating and you don't want to see his temper."

"We're not bothering him, Mother. We're saying hello."

Gramp sat in an old worn-out wing chair in the corner of Gram and Gramp's bedroom, his feet resting on an upside-down wastepaper basket. I remembered him as a big bulky man but this person was so bony and slender he seemed almost hollow inside. The skin at his cheeks and jaw sagged like a bloodhound. Asleep, he leaned forward and the tip of his tongue stuck out from his mouth and dribbled drool down his chin. His snores were rough and shook his whole body. One of the snores was so loud it shook him awake. He gagged and spit a blob of phlegmy gunk into a tin can between his legs, kept there for that very purpose.

The smell in the room was a mix of beer sweat, chewing tobacco, and pee. Overlaying those smells was the cloying sweetness of rosewater that Gram kept in a dish on her dresser. I thought back to the wooly mothball smell that had clung to Auntie and reckoned how much better that smell was to stinky rosewater.

As we stood in front of Gramp, Brother quietly whimpered, probably thinking Gramp was part monster, or part curse. As I stood there, I thought Gramp looked a million years old. He was older than Gram and had had another wife and family long ago. But that wife along with his twin baby girls were whooshed away in a flood. The fact that Gram, Daddy, and dead Uncle Frank were his second family was almost unbelievable to me, except that I knew it to be true.

I squeezed Daddy's hand and he squeezed back as he repeated to Brother, "What did I tell you about crying? What did I say?"

Pointing at Brother, Gramp said, "Boy ain't . . . make it . . . 'fraid . . . Grampa . . . cripessakes."

"Little dope's got his father in him," Gram chimed in from the door. "You were as much of a baby at that age, Adrian."

"But Brother looks like Ma," I said and this made everyone laugh, which hurt my feelings since I'd meant it seriously and I didn't see anything funny about it.

Gramp wiped the back of his hand across his mouth. "Boy know . . . family curse?"

Even though Brother could be shy, he got a mean streak in him when he was made fun of. His little Ma eyes got big and glossy and his mouth pouted red. He took a step toward Gramp and said, "I know it comes from you."

Daddy reached to slap him, but Gramp waved him off. "Curse come . . . great-great-grandpa." Gramp turned his head into his shoulder to smother a cough, then he continued. "Molly Maguire. Know they were?"

Brother clammed up and tilted his chin, same as Ma did when she felt insulted. I went on to brag about the Mollies, the people who fought for the rights of the Pennsylvania Irish mine workers by viciously attacking anyone who took advantage of them.

Gramp nodded, pleased, and I felt my cheeks flush with pleasure. Gram leaned against the door frame, arms folded. "Brown-nose, this one."

Gram and Gramp laughed. Worse, Ma and Daddy laughed too and I felt my eyes sting with hurt and betrayal.

Gramp gripped the armrests, trying to catch his breath. Some sun managed to streak through the curtained window and warm his forehead before getting shadowed out by Gram as she crossed the room to stand by Gramp. "You rest, John," Gram said. "I'll tell it." And Gram went on to tell about the priest, Father Capedonico, who told his parishioners in Centrereach that the Mollies did evil. "What that idiot priest was thinkin', I'll never know. 'Course the Mollies attacked him. What did he think they'd do? Thank him? So they waited for him one night and beat him and then you know what that priest did?"

Gram waited for Brother to answer but he turned his head stubbornly to the wall. Gram flicked his ear with her finger and Brother swatted at her hand like it was a fly. "Well, then," Gram continued, "I'll tell you what he did. He not only cursed your great-great-granddad and the other men who did the attack, but he cursed all of Centrereach. 'In a hundred years,' he said, 'not a single building will stand.' And with the fire they got burnin' there now, that part of the curse is comin' true. All you needin' to come here is proof of that!"

Gram looked at Daddy for confirmation, but Daddy hadn't taken his eyes from Gramp. The look on his face recalled how he'd looked when he'd stood on Auntie's back porch and stared out at the pit that had swallowed her.

Gram placed her hands on Brother's shoulders as if she expected him to turn tail and bolt. "But there's a second curse too," she added.

Gramp puffed and wheezed as he pointed from himself, to Brother, to me, then Daddy. "We're only ones alive . . . got curse . . . in our bones."

Gramp leaned back, breathing heavy and Gram fussed over him, but he waved her aside. Grunting, he leaned forward until his face was on level with Brother's. "Thousand time over—" Gramp launched into a coughing fit so hard he brought up blood.

Daddy finished for him. "Thousand times over your sins will be revisited on your descendants. That was that priest's curse." Daddy leaned toward Brother and wagged his finger. "But the Mollies did what they had to. Don't you ever forget that. They tried to make a wrong situation right. You can never judge a man bad for that."

"Ain't that the truth!" Gram declared and placed her hand on Gramp's shoulder, stroking him like a cat. "The thing to remember, boy, is the curse makes us strong. Other folks just live their lives with nothin' out to get them. But we live knowin' somethin's out there waitin' to pounce." Gram tapped the side of her head.

"And it keeps us sharp. Keeps us on our toes. Almost protects us in a way!" She grunted out a laugh and slapped Brother on the arm to get him to laugh too.

But Brother didn't make a sound. He leaned up against Daddy's leg and his lips scrunched like he had a bad taste in his mouth. I wanted to hug him but I knew Daddy would get mad that I coddled so I just said, "But the curse usually doesn't strike little kids, so you don't got to worry about it till you're all grown-up."

Brother's eyes widened, trying to search out the trick since I'd teased him so often about the curse being the boogeyman in his closet.

Gram sighed as if in agreement. To Ma, she said, "Don't know why you two ever moved back to Centrereach."

Ma tsked her tongue and left the room, leaving us all to share an awkward silence as we listened to church bells play in the distance. When they finished Gram said that they were playing for the funeral of George Malozzi, one of Gramp's old buddies, another survivor of the disaster. "We stopped in at the wake earlier. That's what Dad's restin' from."

"Sorry to hear that," Daddy said. "He was a good man."

"Not many . . . survivors left," Gramp said, shutting his eyes.

"The survivors of the disaster," I told Brother, showing off still with how much I knew. "The disaster Daddy was hurt in."

Gram continued, "Not everyone who should have showed at the wake did. 'Course the fire is what's on people's minds nowadays." Gram walked out and Daddy turned toward the window that framed part of a catalpa tree and a rickety old shed.

"I told Frank to get the men out that day. Told him it was a mistake." Daddy leaned with his bad arm on top of the bureau and his face went ugly with the memory.

"Hindsight twenty," Gramp said, opening his eyes with a sort of wince.

Daddy didn't speak for several moments. His jaw worked like he was chewing something gummy. Then carefully he said, "It wasn't hindsight *then*. At the time, it was foresight."

Three

I t took forever for the sun to finally set on our first day in Barrendale and I was glad to be given the task of helping Gram get supper ready, eager to get the meal over so that Ma and Daddy could go to bed and take with them all the unease they pretended they didn't feel.

I stood at the counter and peeled carrots, glancing through the window every now and then. Dusk seemed to be creeping up the hill, swallowing the last bits of light still drifting around the house. The front lawn where Daddy was pacing grew steadily darker and you could actually see the air turn bluer and bluer. In between the trees you could also see part of West Mountain glowing red and that red glow along with the blue air made an eerie backdrop to Daddy as he paced and smoked a cigarette. He didn't normally smoke and from the taut way he held his body I could tell his thoughts were onto something bad.

At dinner me and Brother devoured everything within reach except for the canned peas and Ma kept saying, "That's enough," and slapping our hands. Then she'd laugh. "They act as if they ain't never ate before."

"Right now," Gram said, "we got it to spare. But that won't last for long. Adrian, Dad put his good name out there for you. Jim Schaffer's grandson runs the shoe department at Kreshner's. He says he could use some help. It ain't much but if it works, maybe it could lead to more."

"Shoes? You mean dealing with people's smelly feet?" Daddy held his nose and made faces to make us laugh.

"Shoes is fine," Ma was quick to say. "Everybody needs 'em."

Through the kitchen entryway we could see Gramp seated in the Barcalounger in the living room. He hacked up something from deep in his chest and spit it in his cloth napkin. He had another napkin tucked in his collar as a bib and he sat with a TV dinner tray on his lap and a TV dinner steaming up into his face. He waved and pointed at something on the hutch.

"Can't believe I forgot," Gram said and she was quick to go to the hutch and retrieve a folded newspaper clipping. It was an article about the disaster, in memoriam of its fifteenth anniversary. Within it was a bio about Uncle Frank that mentioned his high school football achievements as well as the fact that he'd been elected a shop steward after being a miner for only two years. The article ended by speculating that he'd been found dead in a monkey shaft because he was probably trying to rescue one or more of his trapped men.

Gram stood framed in the living-room entryway and read it out loud. When she reached "one or more of his trapped men," she licked her teeth as if she'd missed a morsel of something tasty between them.

Ma said, "Ain't that nice."

Gram sat back down and spread her napkin neatly on her lap. "I'd say it's more than nice. I'm specially glad they mentioned he was a commemorated veteran."

"The word is *decorated*, Mother," Daddy said.

Gram stared at the space to the left of Daddy's head. "He was so brave he volunteered. Didn't wait for no draft." Gram made a sucking sound with her lips and her eyes shifted toward Daddy, then away. "There our Frankie was only seventeen years old, but lyin' 'bout his age so they'd take him. He didn't want to wait no extra year. That's a lesson you kids could learn." Gram shook her finger first at Brother, then at me.

"What the heck kind of lesson is that?" Ma said. "If he'd waited, the war would have been over and he wouldn't had to go."

Gramp grunted and gripped the fork with his fist, the way Brother still did, and shoveled into his brownie before he'd even touched his Salisbury steak.

Gram massaged the top of her hump and sighed. "Sometimes I wonder where Frank would be now. Probably havin' a big house like you see in those magazines. Maybe he'd even be in the movies and have a movie star wife!" The lines in Gram's face deepened as she shot a glance at Ma.

"For chrissakes," Ma said. "You act like he was a saint."

"Not in my house," Gram declared, pointing with her knife at Ma. "No one's takin' the Lord's name."

"For god's sakes," Daddy said. "Enough about Frank." Daddy pushed his plate from him and shut his eyes. "He's gone from us. Let the dead lie."

For dessert Gram served pound cake. She poured us kids two large glasses of milk and talked about the wonders of having a

Roman Catholic president, and an Irish one to boot. "Just shows how far we've come. From no one wantin' to hire us to being president of these here great United States!" Gram wiped a dusting of powdered sugar from the cake plate and said, "Just a shame 'bout his politics, is all. By the way, Dolores, I got you your old job back. Won't that be a kick in the pants!"

Ma shifted in her chair as if she *had* just been kicked in the pants. "Actually, I was hoping for something better."

"Who ain't?" Gram quipped. "I'm still there sewin' up side seams. I'll be watchin' you."

"I'll be watching you too, Rowena." And Ma said *Rowena* like it was a razor at the tip of her tongue.

"What happened to callin' me mom?" Gram said with a tight triumphant smile, like she'd just revealed some telling part of Ma. "But I guess mom's a hard word for you. I understand. I told you my mother was sent to an orphanage too. And she wasn't sent to no nice Pennsylvania orphanage. She was sent to one in Dublin where things was much worse than they ever was over here. Her parents had too many mouths, so they just stuck her in some orphanage. She was right 'round the age you was when your daddy dropped you off, Dolores. I told you I understand. You think I don't, but I told you before I do."

You could just feel the electric rising off Ma and I slouched in my chair, eyeing Brother whose face showed the same concern.

"Was my new stepma brought me there," Ma said. "Brought *me*. Not my little brother. Dirty bitch." And when Ma said *bitch* she said it straight into Gram's face.

"Not in my house," Gram said. "Filthy mouth."

"Enough, Mother," Daddy said. "Remember what I said about all of us getting along?"

Gram bit into some cake and chewed as if it had gone sour in her mouth.

That night I stretched out on the lower bunk. Ma didn't like the thought of having anyone sleep above her, which was why she took the top. We kept the desk lamp on because we'd gotten used to the neon light from the hotel's sign beaming in our window. In the lamp's light my eyes flit from the sag of Ma's rump above me to the picture of a werewolf taped to the wall by my head. The lower bunk had been Daddy's bunk when he was growing up so I was just as glad Ma had taken the top. Looking at the werewolf made me feel close to the boy who'd so many years ago ripped it out of a magazine and stuck it to the wall. I liked the fact that I'd have its steely wolf eye on me all night long.

Above me, Ma flipped through a *Reader's Digest*. "Can you believe they say a man marries someone just like his mother? A whole stupid article they wrote about it. I may not know much, but I know I ain't nothing like that old bitch." Ma flung the magazine to the floor. The mattress squeaked as she rolled onto her side. "Damn it, Brigid! Didn't I tell you not to leave that glass of water on the desk? I swear, sometimes I think you're retarded. Now she'll blame us for the dang ring it leaves!" Ma hung her head down to look at me. Upside down, her mouth and cheeks slouched.

Quick I got up and moved the glass from the desk to the floor. Standing there on the worn carpet I shivered, even though I wasn't cold. But I could just feel Ma waiting for me to get settled so she could start her nightly talking. At the hotel, Ma had gotten into the habit of talking to me before bed, telling me about some bit of gossip she'd heard or movies she'd watched as a kid. But that night, our first night at Gram and Gramp's, I knew Ma's talk would be prickly with all her unspoken concerns.

Gram knocked and opened the door without waiting for an answer, demanding to know why we'd left on the light.

"This room ain't familiar to us yet," Ma said. "We need it on."

"Scaredy-cats," Gram said. "First time you pay an electric bill you can put on any lights you like." She stomped to the corner, head thrust forward from her hump, and flicked off the lamp. In the dark she tramped out and shut the door.

Ma whispered that she'd turn it back on and a few minutes later she did just that. She rolled up one of her old hand-knit sweaters and placed it at the bottom of the door to keep all the light inside. "Alls I know is it can't stay like this. Not for long. You pray to Auntie." Years ago Ma had given up prayers, which included going to Sunday mass. "If God wants to see me on my day off," she'd say, "he can come and tell me himself."

Thinking of Auntie made me think of her all alone buried in the darkness of our backyard. Though we'd had a funeral, they'd never found her body and it still felt to me that she hadn't been put to rest. "We go where we believe we'll go," Daddy had said. Ma said, "*If* there is a heaven, Auntie's sure to be there."

I'd stashed a small brightly painted cross of Auntie's beneath my pillow and right then I pressed my head back hard to feel it. I tried to do what Auntie had so often told me to do, to feel the calm inside myself, but instead all I could think about was the curse's secret, that it lived inside us. In the past whenever I'd thought of Father Capedonico, the priest who cursed us, I'd see him as a short red-faced bulldog of a man and at that moment I imagined a tiny version of him creeping into my ear, trying to goad me into telling Ma the secret so then he could seek his revenge on me as he had on Auntie.

Ma climbed back up the bed ladder and flopped onto the mattress with a huff. She added, "You pray and we'll wait for a sign. Auntie will send it. She won't forget us. You pray to my dead ma too. Sometimes I think she looks out for me. Wherever she is, if she can help, I bet she will."

Then Ma went on to talk about the few memories she had of her ma who died when Ma was only seven. The way her ma spittied her hair with rags at night to make it curl. The way her ma made crowns of flowers with bridal wreath or Queen Anne's lace, buttercup or clover. "But," Ma said, "she also told me kids don't got headaches or problems. Can you believe that? That's something I never told you or your brother. If anyone knows that ain't true, it's me."

Eventually Ma fell asleep, but I stayed up after, listening to her breathe as if each sigh of her breath carried the clue to our happiness.

Four

Those first few days there, me and Daddy walked all over Barrendale. "Exploring," he called it, but "recalling" would have been the better word. He showed me a place called Devil's Well where the water pooled so deep in the river that a boy had drowned. He took me to the field that was no longer a field but a salt rock factory where he and Uncle Frank used to play ball. He pointed out all the spots known to have bootlegging holes, the holes people dug so they could get down into the mine shafts and steal as much coal as they could carry. Daddy was careful to let me know that the people were forced to do this because the coal company wouldn't give them enough work or pay to make a living. Meanwhile, he told me, there was still more than two million tons of coal unused beneath our feet. "What a waste," he said. "And they'd arrest you for taking it when they know there's more down there than they could ever use."

Most of the bootlegging holes Daddy knew about were off dirt roads up in the mountains and were so boarded up there was no way down them anymore. The entry to one of them was inside a cave and Daddy and I hunched outside of it one day and stared at the wood slats the cops had used to seal it off.

"One of Gramp's friends used to own this property," Daddy said. "We helped him dig the hole. In exchange he let us use it. I was only eleven at the time. Your age." Daddy looked at me with wonder as if how old I was had surprised him. "I didn't think of myself as a kid though. There were other boys my age helping out their dads. All the men had their hours cut. All the men had to figure out some way to get by."

I loved to walk with Daddy and think about the ground beneath us that was honeycombed with gangways and shafts and tunnels, the very tunnels Daddy had mined, the very tunnels I'd dreamt of all my life, wishing I could one day see them for myself. I tried hard to imagine a young daddy, a daddy my age, going down that hole in that cave with Gramp. If I pictured him hard enough, if I felt what he felt then, I'd get closer to his heart. I'd concentrate as if my life depended on it, as if my imaginative abilities could somehow prove my love.

During those "exploring walks" was the first time Daddy talked about Uncle Frank and when he talked about the places where they'd worked or hung out as boys, there was a rawness to his voice that was so tender and rough it made me jealous.

"Pity the good one died," Gram had said about Uncle Frank and I thought if I could be as good as dead Uncle Frank had been, maybe one day Daddy would talk about me like that, with an ache in his voice. And I pictured myself dead in a coffin in the pink dress Auntie had bought me with Daddy telling people how good I was, his voice all sweet with the sad.

On those walks, though, Daddy didn't just recall his own

memories. He talked about the original city of Barrendale that burned down in the great fire of 1850 and how the people came together to build it up again. He took me to a little knoll in the furthest part of the cemetery and showed me where some Civil War soldiers were buried and then he showed me a house with a busted-up widow's walk that had been part of the Underground Railroad. "When I was a kid," he said, "the rich old lady who owned this place hired me to set mousetraps in the tunnels between the walls where the slaves used to crawl."

We looked up at the house and then at the house across the street that had a portico with big white columns. We'd entered the north side of town where the rich people used to live and surrounding us were what had once been beautiful homes, most of them Victorian and Tudor and Queen Anne style houses. We shook our heads at the sofas and appliances left out on the porches to molder and rust. Garbage cans were tied to slate hitching posts. An air conditioner jutted out a stained glass window. Turrets capped houses that were so peeled and beaten it hurt to look at them, yet we couldn't stop looking at them. They had so much to tell us about what they once had been and what they'd lost along the way.

Daddy also talked about Barrendale before it was called Barrendale, when it was called Slocum Hollow. Washington Irving supposedly gave it the name Barrendale after being disappointed by a visit to the city. Somehow or other the name stuck. I couldn't get over that the town would give up such a beautiful name in favor of such an ugly one and I found myself saying "Slocum Hollow" aloud every now and then, loving the way my tongue shaped the words.

On some days Daddy talked about the Indians who'd called

West Mountain Black Mountain. "And when the men who started the Delaware and Hudson Canal heard there was a mountain called Black Mountain, they guessed there was coal there."

Daddy showed me the site near the courthouse where the first underground coal mine in the country was opened and he explained how the D&H Canal was built to haul coal from Barrendale to New York City. "They couldn't get the canal all the way to Barrendale though, because East Mountain was in the way. So they had to build a gravity railroad to get the coal over the mountain to the canal. You wouldn't think it to look at this place now, but up until the mines shut down it was like a little Philadelphia for all it had going on."

We'd wandered from the rich section to the center of town, which consisted mostly of empty storefronts and abandoned lots. High up on the brick buildings were the faded names of the stores that used to be there such as J. C. Penney's and Newberry's and Woolworth's. Every building we passed, Daddy could name what shoe store, or appliance store, or law office it once had been. Daddy told me that the D&H Canal Company was the first million-dollar private enterprise in America and that it was all due to the fact that the biggest anthracite coal vein in the world was right below our feet.

"We were a part of something, princess," Daddy said. "We helped make this country great. Don't you ever forget that."

We were standing outside a building that had an old Coca-Cola advertisement pasted to it. We gripped hands and a lady passing by smiled shyly at Daddy. "Handsome as Clark Gable," Ma liked to say whenever she reminisced and the love she felt for Daddy oozed out from whatever dark place she'd hid it.

Daddy's hair was as black and as shiny as the slag littering the lots and his eyes were what's called Madonna blue, the color of Our Lady's cloak. Daddy's what's called Black Irish. There's Spanish in his blood. Hundreds of years ago Spanish ships sank off the coast of Ireland and the Spanish soldiers, so in love with the Irish girls, stayed in Ireland—or so the story goes. Their dark-haired descendants became the Black Irish. Of course that meant I had Black Irish in me too, but wherever it was in me didn't show.

Those days our walks always ended in the fire zone, if ended is the right word. In a way it was what we were headed to from the start of every walk. The zone started about a quarter of a mile west of Gram and Gramp's and covered an area of nearly ninety acres. Surrounding most of the houses were a dozen or so holes that had been drilled to have silt flushed down them. Some houses were propped up from where the ground had sunk from the fire or drilling. On the southernmost edge of the zone they'd started digging a huge pit to try and stop the fire from spreading, and an entire playground had been condemned because the ground was too hot for dogs or kids to play. Here and there remained only a cellar door or a gaping foundation to mark where a house once stood.

Daddy didn't say so but I could tell the fire was much worse than he'd expected. You could see the worry pull creases at his brow like lines tugging on a weight too heavy to bear. "Don't worry, princess," he said. "They're going to spend three years and over two million dollars to dig this fire out. And if they're going to spend that kind of money they're planning to do the job right. They've declared the whole area a slum which means they get to wreck every house and dig down as far as it takes. Dig to the middle of the earth. Dig to China, if they have to."

He took my hand and squeezed it till I gave him a weak smile. "Now what would the middle of the earth look like?" he said and we made guesses to that as we walked all the way back to Gram and Gramp's, swinging hands, coming up with more and more fantastical ways to describe the earth's center, settling finally on a blue ball of ice, as clear and fragile as glass.

Five

That first week in Barrendale Brother and I dreaded starting a new school, but our first day turned out to be easier than expected. Since the school was located in the fire zone, nearly three-quarters of the kids and teachers were either waiting for their houses to be destroyed or were already living in hotels or with extended family. Us being the new kids barely went noticed by anyone but ourselves.

During those first weeks in Barrendale the best part of my day was when school ended and I went to visit Ma at the mill. I'd follow the railroad to the edge of town and I'd veer onto Stone Lane, a long narrow road that meandered along a cliff that dead-ended at the mill's enormous imposing doors. The mill was the largest building I'd ever seen, at least twelve houses wide and two high. It was made of bluestone, which gave it a shimmery bluish or gray quality depending on the light and the top of it was what Daddy called crenulated. I'd never heard that word before. All I knew was that the building put you in mind of a castle. It was easy to imagine it with turrets and a drawbridge. Sometimes when I approached it, the sun would be at just the right angle to make its countless windows glint and the sight of it would fill me with wonder.

Ma, though, I don't think ever had that feeling as she walked to work. Her station was on the second floor of a room that was maybe three times the size of the baseball field in the park. I'd walk up the side stairs that also served as a fire escape and I'd wave to Big Berta, the floor lady, who'd wave back, letting me through to where Ma sat near a window that looked out on tree branches. Sometimes birds flew in the opened windows and snakes dropped from the trees' limbs to slither across the sill.

At the end of a long row of women bent at sewing machines, Ma worked stitching the crotches of pair after pair of underwear. The noise of the machines was so steady it made even your blood thrum. "It gets inside you," Ma said matter-of-factly. "You can't escape it."

Feeling trapped by her work made Ma expressive like she'd never been before. I loved to come by and visit because each time she told me a little more about her life before she had me. It was like one of those children's books where you can slide a picture to the side to reveal another picture beneath it. Slowly Ma was pulling aside the surface part of her to show me a different deeper part of her that I believed to be truer. Just a week earlier she'd told me how after leaving the orphanage, she eventually wound up in Barrendale because she'd heard the mill was looking for workers.

"When I first met Gram I actually thought she was nice. That's how mean the orphanage nuns were. But I'll tell you what your daddy said to me. He said he didn't care that I came from no orphanage. He said his own grandma came from one and so he was orphanage trash too. And the moment he said that, well, I knew right then he was the one for me."

On the day Daddy started his job at Kreshner's department store though, Ma was cranky and out of sorts—more than usual. Just looking at her you could see the tension ready to burst out of her like an overwound spring. Before she and Daddy moved from Barrendale, Ma had been the best crotch sewer the mill had, but since then, she'd become slower. She couldn't see as well. Over and over she'd mention how she wanted to go back to hooking on the knitting machines back in Centrereach.

She talked out of the side of her mouth because she was holding two pins between her teeth. "When I met your daddy, I thought all I'd been wishing and hoping for was about to happen. He was the best-looking man I'd ever seen. Better looking than his brother, that's for sure."

Ma swerved her head to cut a steely glance at Gram who, hunched at her machine on the opposite side of the room, sensed it and looked up. Ma continued, "Your daddy paid me attention right from the start. He noticed the littlest thing I'd do or say. Then when your daddy's arm got all broke in the mine, everyone said I shouldn't marry him. We was only engaged then but I would have felt bad leaving him just 'cause he wasn't useful no more. Besides something happened to him down there. I don't know what it was. I asked him once but what I seen in his eyes made me never ask again." Ma gazed off toward the window and crinkled her nose in thought. "That's what surviving does. Puts something hard and mean in you. I liked that in him. That he'd been through something worse than me."

She pulled the pins from between her teeth to cough out a vicious laugh. Then she covered her mouth and we both looked over to where Big Berta stood, flicking her eyes away, pretending not to notice us. "I was so stupid back then," Ma added, "I thought living with Gramp and Gram would be like a dream come true. I thought I was finally getting a family. That's how stupid I was *then*, and now look at me."

She actually waited for me to look at her. Lines splintered out from her lips and the skin beneath her eyes was veined and yellow. I thought back to that day in the trailer when Brother plunged into her with his first steps and Ma looked like she'd been singed by fire.

"Here I am," she proclaimed. "Back exactly where I started— nowhere. All that wishing and hoping as a little girl turned out to be just a way to pass the time. You remember that, Brigid. That's what wishing and hoping gets you. Nowhere. I sure as heck re- member it every stinking day I walk down Stone Lane."

"Bah-bah-but nah-nah-not for long, Ma." I blinked and stam- mered, mimicking the way Daddy mimicked his manager, Mr. Wicket. I reminded Ma that Daddy said he'd be able to do his new job with his hands cuffed behind his back. "It's that easy, Ma. Daddy will have no problem with it. Auntie or your ma will make sure of it. You'll see. Soon we'll have our own house and you'll never have to work in a place like this again."

Ma slouched in her chair, softened by the prospect of every- thing she wanted. Then she told me about a time long ago when I was just a baby and Daddy had a job selling encyclopedias door-to- door. "He was so good at it they got jealous. They fired him, say- ing he talked too much. That for the time he spent selling one family, he coulda sold two or three. Your daddy's smart. I don't say that much, but it's the truth. I bet what he told those families was all sorts of facts nobody else would ever tell 'em. But none of that mattered. Getting fired took the last bit of oomph out of him." Ma's gaze flicked off Gram. "Don't tell him I never said it but he should of been much more than he is. And now he ain't done nothing in so long, maybe nothing's all he's good at."

Just then Gram interrupted by beckoning to me from the other side of the floor where the side seamers sat. Ma glanced toward Big Berta, stuck the pins back in her mouth, and through clenched teeth said, "You best move on."

At her sewing machine Gram hunched sewing the side seams on one pair of underpants after another. Next to her sat Edna Schwackhammer, Gram's closest friend. The Twit Twins, Ma called them or, depending on her mood, Twin Twits. Not that they looked that much alike. Mrs. Schwackhammer was tall and big boned and unlike Gram, who walked tilted forward from her hump, Mrs. Schwackhammer walked tilted to the side from a bad hip. But they did both wear large clip-on earrings and skirts and blouses that must have been a million years old and they had a way of looking at you that made you feel like you'd been judged and had come out poorly.

That day seated on the opposite side of Gram from Mrs. Schwackhammer was a lady I didn't recognize. She was young and pretty and looked like one of the seniors from the high school. Her lips and cheeks were bubble-gum pink. Her hair was the yellow of the inside of a peach and was swept up into a French twist that left little wisps of curls at the back of her neck.

Gram's hump shoved her head almost up to the sewing machine. She lowered the dark-rimmed reading glasses on her nose and ripped at a thread dangling from a pair of black underwear with the words "Little Angel" embroidered on its front. "This is Brigid," she said to the pretty lady. "The girl of my oldest boy."

"Ah," the woman said. "The son who was wounded in the mine?"

I smiled, pleased that she knew about Daddy. I thought of his hurt arm as a badge of honor. "He tried to tell everyone not to go in that day," I told the lady whose wide pale eyes opened attentively. "If everyone had listened to him it wouldn't have happened. I mean the tunnels would have collapsed, but no one would have died."

"The body of my youngest boy," Gram said, "was found down a monkey shaft. Nobody knows what he was doin' down there. They weren't minin' that shaft no more. But you can bet he was tryin' to stop the disaster. That he was tryin' to warn people. That's the type he was. Once he stopped a runaway colt at the county fair. Another time he got an entire stadium of people to follow him off the football field because he was sure a tornado was comin'. And boy did it come! Tore through those bleachers like they was toothpicks."

Mrs. Schwackhammer chimed in. "I swear, Ro, he was the most handsome boy from anywhere around. Both my girls mooned all over him. Violet sent him secret admirer letters for years."

Gram nodded. "I don't blame her one bit. Senior year, my Frankie was voted number one athlete. Wrestlin', baseball, football—you name it!" She turned to the pretty woman and said, "Shame you two never got to meet. You and him would have made a nice pair. Though of course now he'd be quite a bit older than you."

Gram sent me off with some money and a grocery list and as I crossed back through the room to the stair, I found myself wishing dead Uncle Frank was alive so Gram could see living proof of something Daddy often said, "The body wears down, but brain smarts last forever."

Outside the crisp air tasted of wintergreen and wet rock. Cardinals trilled and red-winged blackbirds called and the feeling of spring walloped me, as it always did, making me ache worse than I ever did in the fall. Which got me thinking of something Auntie used to say—that it hurts worse to open than close.

But that feeling of spring was quickly gone as soon as I stepped inside Kreshner's. The store smelled of damp wool and bleach cleaner and burned in my nose and throat. I didn't even have to look for Daddy. I could hear him talking from where I stood in the main aisle so I simply followed his voice to the back of the store where I found him explaining different grains of leather and the benefits and drawbacks of buckskin versus patent to one of the high school stock boys. The boy nodded and said things like, "You don't say, Mr. Howley?" or "That a fact?"

Several yards from them a woman sat waiting to try on shoes while her two little kids spread their arms and played airplane wars, crashing into each other and the chairs.

I waited by a display of rhinestone clips that were in the shape of bows and circles meant to dress up shoes. I spun the display case around, admiring the way the stones caught the dim overhead lights and sparkled.

After several minutes a man approached Daddy. The man's face was all red and bumpy and every time he talked he blinked his eyes. I knew from Daddy's description that this was Mr. Wicket, Daddy's manager, who Daddy called Mr. Shit-it. Daddy hated the way Mr. Wicket bowed and blinked to the customers as if they were royalty. "Obsequious," Daddy said about Mr. Wicket as if that were worse than being one of the perverts we read about in the paper who touched little kids.

Daddy was dressed in one of Gramp's old suits. His arm must have been bothering him because he held his shoulder up and his elbow pressed to his side. The stock boy retreated through a swinging door to the back room and I could tell Mr. Wicket and Daddy were exchanging words, though I couldn't hear clearly what was said because the two little kids were making sputtering crash noises.

Mr. Wicket pointed to the lady waiting to be served and Daddy pointed at the door the stock boy had just gone through. Mr. Wicket said something else and Daddy put his hand on Mr. Wicket's shoulder and pushed him back a step. Mr. Wicket's big brown eyes blinked slowly closed, then open. He said something else and Daddy turned from him and started walking toward me.

"Princess!" he loudly exclaimed and the sour look that had been on his face so quickly became one of delight that it made my heart hurt. He lifted a pair of clips from the rack and said, "What do you think of these clips? Pretty, aren't they?"

"Beautiful," I said, my voice thick with desire for them.

"Ma'am," Mr. Wicket said, bowing his head slightly toward the woman as he passed her on his way to us. "We'll be with you in a minute."

I looked up at Daddy in surprise. Daddy had made fun of Mr. Wicket's stutter so often that I was shocked to hear him speak with no stutter at all.

Mr. Wicket's face had flushed a deeper red than his pimples. "Mr. Howley, if you leave now, you come back a paying customer.

Your working days here will be through!" Mr. Wicket's voice went as high-pitched as a girl's and his eyes turned weepy.

"Then I guess I'm through," Daddy said as happily as if he'd wished Mr. Wicket good day. Daddy reached his hand out for me and I took it. Together we walked out of the shoe department and into the women's dress clothes, aiming for the door. Daddy blinked his eyes and mimicked Mr. Wicket, "If you leave now, you come back a paying customer."

My laugh was edgy and when we pushed through the doors I felt my insides turn as hard and blank as the slate on the walk. "Daddy," I said. "Ma—"

"Shh," he said. From his jacket pocket he pulled out the rhinestone clips. "They have plenty. They won't miss them."

He placed the clips on my opened palm and for a few moments all I could see was their glinting brilliance. "But, Daddy, are you fired?"

Daddy ran his hand through his hair, his jaw already bluish with growth. He stared ahead as if he was gazing for the first time on some wondrous sight but all that was ahead was a second-hand shop that had a scratched-up rocking horse and a ratty baby carriage out front.

"Daddy?"

Daddy turned to look back at Kreshner's. "Shoes," he said bleakly. "What a joke." He shoved his hands into his pant's pockets and started walking at a fast clip. Together we crossed the bridge into the west side of town and kept walking deeper and deeper into the fire zone, sidestepping cracks and dips in the street. A man called from the doorway of a shingled building that had no windows in it. In faded letters above the door it read The Shaft.

"Adrian. Hey, Adrian, I'd heard you were back."

Daddy waved and crossed the street.

"Buy you a beer?" the man said.

"Daddy, what about Ma? What you promised Ma?" I gripped the elbow of Daddy's jacket but he shook me off. "Please, Daddy," I cried. "You need to apologize to Mr. Wicket. You need to get your job back. Please, Daddy. For us."

The man pinched my cheek. "What's the problem, sweetheart? What's got you worked up?"

Daddy told the man he'd meet him inside and then he pushed me toward the dirt parking lot where someone had dumped a TV and an armchair. The blue of Daddy's eyes went as glassy and dark as night water. His fingers squeezed my shoulder until I imagined them touching bone. This was the part of my daddy I hated. The part that didn't love us and wished us harm. "Get on your way," he said, shoving me in the direction of Gram and Gramp's. "Get on your way and don't come back here again."

Six

The night Daddy came home from quitting his job, Gram and Ma sat at the kitchen table waiting for him, Gram sipping tea and Ma sipping a can of Schlitz, neither speaking to the other, but sharing a kind of general dissatisfaction. Through the window above the sink you could see part of West Mountain glowing red, matching the way Ma and Gram must have felt inside.

"Here you go insultin' the grandson of one of Dad's friends," Gram said as soon as Daddy stepped in the house. "When Dad spoke up to get you the job, no less! Always such a big shot with all your awards and nose in the books, but where'd it get you? Frankie would a taken any job he could get his hands on."

"Shut up, Rowena," Ma said. She stood and tossed her beer can in the sink where it rattled against some forks and spoons.

Gram's face went slack with surprise. "What on earth you stickin' up for him for?" When Gram said *him* she jerked her thumb at Daddy.

Ma stomped toward the hall and as she passed Daddy, her

eyes clouded over like frosted glass, the way they did if he'd lost a horse bet or spent our last bit of money on whisky. "Promises shmomises," she said so softly I barely heard it.

Gramp cleared his throat from where he slumped in the living-room Barcalounger. He waved Daddy toward him and asked what had happened. Daddy said that the little twerp of a manager wouldn't let him take any breaks. "He expected me to work straight through," Daddy said. "Who the hell is he to tell me when I can go to the bathroom?"

Gramp tilted the spit can gripped in his hands and pondered the gunk inside it. "If true . . . should punched . . . his face."

Daddy's eyes misted red as the fog clinging to West Mountain. "I just said it, so why wouldn't it be true?"

Gramp shrugged and hocked up into the can.

That night Ma had me pray extra hard to her dead ma and to Auntie. "Somehow we got to get out of here. Somehow we got to figure a way." And I guess the prayers I said for Ma were answered because less than a week later Ma had something happen she'd been waiting for all her life.

It was a Saturday. On Saturday mornings Ma and Gram worked a half day at the mill and I had a list of chores to do while they were gone. I hated doing them because no matter how hard I tried, Gram was never happy with what I did. There was always some streak she could find on the windows or floor. A powder of dust on this or that molding or lamp shade. But all the drilling and flushing only blocks from the house made it impossible to keep things clean, as Gram herself had admitted the first day we'd arrived. "She ain't a miracle worker," Ma would say and Gram would say, "You got that right!"

In addition to basic cleaning, Gram also had me help with

house maintenance and repairs. She had me cut up old dungarees so that we could go on the roof and patch it by spreading tar over the denim pieces. Together we removed the wooden window screens and replaced them with wooden storm windows. We painted the front railing, hammered down the loose nails on the porch stoop and changed the washers in the tub and faucets.

"See, girl," Gram liked to tell me. "With what I'm teachin' you, you don't need a man. In fact you don't need no one. I never let a sick husband or this hump"—she jabbed her thumb toward her back—"stop me from anything. That's somethin' your ma could use to learn." Gram would repeat this lecture to me often, ending it with a smack between the shoulder blades and a warning to stand up straight. Gram was convinced that she'd gotten her hump from slouching because her mother had made fun of her so much. "But what did Mama know about being a mama, comin' from an orphanage and all? You remember that too." And Gram would give me this telling look that I didn't quite understand and then inevitably complain about how haphazardly I'd washed the windows or hung the curtains.

Ma barely seemed to notice Gram's complaints about my work and I'd learned not to bother complaining to Ma about Gram's chores either. Once when I'd whined that the dust rags Gram gave me were either Gramp's old drawers or hankies, Ma said I was lucky that was my only problem and then she'd tell me how in the orphanage the nuns would make you sit in a corner with a dunce cap on if you didn't do your chores to their standard. When she'd talk about wearing that cap her face would glow with hate as if a bright hot light had been turned on inside her. I could tell Ma considered underdrawers and hankies luxury dust rags and thought I was just acting spoiled thinking otherwise.

That particular Saturday, by the time Ma came home, I'd finished my chores and Brother and I were sitting out on the side porch enjoying the spring weather. Saturdays were especially nice because there was no drilling or blasting. You could actually hear the breeze and the birdcalls and it was like you only right then realized you'd been missing them all week, which crazy as it sounded, made you miss them more. Brother was busy flipping through one of his favorite Superman comics and I was reading a book about Joan of Arc, eager to get to the part where she burned at the stake.

I was so into the book that I didn't even hear Ma come in the porch door. She walked in smoking and when she saw me she winked and started singing, "Somewhere Over The Rainbow." Me and Brother, surprised by Ma's good mood, stole a glance at each other. Ma's smile didn't even quiver when Gram came in and yelled at Ma to put out her cigarette. Gram took one last puff on her own cigarette before smashing it out in a glass plate she used as an ashtray. Ma took a long slow drag as she happily rolled her eyes at me.

"Rollin' your eyes like a little kid!" Gram proclaimed.

"I'll hold my tongue out of respect, old lady," Ma said.

"Fine with me. You got nothin' worthwhile to say anyways."

"Not to you," Ma said, her voice relaxed and playful, the way I hadn't heard it in years, and for some reason or other that unsettled something inside me.

Gram walked around the porch, inspecting my shabby dusting job. She asked how much brains it took to wipe up some dirt.

"What's a little dust?" Ma said, smashing out her cigarette. "Live a little, old lady. I ain't afraid of you."

"'Fraid of me?" Gram said. "Now look at what a fool you sound, Dolores. I'm talkin' about how to teach your child to 'complish a task."

"Complish shmomplish," Ma said and then we heard a sound like a cat hissing coming from somewhere on the front walk. We all turned toward the window and saw standing out between the two ash trees the crazy old lady who Gram had told us numerous times to ignore.

"What's she up to now?" Gram said, stepping behind an aspidistra plant and peering between its large leaves.

"Who cares?" Ma said, not even glancing toward the window.

The old lady was staring at the house and slowly shaking her head from side to side. Her hair looked like she'd cut it herself and its uneven gray locks were crushed where she must have slept on them. Her dress appeared to be stained with gravy, or something worse.

Brother and I knelt on our chairs, hands on the windowsill, leaning forward.

"Go away!" Brother shouted.

"Shhh," Gram commanded from where she stood frozen behind the plant. "Don't go 'couragin' her. Woman's crazier than a loon. Her son goes killin' himself and she blames us. When people can't find nobody else to blame they blame us. You kids remember that. We're what's called escape goats."

Brother's face went red with anger but I found myself studying the old woman with newfound fascination. I'd always known about our own bad luck, but I couldn't get over other people blaming us for theirs.

Ma tapped me on the shoulder and waved at me to follow her

into the kitchen. From her purse she pulled out a folded page of newspaper. She sat down at the table and whispered, "Here's our sign. Right here we got one. This is it."

"What are you whisperin' about?" Gram demanded, clomping into the kitchen. The hump pushed her weight forward and made her heavy on her feet.

"Don't you worry about it," Ma said. "Don't concern you."

But of course those words taunted Gram into peering over Ma's shoulder to see what was going on because as far as Gram was concerned anything happening under the roof of that house *did* concern her.

Ma pointed at a photo of a man and boy above a caption that read BOY HIT BY CAR SURVIVES UNSCATHED. I looked from the photo to Ma's face, which had turned as shiny and pinkish as a pearl. The tip of her tongue sawed her chipped eyetooth. You could feel the expectation all bristly on her.

"Can't you tell?" she asked.

"What on earth there to tell?" Gram said.

Ma raised her eyebrows at me, doing her best to pretend that Gram wasn't there.

I looked back at the photo again and said, "I guess the little boy looks like Brother."

Ma nodded, all justified by my answer. Then she pointed at the kid's daddy and said to Gram, "Know who that is? That's *my* little brother. Told you I'd find him. You said I never would but I told you." Ma said this like it was Gram herself who sent Ma to the orphanage all those years ago, and not Ma's daddy's new wife.

Ma pointed at the name, JEROME CORCORAN, below the photo and her voice got hushed like she was pointing at something sacred that belonged in the church. "And that's *my* real last name.

The way it was before the orphanage changed it to Coran. Can't believe I forgot it. All these years it was right there, at the tip of my brain."

Ma's eyes turned golden, like the creek water with sun on it. Her gaze swerved up and around my face, searching for something.

"Cors-or-ran," I said, feeling Ma's real name settle inside us.

"Cork-run," Ma corrected.

Gram leaned further over Ma's shoulder and squinted. "Just 'cause he looks like John Patrick don't mean he's your brother."

When Brother heard his name, he tromped over, looked at the photo and said the boy looked "runty" which was a word he'd picked up from Mr. Williamson, our neighbor across the street, who'd drowned the runt of his basset hound's litter.

"I tell you I remember the name," Ma said. "Now that I seen it, I remember it. Corkrun," she said and then carefully repeated, *"Cork-run."*

"Well, so what if it is him?" Gram said, stepping back and eying Brother who had his arm elbow deep in the cookie jar. "What you 'spect to happen if you find him?"

Ma didn't answer. She pushed back her chair and jostled me out the front door with Gram shouting after us, "Really, Dolores. What you 'spect to happen? Remember, once a thing's done, you can't take it back. Think, Dolores. Think before you do somethin' you'll regret."

Quickly we reached the point in the road where it turned onto the long crooked hill down to town. We were walking so fast we were practically at a skip.

"I forgot what he looked like too," Ma said. "But don't he look just like John Patrick? His name's Jerry, short for Jerome. I remembered that even though what I called him was Bropey. I used to cry at night, waiting for him to save me from the orphanage. But he was too little. Four or five when they sent me away."

Ma stopped short and jabbed at the tears on her cheeks with the heel of her palm. "Know what that bitch said to my daddy? 'The boy will be useful.' I heard her say it. And my own daddy let her take me away. Can you imagine a daddy doing such a thing? As bad as your father is—"

She didn't finish that sentence and we walked in silence to the library where Ma made a beeline for the phone books. In the Allentown phone book she found a Jerome Corcoran. She got change from the librarian and dropped dime after dime into the pay phone outside the library, telling me to dial the number because she was too afraid she'd do it wrong.

Slowly I dialed, double- and triple-checking each number to make sure I had it right. It didn't help that each time I let the dial roll back into place, Ma made a sound high up in her throat like a wounded animal. Eventually I completed all the numbers and me and Ma waited, staring into each other's eyes. Then Ma said, "Hello? Bropey?" I'd never heard her voice so broken and sad before. "Bropey?" she cried. "That you?"

But as Ma spoke I heard behind her words Gram's words: *Once a thing's done, you can't take it back.*

Through the phone booth's glass door I stared intently at the street as if by concentration alone I could control where we were headed.

Seven

Once a week I accompanied Ma to the pay phone outside the library where she'd call Uncle Jerry collect. My job was to come and stand guard. Ma never said who I was supposed to be guarding her from but I'd understood, without being able to put it into words, that those phone calls were as valuable to Ma as gold or treasure. While Ma stood there talking to Uncle Jerry, she felt like her words needed protection, even though mostly all she said was, "Yeah? That right? Don't say?"

Still, it wouldn't be long before Ma would cry out, "Oh, but this must be costing you a fortune!" And then she'd hang up, promising to call again the following week. Afterward me and Ma would split a vanilla cream soda at the drugstore and Ma's face would get all wistful and soft and I'd pray all the harder to Ma's dead ma and to Auntie that Ma would stay as sweet as this forever.

The mornings broke cool but the afternoons broiled to summer fast and the school year ended early due to the heat. Mrs. Schmidt, our history teacher, actually wept with joy, and that's the first time us kids realized that going to school in the fire zone was even more miserable for the teachers than it was for us. The heat did something to Ma too. As soon as we were out of school she declared that she deserved time to herself. She said "time to herself" like it was a right signed into the Constitution that she'd been denied. So on Saturday afternoons when Ma got home from the mill, Daddy would take me and Brother out of the house so Ma could be free to do what she wanted. I loved this time with Daddy because it reminded me of the "exploring walks" Daddy and me used to go on when we first moved to Barrendale. First we'd wander around the fire zone, passing by blocks where nearly every house stood empty, to blocks where the houses were so well-kept you could believe the rumors that there was no fire and the plan to dig it out was just a conspiracy for the coal company to get the coal cheap.

As a treat Daddy would take us into the air-conditioned space of Kreshner's where he'd dawdle, picking this or that up, to make it clear to Mr. Wicket that he'd returned and was not going to buy a thing.

Those afternoons with Daddy always ended at a bar, usually The Shaft. Me and Brother didn't mind it too bad though because Daddy never drank so much that he needed breath mints and he'd always buy me and Brother a root beer or a Coke.

The Shaft was deep in the fire zone, which meant that most of the houses around it were still standing. It was the houses on the edge of the zone that needed to be wrecked first since the trenches were intended to stop the fire from spreading. In those days at the bar the men mostly talked about the fire. They discussed the layout of the mine shafts and how they expected the fire to burn. They talked about how much money the dig out would cost and the impossibility to move anywhere else on the amount of money they'd get for their houses. They talked about the dangers of black damp and other hazards the fire caused and eventually they'd talk about Cuba and Russia and space flight and which Phillies players they thought were worth their salt.

No matter what they talked about the men always listened to what Daddy said like he was someone important. That's what struck me the most about those afternoons, seeing Daddy being admired the way I always knew he ought to be.

"Smartest in the class, Adrian. That was you," Joe, the bartender, liked to say. Joe always said something nice about Gramp too. One day he talked about the man Gramp had beaten up for sending the men into the mines the day of the disaster. "Broke a beer bottle right across his face," Joe said with as much excitement as if Gramp had done it only days ago and not a million years ago before I was even born. "That bastard never saw out of that eye again," he added. "Right? Right? Am I right?"

Daddy hesitated before he agreed and from the way his eyes got all distant I could tell he was thinking about something else.

"What did Gramp do?" Brother asked as he tried to jam a toy car in his ear to see if it would come out his nose.

"Stop that," I said, feeling a stab of pain, remorse I guess. Auntie had made me promise multiple times to take care of my little brother, and his not knowing about the family history I took as proof of my neglect. "He beat up the fire boss, Jack Novak," I said in a low voice. Jack Novak was a name I'd never said out loud before, though I'd said it in my head countless times, enjoying the rhyme. My tongue got heavy saying it out loud, as if I'd just spoken a secret or a curse word.

Intrigued, Brother paused with the car pressed up to his ear.

I continued, "Gramp beat him up to get him back for sending everyone into a broken mine shaft. For killing Uncle Frank. For letting him get killed in a shaft that the fire boss knew was dangerous. Gramp was protecting us, all the miners, by letting those mine owners know they had to respect us. They had to treat us right."

"So he killed him?" Brother's eyes narrowed and his mouth opened slightly like he wanted to taste the words I spoke.

"No," I said. "But I guess he was trying to." I took the car from Brother's hand, bothered that I'd never before thought that Gramp might have wanted to actually kill the man.

On those Saturday afternoons there weren't only men in The Shaft. Often there was a woman named Star, though Star wasn't her real name. Her real name was Beatrice Kittering. She was called Star because she always wore a star pendant around her neck that she liked to hold and rub between her thumb and forefinger as if good luck or a genie might spring from it. Her long neck and large bulging gray eyes gave her a crazed starved look that reminded me of the goldfish we'd had at Auntie's that froze one January morning in their bowl.

Star had a way of leaning in toward Daddy when she spoke that I didn't like. What I did like though was that, at least in the beginning, Daddy didn't pay her any mind. The first time I met her she said, "Why, when I was your age, I had such a crush on your uncle Frank. Remember that, Adrian?"

"Followed him around like a dog," Daddy said into his beer.

"Like a little puppy," she agreed. "Wasn't till I was a little bit older I also got a crush on you, Adrian."

I pushed up against Daddy's knee so that I could sit with my head resting on his shoulder and I asked Daddy if we could bring an ice-cream cone home to Ma. Daddy cuddled me with his bad arm and kissed me on the side of the head.

Star took a slow sip from her glass of beer. "So, what brings you back to Barrendale, Adrian?

"Dad took a turn for the worse," Daddy said, nudging me back toward Brother.

"Sorry to hear that," she said, rubbing her pendant and lowering her eyes so Daddy couldn't see what thoughts had floated up into them.

Sometimes Star was there alone, sometimes she was with Bear. Like Star, Bear didn't look anything like his name. He was skinny and barely taller than me, but he had a tattoo of a bear on his bicep. On his elbows were also tattoos but those were of webs, which Daddy said meant he'd been in jail. Daddy said this with a note of respect but there was an edge to his voice too. Gramp had been in and out of jail, sticking up for himself or the miners by busting up some place or person. "Disorderly conduct" this was called, but Daddy said there was nothing disorderly about sticking up for what's right. Sometimes Star would hang all over Bear and sometimes she'd act real cool to him and sit on the other side of the bar and tell Joe to tell Bear that she wasn't going to talk to him for the rest of the afternoon.

One of those Saturday afternoons Star offered Brother some Mary Jane candies she'd pulled from her purse. When Brother reached for one she cuddled him up to her breasts and said how she hoped one day to have one as cute as this. Brother took the hug for about three seconds and then shoved off of her with a push.

"John Patrick," Daddy growled.

"It's all right," Star said, forcing a laugh. "Boys are boys, after all."

That day an old man was seated at the bar. He looked at least as old as Gramp and he spoke with a backwoods accent that made him hard to understand. His name was Caleb Delling and as soon as he caught Daddy's eye he started to reminisce about the disaster.

"Saw the rats running by me," Mr. Delling said.

"We'd been noticing the wood beams sagging for weeks," another man said to Daddy. "Didn't you tell them that? But didn't they send us in anyway?"

"What choice did we have but to go?" Mr. Delling said. "With them cutting us a day or two a week, we needed any work they'd give us."

"That day I told Frank to get the men out," Daddy said. "Then there was this tremor and I said, 'Frankie we got to get the men out.' But don't you know, he went deeper in."

"Must have been looking for someone," Mr. Delling said. "That's why he wound up where he was."

"He was looking for trouble," Daddy said.

"Wasn't he always," Joe said.

Daddy continued, "With the next tremor, I raced to the hoist, but then I heard someone shouting."

"The way I recall it," Mr. Delling said, "the hoist didn't work. That's why we lost so many men."

"Yeah," Daddy said, "but I didn't know that yet. So I went back to where I'd heard the call. That's when the beam came down on my shoulder and crushed my arm. I don't even know how I got us out of Devil Jaw and into colliery nine. But by the third tremor, I was out."

"I was with your dad, Adrian," the other old man said. "By the third tremor we were out. He didn't know where you two boys were except that you'd both been farther down, in the worst of it."

The sirens from a fire truck grew, then faded, and everyone stopped talking. In the quiet a cardinal's tweets could be heard through the open door. I didn't want to think about Daddy being in the mine that day. I couldn't stand the thought of him down there, knowing the ground perched above him was about to fall.

Star must have been thinking of Daddy too because she said, "Can't imagine what it was like for all you down there." But when she said "you" she looked at Daddy and shivered.

Bear squeezed the shell of a peanut until the peanut popped out. Then he reached into the bowl for another nut and squeezed that one too. "You Howleys always thought you were God's gift. You and your brother. But look at you." He nodded his chin at Daddy. "Vala-freaking-dictorian. But you didn't turn out to be much at all."

No one spoke. Mr. Delling wiped a cold bottle of beer across his forehead.

Daddy took a slow swig from his own beer bottle, then held it in front of his face as if he was trying to see something inside it. His glance grazed mine, then stuck on Bear. Instinctively I stepped backwards, thinking of Gramp bashing a bottle across that fire boss's face. But all Daddy did was place the bottle down and turn to Star who was standing next to him.

Daddy put his hand on Star's waist, pulled her to him, and kissed her right on the mouth. Afterward he said, "You got that right. Didn't turn out to be much at all."

Joe was quick to offer drinks on the house.

"Now, Bear," Star said lamely as if she were trying to command a dog she knew wouldn't listen. She ran a hand over her bouffant hairdo and grabbed the pendant that hung between her breasts.

"Don't worry," Bear said with a laugh, cracking the shells of several peanuts by squeezing them in his fist. "He ain't worth the bother."

Daddy didn't say anything. He merely motioned to Joe for another beer. But then after that beer he ordered another and another. He drank so much he forgot me and Brother were there and eventually we had to walk home without him so we wouldn't be late for supper.

Eight

During the early part of that summer I spent much of my time reading. The house, stuffy and dark with Gramp's sickness, became a place to escape so I often read outside. Some of my favorite haunts were the shores of the local ponds where I could cool my feet in the shallows that were green and purple with pickerelweed. But I also liked to spend time in the church.

Saint Barbara's Roman Catholic Church was built of gray stone and erected in 1829 when the canal and gravity railroad were being built. It towered partway up a hillside, looking like the back of it had been wedged into the mountain and being partway up the mountain had protected it against the great fire of 1850 and countless floods and tornadoes. To me, that gave it a true feeling of sanctuary and I especially loved being there in the late afternoon when the sun through the stained glass windows sent swaths of ruby and golden light across the wooden pews, the heat making the benches smell woodier. Sometimes that waxy wood smell got so far up into my nose that I could taste it.

Daddy said people got the idea for stained glass by looking at trees that were backdropped by the setting sun, the crisscrossed tree branches framing oddly shaped patches of reddish amber light. Whenever I saw bare trees from a distance I thought of stained glass and whenever I looked at stained glass, I thought of trees. The stained glass windows in Saint Barbara's all depicted saints, each saint representing the type of people who'd worked digging the canals and mines. There was Saint Patrick for the Irish, Saint Anthony for the Italians, Saint Adalbert for the Polish, Saint George for the English, Saint Joan of Arc for the French. There were far more men saints than women and they all just stood there, draped in robes of various colors, staring out blankly as if there was nothing in all the world for them to see.

Saint Barbara was the patron saint of prisoners, artillerymen, and of miners. She was also the saint to turn to during thunderstorms or fires. I supposed if she could be the patron saint of a prisoner, then she could also be the saint of the cursed. So whenever I went into that church I prayed especially hard to her. Ma had only married into the curse, so she shouldn't be as cursed as Daddy, Brother, and me, but I often found myself praying twice as hard for her.

That summer I'd made it my goal to read all of the Nancy Drews. I'd already read all the books that had the words *the clue* in their title and I remember pausing when I'd reach a dramatic part in the book, savoring the moment before Nancy solved the crime. Sometimes I'd catch myself fantasizing that just like Nancy I lived alone with my daddy. In this fantasy Ma was dead and Brother never existed. I'd relish the feeling of all my love being just for Daddy and all of Daddy's love being just for me until I'd get sick with guilt that I could ever wish Ma dead and Brother never born. Then I'd convince myself that it was the curse living inside me that thought such awful things and that it was Father Capedonico himself whispering those ugly thoughts into the chambers of my heart.

On those days when I went to the church to read I always sat near the statue of Saint Barbara on the right side of the altar. Sometimes seated on the left side of the altar, where the statue of the Virgin stood, was a girl. I'd seen this girl many times, both at church and at school. She had spirals of black hair past her shoulders and eyes that appeared either gray or green depending on the light. Her skin was the color of the tea Auntie used to drink, a sunny brown, and speckling her nose were freckles, a darker brown than her skin. At Sunday mass she ignored the service, praying the rosary like the old ladies did, a string of mother-of-pearl rosaries worked bead by bead between her thumb and index finger, continuing to sit even when everyone else stood or kneeled. Even at school she had a way of walking through the halls that set her apart and there were always a couple of boys following her around, taunting and teasing her. Marisol Diaz Sullivan was her name, and whenever she said it, she pronounced *Diaz* like it was a threat, like it was a bit of something sharp and glinting on her tongue. Each time I saw her I couldn't help fantasizing that my blah-brown hair would blacken and my blah-brown eyes would chameleonlike change color.

Usually I watched her from a distance but once during an air-raid drill I got so close that I could smell the baby shampoo of her hair. It was lunchtime and we wound up crouched under the same cafeteria table. The sides of our legs and arms pressed together and I wondered if she ever let any of the boys touch her and if she had, where. As if reading my thoughts, she shot me a snotty glance and I looked away, imagining what would happen if this wasn't a drill, but the real thing and the atomic bomb was actually dropping right outside the window. I pictured me and Marisol laid out together, our faces burned like the photo I'd seen in *Life* magazine of two little Japanese girls who'd been in Hiroshima when we dropped the bomb on them.

That day in the church when I actually met Marisol Diaz Sullivan I thought again of the bomb dropping and I touched the warm clammy skin at the back of my neck. Curled up asleep on the pew behind me was Brother. He looked like a little angel with his wisps of strawberry blond hair and cupid lips, which made me think that Ma was right when she said you could never trust a thing for what it was.

At the time I was reading *The Ghost of Blackwood Hall* and though I was into the story I couldn't keep from glancing at Marisol. She looked to be doing a crossword puzzle, a pencil poised between her fingers, a streak of orange light from a stained glass window coloring her face. Every now and then she reached into a straw purse on the bench beside her for a potato chip that she'd then slowly crunch in her mouth with a dreamy look on her face as if it was the Eucharist itself.

Feeling my stare Marisol turned toward me, but the sound of a door being closed coming from somewhere deep in the dark entry to the rectory snapped her to attention. We both turned in time to see Mr. Edelmann, the church sacristarian, in the entryway off the side of the altar. He wielded a feather duster like a sword and pointed it at Marisol. "You better not be eating in here again." Marisol didn't say a thing and his glance swept over her bag and then up and over me. "What are you two girls doing?"

"Praying," Marisol was quick to say. "Isn't that what church is for?"

He turned on me a bullying stare. I looked down at my shoes that sparkled with the rhinestone clips Daddy had taken from Kreshner's. "Praying," I confirmed, fanning myself with an opened hymnal in my hand. When I read, I always kept a hymnal beside me just in case a priest or a nun walked in. Mr. Edelmann narrowed his eyes into an angry squint and aimed the feather duster at Brother. "Get that kid up. This is the house of the Lord, not some flophouse."

I moved as if to wake Brother but as soon as Mr. Edelmann left I sat back down. Without saying a word, Marisol stood, slipped her bag over her shoulder, and sidestepped out of her pew and into mine. She plopped the bag between us and offered me a chip. The chips were barbequed flavor. As soon as I took one, my tongue zinged with the spice of it.

"Thanks," she said. "Last week he caught me eating in here and said he'd throw me out if I did it again. I said, 'How could you throw me out of church? It's the house of God and my body is a temple of the Holy Ghost so shouldn't the house for God be open for a house for God?'"

She smiled wide, her eyes seeking something in mine. I smiled back. She was two years older than me because she'd been left back twice and her age and experience were something I flat-out admired. Together we reached into her bag for a chip and as we chewed, the rust-colored powder coating our fingers sealed our friendship as good as any Indian blood vow.

Eventually she said, "I know about your family."

"Yeah?" I tilted my head to look at her from the side. I never knew where a comment about my family was headed.

"I heard about your grandfather," she said. "That he never lets anybody push him around. I like that."

"Yeah," I said, looking down at a tear in the cushion of the kneeler, not knowing why the thought of Gramp being looked up to made me feel small.

Then she said that she'd seen me around at school and I blushed, having thought that I'd slipped through the halls safely unnoticed.

"New people interest me," she explained. "I always wonder why anyone would want to come to Barrendale."

I shook my head. "We didn't want to." And then I told her about Centrereach and Auntie and the remedies she'd make. I felt breathless and raw when I described the fire under the fields and how the earth opened up like a mouth to eat Auntie. I'd never spoken about the way she'd died and it made me feel like I was losing more of her, like putting it all into words somehow made Auntie less than who she was.

Marisol's gaze roamed over my body as if she expected to find something wrong with me. Leaning forward, she waved her hand in front of my face like she was washing a window. "Your auntie's spirit is around you. I can feel it."

"Where?" I said, studying the air near my hands and legs. "I can't feel it."

"You're closed to it," she said and crumpled the potato chip bag up. "My grandfather is a *curador*, a healer like your auntie was. What he would tell you is that you must beat your heart open. Whatever that means. Ask me, there's enough people out there who'll do that for you. You don't need to do it yourself."

From that day on Marisol and I became fast friends. She had a way of seeing things and of saying things that I especially liked, and she said that it was exactly her way of saying things that had gotten her left back twice. "Teachers want you to say what *they* want you to say," she explained. I found out that she was born in Barrendale but had spent most of her life living with her grandmother in the Bronx. She'd only come back to Barrendale two years ago to take care of her sick mother whose healing she prayed for whenever she came to church. Often she'd talk about how much she missed her grandmother and her neighborhood in the Bronx, especially the salt marshes.

"The air tastes of the ocean all morning," she'd say, "and smells of faraway places all night." Then she'd go on about how the setting sun turned the marsh grasses pink and how the moonlight made the grasses look like slivers of spirits all moving together in the wind.

I'd never even heard of the Bronx, but I couldn't get over that Marisol could make a place with such an ugly name sound so pretty and the fact that she could made her seem more than ordinary to me. She was like us, I figured. She also walked on fire or air. She had a kind of magic to her.

And I understood that we were not only meant to meet but that we were meant to do something I'd been waiting for all my life. I just didn't yet know what that something was. But with each day that passed, I could feel it coming closer and closer.

Marisol and I met on the afternoons that she didn't work cleaning and doing chores for one of the rich old ladies in town, a widow of one of the mine managers. Sometimes if the old lady had enough work she'd hire me too and Marisol and I would work together, cleaning windows or polishing copper pots. When the old lady was napping or out, we went up into the attic and tried on the dresses and shawls and hats that were packed away in the trunks, most of them Victorian style, their mustiness whispering of a glorious Barrendale past that was almost impossible to imagine.

On the days Marisol didn't work we'd often sit side by side in church or on boulders by a lake and we'd read. In less than a week we devoured *Wuthering Heights* and *Jane Eyre* and while I longed to be loved by Heathcliff and Mr. Rochester, Marisol considered Cathy and Jane fools. "Why haunt a SOB like Heathcliff?" Marisol said about Cathy. "And that Rochester!" Marisol said about Jane, "He tries to marry her when he's *already* married and she *forgives* him for it?"

When we weren't reading we spent our time doing silly stuff that amused us. One entire afternoon we went door-to-door Christmas caroling in the July heat. Sometimes we'd put on accents and pretend to be foreigners from this or that made-up country and we'd ask directions from people or give cashiers a hard time counting our change. And when we weren't doing what Gram called "the crazy that comes from doin' nothin' all day" we boy-watched. We watched them play softball, basketball, and stickball. We hid and watched them skinny-dip at Tinton Falls, deciding that their privates were the least attractive parts of them. We took long walks starting from the farthest reaches of the fire zone on the west side of the city to the farms and hunters' shacks on the east side, all in the hopes of seeing Billy Branigan, a boy who was a year older than Marisol, which meant he was three grades ahead of us in school. He had curly blond hair cut so short it was just a sort of wiry frizz and his eyes were such a pale cold blue they reminded me of the ice covering a winter pond. To me he seemed stuck-up and mean, but Marisol knew things I didn't so I figured there must be something cute and nice in Billy that I couldn't see.

Regardless I didn't mind those long walks because sometimes Billy was with Eddie Battista, a boy whose eyes were the same light brown as Auntie's nut bread and made me feel all sweet inside. If we saw Billy, and we usually did, nothing much would happen though. Marisol would lay on Billy a heated look that Billy would shrug off, his cold blue gaze sliding off her like melting ice. If Eddie was there he'd usually follow us for a block or so and make kissy noises or ask questions like, "Where you headed?" or "What's your rush?" These questions, much to my disappointment, were never aimed at me.

On especially hot days, Marisol and I would hike up the steep streets out of town and into the woods of East Mountain. We'd wend our way through ferny woods, then marshy meadows, and then back into ferny woods. Occasionally we saw coyotes that looked like strung-out wolves and a black bear that resembled the giant black dog the devil was said to come as. We eagerly kept watch for the cougar said to live up there and the snapping turtles rumored to eat small children. In the marshes it was hot and buggy but the bushes were heavy with blueberries and there was a creek that was cold and shallow enough in places for us to walk its bed. Sometimes its rippling water looked jeweled by so many darning needles flitting along it, their lacey wings shimmery with light.

When we walked the creek bed our gaze constantly swept the water, looking for the gold people occasionally panned for, turning over every glittering rock in the hopes of seeing some of the precious metal embedded in its seams.

On one of those walks I took her to the bootlegging hole

where Daddy had taken me, the one that Daddy had helped to dig when he was my age. At the back of the cave the boards of wood the cops had placed to block the hole looked the same as when I'd been there with Daddy. Together Marisol and I hunched and sidestepped into the cave like crabs, our feet kicking up the smell of moldering leaves and wet earth.

Marisol pressed her palm to one of the boards that sealed off the hole. "My father bootlegged coal," she said. "Maybe he went down this hole too."

At first I didn't say anything. Weeks ago when I'd asked her where her daddy was she'd just said, "He doesn't care about us and we don't care about him." So I knew not to ask anything else until she'd brought him up herself.

"My gram says your daddy was in the same class with my uncle Frank," I said. I didn't add what else Gram had said—that Marisol's daddy was a liar and a cheat and had gotten Marisol's mother pregnant and left. I wondered if Marisol could actually be a bastard born out of wedlock. The only girl I knew who'd gotten pregnant when she wasn't married had lived across the street from Auntie and as soon as she'd told her parents they'd thrown her out and locked their doors and for hours through our open windows we'd listened to her cry.

A spider skittered from between the slats of the boards and we both eased our way out of the cave. Marisol said, "They were married only three months when my mother got pregnant. And as soon as she got pregnant he started cheating on her. When my mother found out about it, she told him to leave and never come back. And that's what he did. Left town when my mother was out to here with me." Marisol held her hand about a foot out from her stomach. "Can you believe that? And he never so much as sent a postcard."

I met her eyes, which had turned the green of the moss clinging to the cave. "But your mother told him she never wanted to hear from him again," I said.

"That's not the point," Marisol said, her eyes widening with hurt and disapproval and I immediately regretted my words. I couldn't imagine what it would be like if Daddy left us and I spent the rest of my life never hearing from him again. I looked back at the boarded-up hole in the cave. I'd never before thought of myself as lucky when it came to my family. I'd never thought of us as lucky with anything at all.

Nine

It took weeks and an outrageously short half shirt for Marisol to finally get Billy's attention. The chill actually came off his stare as he took in her exposed midriff and said, "Want to meet up later?"

Marisol shrugged as if she didn't care one way or the other. "What do you think, Brigid?"

I murmured something that sounded vaguely like "I don't know" and Marisol followed with, "Will Eddie be there?"

Now it was Billy's turn to act like he didn't care. "Okay," he said and then he told us to meet them at Old Man Hudson's shack later that afternoon.

"Okay," Marisol said and we walked off slowly to let Billy know we weren't in a rush and to give him a chance to take in Marisol's backside.

"Why Old Man Hudson's shack?" I asked. "Who is he?"

"Who *was* he," Marisol said. "He's been dead for years. The place is abandoned."

The thought of being in an abandoned shack with Eddie was too good to think about. "But Eddie doesn't even like me," I said.

"Sure he does. He just doesn't know it yet."

I stopped midstride. This was Marisol's way of thinking, which somehow or other always made sense. "My parents wouldn't—"

"Of course they wouldn't," Marisol cut me off. "But you'll never get to make out with Eddie until you have a chance to be alone with him."

I said nothing and we continued walking. Countless summer nights I'd kissed my hand imagining it was his mouth.

Marisol misread my silence. "Please go," she pleaded. "The place is in the middle of nowhere. How could your parents ever find out?"

Marisol was right about Old Man Hudson's shack being in the middle of nowhere. It sat in a field of foot-high quack grass and was really more of a bungalow with a little front porch and a hatch to the side for the cellar door. Toward the back was a crooked little outhouse that someone must have used for target practice because it was riddled with holes.

Our skin was gritty with red dust from the dirt road we'd had to walk to get there. Though I was glad we were so far off the beaten path, I couldn't stop hearing Ma's and Gram's warnings to never go somewhere alone with a boy, especially one I didn't know. Both Ma and Gram had followed those warnings with stories about girls who'd been foolish enough to let their reputations be ruined. As we waited for Billy and Eddie on the porch those warnings played like static between my ears.

Billy and Eddie were just two of the boys who hung out in packs, roaming around town, peeping into windows, bending traffic signs. That was what boys did around Barrendale: it didn't mean they were bad. Besides, Daddy and dead Uncle Frank were just as unruly as teens, according to Gram, and she seemed pleased with them for that. Still, I kept thinking about the pregnant girl who'd lived across the street from Auntie. When her parents threw her out she'd gone to live with an aunt in Plattsburgh who'd taken the baby as soon as it was born and never brought it back. Last we'd heard the girl had gone crazy and was being sent to a funny farm.

It was a hazy day and we got hot standing on that porch in the middle of that field and we started to regret agreeing to meet them there. But as soon as we saw them walking up the drive, all our regrets were forgotten.

"God, isn't he to die for?" Marisol gushed about Billy. She rubbed her hand across her exposed stomach. "I think I'll let him feel me up. *Imagine.*" And then she shut her eyes, lost in the fantasy.

I didn't say anything. I couldn't think beyond kissing Eddie. I saw his face getting closer and closer. I saw our mouths almost touching. And then . . . that was it. My imagination dead-ended.

Quickly the boys neared us, their hands thrust deep into their dungarees' pockets, their heads down. Eddie walked with a kind of loose stride that reminded me of Daddy's way of walking. When they reached the porch, Billy said, "We've got cold beer in the cellar."

"Lot cooler down there," Eddie said, giving us both an open, friendly smile. His eyes once again reminded me of Auntie's nut bread, and I was immediately glad Marisol had made me come.

A piece of rope was the only lock on the basement door. The boys went down the thick concrete steps first. Marisol and I followed and then stood at the bottom of the stairs waiting for our eyes to adjust. The only light came from the sunlight streaming in from behind us and a lantern perched on a kitchen table that sat at the center of the small dank room. Along one wall was an old ratty sofa and along another was a mattress on the floor. Hanging above the mattress was a long length of rope tied to a rafter.

Eddie sat on one end of the mattress and patted it for us to join him. Billy opened a can of beer from a case in the corner. He took a swig and offered it to Marisol. She worried the knot tying shut her shirt before reaching for it.

"We got the beer off Darren and Jimmy and all those guys," Billy said, referring to a group of older boys who were notorious for drag racing on Route 6 and for stealing people's firewood to use for bonfires they built in the woods. Billy explained that every couple of weeks the older boys stashed beer somewhere on East Mountain. "They keep changing their hiding places, but we find them every time."

From the smug look on his face you would have thought he was bragging about finding pirate treasure, not a case of Ballantine beer.

Marisol peered into the darkness clustered by the sofa. "*This* is where you hang out? Pretty lame if you ask me."

"That's 'cause you haven't seen it all," Eddie said.

"I've seen enough," Marisol said. She slurped at the beer and then handed it to me. "How 'bout you, Brigid? You seen enough?"

I let the cold beer bubble in my mouth before swallowing. All along our walk Marisol had coached me on the various ways to play hard to get. "Yeah," I said in the most offhand way I could muster.

The smug look on Billy's face briefly hardened. But in a flash the look was gone, replaced by a wink and a half smile. "Nah," he said. "You girls should stay."

"What do you think, Bill?" Eddie said. "Should we show 'em?"

Billy's gaze went down the length of Marisol's body and stayed resting on the floor. "I don't know if they deserve to see it."

Quick as lightning Marisol said, "I know of plenty you don't deserve to see."

Billy's laugh prickled with something like pleasure. "If we did show you," he said, "you'd have to keep your mouths shut. It's the only one the cops don't know about."

"Think you could keep your mouths shut?" Eddie said and I couldn't tell if there was something nasty in his voice or not.

"We know we can keep *our* mouths shut," Marisol said.

"But can *you*?" I asked looking straight at Eddie. He tilted his head to the side, considering either me or the question. When he smiled slyly, I all but stopped breathing. Maybe Marisol was right, maybe we would make out.

The boys yanked the mattress away from the wall and shoved it into a corner. There was a large wood board on the floor where the mattress had been. The board was about half the size of the mattress and was speckled with mildew and dirt. The boys dragged the piece of wood over to the mattress and then Eddie lifted the lantern from the table and held it so that its light shown on what had lain beneath the board.

"Oh, my God," Marisol said.

There in the floor was a hole about three feet by three feet, but even with the lantern's light all we could see was blackness within it.

"A bootlegging hole," I whispered, my voice hushed with awe. Daddy had told me that people had dug holes in their basements and backyards and I wondered if this was a bootlegging hole Gramp and Daddy had gone down, creeping their way into the mine shafts at night, filling their sacks with whatever coal they could manage to carry out and sell.

The boys said they'd gone down into the mine too many times to count and had walked its different tunnels for hours. They told us about walls that were covered in dinosaur fossils and caves that glittered with quartz.

"What about the fire?" I asked.

"Too far away," Eddie said.

"But if we feel it getting hot or we smell sulfur," Billy said. "We need to leave."

Then we all talked about flaming walls, poison gas, flooded shafts, and copperheads as if they were things that existed only in stories and myth. But I knew better than that. I was the child of generations of miners. I knew the air could be bad and you wouldn't even smell it or that a cave-in could happen without any warning at all.

The boys had two flashlights, a headlamp, and a lantern that we could take down for light. They also had two sweatshirts that they'd let us wear. Billy handed Marisol his, which meant I got Eddie's. As I slipped it over my head my insides turned oozy. The sweatshirt smelled musty but beneath that smell was another smell, a coppery scent like blood, a boy's scent. Eddie's scent. I breathed a deep whiff of it.

The boys dropped the rope tied to the rafter into the hole and said they'd go first. "We've got sofa cushions down there," Billy said. "Just climb down as far as you can and let yourself drop. It's not far. We do it all the time."

Billy went down first and tossed the rope back up. Eddie tied the lantern to it and slowly lowered it down to Billy.

"Take a flashlight," Eddie said to Marisol. He tucked the

other one into the back of his pants. "You take the headlamp," he said to me. Then he sat on the edge of the hole with his legs dangling inside it and without even gripping the rope slid his bottom forward and dropped clean down into the hole.

"No problem," he called up. "Just drop down. You'll hit a cushion."

Marisol leaned close to my ear and whispered, "Just give him a chance. He'll like you if you give it time." Then she crossed herself, sat down near the rope and gripped it for a while with her legs dangling into the hole.

"Come on, Marisol," Billy said.

Marisol shook her head slowly from side to side as if there were no way she was ever going to budge and then she slid forward, let go of the rope and dropped down the hole with a high-pitched screech. I heard all sorts of yuck and eww sounds and then she called up, "It's okay, Brigid. Don't worry. It's not that far."

I strapped on the headlamp and repositioned it several times to my forehead but no matter what I did it pressed uncomfortably against my skin. For as long as I could remember I'd wanted to go down into the mines, to experience what Daddy had experienced, to feel closer to him. But as I glanced toward the open cellar door that framed a bit of summer sky I felt an unease come over me. Marisol must have read my thoughts because she shouted, "You can do it, Brigid! Really, it's not that bad."

The boys followed her words with squawking chicken noises.

I stepped near the rope and then sat down on the cool basement floor. Immediately my nostrils burned with the smell of dank mold. I was afraid of going down in the mine, but I knew with a certainty I couldn't explain that this was what Marisol and I were meant to do. That God had planned for it. So as I sat there with my legs dangling in that hole, I knew that I was about to drop straight down into what I'd been waiting for all my life. I was about to drop straight down into my own destiny. I could only hope that destiny would uncover for me the hidden places of Daddy's heart.

I gripped the rope, thrust my body forward, and let go. With a jolt I landed onto the cushions and just lay there for a while wondering how bad I was hurt. I heard Marisol asking if I was all right but all I saw was complete blackness.

"I can't see," I sobbed. My breath snagged in my chest and my heartbeat became thunderous. I thought of Auntie sinking into the earth, I thought of Daddy trapped and terrified in the Devil Jaw mine shafts. "You don't conquer fears," Daddy liked to say. "You bury them deep down where you can't feel them anymore."

Billy and Eddie laughed and Billy said, "That's 'cause the headlamp's over your face, you dumbass."

I sat up and pushed the headlamp back onto my forehead, too embarrassed to say anything. First all I saw was red and white patches but then my eyes started to adjust to the darkness, which was lit dimly a few yards in either direction by our lantern and flashlights.

I felt my way off the sofa cushions, my palms feeling hot and raw from rope burn. I stood up and shivered. It was not only chilly but so damp you felt like you could touch the moisture in the air. My gaze roved over the ceiling, and then down the wall to the floor. The tunnel was probably about eight feet wide and who knew how long in either direction. The lantern was on the ground near a six-pack of beer. There were empty bottles and cans of beer strewn all around and up against the wall nearest me were three kitchen chairs that matched the kitchen table up in the basement.

"You guys are the only ones who know about this?" Marisol said.

"Mike and Georgie come down sometimes too," Billy said and then the boys bragged about how far they'd wandered in either direction of the tunnel and how many times they thought for sure they were lost or dead. Listening to them I got this feeling of déjà vu, as if I'd been in these tunnels many times.

"I don't know about anyone else," Marisol said. "But I don't want to get lost or dead."

Billy opened a can of beer and handed it to Marisol. "We also just hang out and drink." He kicked an empty beer bottle. "Sometimes play truth or dare."

"Truth or dare?" Marisol said. Her voice quivered with excitement. "Haven't played that since I lived in New York."

Despite the chill, sweat beaded on my neck. Truth or dare was a game the older kids played to get other kids to do or admit horribly embarrassing things. Often girls got dared to lift their shirts or to go off into the dark with a boy. In the back of my mind the warnings from Ma and Gram blazed, making it hard for me to think straight.

I nuzzled my face into my shoulder to arm myself with a sniff of Eddie's sweatshirt. The boys arranged the three chairs into a tight circle and Eddie placed an empty bottle in the center.

"But there's only three chairs," Marisol said.

"Sit on my lap," Billy said. "If the bottle aims at us we'll take turns. First I'll go, then the next time it aims at us, you go."

Eddie said, "That's the stupidest—"

Billy cut him off. "What do you care?"

Eddie grunted and looked away as Marisol settled onto Billy's lap. We were sitting close enough that we could see each other fairly well but only yards from us darkness swallowed all of the light and lay there like a presence.

"I'll go first," Billy said. Awkwardly he leaned to reach the bottle and spin it. I'm sure we all knew he was hoping it would stop and aim straight at him and Marisol. But instead it fell short of its mark and aimed straight at me. He actually groaned in disappointment. "Truth or dare?" he said as if it was the most boring question ever asked by anybody.

I did Ma's proud chin tilt. "Truth."

He leaned into Marisol and she snuggled against him making a soft sound of sleep or pleasure. "Then you better tell the truth," Billy said. "Did your grandfather kill Jack Novak?"

I tsked my tongue, irritated at how gossip made lies out of what happened. "All he did was hit him." I didn't add with a bottle, I didn't want to talk about it with someone like Billy.

"That's not how some people say it went," Billy said.

"Who?" I said, standing up and stepping toward him. Marisol said my name as a form of plea and I sat back down, wondering what she could possibly see in such a jerk as Billy. "Who?" I said again.

"Lots of people," Eddie said. He nodded his chin at me. "Your turn."

I leaned down and spun the bottle, hoping it would land on Eddie and not hoping it would land on Eddie. If it landed on him I'd surprise everyone by not daring him to so much as hold my hand. I had my pride. I'd make him tell me who was spreading those lies about Gramp.

The bottle stopped slightly to the side of Eddie. "Truth or dare?" I asked him.

"Dare."

I tongued the back of my teeth like I could find a good dare stuck between them. Billy made kissy-kissy noises and Eddie grunted again and looked up at the ceiling.

"Shut up," Marisol said and the burn off Billy's teasing eased.

I looked off toward the darkness beyond Eddie and my inner eye lit with visions of crystal caves and lacey fossils of creatures no one ever knew existed. I dared Eddie to walk a hundred feet down the shaft and when he readily agreed, I said I wanted to come with him.

"No hankie-panky you two," Billy said.

"Jesus," Eddie said and he swiped up his flashlight and started down the shaft with me trailing him. Then I heard a slap and Marisol playfully say, "Behave. That's off-limits."

"What about here?" Billy said.

"Jesus," Eddie said again.

I was embarrassed by what Marisol was doing and by what Eddie clearly did not want to do with me, but I was also excited by the thought of going deeper into the mine. Eddie moved deftly into the darkness and it was easy for me to focus on following his beam of light. It was easy for me to convince myself that Daddy had at one time or another walked the very ground I was walking and I felt that proved something mysterious and vastly important. For the first time I felt more than merely pride that my great-great-granddaddy had been a Molly Maguire, I felt a connection to him.

Eddie stopped and shone his light at the wall. "Look at this," he said. There in the beam of our lights was an opening in the wall, a narrow shaft that started at chest level and ended a couple of yards below the ceiling. A monkey shaft, so named because only a monkey could maneuver well in it. It was exactly this type of shaft that Uncle Frank was found dead in.

I bent and twisted my head so that my headlamp beamed up into the craggy dark of the chasm where some mica, embedded in the rock, glistened. "Wow," I said. "I always imagined what one would look like."

"Come on," he said, waving me back in the direction we came. "That was at least a hundred feet. Probably more."

We headed back quickly to the sounds of Marisol play-slapping Billy and saying, "Bad boy. No. What'd I say?"

Eddie stepped into the circle and spun the bottle before I'd even sat down. It stopped and pointed directly at my empty chair. "Redo," he said.

"Nah, that counts," Billy said with a wicked laugh.

"Truth or dare?" Eddie said.

I didn't even pause. "Dare," I said.

He leaned forward with his elbows on his knees. His face was less than a foot from mine and my heart hammered at the thought that he'd dare me to kiss him, dare me to kiss him just to be mean.

"I dare you to crawl a hundred feet up that monkey shaft."

"A hundred!" Marisol said.

"Okay, fifty."

"Fine," I said, pushing the headlamp further up my forehead. Then I stood and faced the darkness behind Eddie but I didn't move.

"I'll go with you," Marisol said. Eddie stood to go with us and then Billy did too. The tunnel was wide enough that we could walk side by side and Marisol and I linked arms and Billy and Eddie flanked us. We reached the monkey shaft more quickly than I expected and this time I didn't pause. I reached into the hole, my fingers scraping at whatever purchase I could find and then I yelped as I felt hands on my backend and the boys lifted me and pushed me in. I took a deep breath and coughed on some dirt I'd swallowed.

The hole was high enough that I didn't have to slither and could crawl on all fours. It led upwards slightly and was probably more than thirty feet wide. The cold wet rock scraped my bare legs as I slowly crawled forward, swinging my head from side to side to keep an eye on what was next to me as well as what was ahead.

"Can I touch you there?" I heard Eddie say, followed by a slap and a high-pitched giggle. "What about here?" Billy said.

"This will cut up my knees," I said. "How far do I have to go?"

"I'll tell you when to stop," Eddie said.

"She's in shorts, Eddie," Marisol said.

"Who told her to wear shorts?" he said.

"You all right?" Marisol called to me.

"Yeah," I said, managing to crawl a few more feet. The cuts on my legs and hands felt like badges of honor. Ahead I could see the shaft open up into a wide chamber. "Crawling into the earth's belly," was how Daddy described crawling up a monkey shaft. "You can get so spun around you can't tell your forward from your back," he'd say. "You can get so lost it can feel like no one will ever find you."

As I looked sideways in the narrow space I was sure I was feeling some of the same feelings Daddy had felt countless times and I felt so close to him then, to who he was before the disaster, that I quickly moved ahead, eager to feel even more.

"Okay," Marisol said. "Enough." This time the slap and her protest sounded real. "Come on, Brigid. Turn around. Let's get out of here."

I looked behind me, trying to figure how best to get out. The ceiling of the shaft wasn't high enough to let me easily turn around. It was only then I noticed a sound I couldn't place. It was like a fast ticking clock or water quickly dripping. The rocks were wetter here. Maybe I was near a spring. But then something brushed my arm and shot past me into my beam of light. A rat! I sobbed, "A rat touched me."

"Get out," Marisol said. "Move fast."

"I'm trying," I said and veered to the side but I'd moved too quickly and a small avalanche of rock and coal showered me.

"Crawl slow," Billy said.

"Shit," Eddie said. "I knew we shouldn't have brought a little girl."

Slowly I moved backwards, seeing yet another rat several feet from me and realizing the sound I'd been hearing was them calling each other, doing whatever they do with their tongues in anticipation of food. I whimpered again and kept trying to turn my head to see behind me but all that happened was that my headlamp beamed the darkness to my side.

"Keep coming, Brigid, you're doing all right," Marisol said.

"As long as you keep moving, the rats won't bother you," Billy said.

Backwards I moved first one leg than another and then my skin prickled as if someone was watching me. I could feel the stare coming from somewhere to my left, to the side I was turned away from. I swung my head in that direction but saw nothing except rock. Could bootleggers still be coming down here? Is this where some serial killer or pervert hid? Or could there really be a monster living down in the mines like rumor said?

For one ridiculous moment I feared that this was the monkey shaft Uncle Frank had been found in and that his ghost was there waiting to get me. I knew I needed to follow Daddy's advice and bury my fear deep down where I couldn't feel it anymore, but I didn't know how to do that when all I could feel was dread.

My hand touched something and I snapped it back, but then I saw it was only some miner's old glove.

"You got to straighten out," Marisol said. "You're heading to the side."

I turned my head over my shoulder, aiming the headlamp as best I could and trying to maneuver so that my feet angled straight down to the opening of the shaft. "Better?" I said but then my head knocked the roof and another shower of rock fell on me. I gripped something hard to steady myself and moved a leg backward, lowering my head to see what I was holding. It was a white stick. And alongside that white stick was another white stick and then a piece of cloth and then a rib cage.

A scream stuck in my throat. There, several feet from my hand, was a skull staring at me.

I couldn't move, I couldn't speak. Even when Billy and Eddie crawled up and poked the skeleton with a flashlight, I didn't make a sound. Fear had turned all my muscles as stiff as the bones I was staring at.

They had to pull me out by my ankles, shredding my shins and belly with sooty black cuts. Marisol held me and said the Hail Mary and told the boys that we had to get out of there. Even after we'd scrambled up out of the hole and were standing outside in the bright green of the day, all I could do was merely whimper. I could still feel the empty eyes of the skull looking at me, knowing I was there.

PART II

Ten

Nobody rested well in the weeks after finding the body. A murder down in what everyone called "our mines" was a bad omen and surely meant that the dig-out project would fail and the fire only worsen. And as far as most of Barrendale was concerned, us kids were to blame.

"Couldn't you leave well enough alone?" was one of the questions we heard in those first few days after finding the body. "Don't we have enough problems without you kids digging around for more?"

The postmistress was so angry that she hissed at me over her counter, "Knew once you started hanging around with that Puerto Rican girl you'd be trouble." And I remember how hurt and shocked I was by her saying that, especially when she didn't know Marisol or me at all.

"Don't tell nobody nothin'," Gram warned me. "If they can blame an Irishman, they will. Blame a Howley, even better. Tell them lies if you have to. Tell 'em anythin' but the truth." Gram's face looked as wrinkled as a crumpled sheet as she added, "Specially don't say nothin' about being with two fifteen-year-old boys. Don't you value yourself none, girl? Don't you want to be good?"

Billy's daddy beat him so bad he had to wear a sling on his arm for a week and whenever he saw me or Marisol he acted like he had no idea who we were. Eddie's daddy sent him off to work on a relative's farm in Ohio. "That boy's a bad seed," Mr. Battista would tell anyone who'd listen. "What could I do? Tie him to a tree? I couldn't watch him every second."

Marisol said she'd heard people calling her spic and little bastard. "My parents were *married*," she said to me, her eyes fierce. "And if my mother wasn't *Puerto Rican* people would believe that."

Not everyone reacted with anger, though. For some of the people, especially the ones who lived in the worst of the zone, it grated their nerves further. "Is it true his skull was bashed in? Do they know who it was? Do they know who did it?"

By far though, no one was more angry or anxious about it than Ma. She'd thrash around at night unable to sleep. She'd look at me as if I'd betrayed her worse than her own daddy or stepma had. "How could you a done this *now*?" she said to me. "Everybody knows a dead body is bad luck. What's Bropey going to think?"

In those first few days after finding the body it was Daddy who protected me against Ma's wrath, saying it was crazy to punish me when the image of that dead body would be with me for life.

"Let me get this straight," Ma said. "She goes off with a couple of boys down in some mine somewheres and don't tell nobody and we ain't gonna do a thing? Well, let me tell *you* something, Adrian Howley. That's how come she's a daydreamer. She thinks the world's soft when it's the hardest thing there is."

But Daddy had this look on him, like I was sick or something and it was somehow his fault. Over and over he'd ask me to describe exactly where the body was and how it looked. And though I hated thinking about what I'd seen in that shaft, I loved having Daddy's attention focused on my every word. His eyes would rove from the wall up to the ceiling like he was trying to solve the murder from the little I could tell him. Eventually I'd repeated the details so often that it became like a story I told. It became like one of the tall tales Daddy and I used to tell each other. It was almost a thing of pleasure.

Only when we were alone did Daddy listen that carefully to me. When the detectives were there he acted like he didn't care what I'd seen. Which was how we all acted. It was understood by us all that cops were especially not to be trusted. Gram particularly disliked the main detective who was Greek. "Remember the story 'bout that big horse they sent to trick them people," Gram warned me more than once. "Greeks is sneaky."

Gramp and Daddy agreed and I started to think Gram was right because whenever that detective came by he'd ask the same questions over and over as if eventually he'd trick me into saying something I hadn't said before.

"You can tell us anything," Detective Kanelous liked to say.

"Anything. Absolutely anything," Detective Wolinski would repeat, looking up from his notepad where he constantly scribbled as if I'd said volumes when I never said much at all.

They wanted to know what I saw, what I'd heard—what I'd been doing earlier that day. They wanted to know how we'd found the hole. Whose idea it was for us to go down there. How long I'd known Marisol. How long I'd known Billy and Eddie. They asked the same questions to Marisol, but still I thought it was me they were after. Their questions made it seem like they thought I'd killed the man and dragged him into that monkey shaft. And in a way I felt I had. That people were right when they thought that in finding the body I was to blame for it being there. I guess I felt that in simply wanting to be close to Daddy, to experience what he'd gone through in the mines, I'd been selfish. I'd wanted too much.

Whenever the detectives showed up, I'd sit on Daddy's lap, leaning my weight against his good arm, his bad arm around me like a battered shield. Each time they came, Daddy's voice would get a waxiness to it, his words greased with fury and contempt. "For chrissakes, we go through this each time. Don't *you* know where she found it? Don't *you* know what position it was in? She's only a little girl. You act like you think my daughter did it."

"Not at all," Detective Kanelous would say, passively lowering his eyelids and then widening them as if he could blink his way into my head.

"Not at all," Detective Wolinski would repeat, gripping his pad as though it contained the key to unlocking the murder.

Just as Gram had predicted, once the detectives discovered that Gramp and Daddy had bootlegged that hole, it was Howleys they seemed to blame.

"Know anyone else who used that shaft?" Detective Kanelous asked Gramp and Daddy. He was a big man with the blackest hair I'd ever seen and he spoke in a quick clipped New York way. "Anyone unusual? Anyone you didn't know?"

"Lots men . . . used it." Gramp said, eyes slit, swallowing and gagging on the effort to keep his cough at bay.

"Bootlegging holes are all over this town," Daddy added. "You know how many men used them?"

There were little bumps on Detective Kanelous's cheeks that glistened where his beard came in. "How many?" he asked.

Daddy said nothing and then Detective Wolinski asked Gramp, "About how many would you say, Mr. Howley?" Detective Wolinski had a mustache that curved down toward his jaw and made me think some furry creature perched on top of his mouth, ready to eat his words.

Daddy made his face as blank as stone. "How would *we* know?" he said. "Can't you tell my father's sick? Can't you leave him alone?"

On one of the times after the detectives left, Daddy poured two glasses of whisky and he and Gramp sat out on the side porch, sipping it. The window over Daddy's head was open and I heard Daddy say this would all come back to the Devil Jaw mining disaster.

Gramp grunted.

"You know you can tell me what happened," Daddy said. "You're not the only one who tried to help Frank. I tried to help too."

The juicy sounds of Gramp sucking the saliva in his mouth was followed by him saying. "You tell . . . what happen . . . that day . . . down there."

"I've told you that already," Daddy said, his voice strained. "I went down into Devil Jaw to tell him to get the men out. To tell him he could keep the money and still do right by the men."

Gramp hocked up something. "Make no sense . . . why Frank in . . . monkey shaft."

"Chrissakes," Daddy said. "He's dead. What does it matter why he was in a monkey shaft? You know these cops aren't going to quit until they pin this on someone. How 'bout trying to protect me the way you were always protecting him?"

An explosion in the fire zone shook the house and all of Gram's dishes on the hutch clattered.

"Shit," Daddy said and the pain in his voice drew me out into the doorway where I saw him gripping his hurt arm the way he did when it ached from rain. "Shit," he said again and then he kicked at the screen door, swinging it open. He jogged down the steps and crossed the lawn without once looking back, leaving me for hours after to ponder his words with Gramp. What was it Daddy wanted Gramp to tell him about? Had Uncle Frank been taking bribes? Why did Gramp think Daddy knew why Uncle Frank had been in a monkey shaft? All these things I thought about and for days after whenever I shut my lids I'd see Gramp's and Daddy's faces blurring with Father Capedonico's and then I'd see the white skull with its empty sockets and I'd open my eyes with a shudder.

I should have avoided Ma in those first weeks, but instead I found myself hanging around her more, hoping somehow I could make things better between us. Sometimes I'd even meet her on her lunch break at the mill thinking that if I could get her to tell me stories about her and Daddy's pasts, like she used to, she'd start to like me again and not worry about the dead body.

On one of those days I found her standing in the side yard over by the garbage bins, smoking fast and hard. It was a warm day that smelled of the brown lanky river running below the cliff.

The bluish stone of the mill towered behind us, greenish in the crevices with mold.

"We was already married when your daddy told me about the curse," Ma said, squinting at Gram who stood across the yard beside Edna Schwackhammer, the woman Ma called Gram's twin twit. That day Gram and Mrs. Schwackhammer did seem twinnish in appearance. They stood there with their old lady skirts halfway down their calves and their thick-heeled, square-toed shoes and chunky clip-on earrings. They'd had their hair dyed and curled by the same hairdresser in town and they looked like different-sized versions of the same woman.

Ma continued, "He gave me the same cock-and-bull story that old biddy tries to sell about the curse making you stronger because it keeps you on your toes. But you know what I think about the curse?"

I wondered if Ma knew about the curse's secret and if she was trying to tell me about it. "What, Ma?" I said, my voice hardly above a whisper. I was desperate to talk about the curse's secret, especially with Ma. But she saw how bad I wanted her answer, so she wasn't going to say a thing.

Gram was looking this way and that, squirming under the pressure of Ma's stare. Eventually she called out, "So why ain't you met that brother of yours yet, Dolores? What's keepin' him from you?"

"He's busy with his car dealership," Ma snipped.

"*Used* car dealership," Gram said as if the word *used* was a four-letter curse word. "So? Can't he have you down to him? Can't he invite you?"

"He has. Bunch a times," Ma said but I could tell from the way she held her chin, tilted and up, that he hadn't. "You just mind your own business, Rowena. Ain't seen your brother visiting you anytime lately."

Mrs. Llewelyn, a big fat woman whose feet bulged out of her shoes, stepped up to Gram and got right in her face. "Speaking of minding business, Rowena, I finished that tote. Why'd you go and tell Big Berta I fell short? You're not the boss here. You can't even control your own goddamn grandkid from going down in the mine, you think you can control our totes?"

Mrs. Llewelyn must have heard Ma coming because she turned just in time to get Ma's fist smack in her nose. "You control your own goddamn kids, Linda," Ma spat and then they ripped at each other's hair and fell to the ground and I ran to get the janitor to pull them apart, I was so afraid Mrs. Llewelyn would crush Ma.

Eventually as the weeks passed so did Ma's anger and in its place was something blank and quiet. It was almost like she was still herself, she was still Ma, but somehow less so. She'd collect change to call her brother on one of the pay phones in town and spend evenings smoking out by the catalpa tree, its trunks split three ways like the prongs on a ring that clasped nothing but the starry night air.

Some nights she'd sit on my bed playing solitaire, slow sipping a can of Schlitz, occasionally leaning her head against Daddy's werewolf poster. At night as we lay in the bunk beds, Ma on top, Ma would tell me gossip about the girls from the mill. She'd tell me about the money she'd hidden from Daddy and how much of it he'd found. She'd tell me, voice all whispery, about the times Uncle Frank had tried to get fresh with her and her voice would carry a kind of wary excitement.

Whenever we got into bed we'd leave the light on. Inevitably

Gram would come in and turn the light off and then Ma would instigate her usual fight but there was an emotion lacking to her—"You ain't the only one who pays the bills, old lady"—as if she were merely mouthing the words.

If all the questions about the unsolved murder made Ma less talkative, they had the opposite effect on Gram. It was only then that Gram started talking about when the mines started slowing down in the twenties. She said the slowdown was so gradual that at first they didn't think much about it. They thought people would always want coal and couldn't imagine a time when there wouldn't be a demand for it anymore. "But then slow and sure the railroads cut back more and more operations and then all sorts of businesses cut back, first on hours, then on workers. Before you knew, it wasn't just the miners who was strugglin', it was everybody. It was all of Barrendale."

Gram also told me that during Prohibition she supported the family making shine until the cops shut her down and later, she said, during World War II she worked in a factory in Scranton making bombs. One day while we were outside cementing the cracks all the drilling and flushing had caused in the foundation, Gram told me that it was her hard-earned money that had bought this house and I should be proud to ever do the same. "Lots of women ain't got a house to their name," she said, glancing toward the living-room window behind which Ma was painting her nails.

Gram waved her hand to take in the whole yard and house. "And now look at all I got. And to think when my daddy came here from Limerick not a soul but the mafia would hire him! Nobody else wanted Irish. They thought we were as low as coloreds. Lower maybe. 'Cept for those criminals in the mob. They wanted him to drive one of their trucks. So that's what he did till he heard the mines would take Irish."

On some days she talked about Uncle Frank and how he was always in trouble at school for roughhousing, for smoking in the bathroom, for being with girls under the bleachers. And that she knew he was bad but she couldn't help loving him for it.

I had a putty knife in my hand and I was far enough out of Gram's reach that she couldn't slap me. Cagily I asked, "But if you knew he was bad, why'd you tell Ma it was a pity the good one died?"

"What?" she said. "I never said no such thing." And then she poured too much water into the bucket of cement and clucked her tongue and said that Daddy liked to pretend he was a Mr. Smarty-pants never doing nothin' wrong, but that sometimes he'd been with Uncle Frank and had gotten in trouble too.

School started and Marisol and I were inseparable in our classes and inseparable afterwards, going on long walks in the warm and yellowing September woods and fields. During those walks Marisol liked to wonder about the dead person's spirit. She supposed that it had chosen us to help solve its murder, to be the instruments of its revenge. It was possible, she said, that in a past life we'd wronged the man and that was why the spirit had us find it. It was even possible, she'd whisper, that the spirit was standing right next to us, talking to us at that very moment, not knowing it was dead.

In an attempt to communicate with it we used Marisol's Ouija board, but all it spelled was O-W, which Marisol said meant it couldn't get past its pain, or it spelled H-O-W, which Marisol said meant it wanted us to find out how it was killed. We tried a séance too. We lit some candles on the shore of White Deer Lake and held hands and asked the spirit to speak to us but we didn't hear a thing, though Marisol said she could still feel Auntie's spirit around me, just as she had when we first met in Saint Barbara's church.

"You should be careful," she warned. "I don't feel her as strong as I did. If you're not open to her being there, she'll go away."

And when she told me that I found myself patting my chest as if there were a secret compartment there that might magically open to let Auntie in.

There was one particularly warm afternoon when I walked Marisol home and then continued into the fire zone toward Gram and Gramp's. Talk of the dead body had dwindled and I no longer walked with my head lowered, worried that someone would say something nasty if I looked them in the face. So I'd had plenty of time to cross the street and avoid the crazy lady who sometimes stood outside our house. She was at the end of the block coming toward me and I was curious, I guess, to see her up close. I wondered if you could tell she was crazy just from the look in her eye.

As we neared each other I saw that she was wearing the same gravy-stained dress that I'd seen her in the last time and that she had a faded red Christmas ribbon in her hair. She stepped to the side as if she was getting out of my way, but as I passed she gripped my arm and got right in my face. Her breath smelled as bad as dog dirt. She had the prettiest pale blue eyes I'd ever seen and they looked wildly, first in one direction, then another. "That was my son down there, wasn't it, girl? You tell me what he looked like. You tell me it was your grandpa who done it. I always known it was. I ain't the only one who's known it neither."

Then she pushed me so that I fell back into a parked car. "The cops will find out, you know." She took several steps backward and taunted in a singsong voice, "The cops'll find out, the cops'll find out." She clasped her hands and raised her eyes skyward. "Oh, yes, they'll find out."

Eleven

A t first I didn't tell anyone what the crazy lady had said. Everyone was upset enough that I didn't want to add to it with rumors, but I found myself looking at Gramp more and more. The fingers on both his hands were all crooked from arthritis and breaks and I wondered if that was what a killer's hands looked like. I knew he'd been in and out of jail for beating up on people and wrecking this or that place and for all I knew he'd killed somebody too.

Often I found myself drawn to ponder the photos of a younger him that Gram had framed on the mantel. There was the photo of the two of them married in the church rectory, Gramp's face unreadable, possibly a little proud. There was the one of him in uniform when he returned home from the Western Front, the wedding band on his finger symbolizing his marriage to his then wife, his first wife, who would along with their twin tots soon die in a flood. And then there was my favorite photo, the one of him and a group of other little boys down in the mines. The boys were all lined up like in a class photo with the first row crouched in front and the other row standing behind. They were around my age and their faces and clothes were filthy. They all held lanterns or had a headlamp strapped to their heads. Gramp stood far on the left, the features of his face blanked out by the camera's flash.

When I looked at these photos, I searched for something telling in them, but all they told was that he'd lived through unbelievably difficult times and had survived.

Gramp never seemed to notice or care that I looked at these photos so I didn't think much of it when he told me to fetch an old wooden cigar box from the hutch. He told me to open it and when I did I found inside a clay pipe, worn smooth. Its whitish color reminded me of the ghostly white stems of what people called Indian pipes or corpse plant that grew in damp places in the woods.

"That pipe . . . my granddaddy." Gramp gestured at himself with his thumb.

"You mean the granddaddy who was the Molly Maguire?"

Gramp nodded and for a moment a satisfied proud glint lit his dull eyes.

I held the pipe tenderly, turning it this way and that as if it were a relic. I couldn't believe I was touching something my great-great-granddaddy had touched. My great-great-granddaddy, the legendary Molly Maguire, who'd heroically attacked a priest and for that had gotten us all cursed.

"What was he like?" I asked.

Gramp's mouth opened into a smile. "A rogue," he said.

It was the first time I'd ever seen Gramp smile and I smiled back.

The dead body faded from our lives. People stopped asking

about it, even Daddy stopped asking about it and the detectives stopped coming by. On Saturday afternoons Daddy still took me and Brother for walks so Ma could have time for herself. Sometimes we'd stop in at Kreshner's department store for Daddy to show Mr. Wicket yet again that he would browse there as often as he wanted and not buy a thing. Then we would always stop at The Shaft, but Daddy would only get one beer. If Star was there alone, Daddy barely paid her any mind. But if Bear was with her, then Daddy would take an interest in what she had to say and Star's long neck and face would flush pink and I'd stare at her with a force that I hoped shot little pellets into her heart.

Mostly though we spent those walks doing what we called "pit watching." At that time they were digging the pit closest to us, the one that became known as the East Side Pit. The demolition included all of the homes on Saltmire and Elm streets and cut off all access to the railroad tracks but by the highway on the edge of town. Daddy said that they made the pit V-shaped because they were trying to buttress the fire and after they completed this V-shaped trench, they'd create other trenches all along the outside of the fire to keep it from spreading.

The East Side Pit was nearly three hundred feet wide and a hundred deep. They used steam shovels and dragline shovels and digger trucks and dump trucks and fire trucks and bulldozers and front loaders and backhoes and explosives. They'd scoop out the coal and stone and dirt and dump it in piles that they'd then spray with water to keep it cool. And when they started having trouble with truck tires melting, they started using clay and water to keep the ground cool enough where they worked.

Every now and then a journalist would come from this or that paper or magazine to write about the dig out—we'd already been in *Time* magazine and *The Saturday Evening Post*—and if Daddy saw one of those journalists he'd always stop to talk. Usually Daddy would get the conversation to go from the dig out to the disaster and more often than not the journalist was keen to listen, but I started to notice that each time Daddy talked about the disaster, one or another detail was different.

Sometimes Daddy knew the hoist wasn't working so he didn't run to it. Sometimes he thought it *was* working, so that was the first place he went. Sometimes he got out after the second tremor. Sometimes the third. Sometimes Uncle Frank helped him get some of the other miners out. Sometimes Uncle Frank wasn't mentioned at all.

The first time I noticed the differences in Daddy's story I waited until the journalist was out of earshot and I asked him about it.

"I'm just playing with him, princess," Daddy said. "See what he knows and what he doesn't."

Daddy winked like this was all a great game and I felt the stab of his disappointment when I didn't smile in return. It didn't feel like Daddy was playing a game with the journalist. It felt like he was playing a game with me and I couldn't understand why he'd do that when nobody in the world believed in him as much as I did.

Sometimes when we'd go pit watching Ma would come along and we'd all compete with each other to find the spot that gave the best view. As long as they weren't blasting, we'd get as close as they'd let us. We might sit on a stoop left where a house used to be or lean against a fence marking a property that no longer existed. We didn't talk. It was impossible to hear over the machinery. Sometimes Ma would bring snacks, pretzels or maybe Twinkies, and for the first time since Auntie had died we were happy together as a family, soothed somehow by all the noise and destruction. The dig out would work, we all agreed. Look at the destruction? How could the fire survive it?

But by the start of the fall the Krupskys, an old couple who lived thirteen blocks west of Gram and Gramp's, were killed from carbon monoxide poisoning. The Krupskys lived seven blocks east of the fire zone, well out of the fire's reach, or so we all had thought. But for carbon monoxide to have killed them, it meant that the fire was bigger than anyone had suspected.

"I won't believe it. I don't," Gram said, referring to the fire's spread. Even when one of the government inspectors arrived, waving a detector up by the ceilings and in the corners, checking for carbon monoxide and carbon dioxide as well as sulfur and methane, Gram told him that if he wanted to wreck the house, he'd have to wreck her too.

"No, ma'am," the inspector said. "I don't want to demolish you or your home. I'm just here to monitor the air."

"I don't know why," Gram said. "We sure as heck ain't in the zone."

"No, ma'am," he said. "But we don't want what happened to the Krupskys to happen to anyone else."

When the inspector mentioned the Krupskys, Brother made a mewling sound and Gramp, from his position in the living-room Barcalounger, pointed and shouted, "Don't scared. Howleys . . . survive."

Brother punched the side of his head with one of his tight little red fists. "Retard," Gramp hollered. "Only a moron hits himself," Gram announced. Daddy flicked his eyes at Brother and walked outside, letting the screen door slam behind him.

I crouched in front of Brother and gently punched my own

head. "Ow. See how silly?" I did it again. "Ow. Why would I hurt myself?" I squeezed my eyes shut in mock pain and opened them wide, thinking that Mrs. Mott, Brother's kindergarten teacher in Centrereach, might have been right when she said that Brother should see a psychotherapist.

It was only then I noticed Ma seated at the dining-room table, pasting S&H Green Stamps into her booklet, the smallest smile giving her face a dreamy quality.

Later that night me and Ma moved her mattress from the top bunk down to the floor because gases tend to rise. Gases also tend to hang low in the basement so that night Daddy and Brother had to move their sleeping stuff from the basement to the living room.

"This is the best news I've heard in years," Ma said as we arranged pillows along the wall beside her mattress. "If the fire comes this far, we have to go. We got no choice in the matter." She folded her legs Indian-style and clenched a pillow to her chest. "I was thinking, seeing as it's your birthday next week, why don't we have a party? You'll be twelve after all, practically grown."

I sucked my breath, afraid to so much as breathe. If I acted too excited Ma might change her mind to punish me. To Ma, me wanting a party would mean I didn't appreciate how good I already had it.

Ma let the pillow drop onto her lap where she stroked it absentmindedly. "Still a nice time of year. We could picnic up at Pothole Park. If it rains, we'll go in that wooden thing they got. I'll invite Bropey and get you a present, a present like nothing you ever seen before. What would you think of that?" She paused midstroke, her hand hovering over the pillow until I cautiously nodded. "We'd be a family again," she added. "Like no time passed at all."

That night there was a damp breeze through the opened window that got me thinking again of the mine and got me dreaming of sliding through the bootlegging hole and reaching the bottom to find Ma lying there dead.

At 3:00 A.M. I cried out when I opened my eyes to see a man bending over me. It was the inspector, Mr. Smythe, as we came to know him. "Just checking the air," he said. "Go back to sleep."

Those inspectors were called Guardian Angels throughout the fire zone. Sometimes the floors of the basements they checked were so hot that the bottoms of their shoes got burned. For hours later their gummy soles would stick to the ground as they walked. Their testing equipment made use of little vials and long slender screwdriver-type things and made you think of the terrifying stories you'd heard about old-fashioned medical devices. But those inspectors were all we had to go by that it was still safe to live in our homes. We left our doors unlocked for them to come and go as they pleased and it was more than once that they saved our lives by getting us out of a house when the gases measured too high.

"We got to seal up the cracks, girl," Gram would holler at me as we'd work to repair any we found in the house. When Gram learned that the gases came not just through cracks but also through the water pipes, she started covering all the faucets and drains with tinfoil each night before bed.

"Fat . . . lot . . . help," Gramp would grunt as Gram went from the kitchen to the bathroom with a bag of the crumpled tinfoil she reused each night, shouting, "Use them sinks now, or go dry till mornin'!"

In the evenings Gram would get on the phone to her best friend, Mrs. Schwackhammer, and remind her to block up her faucets. Gram also let me know that she called to make sure Mrs. Schwackhammer was alive. "She got three kids and not one of 'em check on her. Now tell me, why'd she bother havin' 'em in the first place?"

Mrs. Schwackhammer lived three blocks west of the Krupskys, which meant the fire was now below her house too, but it took the government a good two weeks to send her the paperwork slating her house for destruction.

On the day that Mrs. Schwackhammer got the paperwork, Gram had me go with her to deliver a pot of stew. "This news will hit Edna worse than a death in the family," Gram said. "Still, alls you can do is bring food and your dolensces. Makes you feel a fool."

Edna Schwackhammer was ancient, older than Gram, yet she towered over Gram even when she leaned crooked on her cane. No matter what the temperature, red spots surfaced in her skin like her blood boiled up. A lavender scent always stuck to her clothes and whenever she talked about her long-dead husband, Otto, her usually squinting, judgmental eyes would open wide and turn as blank and pleasant as a cow's.

On the day we walked over to deliver the stew, Gram told me that Edna and she weren't always friends. "Edna was top dog of the side seamers," Gram explained. "No one could tell her what to do, not even Boss Betty, the floor lady. When I started at the mill Edna got the other gals not to talk to me and to this day I don't know why. My first three months there were so bad I hoped I'd get hit by a trolley on my way home. The only thing to make my mind worse was right about then Gramp got sick. When Edna heard about it, she started helpin' me out. She worked a shorter shift than me and she'd check in on Gramp on her way home from work. If one of the boys was sick she'd bring over some soup or whatnot. Did more than my own mother ever did, that's for sure! My mother came to stay to help take care of your daddy when I first started at the mill. It worked out fine for a week or so. Then one day I come home from work and there's your daddy, not more than a year old, alone and screamin' in the crib. Turns out my brother's wife had called askin' Mama to come and help out with *her* kids. So that's what Mama did. Took off to watch my brother's kids and left mine alone. That's what Mama was like with her boys. My brothers should finish school but I might as well drop out. 'All you'll ever be is a wife,' she said. But I was the first one of her kids to buy my own property."

Gram nodded her head and pointed to East Mountain. "That's right, girl. I got my own piece of land up in them woods. And it was just last year I made the last payment on the house. Own it free and clear and my own name's on that deed, girl, not just Gramp's. You remember that. Ain't nobody gonna look out for you but your-self."

We stood still, staring off at East Mountain as if we could see Gram's property and admire it from there. "But it doesn't make sense," I said. "Why was she so mean to you?"

Gram sucked at the space where she used to have a tooth. "She wasn't nice to my sisters neither. But to me she was the worst. I got to think she was jealous of the way my daddy loved me. He used to call me his Sweet Rosy Ro. I'd a been a different person if he'd lived past my tenth birthday, I'm sure of it."

It was hard for me to imagine Gram as a little girl being any-thing but like the Gram she was now. And it wasn't so much that I didn't believe her, but that her having a daddy who thought of her as being sweet was as unreal to me as the little angel Gram said sat on my shoulder and told God if I'd done something wrong. "I meant Mrs. Schwackhammer, Gram. Why was she mean to you?"

"I asked her that once and tears came to her eyes. She was sorry, she said." Gram raised her head as far as she could with her hump. "That was all that mattered to me was her sayin' that. I didn't care why else she was mean. Her own husband died of the black lung. She said she was full of regrets over how she handled his sickness and that I looked about as bad as she'd felt then, so it made her feel a little better to help me out. It made her feel like she was helpin' her own Otto in a way, is what she said. And she did help me out. But if you ask me she likes when things go bad. She's drawn to it. Some folks are like that. Other people's bad news makes somethin' feel good inside them."

We'd reached Mrs. Schwackhammer's house, which was a wooden A-frame house with ivy growing all over it. When Mrs. Schwackhammer's husband died, she'd let the ivy go wild because that ivy was the very same ivy she'd rooted from her bridal bouquet a million years ago and to pull it out, she'd often said, felt like she was ripping her marriage farther apart. "He's already in heaven," Gram would say to me. "How much farther could they get?"

As soon as we'd stepped into the foyer Gram started in on that ivy, lecturing as usual about its ability to get into the cracks in the foundation and spread them even more. Most times Mrs. Schwackhammer lectured back about the value of sentimentality and how Gram could benefit from caring about the meaning of things, but this time all she did was sob, "What does it matter?"

"'Course, 'course," Gram said, a look of alarm tightening the wrinkles on her face. Clearly at a loss for words, Gram added, "Brought stew." Mrs. Schwackhammer meekly nodded. "And tomorrow I'll call the mayor's office and the town council. We're not goin' to give up without a fight!"

Mrs. Schwackhammer sat in a wing chair that her large cumbersome body dwarfed. A pool of weak sunlight on the floor by her feet seemed to take all her attention. "Where will I go?"

"You got three kids with houses of their own who you could move in with any day of the week and you know it!"

Mrs. Schwackhammer turned toward the window that was veined with ivy. A moment or two passed before she openly wept.

Me and Gram met eyes, both of us taut with discomfort. "Well," Gram said, reaching for the pot of stew that I still clenched between my hands. "I'll heat you up a bowl. Nothin' like a full belly." And with those words Gram tromped off into the kitchen leaving me alone with Mrs. Schwackhammer who was trying to delicately wipe her nose on her sleeve.

Spying a box of Kleenex on a side table, I plucked several tissues and placed them on Mrs. Schwackhammer's lap, catching a whiff of lavender as I did so. She grabbed the tissues and blew her nose. Then she looked at me. Her eyes were as red as her face and the yellow tint of her hair seemed to softly glow. "Been thinking about you finding that man," she said. "What it must have been like that first moment you saw him. It must have been awful for you." She leaned forward and swallowed as if I was about to feed her a spoonful of something delicious.

There was a clatter from the kitchen followed by Gram shouting, "Didn't break!" There was something stealthy in the way Mrs. Schwackhammer's eyes shifted from the hallway to the kitchen, then back to my face. "Been wondering who that man was who you found and what those detectives keep asking your grandpa."

I stepped back, out of the pool of sunlight that had shifted toward my feet. Irritated by my silence, Mrs. Shwackhammer clucked her tongue. "Well, girl, you must know what they've been asking him. It must be something important. Your grandpa is known for his temper, isn't he? Rowena doesn't mention it, but I know he's been to the county jail."

"Everyone knows that," I said.

"Don't be fresh," Mrs. Schwackhammer snapped, smacking her hands on the arm of her chair.

Gram clomped in the room. "Don't go scrapin' the bottom of the pot, Edna. I burned it. But it's plenty hot for you to have a bowlful."

Gram sat next to Mrs. Schwackhammer at the kitchen table while Mrs. Schwackhammer stirred her spoon through her bowl of stew and talked about the hutch her Otto had stripped and varnished, the shelves he'd built beneath the stairs, the bedroom window where he liked to sit to read his paper. "It feels like I'm dying," Mrs. Schwackhammer said. "Losing this house makes me feel like I'm losing him all over again."

"Nonsense," Gram said. "You can only lose him once." Gram steadily tapped her fingers on the table, looking anywhere but at her friend's face. "Did I tell you John's got blood in the stool?"

"No," Mrs. Schwackhammer said, eyes brightening. "How much? What's it look like?"

Gram gave me a knowing look and then gave Mrs. Schwackhammer an earful of gory detail. Afterward, on our way home, Gram stopped me beside a white fence smothered in yellow roses. "She asked you somethin' about them cops and Gramp, didn't she?"

I nodded. "But I didn't tell her a thing."

Gram looked back at Mrs. Schwackhammer's house and her

mouth scrunched like she'd swallowed something bitter. "Ain't that a woman for you!" Gram gave me a sideways glance that was at least partly appreciative. "You was right not to say nothin' to her. Ain't none of her business what Gramp did or didn't do, ain't that right?"

I didn't answer. My tongue felt heavy as if Gram's words weighted it down and gave my own suspicions greater heft and shape.

Gram repeated, "Our business ain't nobody else's, right?"

I skipped off ahead, blocking out Gram's voice as she called after me. Marisol and I were supposed to meet up at White Deer Lake to finish reading *The Once and Future King* and I couldn't wait to plunge back into the world of Camelot and forget the one I was in now.

Twelve

My birthday fell on a Wednesday that year, but Ma threw my picnic party on the Saturday before. It was Indian summer, the first weekend of October, and the spectacularly red and orange trees looked strange in the hazy heat of the air. It was usually Indian summer for my birthday and I took this to mean that I had some connection with the Indians, even though Daddy had told me that Indian summer was just a slur, meaning anything the Indians did wouldn't last long.

That day as I helped Ma set up the snacks on a picnic sheet in Pothole Park I wondered what the Indians who used to live here were doing on this very spot five hundred years ago. Pothole Park was named for the giant pothole at its center and Daddy said that the Lenape Indians who'd lived here had performed sacred rites around it. If that was so, I wondered what their sacred spirits thought of the trash that the campers and picnickers threw down the hole. But it wasn't just any hole. It was the second-largest glacier hole in the world! The pothole was about forty feet deep and carved out thousands of years ago by a glacier carrying jagged rocks and stones. Whenever Marisol and I hiked in this direction, we always stopped by the hole and counted how many used condoms we could see clinging to the rocky ledges that spiraled down all the way to the bottom.

"Better not be daydreaming like that when company comes," Ma said, handing me the potato salad container to open because she'd just had her nails done and could barely manage to light a cigarette. She'd had her hair done too in what was supposed to be a soft Jacqueline Kennedy style but it looked hard and helmet-like and I didn't care for it at all.

Holding a compact to my face I checked out the eye shadow and lipstick Ma had let me wear for the first time ever. Desperately I wanted a compliment from Ma but I didn't dare ask for it because I knew then she'd say something to make me feel dumb.

"Quit starin' at yourself and help out. Believe me, you're better leaving off boys altogether. They ain't no road to happiness. When I was your age—" Ma breathed out her nose. She glanced off to the shadowy parts in the crook of a chestnut tree that shaded us. "Well, that don't matter. You look real pretty, Brigid," she said, but she got gloomy when she said it and the compliment, instead of making me feel good, just made me wonder about the sad places inside Ma.

Not far from us, Brother lay on a towel dozing in the sun. We were all tired. Mr. Smythe, the inspector, had gotten us all up at three in the morning because the air was bad and we'd had to stand outside in our bathrobes waiting for the house to air out and the danger to pass. More than once Ma had instructed all of us not to mention anything about last night. "And for cripessakes, keep your mouths shut about finding no dead body," Ma instructed. "We don't want them thinking we was bad luck."

We were stabbing melon balls with toothpicks, planning when and how to serve the rest of the snacks, most of them bought fresh from Shnauer's deli. In all my life Ma had never bought deli food so I couldn't help but sneak a cold cut or a bit of pasta salad.

Shaking a cigarette from a pack of Parliaments, Ma nodded at a foot-long present wrapped in paper that was covered in roses. "You'll be so surprised," Ma said, "you'll shit yourself." She stuck a cigarette in her mouth and cupped her hand to light it.

I studied Ma's face for the trick. Sometimes she teased to take me down a peg. There was a glistening sheen to her eyes though, which made her excitement seem pure. Still, I managed to keep my mouth shut and pretend I didn't care what I got for my birth-day. From the way Ma held the smoke before puffing it out, I could tell I'd pleased her. But where, I wondered, had Ma gotten the money for all this stuff? If she could afford deli food and a bakery cake and some fancy present and to have her hair and nails done, then why couldn't she buy me shoes that fit and a bathing suit that wasn't one of her hand-me-downs and didn't cup my boobs like giant shells?

By the time Uncle Jerry and Aunt Janice arrived, Brother had woken and he and little Jerry played in the mushy part of the meadow, oblivious to the bugs sucking at their blood and skin. Uncle Jerry and Aunt Janice sat in two folding chairs they'd brought. Uncle Jerry sat forward in his chair as if he was about to leap onto the picnic sheet where I sat between the melon and cheese platter pouring spiked iced tea from a thermos for the adults. Aunt Janice sat with her back straight as a ruler, hands folded on her lap, the bun on her head so tight even the breeze cutting through the meadow couldn't stir a single strand of it.

Ma sat facing them, an empty folding chair beside her for when Daddy came. When Daddy told her that morning that he'd get to the park when he could, Ma hadn't said a thing. You could see the surprise hit Daddy's face and then you could see him immediately hide it. Ma, I guess, wanted her brother to herself for as long as she could have him so she didn't mind that Daddy was off betting on horses or drinking at some bar. And I suppose Daddy was just as glad.

Ma had taken care to have the chairs arranged in what she called a conversational circle, but the only conversation going on was Uncle Jerry complaining about all sorts of different things: the drive up from Allentown, the students who had nothing better to do than stage sit-ins, the building of the Berlin Wall. I watched Brother and Little Jerry chase ducks while Uncle Jerry recounted the downturn of this great country and the very real possibility of us all being bombed to hell. He sat back and flicked his hands toward the tree as if it were the Soviets or Castro who he said were to blame.

The hair on his knuckles was as curly and dark as the hair sprouting above the collar of his T-shirt. He had pinkish white skin and little red veins all over his nostrils. From the angle I was looking at him, I could see nose hairs sticking out like antennae off a beetle, and I rubbed my smooth legs, shaved that morning for the first time ever, and got afraid that Gram might have been right when she'd shouted at me through the bathroom door: "You'll be as hairy as an ape. Mark my words. Shavin' it just makes it come in thicker and faster."

"Bropey," Ma interrupted Uncle Jerry's tirade against desegregation. "You remember that's what I called you?" Ma was referring to the name she'd called Uncle Jerry before their ma died, before their father remarried, and his new wife sent Ma off to an orphanage, sent Ma off and not Jerry because boys, that horrible woman had said, were useful to have around.

Ma reached into a cooler and picked up the cut-glass salt shaker that Gram usually kept on the dining-room table. "You remember a salt shaker like this? Don't it look just like the one Ma kept in the hutch? Took me a long time to remember why I liked cut-glass shakers so much. But then it just came to me. Just all of a sudden I was back in our dining room seeing sunlight coming through the curtain, dust just hanging in the air, and all that dusty sun making the salt and pepper shakers sparkle."

Uncle Jerry raised his upper lip, which drew deep creases down his cheeks and reminded me of the rats sniffing around where we used to live by the dump. "Well, would you look at that," he said, standing up. He hitched his beige pants, which he wore so high the belt cinched the middle of his chest, and crossed to where Ma sat. The salt shaker had a curved womanly shape, and Uncle Jerry took hold of it lovingly, his fingers caressing its dozens of brilliant cuts.

"Looks like the shaker your mother gave us, Jerry," Aunt Janice said. Aunt Janice added, looking from Ma to me, "For our wedding,"

"Stepmother," Jerry corrected as he crossed back to his lawn chair. From the cheese platter he grabbed a wedge of Swiss. "Have some," he said to Aunt Janice. As he dropped it on her plate, he growled, "Shut your mouth."

Aunt Janice took a swig from her second spiked tea. "Matter

of fact it has the same cuts as the glasses we got from your cousins," she said. "The ones who started a fight in the bathroom?" She looked again from me to Ma, her expression both hopeful and silly as if she were delivering a joke. "What a mess our wedding turned into. You should have seen it."

"Would have loved to have had you there," Uncle Jerry said. He frowned at Ma and added, "If only I'd known where you were. All those years . . ." His words trailed off and he pondered the tea in his paper cup as if it swirled with leaves to read. When he looked up his eyes became like the tea, a kind of orangey brown that looked a bit like mine. "Just think of it, Dolores, if Little Jerry hadn't been hit by that car and the two of us hadn't been in the paper, you and I wouldn't be sitting here right now."

"A miracle," Aunt Janice said, shooting a loaded look at Uncle Jerry and pressing her hands together in a triangle of prayer. She wagged her head and tried to catch Ma's eye, but failing that, snagged mine. She stared deeply at me and described the car that whammed into Little Jerry as he was crossing the street on his bicycle. "He just got up and walked away. Just a few scrapes. We came so close, so close to—" Unable to complete the thought, Aunt Janice dropped her hands, which upset her plate and knocked one of her cheese chunks to the ground.

Uncle Jerry leaned over, picked up the piece of cheese, and flung it behind the chestnut tree. "For Chrissake, Janice, boys ride their bikes in the street all the time. It's not my fault he got hit."

Right then Daddy stepped out from the tree shadows at the edge of the field. He waved to us and walked in that light, loose way of his, body leaning to the left, toward his bad arm.

Uncle Jerry stood, stating how good it was to meet Daddy, but his tone still carried the sounds of complaint. He gripped Daddy's hand, then thwacked him on the back, and Daddy practically danced away from him, his handsome face quirking a smile. Aunt Janice lowered her head as if she were tilting her bun toward him in greeting and he bent down to deliver a sloppy kiss onto the rim of her jaw. Head tilted back, she raised her eyes as if she might find an escape hatch in the chestnut branches crisscrossing above, but the dimples pocking her cheeks hinted that she enjoyed the attention.

"Ain't that hairdo pretty," Ma said, nodding toward Aunt Janice. "Looks like a hamburg bun perched right on top of her head," Ma added.

Aunt Janice's skin turned the faintest shade of bubble gum, making me feel extra bad for her. She hesitantly laughed, mouth quivering, and tilted her head which made her hamburger bun doo aim straight at Uncle Jerry. She knew she was being made fun of but couldn't figure out why.

Daddy maneuvered one of the aluminum folding chairs so that when he sat his knee almost touched Aunt Janice's. I kissed Daddy hello and then sat on the grass by his feet, noticing he smelled of cigarettes and that wintergreen smell of the breath mints he'd sucked when he'd been drinking whisky.

"How lucky am I?" Daddy said. "I get to sit near all the pretty girls."

Aunt Janice giggled nervously and Uncle Jerry grunted, but you could tell he wasn't listening. He told us he'd served two tours in Korea and his eyes went kind of blank when he found out that Daddy's mining accident had kept him out of that war.

"Now let's not go talking about no war on a day nice as this,"

Ma said, swatting at flies. She offered a platter of sandwiches first to Aunt Janice, then to Uncle Jerry, telling me to serve the salads. When she handed Uncle Jerry a napkin, the pink eye shadow she'd used matched the rush of blood heating up her cheeks. "One day we'll have you over to our home," she said. "Soon as we have one, that is."

Uncle Jerry took a bite of a ham hoagie and as he chewed, said, "Well that's something I wanted to discuss with you. With both of you. I've got a job in mind. At my dealership. It could work out well for you, Adrian. It's not that . . . . physical. Paperwork and staying on top of the cars that come in. For repairs and cleaning. You'd be in charge of two guys. Good guys." He turned to Daddy and swallowed, his lip raised in that partial sneer. "During the week you could live with us. Come back here on weekends. Till you get on your feet. Then bring the whole family down."

Aunt Janice quickly added, "Once you find a place of your own." Fast as lightning Uncle Jerry zapped her a look that bolted her upright. "We have so little room was all I meant," Aunt Janice explained.

"I don't want to move," Brother cried from the boulder where he and Jerry perched, each with caps on, each flicking the lettuce shreds and tomato off their sandwiches.

"Shut your mouth," Ma said. Then smiling at Uncle Jerry she added, "Why, John Patrick, you'd be near your little cousin. And we could stay there permanent like. For good." Ma wiped at her eyes and said the heat was making them dry but we could all tell they were wet with tears.

Daddy didn't say a word. He played with a pickle spear, like it was a cigar, and did his Groucho Marx imitation. "I couldn't possibly take a job. After all, where would I take it?"

"If it works out," Uncle Jerry said, "you might get to run your own dealership. I've got plans in the works to set up another in Mechanicsburg."

Daddy bit the pickle and Ma said, "Ah, a job" as if she were saying "Hallelujah" and I knew she was thinking about never having to work at a mill and being like the ladies who lived in the mansions on the north side of town.

"I'd be right there," Uncle Jerry said, "making sure everything went smooth. Nothing to it, really. You'll get the hang of it quick." Uncle Jerry glanced over at Daddy, who was nodding but seemed more interested in rearranging the ham and salami on his roll than in discussing the job.

"Any job that has nothing to it sounds like my kind of work," Daddy said, winking at me.

"How 'bout presents?" Ma said. "Huh, Brigid?"

I knew Ma was looking to distract Daddy from saying anything further about the job for fear Uncle Jerry would take back the offer, but I didn't like the thought of Daddy being away from us all week and I was hoping he'd say something more to blow his chances.

"Look at her." Ma laughed. "Little Miss Something Else. Trying to pretend she don't care what present she got. Trying to pretend she's cucumber cool." With a flourish Ma presented the foot-long box to me, placing it in my arms like a baby.

I turned the box over and slid my finger into the slit where the pretty rose paper was taped so that I could pluck the tape from the paper without damaging it.

"Oh, look at her," Ma said. "Rip it. We don't need to save *paper*." Ma rolled her eyes as if she hadn't screamed every birthday and Christmas—"Careful! You think I'm made of paper?"

I made one practice rip and when Ma didn't say anything, I shredded it all, letting the pretty waste fall to the ground. When I turned the box over, I couldn't believe what I saw. Inside the cellophane window of the box was a doll who looked just like Lady Maribel, the doll Ma had made me leave behind in Centre-reach because we didn't have room for her in the car. This doll though didn't have a chipped nose or ripped lace trim. She had blinking blue eyes and the most beautiful satin dress I'd ever seen. My fingers went limp. It was the nicest present Ma had ever bought me. I felt as soft and pliable as the cloth body of the doll.

"Show her to Aunt Janice," Ma insisted, her face tight with impatience. "And to Uncle Jerry. Go on."

"She looks like you," Aunt Janice said and Ma laughed. The doll didn't look anything like me with her fair unfreckled skin and long golden hair. Uncle Jerry barely nodded at it and then Ma took it from my hands. "Eat your cake," she said. "Don't want her getting dirty. You can play with her later." Ma sealed the doll back up in the box and placed it up against one of the tree's big knotted roots.

I knew better than to whine but I couldn't take my eyes from the box even as Aunt Janice handed me a gift. Without waiting for Ma's approval I ripped at the pink and white paper Aunt Janice had wrapped it in. "Chutes and Ladders," I lamely declared, putting the game to the side. "Thanks."

"Open it," Ma cried with exaggerated excitement.

"But I play this all the time with Brother."

"No, she don't," Ma said.

"Sorry," Aunt Janice said, meeting my eyes. "We thought you were younger."

"Believe me, she acts a heck of a lot younger than her age," Ma said, mouth drawn tight like she was sitting at her sewing machine, clenching pins between her teeth. To me she said, "Thank your uncle Jerry, too."

"Sure, sure." Uncle Jerry said. "She's welcome." For the first time his tea-colored eyes focused on my face. "You know I think she looks a little like Mama. And like you, Doe."

"No," Ma said, "we all know who she looks like."

Uncle Jerry narrowed his eyes at me. "Yeah. A bit."

"Who?" I said. "Who do I look like?"

Ma handed me a plastic bag filled with garbage and nodded toward the pothole. "Go dump it," she said to me. Then to Uncle Jerry, "I'll tell you who really look alike. Little Jerry and John Patrick."

All the adults turned to look at the boys who'd wandered over to the pothole and were busy throwing rocks and trash into it.

"Be careful, Little Jerry," Aunt Janice called. "Don't go falling in." Her voice seemed to get swallowed up by the sounds of sobs choking the air. We all turned in astonishment to Uncle Jerry, who sat wiping at his eyes with the back of his big meaty hand. His voice got all phlegmy as he said, "I always felt so bad. I should have tried harder to find you."

"Nah, don't feel bad," Ma said. "You was too young." Bending her fingers she pretended to admire her extra long, extra red nails. "'Course you could have found me later when you was a little older. But maybe you didn't even know where they put me?" From Ma's squint I could tell she was testing him.

"When I was little they wouldn't tell me where you'd gone. I kept asking and they wouldn't say a thing. So I stopped asking."

He lowered his head in shame. "It wasn't until I was out of high school, had just gotten engaged, as a matter of fact"—he glanced at Aunt Janice who was staring down at her clasped hands as if she expected something terrible to spring out from between her fingers—"It wasn't until all those years later that I asked again. Pop said he couldn't even remember the name of the orphanage. I don't know whether that was true or not. But Mom, I mean Stepmother, remembered."

"I bet she did," Ma declared in the voice she used to talk about the factory ladies she hated.

Uncle Jerry wiped at his nose with a napkin. "All the orphanage would tell me was that you'd left. They didn't know where. Did you run away? I'd guessed you had."

Ma's face scrunched the way Brother's did when he was about to bawl, but she busied herself putting away different foods. "I can't believe you went looking for me," she said. "That we missed each other. All those years." Ma's voice carried such loss that I involuntarily swallowed, as if I could swallow that pain for her. "You know something," she said. "I don't know if you got one to spare, but I'd love to have a photo of Ma. I used to have one. But it got stole from me. The day after I left the orphanage it got stole."

Uncle Jerry reached for the thermos of spiked iced tea and poured some all the way to the rim of his cup. "You bet. Absolutely. I'll make a trip to—" He sipped the drink, smacked his lips and sighed. "I'll take a trip to Elsie's. She has the rest of Mama's things. You can have whatever you want."

"How could you leave them there with *her*?" And when Ma said *her*, spit shot out from her mouth. "How could you not take them with you?"

Uncle Jerry's bottom lip thrust forward. "When Pop died, I don't know. I never thought of it."

"So the bastard's dead?" Ma looked up at a cloud shaped like two wolves kissing.

"Looks like a storm's brewing," Daddy said. "Think we'd better pack it up."

Aunt Janice readily agreed but Uncle Jerry stayed quiet.

"Did he suffer?" Ma said. "I'm his daughter, like it or not. I got a right to know."

Uncle Jerry described a slow wasting death filled with pus and bed-wetting.

"Good." Ma nodded, satisfied. And Uncle Jerry looked off toward the woodsy acres behind us, squeezing his clasped hands so hard his fingers turned red.

That evening, back at the house, we all picked at one of Gram's bready meat loafs. Gramp and Daddy made meager conversation about football and the rest of us ate in silence. The energy that had made Ma talk nonstop that morning had turned into something else and me, Brother, and Daddy shared warning looks to keep out of her path.

"What's everybody's problem?" Gram said. She had an elasticized pink hairnet stuck to her head with curlers nesting below it that looked like creepy fat caterpillars. "Don't know what you thought would happen meetin' your brother, Dolores. If he ain't been there for you in the past, he ain't goin' be there for you now. Anyways, you two don't know each other from two holes in the wall. 'Course things ain't goin' be sweet and nice between you."

Ma fiddled with her fork, her downcast eyes showing all the

cracks in her eye shadow. Hours ago her hair spray had wilted and now her hair just drooped against her head. "Ain't nothing sweet and nice with you, Rowena. We all know that." Ma pushed back from the table and walked out the front door. We could see her through the window, pacing the walk, cigarette in hand, part of West Mountain glowing red behind her. Gram made as if to go after her until Daddy growled, "*Mother.*"

"Leave alone," Gramp said and Gram harrumphed but stayed seated at the table.

After I finished the dishes, I escaped to my room, eager to play with my doll. Carefully I lifted her from the box and placed her on the desk. I couldn't believe she was mine. I combed my fingers through her bright yarn hair and stroked the lace of her dress, hoping some of what made her pretty might rub off on me. I got so lost in fantasy that I never heard Gram open the door but there she was suddenly yelling at me, "What in the Lord's name are you doin'?"

"You said you'd knock," I accused.

Gram stepped in and looked suspiciously from me to the doll. "Twelve years old! Would you believe it?" Wearily she shook her head and sat on the lower bunk, my bunk, where she then gazed up at the empty space where Ma's mattress used to be. She turned as best she could over her hump and clucked her tongue at Daddy's werewolf poster as if she'd never seen it before. "I'll tell you somethin', girl. At twelve my mother wasn't just hangin' around playin' with no doll. She was already out in the world earnin' a livin'! Alone! The orphanage wouldn't keep the girls past twelve years old. Twelve! There she was, just a young girl with no place to go. Nothin' to eat. But she knew she had an aunt all the way over in Limerick. She was up near Dublin. That's the other side of Ireland!

Took her nearly a year of cleanin' people's houses to save the money to get there. And when she did, she knocked on her aunt's door and told her aunt—her father's *sister*, mind you—who she was, and as soon as she said her name, you know what that woman did?"

"No," I said, but I already felt the hurt of it, even though I didn't know Gram's ma, my great-grandma at all.

"That woman, her father's sister, acted like she had no idea who my mother was. Her own *niece*. Her brother's *daughter*. 'Mary Farmer?' she said. 'Don't know that name at all.' She called my mother a beggar and chased her off with a broom. A broom! And here you are with a doll. Doin' who knows what when the door's closed."

Her eyes were full of blame as she looked down at my fingers poised in midstroke on the doll's dress. Dumbfounded, I gazed down at my hand, wondering what terrible capabilities rested within it.

Just then Ma breezed in. "I need a nap, Brigid," Ma said, acting as if Gram wasn't even there. "So shut the door and don't let nobody in."

"Some people just don't appreciate what they got," Gram said, stomping her foot. She then walked out, leaving the door open so Ma would have to shut it, which Ma did with a slam. Ma sat on my mattress and wearily shook her head. Then her pretty face contorted in pain. She pointed at the doll. "Who told you to take her out?" In two quick paces Ma grabbed the doll. "I told you not to get her dirty. How can I return her if she looks all used?"

"Return her?" I cried. Ma placed the doll on my bunk and began to carefully place her back in the box. My voice didn't sound like my own as I said, "But you gave her to me. You said she was mine."

"Mine? Listen how selfish you sound." Ma closed the box and the doll stared stone-facedly out at me through the little cellophane window. I tried to keep my voice calm, knowing it was the best way to handle Ma, but still I whined, "Please, Ma. I'll do anything. I'll stay in my room. I'll do all the chores. I want to keep her so bad."

But as soon as I said that last part about wanting, I knew I'd said the wrong thing. Ma often said she couldn't stand it when I got impatient, but I knew that wasn't what she meant. We'd learned, Daddy and me especially, to pretend in front of Ma *not* to want what we wanted. *That's* what she wanted—as confusing as that sounds.

"Keep your voice down," Ma said. "You know we can't afford no doll. Don't act like you don't know. I do the best I can. The. Best. I. Can." With each word, Ma thrust her thumb at herself. Then she started to cry. She glanced at the door with as much disdain as if the rectangle of wood was Gram herself. "You think I'd be here if it wasn't for you kids. I'm sacrificed so you kids have a roof. Your daddy don't do that. *I* do that."

She came at me and pinched my arm. Then she sat on the desk chair with the doll box resting on her lap. "Don't you dare look at me like that. You know we don't got the money for this. Don't act like you thought you could keep her. Don't make me feel bad when you knew it all along."

My voice came out as thin as a trickle of water. "But you had the money for the deli food. The money to get your hair and nails done."

"And don't I work hard for that! Don't I deserve something too?"

I backed up to the door. My chest felt all dense and tight and my voice came out in stops and starts. "I hate you. I hate you more than anything else in the world."

Ma laughed. "Wait. Wait till you see the rest of the world. I ain't that bad. Compared to the rest of it, I ain't nothin' at all."

Out the door I ran, past Gramp and Daddy who were sitting on the plastic-covered couch watching TV. I ran outside and deep into the fire zone, hoping I'd trip on a borehole and break my neck and for the rest of her life Ma would have to be sorry for what she'd done.

That night in bed Ma shook me and whispered, "Brigid? Did you have a nice birthday? Huh, honey? I need to know. Did you?"

I was lying on my side facing the wall. All I had to do was roll over and say "yes" and Ma's love would have washed over me like sunshine, like rain. But I remained rigid, staring at the werewolf poster on the wall, thinking of Auntie's story "The Great Forgetting." I couldn't wait for the day to come when me and Ma would pass each other on the street and not even know each other's names, when we wouldn't know each other at all.

Thirteen

Our lives changed once Daddy started working for Uncle Jerry. On Sunday evenings Daddy drove down to Allentown where he spent the week working for Uncle Jerry in his used car dealership and living in Uncle Jerry and Aunt Janice's spare room.

"Calling it a closet would be a compliment," Daddy said, referring to the spare room, which fit only a cot and a nightstand. "Calling it a closet would be an insult to closets all over the world."

All week we looked forward to those Friday nights when Daddy came home. When he walked in the door with his jacket folded over his arm and his tie loose around his neck, he walked in a different man. That's what Ma said. "Like he turned back to the way he used to be. Like whatever happened to him that day in the mine just disappeared. Like it hadn't happened at all."

We'd hold supper, sometimes not eating until eight or nine, until whatever Ma and Gram had cooked had dried out or cooled. We'd all sit around the kitchen table with the stove blasting out its warmth and the louvered window cracked for air. The lateness of the hour would give those evenings what Daddy called "night magic," that mystic kind of feeling that comes sometimes with darkness and night.

Those evenings might have actually been magical in that Ma and Gram would use the kitchen together to prepare the meal. Sometimes they wouldn't even be talking to each other and Gram would tell me to tell Ma that Ma's water was boiling, and Ma would tell me to tell Gram that Gram's gravy was sticking. Somehow, though, they always managed to pull off one of Daddy's favorites: pot roast and biscuits, meat loaf with slightly burned oven-roasted potatoes, the salad done with petals of iceberg leaves cupping radish wedges that resembled the hearts of flowers.

Ma wore her hair up the way Daddy liked it and put on one of the dresses she'd made styled after one she'd seen Mrs. Jacqueline Kennedy wearing in a magazine. As soon as Daddy walked in the door he'd wolf whistle and spin Ma around and tell her she was the prettiest girl in the world. And I think just like with Daddy, Ma turned back to the way she once was, the way I remembered before her heart turned bitter. Brother must have felt it too, even though he was too little to remember her back then. He'd cling to Ma, standing beside her chair and nuzzling into her armpit like a sad little calf. Sometimes he'd sit on her lap snoozing against her shoulder as if he was afraid that when he opened his eyes she'd be back to the bristly ma we'd all gotten used to.

On those nights Gramp, who usually went to bed at eight, would stay up no matter how late the hour and Gram would hold off putting her Friday-night curlers in until we'd sat long over dessert, listening to Daddy tell stories about the customers, and the other workers, and the people he met in Allentown. He told funny stories about something dumb someone said. And he'd tell

sad stories about car accidents and deaths and divorces and bank-
ruptcies that had made people lose their cars or need to buy a used
one.

Most of Daddy's job was making sure all the paperwork for
the cars was in order and making sure the two men under him,
Joe and Phil, had done their jobs, which was to clean and repair
the cars. We knew all about Joe's mother's glaucoma and Joe's
hammertoes and about Phil's wife who would sometimes leave
the baby alone in the afternoon to go to the corner bar and how
Joe would hear about it from neighbors and would have to give
her the "what for" all over again.

Daddy was proud of how well the men liked him. "I tell them
I don't care if they take an extra five minutes here or there, as long
as they get the cleanup and repairs done. I tell them flirt with
Norma all you want. As long as your work gets done, it's no skin
off my nose."

Norma was the office girl. She had a boyfriend who she was
afraid was never going to propose and a father who was such a
drunk he sometimes locked her out of the house because he didn't
recognize who she was. "She's a bit of a ditz," Daddy said. "But I
never talk down to her. When I tell her to get my coffee, I always
say please and thank you. A little politeness goes a long way. Especially with women."

Daddy told us about the things they'd find in the cars: loose
change, buttons, a baby's shoe, the last page of a breakup letter,
torn photos, shopping lists, shell casings, a box filled with potted
meat. "And other things," he said ominously. "Grownup things."
When I pleaded to know what those were, he winked and Ma
and Gramp laughed. "Don't you dare tell," Gram said.

"Slimy rubbers probably," Marisol informed me when I asked

what Daddy could be referring to. "I bet the seats are sticky from where people did it. I bet he's found bloodstains and poo stains and who knows what else."

I started picturing those cars as violent wrecks, horrible museum pieces of people's lives. And I got worried for Daddy that something bad would happen to him.

When Daddy came home those Friday evenings, he didn't only tell stories; he also did what Gram called "wicked imitations." "Imitations that make you burn in hell, Adrian, if they weren't so funny." Legs crossed, Daddy would dangle his shoe off his foot and do Norma filing her nails or snapping her gum. He'd do Phil belting his wife and Joe hobbling around on his crooked toes. And he always did a rendition of Aunt Janice that would leave all of us—Gram especially, who'd never even met Aunt Janice—breathless.

"Little Jerry, Little Jerry," Daddy called out, his voice high-pitched and quivering with tension. "You need help wiping your butt? Should I come up and wipe it for you?"

Trying to hold back the laugh, tears oozed out Gram's eyes and even Gramp hacked out a chuckle. The only person Daddy never made fun of was Uncle Jerry. All his life Daddy was careful of the places where Ma was tender.

Sometimes it was close to midnight when Daddy finally fell quiet. He'd pick up Brother from where he'd be sleeping, either on Ma's lap or curled up on the floor mat by the sink, and I'd be left to wash the dishes. Usually Ma would open the front door and stare out at West Mountain, which steamed worse in the cold weather, and tell Daddy how he'd nailed those people exact. "Feels like I know them already, Adrian. Like I known them all my life."

On Friday night and Saturday night when Daddy was home,

he slept with Ma in his and Uncle Frank's old room and I was stuck having to sleep in Gramp's smelly old Barcalounger. The first thing Daddy did in his old room was to move his mattress from the bottom bunk to the floor next to Ma's mattress and the second thing he did was to pack into boxes all of Uncle Frank's athletic trophies and photos. He even peeled off the werewolf poster, stuck to the wall by his bed, leaving a rectangle that was a much brighter shade of blue from the rest of the room.

"Burn it all, Adrian," I heard Ma say about Uncle Frank's photos and awards. "That'll get her. That's the only thing that hurts her—losing him."

To Gram's protests Daddy said, "Wasn't any room to breathe in there, Mother. Much less room for the girls to put their things. But if you want, I'll put it all back when we leave."

"Leave? So you can be a used car salesman? Ain't no one in the world trusts one of them. They cheat anybody, even their own people."

Gramp spit into his can, making a hollow sound of agreement.

"He's working a respectable job!" Ma shouted. "What more do you people want?"

"Well, at least he gets a paycheck," Gram said. "That's somethin'. But I'll tell you, Dolores, you better make sure that brother of yours is on the up and up. You don't know him from Adam. No tellin' what reasons he got for wantin' you down there."

"What you mean what reason, Rowena?" Ma said. "What better reason than having his own sister back in his life. You're just jealous 'cause there's no one on this whole planet who'd want you anywhere."

Then Gram said all sorts of stuff about how Ma should be grateful Gram took her in all those years ago when Ma had nothing to her name but the clothes on her back. "But I understood what it was to be an orphan, Dolores," Gram said. "Didn't I? How many mother-in-laws would a been as nice about that?"

"Nice about it? You call telling anybody who'd listen that my daddy gave me away, *nice*? You call promising me your grandma's ring and then not giving it to me, *nice*?" Ma held her ring finger up like it was her middle finger and wiggled it at Gram. On that finger was the same plain silver ring she'd worn since she was married, the same silver ring she told people was white gold.

With a yelp like she'd been struck, Ma turned and ran into the bedroom. Me and Daddy followed and found her curled up on her mattress like a baby, bawling her eyes out. I was still so mad at Ma for taking back my doll that I just stood there, watching her, even though each sob raked me hard like a claw.

But Daddy knelt on the mattress and stroked her hair. "Mother wants to goad you, Lores. When will you learn that? You're giving her exactly the reaction she wants."

Ma sat up and wiped her nose against her arm. She looked like she had a cold, her face was so puffy and red. She spun her ring around her finger. "I told you no one will ever respect me if I don't have a proper ring."

Daddy took Ma's hand and kissed it. "I was going to keep this a secret"—he nodded at me to shut the door and lowered his voice—"but I might as well tell you now. Jerry and I have been looking at apartments. Soon we'll be out of here, living near your brother, just like you always wanted."

Ma's mouth opened and her bottom lip trembled reminding me of a baby bird I'd found and fed with a dropper. Ma pressed Daddy's palm to her cheek. "Oh, Adrian, how soon can we go?"

"But I don't want to leave," I said. "I've got friends here."

"Can't you think of anyone but yourself?" Ma snapped.

"Can't you?" I snapped back and flung open the door and bolted before either of them had a chance to smack me.

Later that night Daddy found me out by the catalpa tree and put his arm around me. He said not to be mad at Ma for taking back the doll. He said she was so overcome by finding her brother she couldn't think of anything else. He told me that he was proud of me for being as nice to Ma as I generally was, even though sometimes Ma said thoughtless things.

He kissed the side of my head, pointing first at Taurus romping around the sky, then Orion readying for battle, then the sweet sad little cluster of the seven Pleiades sisters, the seventh little sister twinkling in and out, so difficult to see. It was then Daddy told me something crazy. He said that Gram and Ma fought so much not because they hated each other, but because they loved each other. He said they each wanted the other's love so bad they could taste it. "One of them has got to give the love first, though," Daddy explained, "and they're each so stubborn they won't do it. So they hold on to the love for each other and it turns all ugly inside them."

We pondered that in silence for a while and then Daddy asked me all about school and what I'd been up to while he was away. He was especially interested in my teachers, wanting to know if they were mean or nice and it reminded me of countless afternoons in Centrereach when Daddy would pick me up from school and ask about everything that had happened to me that day. If it had been something bad, he'd make up tall tales to make me feel better, returning often to my favorite stories, the library monster who was going to eat mean old Mrs. Blot or the fairy angel who would sprinkle star dust in my eyes and make anything that upset me disappear.

That night by the catalpa, Daddy leaned against the tree's trunk and his face caught some of the living-room window's light. His cheeks looked thin and his eyes hollowed out and I realized that working in Allentown must have been a horrible strain on him.

"Daddy," I said, "something happened while you were away." And I told him what crazy old Mrs. Novak had said about the dead man being her son. And I told him that she thought Gramp had been the one to kill him. And then I did something that we hardly ever did in my family: I asked a question that I knew Daddy wouldn't want to answer. "Could it be, Daddy? Could she be right?"

Daddy shook his head and said, "Jack Novak had a lot more enemies than friends, but then being a fire boss who takes bribes—" He turned to me and stopped talking. He shook his head some more before he continued, "No, princess. That dead man isn't Jack Novak. Jack Novak killed himself. He was seeing this girl over in Minisink Ford. One day he walked right onto the Roebling Bridge and dived straight off it into the Delaware River. People saw him do it. A fisherman even tried to rescue him. They never found his body. Old Mrs. Novak just can't accept what happened. It made her crazy, I guess, pretending that he was missing or had died some other way." Daddy sniffed and wiped at his nose. "That bridge was actually built by John Roebling. The same man who built the Brooklyn Bridge. It used to be the Delaware Aqueduct and was part of the Delaware and Hudson Canal. Actually, it's not far from a Revolutionary battle site." Daddy went on to talk about that battle and what was at stake for the colonies until I shivered. The night had grown starkly cold as we'd stood out there.

"We should head in," he said and reached out his hand for me to take it.

"You're the best daddy ever," I said, playing the game we used to play in Centrereach, a time that seemed so long ago it felt separate from me, as if it was some other little girl and her daddy that I was remembering.

Daddy smiled, playing along. "And you're the most wonderful princess in the world," he declared.

As we walked to the house I made him promise to always be my daddy and always be Ma's lover boy.

"Of course, princess," he said. "All I am is a daddy." And then he told me about the first time he saw Ma standing in the great big doorway of the mill and how she'd stolen his heart that very moment. "That's right, princess. She stole my heart. And don't you know your ma. Once she takes a thing, she never gives it back."

And we smiled in sympathy with each other at Ma's hard, edgy ways.

Fourteen

Ma slept poorly in those weeks after Daddy told her we'd be moving to Allentown. She'd toss and turn, wanting to gossip about the mill girls or discuss decorations for our new apartment. I did my best to fake sleep and ignore her, but that didn't last for long. No matter how much I wanted to keep my heart hard to Ma, I couldn't do it.

"I knew if I waited long enough," Ma told me, "everything I wanted since I was little would happen. I'd almost given up. *Almost*," Ma repeated as if she *had* finally given up, the good stuff would never have happened at all.

Often during the night I'd wake up at 3:00 A.M. to hear Ma talking to Mr. Smythe. Ma usually asked about the gas levels in the houses nearby and then she'd say something like, "Well, we don't got to worry about that no more. We won't be a bother to you soon enough." Or she'd tell him yet again how her brother invited us down to live by him. "In Allentown," she'd add, "where they ain't got no fire."

Mr. Smythe's response was always the same, "Glad to hear it, Mrs. Howley. Now go to sleep."

In the weeks after Daddy told us we'd be moving, me and Marisol spent even more time together. Sometimes we'd hunt for hawthorn or wild thyme or other herbs Marisol's mother wanted to brew in teas to help her breathe better. And it would remind me of the many times me and Auntie went on what we called "herb hunts," taking long hikes to find the weeds and flowers she needed for her remedies. Auntie and me would wander the woods and overgrown fields along the highway, the sun streaking the dusty air, Auntie humming tunes I'd never heard sung by anyone but her. The way the sounds of the approaching, then passing cars grew, then faded, always turned me lonely inside. So on those herb-hunting walks with Marisol I got to feeling wistful and sad and happy all at once.

Marisol was especially worried about her mother's health. She was sure her mother had taken a turn for the worse because Detective Kanelous had been to the house three times in the last two weeks and had asked questions about her father.

"Next time he comes," Marisol said, "I'm going to tell him to come straight out and say my father is the killer."

I stopped short on the fire trail we were walking and pretended to be interested in the lichen greening up a tree. "He thinks your daddy did it?" I shook my head as if that could help me get my thoughts around such an idea.

Marisol kicked at the hunk of artist fungi that was growing off the tree's bark. "He keeps asking the same questions about him and I keep saying the same things—William Sullivan was a cheater and a liar and the only good thing he ever did was listen to my mother and get out of our lives."

"You told Detective Kanelous *that?*" I said, my eyes widening with shock and respect—and hope. Maybe Gramp hadn't killed that man down in the bootlegging hole, maybe Marisol's father had.

"You bet I told him that. I'll tell you something else too. I hope my father did bash that guy's brains in because if he did, then the cops will find him and I'll get to tell him right to his face how much I hate his guts."

We'd stopped in a patch of sun and Marisol's eyes in that light were such a deep green they were nearly brown and you could see glistening within them little flecks of hurt. "Actually," she continued, "I wouldn't give him the satisfaction. I wouldn't talk to him at all."

We spent the rest of that afternoon at Marisol's. She and her mother lived in an apartment building on the south side of Barrendale, seven blocks from the river that divided the main part of the city from the fire zone. We sat on an old sheet on the floor of Marisol's room making grapevine wreaths from vines we'd yanked off the fence in the lot behind Marisol's building. We used wire and pliers and twined the long vines into something resembling circles that we planned to sell, but where we'd sell them we didn't know.

That day as we twisted vines, Marisol talked about her grandfather and told me about something called Espiritismo. Ever since she was little, she said, she'd seen spirit shadows. "I didn't want to scare you, so I didn't say anything, but the week before we found the dead body I saw a shadow. It was the size of a cat and it ran out from the kitchen table and then just disappeared." Marisol flung her hands up and made a whooshing sound. Then she pointed at the space between the radiator and bed. "And just this morning, I saw another one right there. It must be the soul of the dead man. He must want something."

"Like what?" I said with a wariness I'd heard Ma occasionally use.

Marisol shrugged. "Depends. If my father was his killer maybe he wants to seek his revenge on me. Or maybe he wants to seek his revenge on us—for something we did to it in a past life." Marisol said this coolly but the muscles around her mouth tightened into a frown.

I stared at the space between the radiator and bed, afraid that I knew exactly what that spirit shadow wanted, and I prayed hard that it would never tell us that Gramp had been its killer. My cheeks flushed with the effort of the prayer and I could feel Marisol looking at me, her gaze bright and glossy. Could she feel my thoughts the way she could *feel* Auntie around me? But all she did was brush the dust off the head of one of the saints' statues on her dresser. Her dresser top was crowded with statues and bottles of holy water and rosaries of various colors. She took her time describing to me the different rituals and prayers needed in order to get good health or money or love.

"What if you don't want to pray for something you want?" I asked. "I mean what if there's something you don't want? Like bad luck or a curse or something?"

"My grandfather says that a curse comes from an ignorant spirit who is angry because of something the cursed person did to it, in a past life or this one. When someone cursed comes to him, he goes into a trance." Marisol shut her eyes and swayed. "He tries to get the ignorant spirit to understand it's dead and to be sorry for all the evil it's done to the cursed person." She opened her eyes and shook her finger at me. "But he says not to be afraid of ignorant spirits because as long as your own spirit is strong, the bad spirit can't bother you. That's why he says it's important to pray and do good—so you're strong enough to keep evil away."

My hands and arms stung from scratches I'd gotten off the vines. A woody green taste was in my mouth from when I'd tried to gnaw a vine I hadn't been able to cut. Suddenly I felt tired and worn out and beaten. Desperately I wanted to tell Marisol about the curse, but I was scared of what would happen. I'd never told anyone about it before. Instead, I asked her what kind of prayers would keep the bad spirits away.

"Next time Mommy calls home I'll ask," Marisol said, pleased, I could tell, that I was interested in her grandfather's work.

From out in the living room came the sounds of Mrs. Sullivan walking in the door. Her keys hit the table, she coughed. Then we heard a knock and Mrs. Sullivan invited someone in. I recognized Detective Kanelous's voice immediately, it was so fast and ugly with hints of New York.

Marisol shushed me with a finger to her lips. Stealthily she opened the door and stepped out. At first I heard little else but Mrs. Sullivan saying yes to Detective Kanelous's muffled words. I lied down on the bed and tried to think of ways I could be good. I'd have to be more than good, though, to get rid of a century-old curse, a curse that damned my whole family, not just me. I'd have to be like Joan of Arc, I thought, getting lost in a fantasy where flocks of people cheered me as I was wheeled on a horse-drawn cart to the stake. I was so lost in the fantasy that Mrs. Sullivan's wails followed by Marisol shouting "Liar" snapped me upright, confused as to where I was.

Detective Kanelous raised his voice to say, "Sorry, but it's true."

And Marisol screamed, "Get out. Get out and don't ever come back!"

My blood pumped so loud in my ear that I couldn't understand what Marisol was saying to her mother. Mrs. Sullivan was sobbing and Marisol was saying things, possibly in Spanish. Had Detective Kanelous just told them that Gramp was the killer? That I'd known he was the killer all along?

Briefly the window lit golden and then the sun sank deep into the fire zone and dusk gradually speckled the air gray, then blue. I needed to get home. I hadn't yet set the table for supper and Gram would be raising holy hell about that by now.

It was totally dark outside by the time the bedroom door slowly creaked open and Marisol stepped inside. "I gave her a pill. She's sleeping now." As soon as Marisol flicked on the dresser lamp, her shadow spiked up the wall. "It was my father," Marisol said, her voice flat and dull. "The dead body was, is, my father. I can't believe it." She crossed herself and shivered. "He must have wanted us to go into the mine. He must have wanted us to find him. Maybe he wanted me and Mommy to know he'd never left us. Maybe he'd wanted us to know that he was killed and that's why he never came back home." For some time she stared at the space beside the radiator.

I said nothing. My blood was still throbbing hard in my ears and my breathing was so shallow that my chest hurt. I was relieved when Marisol finally broke the silence.

"It must have been his spirit shadow I saw this morning," she said. "He must have known the detective would tell us today. He must have been hoping I'd understand what he was trying to tell me." Her gaze flicked onto her startled image in the mirror, then roamed over the statues on the dresser. Her voice was hushed as she said, "All my life I thought he never wanted to talk to me, but he's probably been trying to talk to me all along. I think we need to Ouija. I think he wants me to find his killer. I think he wants revenge."

She knelt and reached her arm beneath the bed for the board. Then she sat Indian-style on the floor and unfolded the board and placed the wooden wedge on top of it. "I'll do it alone this time," she said. "You force it. You don't let it say what it wants."

I grunted a response, part denial, part agreement. Resting her fingertips on the heart-shaped piece of wood, Marisol shut her eyes. In the soft light of the lamp the freckles splattering her skin appeared to flicker. "Spirit, are you my father?"

Beneath her hand the wedge moved to the letter H, then O, then W.

"How?" she said. "Why do you keep saying H-O-W? How what? Spirit, what are you trying to tell me? How it happened? How you got killed?"

"Maybe you shouldn't ask it," I said, breathing in gulps as if I desperately needed to catch my breath. As the wooden piece moved from L, then E, then Y, it felt like each letter branded a tender spot inside me and I flinched with the burn. "Don't ask it any more," I pleaded. "You don't need to know."

"L-E-Y?" she said and her tongue clucked with exasperation. "What is that? Lee? Lay? Finish the word, Spirit. L-E-Y, what?"

Again the wedge moved. This time it spelled: HOWLEY.

I whimpered, looking helplessly from the board to the mirror above the dresser. I gripped the bedspread as if I was about to fall forward into the horrible place where we were headed.

"Okay," Marisol said, "I get How. But what is L-E-Y. Lee? Lay? Tell me."

I didn't dare breathe, my eyes hurt like bits of salt were in them. When Marisol turned to me, all the angles of her face tensed. "How-lee?" she said. "How-lee?" But then recognition relaxed the muscles around her eyes and she stared at me with a look of amazed horror.

"No," I said, grabbing the wedge and setting my jaw the way Daddy did when the dark place surfaced in him. But my eyes stung so bad I couldn't stop blinking and my fingers trembled so hard I felt ridiculous.

Marisol snatched the wooden heart from my hand and placed it back on the board. "Spirit, are you my father? Is it Howley who killed you?"

We both waited breathlessly as the wedge shifted to yes.

"No," I defended. "You asked it two questions. It's confused. The curse is trying to confuse it. My family's curse." In a rush I spluttered details about the Molly Maguires and the priest's curse.

"A priest cursed you?" Marisol leaned back as if I was a snake poised to bite her. She stood and backed up until she was against the wall. She crossed herself and kissed her fingers. For what felt like forever I listened to her shallow breaths. Then she pointed at me. "Get away from us. Get away from me and my mother and don't ever come near us again." Her finger moved from pointing at me to pointing at the door.

Unsteadily I stood. "You don't understand," I said again and walked proudly, tilting my head the way I knew Ma would if she'd been there with me. My shaking hand gripped the doorknob. "You're making a mistake," I said, but as soon as I said the words I recognized them as a lie.

Flinging the door open, I ran past Mrs. Sullivan sleeping on the couch. I fled down the stairs and out the building and then I kept running, running away from the fire zone and Gram and Gramp's. I ran with the knowledge that Marisol would never have stayed my best friend, no matter what I did, because I was a Howley, because I was cursed.

Fifteen

It didn't take me long to reach the outskirts of the city and the start of East Mountain. I'd taken the side streets and back roads that were as familiar to me as the face of the moon that lit my way that night. I had no plan of where to go, just to go, and I soon found myself at one of Marisol's and my favorite haunts, White Deer Lake, a small deep glacial lake up on East Mountain where I didn't expect anyone to find me for a long, long time.

The moon that night was not quite full with the shadow of part of it showing, and it cast a cold white light that made me feel sorry for running away, but foolish to return. I crouched up against a boulder near the rocky boat launch where Marisol and I had dried strands of duckweed to later paste on to cardboard flowers and where we had sat countless times to read or skip rocks.

As soon as I sat, I felt how tired and hungry and cold I was— and afraid. All the night noises, every crunch and splish and trill, convinced me that some monster or killer was about to get me and I caught myself picturing first Father Capedonico, then Marisol's father, rising out of the mist on the farthest edge of the lake, rising to the height of the trees, to glide across the water and hunt me down.

When I heard the slow gravelly sounds of a car coming toward the launch, I hid in a dense clump of blueberry bushes by the shore and watched the car drive down the launch and park at the water's edge.

The interior light went on and I recognized Detective Kanelous's profile as he lit a cigarette and then shut off the light. His windows were open; I could smell the smoke. I hunched down low. We were only a dozen or so feet from each other, separated by the bushy branches. I shivered, the ground damp had seeped into me.

He smoked for some time before reaching over to open his passenger door. "I know you're there, Brigid. Your mother called worried about you."

He tossed the cigarette toward the water and waited until I came out, lured by the warmth and protection of the car. Cautiously I walked, glancing toward the shadowy places in the boat turnaround. Then I practically dove into the passenger seat and shut and locked the door.

"Were you looking for somebody?" Detective Kanelous asked all friendly, but you could hear the suspicion in his voice.

I shook my head.

"Did you come here with someone?"

I shook my head some more.

"Someone follow you?"

I didn't answer. He was one of the last people I'd ever want to tell about Father Capedonico's curse or Marisol's father wanting his revenge.

"You just get spooked out there?"

I nodded.

"I would have too." He shut the windows and started backing into the turnaround, telling me that Ma had called and told him the different spots where me and Marisol liked to hang out. I was surprised, having thought Ma had no idea where I went when I left the house, and I stared out the windshield at the setting moon, which now rested above the trees across the pond as if it perched there.

He tuned the radio to an all-night doo-wop station broadcast out of Wilkes-Barre and slowly drove out to the road, all the while talking about the neighborhood in Queens, New York, where he grew up. He described houses that were all attached with no back-yard except for a long shared driveway with garages. "But we all knew each other. It was real close-knit, you know what I mean? So I think I understand what it's like growing up in a small town. People wouldn't think I'd understand that with me coming from Queens and all, but I do."

As he pulled up in front of the house, he flicked on the interior light. He shifted the car into park and turned to me. Around the brown of his irises was a rim of orange that made me think of a cat's eyes that were all-seeing and distrustful.

"I hope you'll take some advice," he said. "You can't let what you saw down in that monkey shaft get to you. You know what I mean? You have to try and forget it. You have to try and put it out of your mind."

I nodded, eager to get out of the car before he started asking me questions again about the dead body.

"You let me know if you need me, you hear?" He squinted and looked deep into my eyes and repeated, "You let me know, hear?"

I opened the door, certain at that moment that he knew Gramp killed Marisol's father and that he was trying to goad me into admitting it. I fled to the front door where Ma slapped my face and then hugged me so hard I couldn't breathe.

"Jesus Christ!" she kept saying until we finally both relaxed in each other's arms. Even Gram was glad to see me. She didn't say a word about Ma taking the Lord's name and she made us all a big pot of tea and let me put as much sugar in it as I wanted.

In the days that followed I skulked around the house, not wanting to run into Marisol or her mother. The newspaper had identified the murdered man down in the mine as William Sullivan. I figured soon they'd name Gramp as his killer and all I could do was pray that Marisol was wrong about her father's spirit wanting revenge. And I blamed myself for going down in that mine, for thinking I was meant to go there in order to get close to Daddy. I blamed myself because I'd mistaken the curse for fate so it was my fault all this had happened.

"How many times I got to tell you to set the table or chip the ice off the steps," Gram said to me more than once, irritated by my distraction. "What on earth you thinkin' about anyways? Try havin' worries like I got. That'll keep your brain fixated. Try those worries on for size."

It wasn't until Saturday morning that I finally managed to get Gramp alone. From the closed-in porch I watched Gram and Ma leave for their Saturday morning shift at the mill. They teetered along the bluestone sidewalk that was broken and jagged from the tree roots pushing up and the ground sinking down. Even though they walked near each other, there was still something resistant in Ma's steps that made her look as stiff as one of the tree trunks they walked past.

From the living room came the sounds of *Captain Kangaroo*, turned down so Gramp could doze if he wanted. It was early enough that Daddy was still asleep, and Brother was outside, sitting in the hollow spot where the trunk of the catalpa tree had split, trying to hit birds and chipmunks with his slingshot.

If I was going to say something to Gramp, I needed to do it soon, before Brother came in for a snack or Daddy woke, and I felt the pressure of time squeezing me like a vice. Clasped in my hand was the newspaper article about William Sullivan. The fact that his name was in print for everyone to see made his murder and his dead spirit anger even more real to me and with each minute that passed, I felt more and more helpless. Slowly I walked into the living room and it wasn't until I saw Gramp's alarmed face that I realized I was blinking away tears.

"You hurt, girl? What wrong?" He pushed his hand against the armrest, struggling to lean forward while I stood there, speechless, stupid with surprise at his concern. His breathing got ragged as he pushed against the armrests to sit up. "Boy?" he said. "Boy . . . hurt?"

Slowly I walked until I stood within a foot of him. "I know," I said, unable to say more, worrying the newspaper article in my sweaty hand.

He reached for his mug of hot water on the end table. His eyes were murky like a dead fish that had gone bad. "What . . . hiding?" he said.

I'd fisted the article and I stared dumbfounded at my clenched fingers as if waiting for something to unlock and open my hand. I swallowed. "I know it was you." I said. "My best friend's daddy. Why him? Why'd you have to do it to him?"

He curled his finger to beckon me closer. On the TV *Captain Kangaroo* had ended, replaced by a man reading Robert Frost poetry: "But he knows in singing not to sing. . . ." I took a step forward.

"Throat . . . hurt," he said. "Lean . . . close."

Looking into his glassy eyes I actually wondered if he meant to strangle me or whisper in my ear. My fist tightened until my fingernails cut my hand. I bent down and felt his breath on my neck.

"Your . . . daddy," he said.

I stared at a faint crack in the wall that made the plaster look as thin and fragile as an eggshell.

"Your . . . daddy," he said again.

"What about him?" I said, trying to contain the fury building inside me, knowing his next words would be insults about Daddy. "Don't say nasty things about my daddy. I'm talking about *you*. What *you* did."

Fast as a snake his hand lashed out and gripped my arm. His thick sharp nails bit into my skin.

"Let go," I screamed. "Daddy!"

Gramp released me so fast I lost balance and had to steady myself by gripping the coffee table. Then I bolted for Daddy's bedroom and flung open the door. Daddy was sitting up on the mattress, dazed, his hair sticking straight up like he'd been the one who got scared and not me.

"Gramp," I said. "He tried to hurt me."

Daddy shook his head, stood, and cleared the room in a few quick strides. Then he stopped short in the living room and said, "Jesus Christ."

Gramp's body had gone slack like a doll. The corner of his mouth sagged, an eyelid drooped. His arm dangled helplessly off the chair toward the floor.

Slowly Daddy went up to him and knelt. First he felt for the pulse at Gramp's neck, then at his wrist. Then he pressed his ear to Gramp's chest and right then Gramp gurgled.

"For the love of God," Daddy said, his face inches from Gramp's, his hands clasping Gramp's shoulders. "Tell me while you still can. Did he know about the money? Is that why you did it? Was there *nothing* you wouldn't do for him?"

"An ambulance, Daddy?" I said. "Should I call an ambulance?"

Daddy nodded and I went to the phone, feeling like it was someone else who spoke into the receiver, someone who had no relation to the moment at all. As I walked back to the living room I guessed Uncle Frank was the him Daddy was talking about and I didn't want to guess what it was Daddy thought Gramp had done. "They'll be here soon, Daddy," I said.

"It doesn't matter. It's too late." Daddy stood and gazed out toward the porch. Already we heard the sirens coming. "He's dead and now I'll never get an answer."

I stood there clenching and unclenching my fingers on the article that had smeared my hand with its print. *Body identified as William Sullivan . . . Foul play suspected . . . Wife and daughter stunned*. My gaze took in the photo on the mantel of Gramp as a little boy down in the mine, his face all whited out by the flash. Whited out now, forever.

"Oh, God, Daddy," I said. "I think I did this to him. I upset him."

"No, princess. He was sick. It was his time."

A vastness opened up inside me as big, I supposed, as eternity. I walked up to Daddy and took his hand, wanting to comfort him in what I deemed the worst loss imaginable, the loss of a father.

Together we opened the door for the ambulance workers.

Daddy was all business, like we were dealing with the death of a stray animal, but I could see in his eyes something brewing that I knew must have to do with whatever Daddy wanted Gramp to tell him. With all my heart I wished I could take whatever that was and fling it far from Barrendale. Far from us.

Sixteen

It felt like Gramp's death stoked the fire. Within days of his funeral, the fire spread all the way east and north to Spruce and Electric streets, which put our house solidly in the fire zone. Black boxes, like the ones Daddy had been waiting for us to get in Centrereach, were installed in various corners of the house as a way to monitor the carbon monoxide levels at all hours. The boxes ticked like clocks (or like bombs, Ma said) and shrilled if the gas levels went too high. Us kids especially were warned to keep our distance from woodwork because the gases were said to collect there, but Brother took warnings as taunts and many is the time me, Ma, Daddy, or Gram had to pull him off from sniffing a molding or a window frame.

Gram sat at the kitchen table reading the notice the county had sent. "The Appalachian Mine Fire Control Project Number Twenty-four B, they're callin' it. How many of these godforsaken projects they got?"

Gram looked up as if waiting for an answer and I said, "Twenty-four, I guess."

I expected to get a cluck of tongue or a "Thank you, Miss Smarty-pants," but Gram's eyes had gone stark with fear. She peered through the doorway to all the mass cards for Gramp displayed on the mantel. Then she shook the paper and continued, "They say we got a blight belowground and they got federal funds to take down everything. That's how come they get to take our homes. They're callin' us a slum."

"They can call us anything as long as it gets us out of here," Ma said.

"You ain't got no heart, Dolores," Gram said, "to say that to me now. With John not even cold in the ground and this house all I got in the world."

Ma's spiteful face crashed with regret, but all she did was raise her head and walk away. There was no way in this world or the next that she was ever going to say sorry to Gram.

"I think this must be the curse come to get me," Gram said, looking over at the bowl of crumpled aluminum foil she reused each night to cover the faucets. "Now with John gone, it's me it'll be after next."

"But remember what you said, Gram," I reminded her. "The curse keeps us on our toes."

Gram harrumphed agreement. "Well, I'm on 'em!"

Edna Schwackhammer started coming on Thursday evenings for supper, during which she'd inevitably cry over her Otto and her house, which hadn't yet been demolished. Mrs. Schwackhammer would talk about which part of her basement was too hot to touch and how many tomatoes had ripened in what should have been the frostbitten ground in her garden. She'd complain that even the cold water from the faucet ran lukewarm and that the wallpaper in her living room had started to peel. Inevitably she and Gram would gossip about this or that theory involving the county and the state and the coal company, all of who were said to be conspiring to get the coal beneath the west side of Barrendale as cheaply as possible.

"They don't care how many houses and families they wreck," Gram declared, "as long as they get every last flake of coal down to the bedrock."

As for me, I tried to follow Detective Kanelous's advice and not only forget what I'd seen down in the mine, but forget that we were in the fire zone, forget that Marisol and I weren't friends, that her daddy had been killed, that we Howleys were cursed— but I found that in thinking about forgetting, I thought about everything worse.

To Ma though, the news of us being a part of the Appalachian Mine Fire Control Project was the best news she'd ever heard. "Now nothin' can stop us from gettin the heck out of here," Ma said to me, her eyes glinting as hard and bright as mica chips.

On Thursday nights when Mrs. Schwackhammer visited, me and Ma would go out to survey the progress of the destruction. The East Side Pit, the trench nearest us, was now large enough to hold a battleship. Buckets that could hold ten tons of dirt swung off enormous draglines. Ma liked to repeat proudly, as if she was responsible for it, that after they got finished digging, they would have dug out more earth than they did for the Panama Canal.

Clouds of smoke hovered over the area and whenever we got close enough to the edge of what had become a man-made valley, we'd see flames flicking through the coal chambers that had been opened up to the air. All around us the night glowed eerily pink from the heaps of dug-up coal that burned a hot smoky red.

"Worse than anything I ever seen," Ma would say as if that were the highest compliment she could offer. "Anything I ever imagined." The lines of her face would smooth, the sight of the wreckage seeming to satisfy and console her.

In the weeks that followed Gramp's death, it wasn't only the fire that was let loose. It loosed something in Gram too. Suddenly she was at the ready to talk my ear off as I peeled carrots in the kitchen or as I knelt scrubbing the bathroom floor. She'd interrupt me as I read on the ratty sofa on the porch or tried to work on my math equations at the dining-room table. Her voice would become somewhat breathy as she told me gossip about the rich Barrendale family she used to do laundry for when Daddy was little. She could go on for hours about the mansions and theater and music festivals that once existed in Barrendale as if she were describing some mythic lost world.

She especially liked to talk about her sisters. "I was the oldest girl," she told me. "Mama said the boys needed school and I didn't, so after Papa died I dropped out and started cookin' and cleanin'. As soon as my sisters were old enough, they left and went to New York City. Four of them, Mary, Louise, Kate, and Franny. They all got jobs sewin' at some factory and they got themselves nice young men too, all Catholic. And as long as they weren't Italian, Mama approved. So I thought, what's to stop me from goin' to New York City too? Mama didn't need me at home no more. But do you know what those girls said to me—my own *sisters?* They said they didn't have no room for me. And after all I done supportin' them all those years!"

Gram looked wistfully at a loaf of bread waiting to rise on the shelf above the stove. "If only I'd had the gumption to pick up and go to New York anyways, on my own. Imagine where I'd be now! My life would be so different I bet I wouldn't be able to recognize myself!"

Ma and Daddy were so involved with our move to Allentown that they didn't even notice I no longer hung out with Marisol. Gram was the only one who said something about it. "Why ain't you never with that Puerto Rican girl no more? Lord knows what her daddy did to get dead that way, but one thing's for certain, you're better off without her."

I was out on the closed-in porch, under a heap of blankets, reading one of my *True Confessions* magazines. I didn't even think about it, I just said it, "There are rumors going around that it was Gramp who got her daddy dead that way. There are people who are saying it was Howley who done it."

Quick as anything Gram ripped the magazine from my hands and flung it across the room. She stuck her finger so close to my face it touched the tip of my nose. "Don't you go sayin' rumors like that in this house! Don't you go besmirkin' your own flesh and blood! You got to have pride, girl. Words ain't just words. They got an awful power. Don't go helpin' them along by repeatin' them yourself!"

Daddy started working every other Saturday and on some of the weekends when he worked, he didn't come home at all. When he did come home though, he and Ma only whispered about moving to Allentown, but that didn't fool Gram. "If Frankie was alive he wouldn't leave his own mother alone to fend for herself. He was the type to think about more than just his own good."

"That's what you think," Daddy said.

"The green's showin' on your face, Adrian," Gram declared. "The green of jealousy. And it ain't pretty!"

To make Daddy feel better Ma told him that parents are supposed to want the best for their kids. "If she was a good ma, she'd want us to go. Down the line, you can send her some money. Now and again, not regular. That's all we can do." When all Daddy did was grunt, Ma added, "How much has that old biddy ever done for us? You need to think about your own family. You need to think about me."

At school I kept my distance from Marisol who, if she looked at me at all, stared through me like I was a window, like I wasn't there. "Stay away from her," she told Ellen Adwood, her new best friend. "Howleys are bad luck." Briefly I saw surprise light her face when I didn't so much as flinch at her words. Gram was wrong: words *were* just words. And I was resolved not to care what anybody said about me or my family anymore—no matter how bad it hurt.

Every now and then flashing through my mind were pictures of Daddy tossed out of a car's shattered windshield or of him bloodied and broken at the base of a mine shaft. When Daddy came home from Allentown on Friday night and when he left again on Sundays I took to sitting on his lap like a little girl and clinging to his hand when we went on our Saturday walks. "Stickin' to him like a piece of tape," Gram said. "Like super glue," Ma added.

One Sunday night dinner Gram said, "You 'fraid, girl, that a pit goin' to open up and eat you like it ate Auntie?"

"No," Brother wailed, pulling at the cowlick on top of his head.

"Shh," I said to him. "That's not going to happen."

"No, it ain't," Gram agreed. "Just 'cause they say fire is beneath us, don't mean it is. You kids remember that."

"Things like what happened to Auntie don't happen to a family twice," Ma said. She looked first me, then Brother, smack in the face with a conviction I'd never seen before.

Later that night I followed Daddy out to the car and pleaded with him not to go to Allentown for the week. He nuzzled me into the crook of his bad arm and I pressed my nose to his coat, smelling past Ma's cigarette smell to the musty, metallic smell that was Daddy's.

We walked into the yard and looked up at the stars and Daddy talked about the possibility of life on other planets and how small we were in the context of things, and his talking about space aliens and other planets got me thinking about what he said after Gramp died—"He's gone and now I'll never have an answer." What did Daddy want an answer to?

I walked Daddy to the car and hugged him hard. His face, whitish from the streetlight that flickered between the pines, looked ghostly and sick and I got afraid that I'd never see him again and I guess that fear made me brave enough to ask questions. "Daddy, what did Gramp mean when he said it didn't make sense? When he was talking to you about Uncle Frank being in the monkey shaft? I heard you both when you were out on the side porch. Why was Uncle Frank in a monkey shaft they weren't mining anymore anyway? What did you say that didn't make sense?"

Daddy looked toward the house with its lit windows all cracked for air. He beckoned for me to walk down the street and then he crouched so that he was looking up at me. "I told him that Frank was down by that monkey shaft because it wasn't being worked anymore. Frank would go there from time to time to meet with people he couldn't be seen with in the light of day. People he shouldn't have been meeting with once he became a shop steward.

Gramp didn't want to believe that about him. That he was doing anything against the union, the workers." Daddy patted my shoulder and stood. "You'll understand better when you're older."

"Okay," I said, not really meaning it. When I spoke my throat was so dry that my voice came out low and hoarse. "What about when Gramp died? What was it you wanted him to tell you?"

Daddy took my hand and we started walking slowly back to the car, careful to avoid the dips and cracks in the street. "I wanted to know where the treasure map was. To the pirates' gold. What else would I be asking him?" And Daddy tugged on my arm to get me to smile, but I wasn't looking for tall tales. I was looking for truth, or as close as I could get to it. I shook my head, trying to make sense of the little Daddy had told me.

"But, Daddy, why was Uncle Frank *in* the monkey shaft? He couldn't have been meeting people inside it. It's too narrow. He must have been meeting people outside it, right?"

"One of the tremors must have thrown him inside it, princess. I don't know. I wasn't there."

"But, Daddy—"

"Jesus!" Daddy said. "Is this what I have to come home to? I'm tired, princess. I'd like to enjoy myself in the little time I'm here."

"I'm sorry, Daddy," I said, and then we leaned against the hood of the car and Daddy talked about the president's promise to put a man on the moon, saying that one day we'd fly around in space just like we did in airplanes. Then he kissed me on the side of the head and got in the car. "Be good," he said and when I didn't answer he said, "What I wanted to know was why he was never proud of me. But that was a foolish question."

Daddy shut the door and pulled out of the drive, leaving me to wonder why that could ever be a foolish question. I waved and watched his car vanish into a cloud of pinkish smoke at the end of the block. I stood there staring into that pink cloud as it appeared to grow and come toward me and I thought about what else I'd wanted to ask Daddy. Hadn't he told me once that the first tremor hit while he was with Uncle Frank? And wouldn't that have meant he was with Uncle Frank when the collapse started? I couldn't remember for sure. Maybe it was something he'd told one of the journalists to test, as he'd said, how much the man knew.

It was a long time before I finally walked back to the house, but as I did, I felt as unsettled as the ground beneath my feet.

Seventeen

On our first trip to Allentown it snowed. Big fat flakes stuck in Uncle Jerry's hair as he picked me, Ma, and Brother up from the bus depot. He kissed Ma on the cheek and patted me and Brother hard on the head, asking how our trip was. "Great," Ma quickly said, though the ride from Barrendale had been long, cold, and smelly. When me and Brother balked, Ma said, "Shut it." Sheepishly she added to Uncle Jerry, "What do these kids know from bad?"

Uncle Jerry grunted agreement and at Ma's request drove us first thing to the house Uncle Jerry's friend was fixing up for us to rent. Ma had spent most of the bus ride talking about the white eyelet curtains she planned for the kitchen windows and the fluffy white towels she planned for the bath. "The whole place is getting redone, so as everything will be new. New stove, new carpet, new paint on the walls!"

The house was on Furlong Street, which consisted of several

blocks of attached houses, all identical with yellow shingles and two front windows that stared out at us like blank eyes.

"The suburbs," Ma whispered to me as Uncle Jerry walked ahead to unlock the door. "Don't matter how bad our shit stinks, we'll be middle class by Tuesday."

As Uncle Jerry pushed open the door and stepped inside, he instructed us, "Don't see it the way it is, picture it like it will be."

There was a hole in the hall wall the size and shape of a cauli-flower. A brown stain on the front carpet. The kitchen had one of those old double sinks with a sink and tub to scrub laundry in. The kitchen window that Ma had wanted to drape in eyelet curtains was repaired with a piece of cardboard.

Uncle Jerry slid the dead bolt open on the back door and we all stepped out onto a small concrete stoop. From the next yard we were greeted by a man whose face was all bandaged on one side. "My dog done bit me," he said, talking out the side of his mouth.

Ma's eyes were as dull as the cardboard taped to the window. "Ain't that nice," she said.

"Can I see?" Brother pleaded to the man, whose mouth, where it wasn't bandaged, appeared to grin.

Uncle Jerry ushered us back inside. "After what the last tenants did to the place, Jimmy's sure going to be glad to have you here. The guy he's got working on it had a couple of delays. But by spring you won't recognize it." Uncle Jerry waved his hand like a wand at the linoleum floor that was burned where maybe a pot had dropped on it. "Can you picture it, Dolores? Can you?"

Ma had on her stoic "I'm tough as nails" expression, but her eyes were rolled up, looking at the kitchen globe that shook on the ceiling.

"We're near the train," Uncle Jerry explained. "So you'll get a few vibrations. Big deal. Jimmy will let you have this place for a song. Don't worry, Dolores. It's all going to be fine. Things are working out with Adrian better than expected. You'd never think he'd been out of work at all. He just needed someone to believe in him. Give him his confidence back. Every man needs that."

Ma's brave face wobbled and she began to cry. "I tried. After I married him I tried. But how long can a girl be expected—"

"Sure, sure," Uncle Jerry said, awkwardly patting her on the shoulder. "Of course, sure," he repeated.

We found Daddy at the back of Uncle Jerry's used car lot with his hands thrust deep into his coat pockets. He stared up at the frozen gray sky, which was tinted pink in the way that told of snow. Here and there a big wet flake stuck to his coat, then melted. "There you guys are," he called. "Was getting worried."

Daddy was quick to bring us inside the building. He introduced us to Norma, the office girl, the one we knew had the drunk father who locked her out and the boyfriend who she was afraid would never propose. "So this is Princess?" she said to me and though she winked, I couldn't tell if she meant it nice or if she was making fun of me.

Brother reached for a seashell paperweight on Norma's desk. "Put it down," Daddy yelled but Norma just laughed. "He can keep it," she said. "I got all I want now." And then she showed us the ring on her finger. It had a bunch of little diamonds on it so small you had to squint to see them, but that didn't stop Ma from declaring, "Every girl deserves a nice ring like that, don't they, Adrian?" Ma looked right at Daddy who bobbed and weaved his head like

Ma was throwing punches, not words. Ma added, "Your fiancé must love you a lot to give you a ring nice as that. Me, I never got a proper diamond ring, but then we all can't get what we want, can we?"

No one dared respond and Uncle Jerry told Norma to go in the back room and make us all hot chocolate. At his desk he lifted a brown envelope from where it perched on top of a stack of papers. He hitched up his pants and handed the envelope to Ma with a smile that pushed out his mouth and made his cheeks bulge. "Here you go, Dolores. They're all yours. I told Elsie to give me every last one she had. I told her not to hold anything back."

Ma opened the envelope and slid out several dog-eared photos. Slowly Ma shuffled through them, her face reminding me of the frozen gray sky. "But there's none of Ma," Ma said. "And there ain't none of me neither."

Uncle Jerry noticeably swallowed. "What do you mean?"

"I mean there ain't one of Ma. And there ain't one of me. There's one of Daddy. There's a baby one of you. And these"—Ma fanned three photos—"I don't know who these people are. I bet that bitch ripped up all the ones of Ma and me. I bet she wanted to get rid of any trace of us because we was her competition."

Norma had stepped back into the room with a tray of mugs in her hands. "Where should I put these?" she said, holding the tray out from her as if it held something flammable.

"Bring them back later," Uncle Jerry barked and Norma's gaze slipped sideways to Daddy before she turned and left the room. Uncle Jerry took the photos from Ma's hands and helplessly flipped through them. "I could have sworn we had some of Mama. I don't know. I'm not sure anymore. I don't know if we ever had any of you, Dolores."

"Well, you must have. They were taken of me. I can tell you that. I remember one of them being taken anyways." Ma stared at the little Christmas tree in the corner all lit with fat colored lights. "It was Christmastime. I remember because we made a trip special to Pittsburgh to visit Daddy's sister. She had this beautiful house with the biggest tree I'd ever seen and they took a photo of me, Ma and Daddy standing in front of it."

"Well, I don't know. I just don't know." Uncle Jerry said as he kept flipping through the photos as if suddenly Ma's face might magically appear within them. "Maybe Aunt Rose's kids have that photo. If they took the photo there, they probably kept it."

"No. If they'd kept it, how could I remember seeing it? I bet that bitch got rid of that photo because she didn't like seeing me and Ma with Daddy. I bet she didn't like having no reminder of me neither—seeing as what she done to me."

Ma's eyes lit with such a ferocious intensity that Uncle Jerry instinctively took a step back from her. He placed all the photos facedown on his desk. "Well, I'll just ask her then. Next time I talk to her, I'll ask if she remembers seeing any pictures of you or Mama."

"Like the bitch would tell you if she did." Ma folded her arms and hunched her shoulders.

"Well, then I'll check the photo albums myself," Uncle Jerry said. His eyes moved from one place in the room to another as if he was looking for the photos right on the walls of his office.

Daddy stepped closer to Ma and murmured her name but he knew not to touch her. When she was angry or near tears, a hug was the last thing she wanted. "Now I ain't never gonna see no picture of myself," Ma said. "I ain't never going to see clear what Ma or me looked like. If only I could remember." Then suddenly she lunged forward and gripped Uncle Jerry's arm. "You must remember, don't you? What I looked like?"

"I was so young, Dolores." Uncle Jerry's face had gone white as if Ma had gripped him so hard she'd stopped his blood flow.

"Nah, you weren't that young," Ma said. "Not much younger than John Patrick here." Ma pointed at Brother who looked up guiltily from where he sat on the floor by the tree gazing into the paperweight as if it were a crystal ball.

"You had long braids," Uncle Jerry said. "You dug in the mud pit with me."

"Ah, the mud pit," Ma said, her voice all hushed as if the pit had been something sacred. "I can see it almost. Sort of." Ma turned to Daddy. "You was right. My mind was blocking me from it. Maybe more will come to me if I let it. Maybe I'll remember it all."

Ma turned to Uncle Jerry, but she wasn't really looking at him. You could just see from the way her eyes went dark that she was looking deep into memory. Uncle Jerry gazed off at the wall above Brother's head. "Maybe you will remember it," he said with not a hint of belief.

"Why sure you will," Daddy said, putting his good arm around Ma and kissing the side of her head. "If you want to remember, Lores, you will."

Eighteen

Ma's hometown of Loppsville, Pennsylvania, was on the other side of the state and Ma agonized about going there as if she had to walk the two hundred miles, and not merely drive. But Daddy told her she'd never have any peace until she finally went back and saw her stepma face-to-face. So on the Saturday before Christmas me and Ma made the trip. Uncle Jerry had given Daddy Saturday off so he could drive home Friday night so me and Ma could use the car early Saturday morning.

"You'll be sorry," Gram warned through the side porch window as me and Ma got in the car.

"One thing you don't know nothing about, old lady, is being sorry," Ma muttered but the windows were up on the car so Gram didn't hear her. Daddy was still asleep and Brother was faking sleep and sulking because Ma said he was too little to come, so Gram's words were the last ones we heard as we started our trip and they kind of got stuck, hanging there in the compartment of the car for us to ponder for all the hours Ma drove.

When we finally arrived, Ma parked on a side street several blocks from the house because she didn't want Stepma to see us coming. A layer of snow coated the street, a sight so rare in Barrendale where most snow melted on impact that me and Ma kicked and skidded in it, stretching our legs that were stiff from the long ride. There was a different feel to this side of Pennsylvania. Surrounding the town were mountains more jagged than any I'd ever seen. Glinting foil wreaths hung on most of the doors. Happy-looking paper Santas and reindeers were taped to windows. Wooden mangers adorned lawns. The wonderful, magical feeling of Christmas was alive here, not like it was in dreary Barrendale where the fire had burned out even the spirit of Christmas.

Ma twisted up her hair and stuck it under a knit hat that she pulled low on her forehead, saying she didn't want to be recognized.

"Do you really think someone could recognize you, Ma?" I said. "You weren't much older than Brother when you left. You must look different now."

"Maybe. Maybe not. We're about to find out, though, ain't we? Soon I'll have a picture of myself in this very hand." Ma opened her gloved hand and looked at it as if it belonged to someone else and she didn't recognize it at all. Then she raised her head and sniffed the air as if she could find the house by smell. "This way," she said, jabbing her thumb behind us.

As we crossed first Church, then River Street, Ma spoke about her memories of her stepma and her daddy. "My ma died in the spring," she said, "and Daddy remarried by that summer. 'Here's your new stepma,' he said and believe it or not, I was happy because she was nice to me. She held me and stroked my hair when

I cried about my ma. My ma had been sick for so long, I was grateful, I guess. I wanted someone to take care of me."

Out front of a white wooden building Ma stopped. The sign on the door said KINLEY KINDERGARTEN but when Ma went to school there it went up to the fourth grade. "Two grades per room," Ma said. "I was in first grade so we sat on the left side of the room. Second grade sat on the right."

She glanced over her shoulder as if she expected someone back there. "Everything feels different than it did. All them years at the orphanage waiting for my daddy to rescue me. What could stop a daddy from getting his little girl? What could that horrible woman have said to make him not come?"

Hand in hand we headed down a sloping snowy street that was crunchy with ashes and gravel that had been spread for traction. A bright sun took the bite off the air. I swung Ma's arm and she swung back as we made fun of stupid things we saw on the houses we passed: a gate that wasn't attached to a fence, a manger with an angel missing one of its wings. There was something so sweet and nice about Ma when she was hurting that I wanted us to keep walking around like that forever. We kicked through a crust of sparkly snow and I remembered something Auntie used to say about holding the good moments inside you so that you could pick through them later like a drawerful of tiny treasures. I was certain right then that that was a moment I'd be picking through years in the future when I was an old woman, and then I realized that by the time I was an old woman Ma would be dead. My chest got so tight it stopped my breath.

"Let's go down every street in town, Ma," I pleaded. "We can see if you remember anything else. Stepma can wait."

But Ma didn't respond. She turned a corner and stopped, staring at a narrow house with a flaking white porch at the street's end. A white fence rimmed a yard that contained a shed and two large sycamores. The house's lace-curtained front windows, upstairs and down, were parted to display tin wreaths. "That's it," Ma said.

"You sure?" I said. "That's not how you described it." And I went on to point out all the things it had different from Ma's memory: it was white, not yellow, and had no porch swing or vegetable garden.

But Ma wasn't interested in differences; her pretty eyes squinted as she stood there. "A white picket fence," she said softly but the crisp snow-covered day seemed to broadcast her words and she covered her mouth and giggled. "I always loved white picket fences and never knew why. But I guess you remember home no matter what, no matter if you remember it at all."

We crossed into the street and moved quickly to the front gate where Ma didn't so much as pause. Swinging it open she stepped through into the yard and led me between the two sycamores, their trunks spotted brown and white. At the back of the shed was an ugly beige car seat beside a dented animal cage. Several yards out, a patch of woods harbored a rotting hunter's blind.

"I remember that," Ma said, pointing to the seat, which was the color of vomit. "Ugly as sin. My daddy would sit there smoking a pipe and looking at the cageful of rabbits. My pet rabbits. But then one day Daddy killed them. 'Just 'cause they're fluffy and cute don't mean they ain't fresh meat,' he said. But I knew it was Stepma who'd put him up to it. He'd never had done that if my ma had been alive. For weeks I starved myself at dinner, afraid of what was on my plate." Ma gripped her stomach and added, "Makes me sick just being back here."

We stepped away from the shed and stood beneath the trees. Ma looked up to the wild net of bare tree branches above our heads and said, "I was hoping coming back would make me remember my ma better. But it don't. Every year I can picture her less and less. Every year I lose her a little more."

We walked back out from the woods and stood in the yard. The wooden shingles at the back of the house were chipped and in need of paint. We stood there for so long I started to shiver and it wasn't until we saw the curtain in the upstairs window move that Ma said, "That must be the old bitch." Ma put on her sweetest smile and waved. "Wave and remember to look cute. Uncle Jerry told her about us, but not that we was going to come today."

Together we made our way to the front of the house where the door swung open and there stood Stepma looking nothing like I imagined. I'd pictured her as Snow White's wicked stepmother or as a Jezebel-like slut, but never as a roly-poly Mrs. Santa Claus with jam-red cheeks and a grandma smile. She was littler than me and Ma and more than plump. She was bordering on fat. Her brown and white hair curved in soft waves to the top of her neck. But from the way her forehead wrinkled as she took in me and Ma it was obvious she couldn't see well.

"You're Elsie Corcoran," Ma said in the voice she used years ago to sell Tupperware door-to-door. Yanking off her cap, Ma tossed her hair loose. "I'm Dolores Corcoran. The one you sent away."

Stepma tilted back and swung her hands up in front of her face as if she expected to get hit.

"If I was going to deck you," Ma said, "I'd a knocked you flat already."

The woman lowered her hands to just below her eyes where her spread fingers quaked, reminding me of bird's wings.

"Please," I said, "Stepma. I mean Grandstepma. Stepgrandma?" I looked questioningly from Ma to the woman and Ma laughed, exclaiming, "Ain't she a pip?"

Stepma dropped her hands from her face, and we all stood there openly looking at one another, not saying a word.

Finally Stepma tilted her head, taking me in. "My, my. Look at you." She tongued her lips, an odd expression on her face like she'd just eaten something she wasn't supposed to.

"I know she looks like him," Ma said. "My daddy's one of the few things I remember. That, and how nice to me you was. For the little while I was here with you. That was the unforgivable part. That you could be so nice and then do what you done."

"So it's your daddy I look like," I blurted, brimming with this newfound knowledge about myself, feeling like I had a deeper connection to Ma because of it. Until then I had never felt close to Ma's family—only to Ma—and I peered into the dim entry of the house wondering what else of me I'd find there.

Stepping onto the porch Stepma looked past us to the street as if she expected someone to come to her rescue.

"Who you expect to see? It's only me and her. We come to get my ma's things. And don't tell me you ain't got 'em. Bropey told me you do."

Stepma gripped a hand to her throat as if she might strangle herself. "Bropey? I haven't heard that name since—"

Ma finished, "Since you dumped me at Saint Augustine's Orphanage for Girls. Don't I know it. How 'bout we go inside and give Bropey a call? He'll tell you he wants our ma's stuff too. It's not just me that wants it."

Wincing, Stepma let loose a sigh. She led us into a dimly lit hall that opened onto a yellow kitchen with a black phone hanging beside the fridge. Lifting the receiver Stepma slowly dialed. "Yes," she said. "Hello, Norma. This is Jerome's mother." When she said "mother" Ma said, "Hah!" and Stepma turned away. Then all she said into the receiver was "I see" and "Fine."

Behind her back Ma made faces and I made like they were funny but really I was concentrating on Stepma's voice. It sounded like she had clump of dust stuck in her throat. Finally Stepma said, "Of course, Jerome. You know I only want to help."

Ma's clown face went sour. She reached for the receiver at the same time that Stepma hung up.

"He had an appointment to get to," Stepma said, firmly clicking the receiver into place. She suggested we sit in the living room while she searched for the items in question. "Don't get your hopes up, though, Dolores," Stepma said. "Your mother's things were packed away a long time ago and I haven't seen them in years." Stepma held her hand up in a stop sign to Ma's protests. "I'm not saying they're not somewhere in this house. I'm just saying, off-hand, I don't know where. I told Jerome I'd look for them. I wish you'd called. I could have saved you the trip. When Jerome comes for Christmas . . ." Her voice trailed off.

From Ma's tight smile I could tell she was working hard to hold back the slice of her tongue. "Whatever there is belongs to me," Ma said. "Me and Bropey. You have no right to it."

"You're treating me as if I've stolen your mother's things, Dolores. I don't want to keep any of it. I just have to find where they are. My husband, your father, God rest his soul—"

"Don't talk about my daddy to me. Not after what you done."

In the living room we sat on a checkered sofa facing a Christmas tree with blue lights. Beneath the tree were presents wrapped in paper that was covered with tiny little Santas. Flanking us were two end tables, each displaying photos of Uncle Jerry as a kid. In one of them he rode a bicycle. In another he was dressed in a Boy Scout's uniform. In still another he stood in cap and gown. There were also photos of Little Jerry and a wedding photo of a thinner and younger Stepma standing beside a man who must have been Ma's daddy.

Ma sat, glaring through an archway at Stepma who was searching the bottom drawers of a hutch. I reached for the wedding photo and studied Ma's daddy's face, amazed to see him wearing an expression I'd seen in photos on my own face, a half smile with a bit of squint.

I shivered, feeling as if one of Marisol's spirit shadows was somewhere in the room with us. It was eerie to think of what lurked inside you that wasn't of your own making, that came from ancestors you didn't even know.

Ma made a noise deep in her throat like a growl and I shifted away from her toward the armrest. I almost felt bad for Stepma, for making an enemy out of Ma, and I had to remind myself of the awful thing Stepma had done, which reminded me of the awful thing Gramp had probably done. I felt sick and told Ma I needed the bathroom but Ma wasn't listening to me. She'd gotten up to read the tags on the presents. "To Jerry," Ma read, "Love, Mom. To Little Jerry, Love, Nana." She made her voice tight and snotty as she read each of them. Her voice was so bitter that her mouth screwed up as she spoke and she didn't even notice me walk out to find the bathroom. For some time I stood over the toilet waiting for something to come up that never did. When I came out, I heard Stepma announcing, "I'm not saying I did the best I could, Dolores. I'm not saying that."

Stepma stood in the entry between the living room and dining room, holding a shoe box in both her hands. The plumpness of her cheeks appeared to sag and her eyes darkened.

Ma stood not an arm's length from Stepma and demanded, "How could you have done it? If you'd hated me that'd be one thing. But you was nice to me. That's what I can't forgive."

Ma stepped forward, wagging her head, and Stepma cowered, raising the box up to her face for protection. On the side of the box written in black ink were the words "Mooney Family Photos." Slowly Stepma lowered the box. Her eyes, veined red and yellow, roamed up toward the ceiling as she announced, "Forgiveness is the path to glory, Jesus says."

"Jesus never helped me once."

"He's not there to help you," Stepma said with a wedge of contempt. She held the box out to Ma who warily read the label out loud.

"Mooney's your mother's maiden name," Stepma said. "She and I went to the same school. I was a few years ahead. I didn't know her well, but I didn't hear of anybody who didn't like her."

"'Course everyone liked her," Ma snapped and took the box over to the sofa where I followed. Ma looked Stepma dead in the eye and added, "She was an angel. A real angel, not just one pretending to be nice."

As Ma opened the lid on the box, I sat down next to her. Dozens of black-and-white photos of people lay inside. Groups of unrecognizable children and adults—Ma's family, *my* family. They stood on rickety porches and in front of old-fashioned automobiles. These people were my family but looking at their unfamiliar bleak faces only made me feel empty inside.

Stepma said she'd check the basement to see what else she could find. We heard a door creak and then the slow thud of her steps downstairs. Ma waited barely a minute before she started rifling the drawers of the end tables, then of the cabinet beneath the TV. I stayed put on the couch, searching through the box of photos. Sometimes flickering beneath Ma's face was another face, sweet and helpless. A little girl's face. Ma's face, young. I knew all I needed to do was find that face in the photo album and I'd have found Ma.

When I hit on a photo of Ma's daddy standing beside a different bride, I pulled it out to study the face of Ma's dead ma. There was such a gentleness to the soft roundness of her forehead and to her large doe-looking eyes that for the first time I felt the loss of this woman who would have loved all the hard edges off Ma. I put the photo to the side and then rummaged the rest of the box until I found a photo of a little girl with fat dangling curls. Just a glance and I could see in that girl's face the shy, tender parts that I sometimes saw in Ma.

I placed the two photos beside me on the couch and closed the box. My limbs felt so quivery I couldn't move for a few moments. I couldn't believe I was going to get to give Ma what she craved most her whole life. I was going to get to give Ma, Ma, and at that moment there was nothing in the world I wanted more to do.

By that time Ma had made her way to the kitchen where I found her picking off spoons from a display case on the wall and dropping them into her pocketbook. "Ma," I said, "I got what we came for. You don't need to take anything else." First I handed her the photo of her mother because I wanted to savor handing her the one of herself. "Here, Ma," I said. "Look. Your ma."

Ma wiped her hands as if they'd gotten dirty from touching the spoons. When she took the photo, she held it up inches from her nose and her face got all soft and swollen like she'd been crying.

She talked about how in the orphanage she used to picture her ma coming to her at night. "But she didn't look nothing like this. I remembered her wrong. Even when I pictured her I didn't have her right. She wasn't even there in my memory." Ma's shoulders curved in and her head hung low like she wanted to curl into herself.

But she was in your heart, I thought, but didn't say out loud. For the rest of my life I'll regret not saying those words to Ma right then when she needed to hear them the most.

Stepma called to see where we'd gone and when she found us in the kitchen her eyes shifted from one to the other of us suspiciously. In Stepma's arms was a small box and perched on top of that box was a rusty green and gold tin. I slid the photo of Ma into my pocket as Ma grabbed the tin from Stepma and then handed me the box. "You sure this is everything?" Ma said. "Bropey will know if you're trying to cheat us. He might be younger than me but he remembers his ma too. And he'll come here and look through every last inch of this place if he thinks you're lying."

Stepma's mouth pursed like she was about to blow a kiss but instead tears glopped down her chubby cheeks and the flab on her neck quaked.

"Don't cry, old lady," Ma said. "This stuff belongs to me. Me and Bropey. You should have given all of it to him long ago. So he could have known his family right from the start. So he could recognize them for God's sake if he saw them on the street."

"But he did know his family," Stepma said. "*My* family. I raised him. I was his mother."

Ma moved forward holding the tin in her hand like she was about to hurl it. Her words were a growl. "You're once removed from a mother and don't you ever forget it. You're just his stepmother is all." Ma sucked hard on her breath like she had a sourball of air in her mouth. "You just tell me one thing, Elsie Corcoran. Did my daddy know where I was? Did you even tell him where you sent me?"

Stepma eased down onto one of the kitchen-table chairs. With slow hard circles she rubbed at her hip. "Sure he did. He had to sign the paper to get you there."

Ma banged the tin down on the kitchen table and Stepma jolted. "Then you tell me what you did," Ma demanded. "You tell me what you did to make him not come to get me. And you tell me the truth. You was afraid I'd hit you before and I swear I'll knock your face clean through that wall if you lie to me now."

Stepma's fingers stopped in midrub. Her thumb pressed deep into her flesh as her eyes shifted toward the half-empty spoon rack on the wall. Within seconds, though, the surprise on her face quickly became something else and her gaze roamed down the length of Ma's body until it fixed on the lime green linoleum square beside Ma's shoe. "If you remember him at all," Stepma said, "then you remember he did anything he wanted. On his own account he promised never to go get you and at least with that, he kept his word."

Ma's voice came out soft and low. "Then you're a wicked woman for taking that promise. And you can be sure there are some sins Jesus never forgives."

Stepma's cheeks turned the color of grits. Her stare broke from the floor and stuck onto Ma's face. "But I was saving you," she said. "I saved you."

Ma squinted and leaned forward like she was trying to see Stepma better. "Saved me? From what? My home? My own brother and daddy?"

"Yes, from your daddy. From him touching you. Don't you remember?"

Ma took two quick steps across the floor and slapped Stepma's pasty-white cheek. "You're a hateful woman. I'm taking my ma's things and that's the last I ever want to hear of you and your lies again. All those years my daddy could have come got me but your sick lies kept him from it." Ma broke down sobbing and stumbled into the living room where she kicked one of the presents beneath the tree. Then she grabbed the box of photos from my hands, told me to take the rest of the stuff and fled outside.

Dazed, me and Stepma stood in the hallway staring at the opened front door, which framed the snowy street and Ma fleeing down it.

"I only wish I could have checked on her but I didn't dare," Stepma said as she walked behind me down the hall to the front door. "It seemed best to leave things as they were. For all of us to forget. God forgive me for it."

I paused at the threshold, tasting the snowy cold on my tongue. "What is it her daddy done?" I whispered, afraid to really ask, to really know, but I could feel the weight of it already inside me, pulling me down.

"Little girls shouldn't think of such things," Stepma said and squeezed my shoulder, nudging me out the door. "You take care of your mother. She needs you. She needs all the help she can get."

Then Stepma shut the door and left me there with the knowledge of what had happened to Ma and of who my granddaddy was, this man I resembled. My legs felt heavy and tired like I'd run miles on them and it seemed to take a while before I reached Ma at the spot where she leaned up against a tree. I stood a distance from her as if the things her daddy had done were laying right there at our feet, ugly and shameful. Without a doubt I knew that Ma would hate me if I paid them any mind at all.

"Ma," I said, slipping from my pocket the picture of her as a little girl. "You can stop looking. I got you what you wanted. Here, Ma." I handed her the photo. "Here you are."

Ma barely looked at the photo before slipping it into the box of her ma's photos that she held in the crook of her arm. "Yeah. Ain't that something," she said. "There I am."

Nineteen

Ma and Daddy's anniversary fell on a Saturday that year. Daddy got the day off so he could take me, Brother, and Ma to a Chinese restaurant to celebrate it special. It was late February and the sun was such a pale white with a coating of clouds pasted to it that it was easy to look at. Here and there in the fire zone patches of crocuses came up from the heat and in one spot we even saw a daffodil. But in other places in the zone the ground was blistered and the shrubs and trees were budless and dead. The restaurant though was far away enough, right on the border where the rich people used to live, that the snow kept and there were mounds of it left over from a blizzard the week before.

Ma had walked from the house in a raincoat and rubber boots to protect her pretty dress from the ash and mud and when we crossed the bridge out of the zone and into the east side of the city, she took them off in the empty parking lot where the Sears used to be. She then spit on a hankie and wiped the grime from my and

Brother's face. Daddy, Ma said, wore the dirt well and didn't need a wipe. And she was right. He looked as handsome as ever as he removed his jacket to enjoy the feel of the sun on him. Brother ran ahead and threw bottle caps at the holes in the asphalt where the brick showed through and we walked the long way so Daddy could, as he said, "Show off his girls."

At the restaurant we had sweet and sour pork and chop suey and Daddy ordered us fried dumplings and spare ribs, which were things Daddy had eaten in a Chinese restaurant in Allentown and thought we'd like.

Both Ma and Daddy talked about our new house on Furlong Street in Allentown, which was supposed to be ready for us in a month. "We'll hang our laundry in the backyard, respectable like," Ma said. "I ain't going to have no clothesline going across the front porch. Maybe we'll even get ourselves a dog. We'll be living proper. With our own house, and with family living practically just down the street."

Brother had bitten into three dumplings and spit the ball of meat out onto the plate and he sat there looking down at them as if they were three little turds. Ma flicked her eyes from his plate to the window and then she lifted her orange soda in a toast. "To our new home and family. Well, they ain't new. They're old family but we're only getting to know them *now*, I mean."

Me and Daddy clicked glasses with her and neither of us mentioned that Uncle Jerry lived nearly half a mile away in a neighborhood where the houses had garages and big front yards. Brother picked at an egg roll, eating some of its fried skin, his blue eyes widening in pleasure. Ma was like the weather for us. If her mood was all sunshine and warmth so was ours and for the first time I started to look forward to our move to Allentown, to putting everything that had happened behind us. To not ever having to watch Marisol ignore me again.

The sun hadn't yet set but that part of the city was in shadow. The overhead lights went on and the waiter served us ice cream and fortune cookies. As soon as the waiter walked away, Daddy stood, put on his jacket and got down on one knee beside Ma.

Ma giggled with nervousness as he took her hand. He kissed it and Ma's eyes swerved here and there to see who was watching, wanting the moment to be seen, but there was only one other customer, an older man sipping his soup from a bowl and both him and the waiter pretended like they hadn't noticed a thing.

From his pocket Daddy drew out a small jewelry box. When he flicked it open, me and Ma sucked our breath. There against a black velvety background lay a gold ring glistening with diamond chips. "Oh, Adrian. Oh, my God." Ma's hand quivered as she held her fingers spread in anticipation for Daddy to slip the ring on. When he did, she cupped her hand as gently as if some wounded creature trembled on her palm.

"I can't believe it," she said, crossing her arms and squeezing her shoulders in a hug. "I got my brother, I got my ma's things, and now I got an honest-to-god wedding band. I got everything I always wanted." And then she sobbed uncontrollably and me and Daddy hovered over her, knowing how helpless she felt when she cried.

Out on the street, Ma gained control of herself. She held the ring up to the dying sunlight and said, "Just wait till all them bitches at the mill see this. Just wait till Rowena sees this." Suspiciously her eyes shifted toward Daddy. "We own it free and clear?"

"Free and clear."

"How'd you ever get the money? Or don't I want to know?"

"You don't want to know. But a little luck isn't a bad thing."

Ma, who always lashed out at Daddy when he mentioned luck or anything about gambling, surprised us all by saying, "Well, I guess a *little* luck ain't so bad."

"Nah, it's not so bad," Daddy said. "It's only good that's going to happen from now on, Lores." He looked from Ma to me with his jaw set to show he meant it. "We're owed some good luck, after all. And I tell you, I can feel it coming our way. One thing's for certain, I don't want either of you worrying anymore, you hear me?" He pointed from me to Ma and we both giggled with pleasure and relief. No matter what Daddy had done in the past we always wanted him to take care of us.

That evening when we got back to the house, Ma stuck her hand in front of Gram's face. "See this, you old biddy? I don't need nothing from you no more."

Gram was standing beside the Hoosier cabinet with the phone pressed to her ear. "'Scuse me, Edna," Gram said into the receiver before cupping her hand over it. To Daddy she whispered, "How many horse races you win to buy *that*?" She pronounced "that" like it was some hot, burning thing in her mouth, then she turned her back on Ma and tugged at the phone cord, stretching it so that she could walk to the stove. "No, Edna, really. Legally they ain't got the right to take it away."

Ma walked to where the phone hung on the wall and calmly pressed the lever to disconnect the call. Gram banged the receiver against the side of the stove. "Like a little kid, I swear."

That night Ma called me into the bedroom to brush her hair. "Hundred strokes, remember?" she said, hearkening back to a long-ago time when me and Ma brushed each other's hair every night.

Ma sighed and held her hand out, turning the ring this way and that. "Ain't it pretty?"

"It's the most beautiful ring I've ever seen, Ma," I said, my gut aching with desire for it. Through the shut door we could hear glassware clinking in the kitchen and Gram singing "My Bonnie Lies Over the Ocean."

Ma scratched at the stones on the ring to test the settings. "That bitch might act like she don't care I got this, but believe me, it sticks in her craw. It's what we fought about all those years ago when I said I'd never speak to her again. It all started with her wanting me to bring ambrosia for Easter Sunday, but I had to work a double on Holy Thursday and I was tired and I didn't get to the store for the marshmallows and pineapple so I brought rice pudding instead. Pudding I made myself. But don't you know that damn pudding wouldn't set right and Gram went on and on about how awful it was, how I'd promised to bring stupid ambrosia, and how she could never trust me to make no promises again.

" 'Promises?' I said. 'Who in the heck are you to be talking about promises? Wasn't it you,' I said, 'who promised me your grandma's ring on my wedding day? That was over seven years ago and I still ain't got that ring so don't you go talking about promises, old lady.'

" 'Well,' she said, 'the only way you're ever going to see that ring is over my dead body.' And I said I got no problem getting that arranged and then she said she didn't know why Adrian ever married me and it was a wonder what a man would do for sex and I told her that Adrian married me because he loved me and he wanted to take care of me and she said that was horsepucky and he only married me because he knew no one but some dumb orphanage trash would be stupid enough to marry him with his arm all broke and I said that dumb orphanage trash was at least smart enough to know where and when she was welcome and that she'd never step foot in that godforsaken house again!"

Breathless, Ma finished her story and said she needed a smoke. Ever since Gramp died, Gram didn't care if Ma smoked inside so I went out to the side porch to get Ma's cigarettes, which was when I noticed Uncle Jerry's car pull into the drive. I rushed back to the bedroom but not before Uncle Jerry was already pounding at the door and Gram was saying, "Who is it?"

"Where's Adrian?" we heard Uncle Jerry ask in his booming voice.

Ma clenched at her neck. Her eyes darted from wall to wall. Then she cupped her face and patted her cheeks as if to make sure she was really there. "What's Bropey come for? What do you think he wants?" Wildly, Ma searched my eyes for an answer.

"I don't know, Ma," I cried. "I don't know."

Ma's eyes had a crazed glow to them. "I'll talk to Bropey. But it's your job to keep that bitch from saying something awful."

I couldn't imagine any way to stop Gram from doing anything she wanted. My breathing got shallow and I had to suck for air. "How, Ma?" I said. But she'd already whipped open the door and breezed down the hall, her voice all false and syrupy as she said, "Bropey, what a wonderful surprise."

I moved out into the hall and stood in the doorway watching Ma kiss Uncle Jerry on the cheek. Gram was in profile, her hump shaping her into a hook aimed right at Ma. "Well, since nobody's polite enough to make no introduction, I'll do it myself. I'm Rowena Howley."

"Pleased to meet." Uncle Jerry nodded. "Sorry to be trouble, but I'm looking for Adrian."

"He's probably at The Shaft," Gram said bitterly. "Or O'Malley's. That's the likely guesses."

Uncle Jerry looked from left to right as if he were about to cross a street. Then he wiggled his finger at Ma, beckoning her to follow him outside.

Me and Gram stood watching from the side porch window but we couldn't hear most of what was said. Uncle Jerry lit a cigarette and took one puff, then tossed it to the ground where he scuffed at it with his shoe over and over like a bull getting ready to charge. Ma pressed her hands to her face and seemed to sob.

Gram shook her head. "Told her, didn't I? You was there. I told her don't no good come from lookin' up your brother. Isn't that what I said, clear as day? You remember that, girl. Blood is just blood and no more and the past is best left where it is—in the past!" Gram trudged out of the porch and into her bedroom all the while wagging her head.

Eventually Uncle Jerry held Ma and patted her back. He stared across the street at the Williamson's front porch, which had sunk partway into the ground, and he said loud enough for the Williamson's to hear, "Like hell on earth. You remember what I said, Dolores. You think about it. You'd be welcome any time."

Hours later when Daddy came home, Ma walked straight up to him and while he stood shaking off his coat in front of Gramp's empty Barcalounger, Ma pounded at his chest and slapped his face. "My brother! My brother you had to steal from? Why didn't you steal from any other goddamned person but him?"

Daddy gripped Ma's wrist to stop her from hauling off and whacking him some more. The lines of his face went limp with confusion. "How'd he find out? He wasn't supposed to be back in the office till Tuesday. They were driving to Janice's family in Albany. I was going to put it all back in the safe on Monday. I swear. He never would have known." Daddy dropped Ma's wrist and clasped both her shoulders.

Ma's spine went from rigid to practically collapsing in Daddy's arms. "You mean you got it? You got the money you took from him?"

Daddy disappeared into the basement and returned with a wad of cash. Slowly Ma counted it, then counted it again. "So it's all here?" Ma asked, her voice quaking with disbelief.

Daddy was staring at the darkness framed in the window. "I had a sure thing," he said. "I almost tripled Jerry's money. I had enough to pay him back and buy you the nicest ring in the shop. I was going to put it all back on Monday. He never would have known."

"But he does goddamn know," Ma said, squeezing her ring finger so hard it turned white. "You think Jerry cares that you got all his money? You think he don't mind that you took it to gamble? What if you'd lost it all? What then?"

"But I didn't lose it. All I did was borrow it so I could get you a ring. How could he hold that against me? How could he not want his sister to have the ring she's always wanted? He wanted to find you all these years, Dolores. Of course he wants you to keep the ring."

With Daddy's words Ma wept and eventually she let Daddy hug her and stroke her hair. "You think he'll forgive us then?" she said.

"Of course he will," Daddy murmured, kissing her gently on the side of the head. "Why wouldn't he? He's your long-lost brother, after all."

But Uncle Jerry didn't forgive Daddy. The next day Ma took

off work to drive down to Allentown to return the money and to collect Daddy's things from the dealership. She had me miss school so I could make the trip with her and we met Uncle Jerry in the parking lot of a Giant supermarket because Ma was too ashamed to have Norma or Joe or Phil, Daddy's workers, see us.

"I won't bring him up on charges, Dolores," Uncle Jerry said, handing Ma a paper bag filled with Daddy's things. "That's the best I can do. But don't you forget my offer. And you"—Uncle Jerry pointed at me and barked—"you be good to your mother. You're lucky she doesn't stick you in an orphanage with all she's got on her plate."

I turned away, but just before I did, I shot Uncle Jerry the nastiest look I could muster and secretly smiled when his mouth flinched in response. "My ma would never do that," I said.

"Come on, Brigid," Ma said, her voice weak and her body bent like she'd just been punched in the gut. "We got a long trip ahead."

On our way out of Allentown, Ma drove slow on Furlong Street past the house that Uncle Jerry's friend had been fixing up for us. "Say goodbye to it, Brigid," Ma said with a type of longing I'd never heard before in her voice. "Say goodbye to everything your daddy took from us."

"It's the curse, Ma," I said. "Not Daddy taking it away."

"Don't I know it. Your daddy's curse."

I said nothing. It felt like the core of me was hollow and Uncle Jerry's words about Ma leaving me in an orphanage were echoing inside that place over and over.

When we got back to Barrendale Ma got into bed, pulled the quilt to her eyes, and voice muffled, told me to tell Daddy that she didn't want to talk to him. But Daddy didn't come back that whole afternoon and later when I knocked on the door to bring Ma supper, Ma said, "Go to hell, Adrian. Go to hell and don't never come back."

"It's me, Ma," I said. "I got some of Gram's meat loaf."

Ma didn't say anything so I stepped inside and saw that Ma had spread out on her mattress everything Stepma had given us, all that remained of Ma's dead ma. Looking at the objects made me think again of the bad things Ma's daddy had done to her, the things perverts were arrested for, and I shivered even though the room was steaming hot from the radiator pumping.

Ma's face was grayish, coated with sweat and the grime that coated everything inside and outside the house. She sat Indian-style on her mattress, holding in one hand a tortoiseshell comb with one of the teeth missing. On her lap was a small crocheted white purse and a single long black glove. Spread around her were some hair curlers, a porcelain figurine that spun on a music box, lace collars, and oblongs of lace with snap buttons on them.

Ma dropped the comb and patted the mattress for me to sit. I put the plate of food on the desk and knelt beside her. Ma hadn't let me look through the box of her ma's things so I looked with interest at a porcelain bride with hardened lace on its dress and the little metal barrettes with stiff ribbons glued onto them and the crochet-edged hankies folded neatly in thin cardboard boxes.

"I thought getting married and having my own family was all I ever wanted," Ma said. "I thought having my own family would make me forget the one I came from, but all it did was make me think about them worse."

I didn't know how to comfort the pain in Ma's voice so I reached for a folded yellowing hankie and cradled it against my cheek.

"Jesus Christ, Brigid." Ma slapped the hankie from my hand. "You gettin' it all filthy."

"It's already filthy," I said, streaking a clean spot on the porcelain figurine with my finger. All the stuff was coated with the dust from years of storage as well as the house's general dirt. I wiped the dirt from my finger on to my pant's pocket and wondered how Ma's dead ma could be as saintly as Ma said if she'd let what had happened to Ma happen.

I picked up the photo of my grandma that Ma had propped on the pillow. "I wish I'd known her," I said, trying to get at what I was thinking.

Ma nodded, then pressed her lips tight like she was in pain. She reached for me and clutched me to her. "Ah, God," she cried. "I got everything that's left of her. I got everything there is to get and it still ain't enough. I still got a hole inside."

Ma let me go and thumped her chest like she was drumming the hollow of her heart. Then she lay down on her mattress and I stroked her hair until she quieted. It was only early evening but Ma slept through till night and when I went to bed, I could hear her breezy snores. I tried to stay awake to hear when Daddy came home, but sleep got the better of me and I didn't wake until 3:00 A.M., in expectation of Mr. Smythe's nightly gas check. I rarely slept through it, but when I woke he wasn't there. Through the window, fingers of white moonlight stretched out on the floor to aim straight at Ma's mattress, which I saw was empty. From the kitchen came noises. I guessed Ma had gotten up to make herself something to eat.

"Shh," she said when I stepped into the kitchen and found her at the counter making two cheese sandwiches, one with ketchup on it, the way only Brother liked it. I looked from the sandwiches to the suitcase, Auntie's old green one, which was propped by the door.

"What are you doing, Ma?"

"Me and John Patrick is taking a trip. Don't you mind about it." Ma held her arm up and licked ketchup from where it had globbed on her skin like blood. "Don't go making me feel bad. Uncle Jerry ain't got room for you. John Patrick can stay in Little Jerry's room. There ain't room for me and you in the guest room." She looked toward a crack in the wall that had grown crooked and long during the night. "It's just temporary, Brigid. Don't go giving me a hard time about it."

Ma tiptoed into the living room past Daddy who was loudly snoring in Gramp's Barcalounger. She lifted Brother from where he curled on the couch and carried him with his head on her shoulder and his arm sloped around her neck. "I'm the one who has to get out of here," she whispered. "It's not just you who's suffering. You can't just think about yourself."

In the kitchen she quieted Brother by cupping the back of his head with her hand. "Now don't go making me feel bad, Brigid. I don't want to do this. He don't have room for you is all. That ain't my fault. No one can say it is." Her glance toward me was uneasy. We didn't meet eyes.

"Is this because of your daddy?" I asked.

"What?" she said, the word quick and sharp as a dagger.

"Is it because I look like him? You said I did. Is that why you don't want to take me?"

"This is no time for your foolishness, Brigid. The ridiculous things you say!" Carefully she opened the door, mindful of how it squeaked. Slowly she then slid Brother down to his feet and told him to walk to the car. She picked up Auntie's old valise and stepped out onto the moon-shadowed ground. She didn't look back but she stood there for a moment as if pondering West Mountain glowing red between the trees.

My body went so slack and heavy that I felt as if the bones in my legs had left with Ma. I managed to pull out a kitchen chair and to kind of collapse into it, leaning partway on the table for support. I heard the car motor turn over. I heard the tires crunch the gravel on the drive and then I listened to the fading sound of the car as it drove off. Long after it had gone, I stayed at the table, unable to move.

Eventually Mr. Smythe quietly opened the screen door. He smiled, seemingly not surprised to find someone, even a little girl, up in the middle of the night. "Can't sleep," he stated, shaking his head. He helped himself to a bottle of milk from the fridge and poured a glass. He set the glass on the table and patted me on the head. "Don't stay up too late," he said and then he reached in his back pocket for his gauge meter and waved it up by the ceiling.

Gradually night gave way to bluish, then gray light. A woodpecker worked on a nearby tree. When I heard Gram shuffling around her room, I attempted to get up but the heaviness in my legs had given way to a quivering sensation and I still couldn't move.

"What on earth?" I heard Gram declare. She was staring at the crack in the wall, which no matter how many ways she'd tried to stop its growth, still lengthened by degrees every night. "Lord, girl, what the heck you got the door open for?" Gram trudged toward the door and stepped in front of the dusting of dirt that had blown in a foot or more across the linoleum.

I cringed, waiting for the slap I'd get for leaving it open, but instead Gram lifted a note from the counter. She held it at arm's length and read out loud, "Time to look out for myself since it don't seem no one else will."

Gram peered out the screen, then shut the door. "Guess her brother gave her the gas money. Lord knows what he'll want from her in return."

I said nothing, my leg had stopped its involuntary twitching and now felt heavy as rock.

"Well, you just goin' to sit there?" Gram crumpled the paper and tromped over to the trash where she dumped it. "Even if your ma's gone, you're still here. And it's still Saturday, your day to clean the floors. And you got a mess right there you can start with." Gram pointed at the patch of dirt by the door.

I gripped the edge of the table, leaned my hand against it, and pushed myself up from the chair. But instead of standing, my numb legs collapsed and I found myself flat out on the floor, staring at a table leg, stunned, having never had my body fail me before.

"Get up, girl! Get up!" Gram shouted.

Out of the corner of my eye I saw one grungy pink slipper coming toward me.

"Get up," Gram said. "Don't go lyin' there like a slug." She nudged my shoulder with the tip of her slipper and when I didn't respond she kicked me with it. "Get up, girl. Get up. She ain't worth it, you hear?"

I started to cry. Gram sat down on the chair, bent down and slapped me hard on the cheek. But I only wailed harder so she slapped me again, striking my cheek, my nose, the ridge above my eye. "You deserve better than her. And don't you ever forget it, you hear me?"

I rolled to the side and then pushed up out of Gram's reach, gagging on a sob, my vision clearing. From her bathrobe pocket Gram pulled out a wad of crumpled tissues. She picked out a clean one and offered it to me. "Let it go, girl. Let her go. She can't give you what you want. Let her go. You can do it if you try."

I crawled forward to take the tissue from Gram's hand and as I reached for it Gram said, "It's not your fault who your ma is, you remember that."

Through a haze of tears I focused on Gram's face, surprised beyond all words to see kindness softening its creases.

PART III

Twenty

Spring never came that year. Winter lasted into May with a blizzard blanketing the fire zone in such a thick fog that on Mother's Day weekend Route 6 was closed to traffic and by that following weekend it was closed again because 86 degree days had flooded the road with snowmelt.

Spring was Gram's favorite month and the shock of its absence unhinged something in her. Suddenly she couldn't take a trip to the store or clean a gutter without saying a prayer to this or that patron saint first. On her way to the Hi-Lo market she'd pray, "Saint Christopher, get me there safe, you hear?" As she'd stand on a ladder, swiping her long fingers through the gutter, she'd shout, "Keep me from fallin', Saint Sitha!" Since Saint Sitha was not only the patron saint of housework but also of people who'd lost their keys, she'd usually add, "And don't let me lose my keys!" Of course after such a prayer she wouldn't be able to find the keys to the car or to the little jewelry box where she kept her wedding ring while she cleaned.

Saint Brigid crosses hung above every window to protect against fire and evil, and in every room she'd positioned Saint Joseph statues to protect the house. There was hardly a place you could stand where you weren't fixed with his eerie painted-eye stare. Twice a day she said the rosary when she used to not say it at all and she started holding prayer meetings in the living room, all in an effort for God to deliver us free of the fire and save the house from destruction.

I came to learn there was a patron saint for pretty much anything. A patron saint for stomachaches and one for headaches. There was a patron saint for different types of animals as well as for bakers and brewers of beer. There was a saint to pray to if you were accused wrongly and one to pray to if you were accused rightly. There was a saint to pray to if you wanted children and one to pray to for unwanted children. There was a patron saint of children. I also came to learn there were multiple saints for mothers and orphans and that some saints had more than one specialty. Saint Monica, for instance, covered both mothers and drunks and it was she who Gram said I should pray to "every second of every minute of every day for both your ma and daddy." But I couldn't do it. I'd had enough of praying with no good ever coming from it. For the first time I felt for the people in Auntie's story "The Great Forgetting." I used to think their belief that God ignored them made them foolish, but I'd come to realize that it made them wise instead.

The unusually humid and breezeless afternoons put a glaze on everything. Distances looked like you were seeing them through a filmy glass. Anything that could shone and sweated, and the still glossy surfaces of the lakes reflected sky and made you feel the world had turned upside down. At Pothole Park numerous springs shot out from crevices in the pothole, carving the hole further, the water seemingly spiraling down to the center of the earth.

The heat had its effect on me, Gram, and Daddy too. It was like all our worst feelings rose to the surface, clinging to us as damp and sticky as sweat. The lack of spring weather didn't stop Gram from spring-cleaning and as she and I took down storm windows and washed curtains we were snippier with each other than usual. Daddy, who'd normally lecture about the origins of spring-cleaning or the various uses for baking soda or aluminum foil as a cleaner, didn't say anything except correct Gram when she pronounced the word *perennial* as *peri-en-ul* and shake his head when he saw us dibbling holes to plant bulbs that would bloom in the fall. I thought it was sad and silly to plant flowers that would bloom after the house had been wrecked too, but I didn't tell Gram that, not when she was so busy praying to Saint Fiacre, the patron saint of gardening.

As much as I hated doing the spring-cleaning I was glad for it because when Gram wasn't cleaning or praying she was ragging on Daddy, wanting to know what kind of man would let his wife leave and would drink and gamble his life away. Then Daddy would rag on Gram, pointing out all the ways she spoke or thought wrong and then he'd say the word *mother* like it was the worst word in creation. And it would get so I'd want to be anywhere but in that house.

Of course Gram also had her opinion about Ma leaving. "Don't she think we all want to just up and go? Who'd be around if we all just acted on our impulses?" But she said it *imp-pulses* and when I laughed she wagged her head at me. "I'll tell you one thing, Mama might not have won no awards as a mama, but she'd never have just ditched one of us kids. She knew her 'sponsibilities and if your daddy's got any ideas about just stickin' you with me, he's got another thing comin'."

Fast as a whip I snapped, "Daddy would never leave me anywhere. And certainly not here."

"You watch yourself, girl. I'm hearin' your ma in your voice. I've opened up my home to you, haven't I? Now that's no small thing, am I right?"

I stared at her, chastised but unwilling to admit it.

"Now tell true, girl," she asked one day, "ain't livin' easier without her?"

I didn't say anything. Ma was still my ma and I couldn't bring myself to speak against her, but I knew guilt showed on my face and gave away the answer. Mostly it *was* easier living without Ma, but that didn't change the hurt me and Daddy felt. Most days Daddy drank, rousing himself only for his part-time evening shift as janitor at the mill. After all the crotch sewers and side seamers and appliqués left for the day, Daddy cleaned the toilets and swept up and took out bin after bin of garbage to the huge Dumpsters in the back. Often I'd find him out there standing at the cliff, looking down through the trees to the brown river that flowed sometimes as thick as melted chocolate. Sometimes he'd put his good arm around me and sing "Cockles and Mussels" or "The Wild Rover" and then he'd let me pick through the Dumpsters where I'd fill a paper bag with leftover bits of trim and lace and ribbon that Gram would then use to spruce up hand towels and my dresses.

Those evenings when I'd visit Daddy at the mill he'd send me on my way saying he'd see me in a few hours, but as the weeks passed he often didn't come home until the middle of the night.

Sometimes I'd hear him talking to Mr. Smythe at 3:00 A.M. or later. Daddy liked to talk when he'd drunk too much and I could tell during those late-night chats with Mr. Smythe that he'd been drinking because his voice had a clearness to it that it only got from liquor. Daddy liked to say that drinking helped him see his thoughts better and I suppose as long as he wasn't drunk that was true.

Those nights when I'd listen to him and Mr. Smythe talk, I'd find myself wondering what Mr. Smythe thought about the fact that Ma and Brother were suddenly gone. I wondered what other things he'd noticed and seen in the many fire zone houses that he went into in the middle of the night. Sometimes I even comforted myself by imagining this or that awful scenario that had taken place in these homes. I'd picture daddies who beat their wives and mas who beat up their own mas or starved their kids even though they could afford to buy enough to eat. Sometimes I pictured houses that had instruments of torture in their basements, the like of which I'd read in my historical romances. I'd see an iron maiden beside a furnace or a rack at the bottom of dark stairs, but I always left those devices empty, never wanting to picture anyone in them— not even Ma. Though once in a while I'd think about sticking her skinny body into the chamber of the iron maiden, I never let myself go so far as to actually see her in it, as if just the image itself might have power. And it must have had some because merely trying to keep it from my mind made me feel so terrible that it became its own form of torture.

"I speak to Dolores every week, *Mother*," Daddy told Gram when she was on him about allowing his wife to leave. He'd add, "She'll be back."

And then Gram would complain about the cost of the phone

bills until Daddy's face would turn so ugly that even Gram knew to stop. But I knew Daddy didn't speak to Ma each week. He called each week when he knew Uncle Jerry wouldn't be there and Aunt Janice would tell him that Ma wasn't home, even though Ma was.

Ma told me about Daddy's calls each time *she* called *me*, which was usually once a week at times during the day when she figured both Daddy and Gram wouldn't be around. "I ain't speaking to him or her ever again and I'd a hung up now if either had answered!" But then she'd ask how Gram's house repairs were going and if Daddy was eating well enough and I came to suspect that Daddy was right both that Ma would eventually be coming back and that Ma had always wanted Gram's love.

On one particularly muggy Saturday afternoon Gram came back from her morning shift at the mill in a particularly sour mood. Edna, she said, had jabbed her finger so bad with a pin that she couldn't keep up with her totes so Gram had had to work double to cover for her. The extra work had made Gram's vision blurry and she sat at the table for a while rubbing her shut lids to get the blood flowing. Then she pushed back the chair, stuck a pair of Gramp's old underdrawers on her head to keep her hair from getting dirty, and went about dusting the living room in preparation for that afternoon's prayer meeting. Normally one of my chores was to dust but she didn't trust the job I'd do for the prayer ladies' visit so on those days I got stuck with snack prep.

Gram stood in the entry from the kitchen to the living room and barked orders at me to make the iced tea and wash the watercress real careful to make sure I got all the snails and muck out. Though I loved wading through the creek and picking the watercress, I hated cleaning it and I felt put upon to have to both pick and clean it and make the sandwiches with the crusts cut off.

I stood at the sink lamely rinsing the greens, making sure my glances at Gram were as surly as possible.

"Don't go givin' me that look," she said and pushed at the underdrawers that had sagged over her left ear.

"Do you really have to wear that on your head?" I said, horribly embarrassed even though there was no one else but me and her to see it.

"Don't you mind what I'm wearin'," she said, but then her mouth slouched into a frown that trembled as she added, "Makes me feel close to him is all." Slowly she raised her hand and pointed her finger at me as she called on Saint Lawrence, the patron saint of cooks to give her patience. "I can see a snail stickin' to that cress from all the way over here! Forget it, girl. I'll do everything, just like I always done. All the cleanin'! All the cookin'! And I'll do all the prayin' for this house too!"

"What a racket," we heard Daddy say from down the hall. I turned off the faucet and dried my hands on a dish towel, annoyed that Gram's words stung the place inside me happy to get out of doing the work.

"Looking lovely as ever, Mother," Daddy added as he came up behind Gram and passed her with a look that was all vinegar and salt.

Neither Gram nor me said anything, we were so surprised to see Daddy up that early in the afternoon. Usually he slept till two or three. But that day he was not only up but dressed and looking better than he had in a long time. I guessed there was some special horse bet or craps game he was headed to and I was reminded of how handsome he'd been back before the strain of working in Allentown had thinned him out.

Gram looked at Daddy like he'd stepped in the room naked. "You're a married man," she said, "and don't you forget it!"

Daddy put some water to boil for his coffee and then he sat in a chair with his arms folded, waiting for the kettle to whistle.

"Don't you think people talk?" Gram said with a shifty glance at me. "You think you can go runnin' 'round and people don't know. Shameful enough to have your wife leave you, but now you're puttin' your soul in the devil's hands, Adrian Howley. Even Dad must be rollin' over in his grave!" And with those words Gram stepped forward and slammed her hand on the table and a Saint Joseph statue eyeing us from the Hoosier cabinet jumped.

I was leaning with my back against the sink and I balled up the dish towel and threw it on the table in protest at what Gram was hinting at.

"I'm sure he *is* rolling over in his grave," Daddy agreed, "seeing you with his underwear on your head."

I laughed extra hard, wanting Gram to feel as hurt as I did at what she was saying and I expected Daddy to meet my stare with an appreciative one but he didn't. When he looked at me, his eyes were as steamy as the East Side Pit. "You want to talk about shaming the family, Mother? You really want to talk about that?"

Gram's head tilted back as far as her hump would allow and she looked at Daddy out of the corner of an eye.

"That's right," he said. "I know. I've known all these years."

Daddy unfolded his arms and tilted back on the two hind legs of the chair, something Gram strictly forbade. Gram's eyes lowered to the floor. Slowly she eased the underwear off her head. Then she pat at her curls to fluff them. "What you know, Adrian, could fit

into a thimble and there'd still be room to stick my pinky in."
Gram wriggled her pinky at him. "It's what you *think* you know,
that's what there ain't no room for in the whole darned city of
Barrendale!"

Daddy inspected his fingernails, which were trimmed short
and looked almost polished. "Didn't you *have* to get married,
Mother? Isn't that why you resented me all these years?"

Gram said nothing and merely felt at the wall to steady herself. I felt off-kilter too and gripped at the counter until I could
feel the edge of it press into bone.

Daddy pushed back his chair and walked out the door, not
bothering to close it. We watched him through the screen door as
he stood on the lawn and gazed out on West Mountain. Then he
walked off to wherever he'd been headed to in the first place and
me and Gram didn't speak again until all the church people had
left and it was time to get supper ready. But then our conversation
was full of pauses and uneasy glances, like what Daddy had said
about Gram was there between us as poisonous and invisible as
the gases seeping up through our pipes and walls.

Twenty-one

After school on those hot May afternoons I took to hanging out in Saint Barbara's, the way I had when I first met Marisol. Every day as I walked up the hill toward that pretty stone church, I hoped to find Marisol sitting on one of its worn wooden pews. Yet each time she wasn't there I was almost glad. I didn't know what I could ever say to her that would let us once again be friends, and every time I looked for her and didn't find her, I felt spared the hardship of having to try.

Often after I'd leave the church I'd go up onto East Mountain and walk the creek beds where me and her used to hunt for gold. Other times I'd walk the blocks me and Daddy used to walk in our "exploring walks," almost always ending up down by the mill, amazed that there once was a time when I couldn't wait to visit Ma there to hear stories about her and Daddy's pasts. Now I was almost afraid to hear of their pasts. It was like them not talking about the years before they'd had me had made those years bigger and darker than they had been to begin with. Even Gram's past had its own terribleness to it and as I'd sit in Saint Barbara's I'd stare at Saint Barbara's statue, at the expression on her face that was so sweet it was almost dumb, and I'd think of all the words that I now knew referred to Gram: loose, fallen, easy, floozy, harlot, whore. But none of those words even hinted at who Gram was and I didn't know how to make sense of that. Gram was, well, Gram. The furthest thing from a loose woman imaginable and then I'd feel a twinge, afraid that the rumors she'd heard about Daddy might be true. And if they were, what was he? I thought of words I knew from church: *fornicator, adulterer.* And though those words rang with the judgment of God, they were meaningless to me. If Daddy was messing around with another woman there was no word I could think of to express the hurt it would make me feel.

At home, we all sort of went about our business even as we ignored each other. Gram and Daddy hardly spoke to each other and though they each spoke to me, neither one of them looked me in the eye. I think it was right around then that we all realized that by the time the spring-green leaves turned brown and fell, the house would be destroyed and we'd have no place to live. It was like an hourglass of time was running out on us with each day that greened the leaves up more. It was hard to look at a blooming flower without thinking that soon it would be just dried-up petals mucking up the ground.

Now when I'd overhear Daddy's late-night talks with Mr. Smythe there'd be a slur to his speech that told me he'd drunk too much and in Gram's prayers to this or that saint there was a feverish quality that scared me and got me to sit in on her prayer meetings, even though I no longer believed in prayers.

"So you're not the only one of us praying," I said to her, thinking back to the scolding she'd given me while I poorly washed the watercress. She nodded and the million wrinkles on her face softened as she bared her teeth in a smile.

But what I came to discover about those prayer meetings was that they were more talk than prayer. It was about Mrs. Pasternak sobbing that her blind son wouldn't be able to find his way around a new house. "He knows every inch of our home," she'd wail. "I don't have to worry about him when he's there." It was about Miss Henley's concern for her senile mother who might, as she put it, lose all her marbles in an unfamiliar place. She'd grimly add, "The house is one of the few things she *remembers*, for God's sake." It was about Mr. Wurm's anger over the amount he was to be paid for his house. "They're paying me what I paid for it fifteen years ago. *Fifteen* years. What do they think I can buy for that *now*?"

We'd hear about Mrs. Hoppe's or Mrs. Straumonger's or Mr. Kryzak's homes that had been in their families for generations and had been built by ancestors who'd come to Barrendale to help dig the canal. And of course we'd always hear from Mrs. Schwackhammer, who'd quietly weep over losing the house her Otto had lived and died in.

One time even Daddy sat in on a meeting. It was a Saturday afternoon. He was up earlier than he usually was and dressed as nicely as he had been on the Saturday Gram accused him of running around. Gram looked at him and managed to smother a flinch of surprise. Her shoulder merely twitched. Daddy didn't seem to notice or care. He talked with Mr. Wurm about the cost of the dig out and the possibility of getting more federal funds and Gram and Mrs. Schwackhammer loudly debated the best ways to clean filth off furniture.

An explosion jittered the floorboards and put everyone in an upset. "They're supposed to warn us when they blast, for God's sake," Miss Henley said, her voice as sour as the rhubarb pie she'd brought with her. "It's a Saturday," Mrs. Pasternak accused. "They're not supposed to blast on Saturday."

"That was so close it nearly shook the house off its foundation," Mrs. Schwackhammer declared.

Gram pressed a hand to her chest and her face went as slack as Gramp's had when he died.

"Gram!" I cried, rushing up to her. I put a hand on her hump and peered into her eyes, relieved to see the hazel of them was still clear and bright.

"I'm fine, girl," she said. She stared up at the ceiling as if she was amazed by its off-whiteness. "You got a point, Edna Jane," she said. "You got a point indeed. It did almost take the house off its foundation!"

She turned a daffy smile on Mrs. Schwackhammer and we all shifted around uncomfortably, afraid Gram had finally lost it. But then Gram made a grand gesture like she was Mr. Lawrence Welk himself conducting his orchestra and she started us off on a novena to Saint Jude, which sent all of us scrabbling for chairs and Daddy scrabbling for the door.

Gram waited for everyone to leave and for all the dishes to be washed and dried before telling me what had happened to her that evening.

"I had me a vision, girl," she said. Gram spread her hands before her face as if the vision was coming into focus right there in the kitchen. "It came to me as soon as Edna said the house had almost shook off its foundation. I saw it all—the house up on one of them flatbed trucks movin' down the street as smooth as if it glided on water. Must have been my guardian angel showin' it to me." Gram turned her head back toward her hump as if her guardian angel were right there casting the vision. "We can lift the whole house up, floors and all, right off the foundation and plunk it down on the property I got over on East Mountain. Alls we need is the land cleared! What's to stop us?"

I was drinking a mug of hot bitter coffee, the like of which I'd taken to recently. I felt the burn of it down my throat and didn't say anything. I imagined there was a lot to stop us.

"How could I not have thunk it before? Your ma livin' under the same roof must have clouded my brain! What do you think, girl? What?"

Gram sat down across from me and looked me clean in the eyes, the way she hadn't since Daddy spilled the beans on the way he'd got made. I put the mug down and felt my mouth twitch toward a smile.

"I think it's great, Gram," I said. "It's a great idea." And that's what me and her came to call Gram's plan to move the house, the Great Idea, and it wasn't long before I believed as much as Gram did that she could pull it off.

Twenty-two

Once Gram had her Great Idea she spent all her time working on it. She switched her weekly shift at the mill to the early mornings so she could use afternoons to make phone calls and write letters to this or that office and agency requesting that she be allowed to move the house. Then she spent her evenings planning how to adapt the house for country living.

The first change she wanted to make was to turn the pantry into a mudroom and cut a back door in one of the walls. "We'll get started straight off," she said to me and when I balked that we could never do it, she said, "Who in heck you think closed in the porch? That was me and Frank done that and believe me *he* was the helper, not the other way 'round." Then she drew one after another sketch of a possible mudroom explaining to me that any new construction had to fit in with what she termed the "architexture" of the house. "It's got to *feel* right, girl. Know what I mean?"

You'd think having a vision sent by God would make her pray more but it didn't. She prayed less and picked on Daddy hardly at all and it was almost as if Daddy needed Gram ragging on him because once she stopped, he stayed out later and drank more. Though we never talked about keeping the Great Idea a secret from him, both me and Gram did, on instinct I guess. Probably it was our newfound hope that blinded me a while to how much more Daddy was out, especially on the weekends, and how much care he was taking with his looks, making sure his hair was kept trim and his face shaved. More likely though, I just didn't want to know what he was up to when he was away from the house, not until Marisol told me that she knew where he'd been.

We were in the playground of our new school. The week before a sinkhole had opened up in the playground of our old school in the fire zone, forcing the county to condemn it and the east side school to take all of us in. Marisol and me stood within a cluster of birch trees in the far corner of the playground, the only area that wasn't packed full of kids. The school was so over-crowded from taking all of us that there wasn't even room to play ball. We all just sort of milled around looking to get into or out of trouble.

"Bet your father doesn't come home as often as he used to," Marisol said. "That's because he's with that idiot everybody calls Star. She lives in my building. Every time I see them I laugh right in their face."

Part of the playground fence was dented in like a car had rammed into it and I stared at that dent a while trying to take in what she'd said about Daddy and Star. Would she say something like that only to be mean? Cagily I said, "Just because your daddy had a girlfriend doesn't mean mine does."

"No," Marisol said. "But that doesn't change the fact that your father *does* have a girlfriend."

"You know just because the Ouija spelled out Howley doesn't mean anything," I countered. "It could have been wrong or it could have been trying to tell us something else." I did my best to glare at her, hearing the advice Ma had given me countless times—"Any lie can sound true so longs as you tell it right"—but then my gaze softened. "I'm sorry about your daddy. Real sorry. I don't know what I'd do if I ever lost mine."

But then the bell rang and Marisol walked away and continued ignoring me with the same vacant stare she'd been using on me for months.

Later that afternoon I found Star's apartment by looking for the name Beatrice Kettering, Star's real name, on the doorbells of Marisol's building and for nearly a week I hung around outside her door. I'd sit in the hallway and do homework for a good hour or so at a time. Nobody seemed to care. Occasionally I'd get the nerve to put my ear to the keyhole, but I never heard much beside a radio playing rock 'n' roll and once I heard Star on the phone saying, "You bring that up every time I call. I can't change the past, Mama."

Sometimes while I waited there in the dusky light of that hallway, I'd think of all the different ways Daddy had described the disaster to various journalists. I'd think of our long-ago "exploring walks" and the sweet way he'd talked about Uncle Frank and then I'd think of the bitter, ugly way he'd talked about Uncle Frank taking bribes and I started to think that maybe nothing Daddy said was true. Maybe he *had* stolen the money from Uncle Jerry and not taken it as a lend. Maybe Ma was right that surviving the disaster had put something mean and cruel in him. Maybe she was right to go away. Maybe she really had no other choice but to leave me behind.

And then on one of those days as I sat outside Star's door the thing that I'd been dreading would happen happened. I heard Daddy's joking voice, the loud somewhat gruff voice he used whenever he was teasing or telling jokes. My chest tightened as if my ribs were squeezing in on me. I pressed my ear to the door and stared down at the rhinestone clips on my shoes, the same clips Daddy had stolen more than a year ago when he was fired from Kreshner's department store.

"I'll start the shower," Star said.

"Be there in a minute," Daddy said. And then the apartment quieted and all I heard was the sound of running water. Slowly I turned the knob and pushed the door open. Slowly I stepped inside. The apartment was mostly just one large room with an unmade sofa bed at its center. Daddy's shirt lay sprawled on the green carpet. His pants were neatly folded over a chair. A silky embroidered bathrobe had been cast off onto a pillow. On a side table draped over a tissue box was Star's star pendant necklace.

There was a small kitchenette against the far wall and, in the corner, a partially closed door to the bathroom. I could hear their voices in and out over the fast, hard spray of the shower.

Star laughed a deep throaty laugh that gave way to a long throaty moan. I picked up the necklace, gripped it in both hands, and yanked with all my strength until the catch broke. Then I dumped it back on the table, my breathing coming in such gusty huffs I was afraid they'd hear me. Quickly I moved for the door but my foot caught on the sofa leg and one of my rhinestone clips snapped off. Looking down at that clip the idea just came to me to take off the other one and plunk them both down on the table next to the necklace. So that's what I did. I put the clips next to the broken necklace and then I ran like hell from the room. I ran right out into the hall and down the stairs. But as I fled into the vestibule someone gripped my hair, pulling me up short. I hissed in pain, not wanting to scream and draw attention to myself.

It was old Mrs. Novak, the crazy lady, who said Gramp had killed her son. The shoulder of her dress was ripped and her brassiere strap showed. She let go of my hair. "What did your grandpa do to my boy?" she said. "You tell me, girl."

"Your boy died jumping off a bridge," I said. "My grandpa had nothing to do with it." But in the hallway my words echoed with their untruth. After all it was Gramp blinding him in one eye that probably led him to want to kill himself and for all I knew Daddy had lied about Jack Novak jumping off that bridge.

Mrs. Novak clawed at a button on her dress. "Wasn't just my boy he killed. Was that Billy Sullivan too. All because both them boys knew about the bribes that Frank Howley was taking. Wasn't just my boy taking bribes. Was that Frank too. *He* let all them men die. Wasn't just my boy."

The old lady took a step toward me and I backed up to the wall. Her eyes had a suspicious cast to them as she turned her gaze to the stairs. "Bet that daddy of yours knew about the bribes them boys were taking. Wouldn't put it past him to have killed my Jack neither. Them Howleys act like their own shit don't stink, but it does. It does!"

"My grandpa and daddy didn't do a thing," I said weakly.

"Then this is for them not doing nothing," she said and spit straight in my face.

I grunted like I'd been slapped and glanced down the hall, embarrassed someone might have seen.

"Now I'm all alone," she said, "with not a soul to look out for me."

Cautiously I circled around her to the front door.

"All alone, all alone," she chanted as I opened the door and stepped out. Even once I was down the block I swore I could hear her singsong voice calling, "Not a soul, not a soul."

Twenty-three

School ended abruptly due to the heat and Ma invited me to spend a week in Allentown. It was her and Brother who met me at the depot, and as soon as I stepped off the bus Brother hugged me hard and wouldn't stop. Ma had to actually peel his arms from my waist.

"Where's Daddy?" he said.

"He'll be coming," I said. "Eventually." Then me and Ma looked away from each other but not before I saw a fleck or two of regret shimmering in the dark auburn of her eyes.

It was Sunday morning and we were all invited to a breakfast at Uncle Jerry and Aunt Janice's church, but it wasn't a Catholic one, it was Baptist. When I complained that we'd be sinning against God going to a Baptist church, Ma said "Church smurch," and then she stood in the pew in her white gloves and her pretty blue pillbox hat, belting out songs, saying afterward as we all sat at a table in the church basement that any church that was her Bropey's church was her church too.

Aunt Janice wiped at some egg at the corner of her mouth. "Just so long as you realize we don't take any orders from the pope."

"Shut up," Uncle Jerry growled.

"I meant it as a joke, Jerome," Aunt Janice said. Then she added, "It's just so strange you're Catholic, Dolores. That's all I meant."

Ma looked like her girdle had squeezed all the air out of her. Her mouth opened and her eyes bulged. Eventually she cleared her throat and her voice came out louder than it should. "Well, you got to remember Jerry ain't really Baptist. He was brought up Catholic first. Ain't his fault that bitch raised him Baptist after."

Ma lifted her chin proudly and nodded at the nice-looking blond family who was seated farther down the table pretending they hadn't heard what she said.

Aunt Janice's face turned the same yellowish white as the eggs on her plate. Ma nodded at Uncle Jerry who kept busy shoveling food into his mouth. "You was just a little baby, Jerry, so how could you remember, but you was baptized Roman Catholic. One of my earliest memories is being by the fountain in the back of the church and both of us wailing. I guess I thought they was hurting you with the water the way you cried."

Ma wiped at a smear of something on her white gloves. "You being baptized is probably the earliest memory I got and I read once in the *Reader's Digest* that your earliest memory tells something." Ma tapped at the lace trim of her collar. "It tells about who you are. Inside, I mean. I guess that memory tells how much you meant to me, right from the start. Before I even got took away." Ma's eyes opened wide as she stared at Uncle Jerry almost in wonder.

Uncle Jerry stopped in mid-chew but didn't look up from his plate. Then he swallowed a wad of biscuit and had to guzzle his whole cup of coffee to get it down.

Back at the house Ma led me to what had become her room, the little room that had once been Daddy's. Ma sat on the window ledge and brushed her hair with short, snappy strokes. As she brushed she talked about the possible jobs she could get once her money ran out from pawning the ring Daddy had bought for her. The most likely job seemed to be the one Aunt Janice was trying to get her at the accountant's office where Aunt Janice used to work before she got married.

"But we have to go on a trip, Ma," I said bending up my legs and resting my chin on my knees. "You promised we would. Just the two of us." Ever since Ma had moved into Uncle Jerry's me and Ma had been planning a vacation. "Just you and me," she'd told me on the phone several times. "A chance for just us girls to be together, no boys allowed."

"Well, I ain't got enough money for no vacation," she said, "but I made some calls to see about Auntie's house. The money should be coming through on that soon and then we can go anywheres in the world we want." Ma laughed and we both came up with more and more outrageous places we could go, Hawaii, the Arctic. "Anywhere where they ain't got no dang fire," Ma said. Then she talked about the nice apartment we'd be able to get and Ma whispered, "Nicer than the one Bropey had planned for us." And the mere mention of that apartment seemed to color the very air with its dinginess and our mood changed as we both thought about the reason why we weren't living there.

Daddy never talked with me about my going into Star's apartment or breaking her necklace. All he did was drop the rhinestone

clips on my bed with the warning, "Don't go thinking you understand things you don't." And I thought, what's there to understand about a daddy cheating on his wife? Only it didn't feel so
much like he'd cheated on Ma, it felt like he'd cheated on me. I
didn't say that to Daddy though, partly out of pride. If he didn't
care enough about us not to do what he'd done, then I wasn't going to let him know I cared about him. But mostly I didn't say
anything because of what I saw in his eyes. It was the dark part of
Daddy, the hateful part, and it put a hardness to his gaze and a
sallowness to his skin that put me in mind of the werewolf poster
that used to hang beside his bed. It felt like ever since we'd moved
to Barrendale he'd become something else. Someone he couldn't
control.

Cagily I asked Ma, "Don't you want to know anything about
Daddy?"

"What's there to know?" Ma said. She put the brush down on
the nightstand where she'd laid out some of her ma's things: tortoiseshell combs, hankies, a pretty glass perfume bottle. From the
top drawer she pulled out a pack of cigarettes and shook one free
from it. "Do I need to know he lost your bus money on some dang
horse bet and now that old biddy thinks I owe her the fare? Why
don't she ask her own son for the money? Why she got to tell *you*
to tell *me* I owe *her*?" Ma puffed furiously at her cigarette as if it
were a source of revenge against Gram.

From downstairs came the sound of a knock on the door, followed by the doorbell buzzer. Ma put her finger to her lips. We
heard Aunt Janice say, "Hi, Mom, how was the trip?" and then we
heard, "Fine, sweetheart, just fine."

I stiffened, recognizing Stepma's voice. Ma must have recognized it too because her finger remained glued to her lips, her eyes swerving back and forth like the gong of a clock.

Uncle Jerry's voice boomed out from the downstairs hall, asking Stepma about traffic and the potholes on Route 80. "Didn't expect to see you, Mom," Jerry said. "But always glad to have you here. Why don't you follow me out to the kitchen? There's something I've been meaning to show you." And you could tell in his voice that he was about to take her deeper into the house to talk about Ma.

"*Mom!*" Ma said and her eyes stopped in their swing, fixing on the opened doorway to the upstairs hall. "*Mom?*" She cupped her fingers around her mouth, her hands curved like question marks, her brow creased with thought. In that position she remained as if she was about to shout out to someone but the only sound that came from her mouth was the quick rhythmic sound of her breathing. Eventually she stood and walked out into the hallway toward the stairs.

"Ma?" I whispered. "Wait." But she didn't so I followed her and together we arrived at the bottom of the stairs where we found Stepma in a white dress that had such a wide collar it made her head look like it was on a platter. Stepma was flanked by Uncle Jerry and Aunt Janice and the tight bun perched on Aunt Janice's head was tilted toward Stepma seemingly in protection.

"I cannot stay in the same house," Ma announced and turned her face to the wall.

"Well, it's not your house to stay or not stay in," Aunt Janice said.

Uncle Jerry coughed. "Plenty of room for everyone. Right, Elsie?"

Stepma's voice came out small as a mouse. "Of course, Jerome. Whatever you say."

"Right, Dolores?" Uncle Jerry said, not bothering to hide the plea caged up in his words.

"'Course, Bropey," Ma said. "For you I'll agree to anything. Speaking of room, I'm going to mine now." Ma turned abruptly and headed back up the stairs.

"Sure, Dolores, sure," Uncle Jerry called up to her. "You rest as long as you want."

For what felt like hours me and Ma sat on Ma's bed playing gin rummy. Through the window we could see Brother playing with his toy cars in the tree house Uncle Jerry had built. The tree house was two floors and wedged cockeyed into the branches of the mulberry tree. The boards of the house were streaked with purple and white bird poo and resembled one of those modern dot paintings Gram said wasn't worth the board it was painted on. We played cards until the sun became a golden ball between the mulberry branches and Aunt Janice called, "Supper's ready."

Ma sent me down alone and we picked at the platter of hamburgers and franks in silence for so long that I found my foot tapping the rhythm of the ticking clock.

Eventually Stepma carefully placed her fork and knife at the top of her plate and her eyes combed over me. "Maybe I shouldn't have come."

"Bullcrap," Uncle Jerry said with a smile frightening in its scope. "Janice should have mentioned it is all."

Aunt Janice slowly chewed her last bit of frank like a cow working on its cud. "I thought I—"

But when she got a look at Uncle Jerry's face she didn't finish the sentence.

"Hate for there to be any problems," Stepma said.

"No problem," Uncle Jerry said and then he went on to complain about the president. "Those Kennedys and their civil rights," he said. "I'd like to see those freedom fighters get in a real fight. It's gotten to the point where you can't turn on the television without hearing somebody boo-hoo over colored's rights."

Aunt Janice's face went as smooth and white as the porcelain cups she served the coffee in. She shook her head in amazement. "And only a hundred years ago they were slaves."

Uncle Jerry nodded, "That's right, Janice. That's right. And believe me we're looking at a time in our future when the white man won't be top dog anymore. And it's not as far away as you'd like to think. It'll be in our lifetime. You wait and see."

Uncle Jerry looked at Stepma for agreement but all she did was sigh and move her eyes up toward the ceiling. It was right then I guessed she was thinking about Ma and I felt a little bad for her.

After dessert I played with Brother in the yard. Dusk was still a ways off but the sun had turned orangey and within its long summer rays Brother was trying to set ants and leaves on fire with his magnifying glass. Little Jerry was playing in his mud pit, eager, I figured, to keep out of Brother's way.

Suddenly Brother looked up from his magnifying glass and his pointy little Ma face went soft and sulky. "Want home," he said, reminding me that he'd said those same words when we'd moved from Centrereach to Barrendale, and I had the awful feeling that for the rest of our lives home was something we'd always be wanting.

"So do I," I said, remembering how gloomy Auntie would get when she'd talk about never being able to go back to her home in the Ukraine. For the first time I understood a little of what she must have felt and oddly enough that warmed me. To share even this sad thing with my long gone auntie brought her, for a little while at least, close.

Once it was fully dark Stepma announced that she was going to leave that night, not stay over, and she wouldn't listen to anything Uncle Jerry or Aunt Janice had to say about it. She also wouldn't listen to them about *not* saying good-bye to Ma. She gripped the wooden railing of the stairway to the second floor and walked so slowly up it I got the feeling she was hoping somebody would stop her. I shot past her up the steps, afraid of what she'd say to Ma, and I suppose I nearly knocked her down because she whimpered and took twice as long climbing the rest of the way.

Ma sat on the cot, looking out the window, and I wedged myself between her and the pillow so that I'd be nearer to the doorway where I hoped to somehow protect Ma from Stepma's words.

"You ought to know he was mighty sorry for what he did to you," Stepma said. "The awful things he did, to you, his own daughter. If he'd lived, he might have found you to tell you that. He was saved in the end. He accepted Jesus in his heart."

Ma flinched as if struck, but she didn't turn her head. "He coulda accepted shit in his heart for all I care. Don't you go talking about what he'd done. You're the one who done something to me. Sending off a little girl. Because you was jealous of her. Jealous that she had her daddy's heart."

Ma stood and looked Stepma dead in the face. "That's what you couldn't stand, Elsie. Tell it true. You couldn't stand that he loved me more. So you sent me off. Separating me from my daddy."

And when she said *daddy* her voice splintered and she gazed down at the nightstand and all the trinkets it displayed.

"You're the lucky one, Dolores," Stepma said, taking a step forward and crossing the threshold into the room. "Can't you see that? I'm the one who had to live with him knowing what he'd done to you."

From the nightstand Ma lifted a porcelain bride that spun on top of a music box. It had been one of her ma's things and Ma had told me she guessed it must have been a wedding gift from her ma's parents.

Ma's eyes slid from the figurine to look at Stepma sideways. "Yeah? If living with him was so bad, why didn't you leave him then?"

"He wouldn't have let me leave with you two kids. I did all I could think of to do. But tell me, Dolores. I can see it in your face. You remember now, don't you? You do, don't you?" Stepma took another step forward and rested her hand on the doorknob.

"What I remember is that he let you do it. He let you get rid of me."

Stepma lifted her foot as if to take another step but instead she stood there with her heel lifted, rocking on the ball of her foot. "The shed, Dolores. The car seat behind it that faced the rabbit cages. Remember how I found you there on his lap with his hand—" Stepma dropped her heel and turned aside, glancing behind her into the darkness of the hallway.

Ma fingered the delicate veil on the figurine. It was made of lace dipped in a hardener that made it all sugary looking. Softly she said, "He killed my rabbits because you asked him to."

"Remember you were holding one of the rabbits and squeezing it so bad it squealed and I screamed and—"

Ma bent back her arm as if to hurl the figurine like a dagger at Stepma's head. For a full minute it seemed she stood there poised, quavering in that position, until she suddenly brought the statue down onto the edge of the nightstand where it broke and fell. Then Ma stared at her cut bleeding hand as if it belonged to someone else.

I cried out and rushed toward Ma, but she pushed me away.

"It wasn't you, Dolores," Stepma said. "Don't you understand. You didn't do anything wrong. You couldn't have stopped him. Forgive him. Forgive yourself." Stepma lowered her head and took a step back. "Someday I hope you'll forgive me."

Ma yanked open the nightstand drawer and grabbed a white sock that she pressed to her cut hand. "I ain't never going to forgive you for nothing. I hate you with all my heart. I hate you with everything I got." Ma tossed the bloodied sock at Stepma's feet and then pushed her out of the way to run down the hall into the bathroom.

Stepma and I stared at each other as we listened to the sounds of Ma heaving up her church breakfast. Once Ma got quiet, Stepma tiptoed down the hall to the bathroom door. She leaned her head toward the doorknob and said, "I want you to know it's still your home, Dolores. He's gone now and it's still your home. I'm going to leave it half and half between you and Jerome. And if you ever need it, there's always a room for you. For you and for your children, Dolores. I hope that makes it up to you somewhat. It's all I know to do."

Then Stepma lunged toward the stairs as if afraid Ma was about to come out and beat her to mush. There was no sound from inside the bathroom though, so Stepma paused, gripping the rail, and looked over to where I'd poked my head out through the doorway. "Pray for her forgiveness, girl. For her to forgive." Then she slowly trod down the stairs.

It was a while before Ma left the bathroom. She didn't even ask if Stepma had left but she must have heard the commotion from the downstairs hall of Aunt Janice pleading with her to wait to leave till morning.

Ma handed me a tin of Band-Aids she'd taken from the medicine cabinet and then silently held her hand out for me to stick the things all over the various cuts on her hand. When I was done Ma's hand looked like Brother's baseball glove that was marked all over with tape from where it had gotten busted. Ma then directed me to sweep up the pieces of the porcelain bride and to throw them in the outside garbage can because she didn't want to have to look at them in her own wastepaper basket. Then she asked me to set warm wet washcloths on her forehead and wipe the toilet down with disinfectant because she didn't want to hear nothing about no mess from Aunt Janice.

Ma shut her eyes and said, "Try to keep quiet, Brigid. I need to rest."

So I did just that. I sat on the edge of Ma's bed and looked from Ma to my reflection, vague and wavering in the darkness of the window. I wondered if Ma thought about how I looked like her daddy, how I had his way of looking. And I wondered if that was why she'd never loved me as much as she'd loved Brother.

The next day Aunt Janice got Ma an interview at the office where Aunt Janice used to work before she married Uncle Jerry. The job was to be a file clerk for two accountants. All Ma would have to do was keep track of their clients' files, answer the phone, make appointments, and handle incoming and outgoing mail. From January until April fifteenth, Ma would have to work long hours. But otherwise she'd only have to work half days on Fridays.

I went with Ma to the interview and waited on a bench in the park across the street from the office. When Ma walked out, she teetered slightly, pointedly ignoring the man who stood by a parking meter looking her up and down.

As she neared the bench, she rolled her eyes and said, "What a bunch a retards they got running that place. Made me take a dumb test. Like I was a little kid! Wanted to see how I'd type a letter, they said. When things got busy they might need me to handle their correspondence, they said." When Ma said *correspondence* her mouth turned downward in an ugly way. She lifted her hair and fanned the back of her neck with her scabbed-over hand. "They was all stuck up like Aunt Janice. But I convinced them by the end there was nothing to it. I can type good enough and what's the big deal about answering the phone?"

By the following afternoon Ma was all agitated, waiting for the call. "They said they'd call today and now it's after three o'clock and that dumb bitch ain't been off the phone since she woke up!" Ma said about Aunt Janice. "I think she's talking about me too. You hear how much she's laughing?"

We were in the kitchen nosing through the refrigerator because Aunt Janice hadn't bothered to make us lunch. Brother and Little Jerry were watching an old Western on the TV in the living room but still we were able to overhear Aunt Janice on the phone in the front hall. Laughing, Aunt Janice said, "Can you believe it, Linda? She actually handwrote part of the letter and some of the words are so badly misspelled you can't even figure out what she meant. She thinks *could* is spelled c-l-u-o-d."

Ma's head swung up like she'd heard a gunshot and next thing I knew she was running down the hall. Aunt Janice, seated at the little telephone table, looked up and screamed as Ma rushed toward her and grabbed the letter from out of Aunt Janice's hands. "How you even get this letter? Was it all just a joke? Were they serious at all?"

"Yes, they were serious. You should have told me you had no proper schooling. You know how embarrassed I am? You're my husband's sister. I recommended you."

Ma held her hand like she'd claw Aunt Janice's face and Aunt Janice leaned back until her head was touching the mirror hanging behind her.

"I had to handwrite it 'cause the cheap ribbon they gave me got all locked up," Ma said. "Look at you with your bird's nest hair and your phony way of talkin'. You're the dumb bitch. If there's any dumb bitch here, it's you."

Ma then pounded up the stairs, sobbing so hard that she fell down halfway up them and had to yank herself up by the rail. Aunt Janice hadn't moved and all she did was blink as Brother started pelting her with his little plastic soldiers. "Take that!" he shouted. "And that!" Little Jerry then started throwing little plastic toys at her too.

"Shut up!" Aunt Janice screamed as I grabbed Brother and started dragging him up the stairs.

In Ma's room me and Brother found Ma seated on the cot, staring at the wall. "She thinks she can treat me like shit and get away with it? I won't let her, I won't let her." And Ma pounded her fist over and over into the bedspread.

And that was it. Ma packed her clothes and her ma's things into Auntie's old green valise. She had me shove Brother's stuff into a couple of brown paper bags and within a half an hour we were standing out by the car and Uncle Jerry was handing us money. His mouth flexed like he was trying to form words but couldn't. Finally he said, "Do you really have to go, Dolores?"

Ma squinted her eyes at the house where we could see Aunt Janice on the phone pacing back and forth behind the living-room picture window. Ma worked hard to hold her tongue but you could see it there poking out beneath her chipped eyetooth like it was scratching an itch. "Don't you worry now, Bropey. I hate seeing you upset. I'll manage. I always have."

And Ma's words set Uncle Jerry off and he sobbed again like he had at Pothole Park. His meaty red hands rubbed at the slobber on his face.

"Don't worry," Ma repeated. "I been on my own before. I been on my own practically from the start. I can do it again."

"But *we're* with you, Ma," I said. "You're not alone." I touched her arm, wanting to hug her but there was something resistant in Ma when she was upset that wouldn't let you near. It was like an invisible shield that kept us from touching her when *she*—when *we*—needed it the most.

Uncle Jerry sniffled. "You're the strongest woman I know, Dolores. Maybe even the strongest man." His face turned red and he swatted at the air like he was swatting at his words that didn't make sense. He added, "You know what I mean."

Ma's glance toward Aunt Janice in the window could have sliced the woman in half. Ma tilted her chin proudly as if Uncle Jerry had been offering praise, but with the way his hands were clasped before him and his head was lowered, he reminded me of a mourner at a funeral. Ma's strength was a kind of weakness for her, we all saw that. Maybe even Ma did because her eyes softened to a warm amber and she said, "I love you, Bropey. Thanks for taking me in."

Then she closed her hand on the money and called us kids to the car and told us not to look back, not even once. "Because if you do," she said, "it'll burn your memory for the rest of your life."

Twenty-four

We didn't know where Ma went after she left Uncle Jerry's. She'd brought me to the bus stop with enough money to buy my ticket and pay back Gram. She let Brother hug me first, then she squeezed me tight. "Don't go worrying about us or making things worse than they are," she said. "I got a friend I can go to. I'll call you soon."

But she didn't. A full week went by before Uncle Jerry called saying she was in Easton and doing all right and he'd let us know if he heard anything else. He made me put Daddy on the phone and they spoke for several minutes, but all Daddy told me of the conversation was that Uncle Jerry was sorry for how it had all worked out.

"You think she'll come back?" I asked, hardly able to look at Daddy since finding him at Star's.

"Of course she will," he said. "You know your ma."

And that statement just hung there for a while for us both to ponder. Then Daddy said, "Listen, princess, it's over. You know what I mean. I don't want to talk about it again." And then Daddy left the house but he didn't stay out that late and when he greeted Mr. Smythe at 3:00 A.M. his voice was only slightly slurred.

It was early July and warm but cooler than the hot spring had been. Fireflies lit up the dark hollows of the woods and no matter how bad things were, I couldn't help but look on their glow as something magical. Sometimes late on clear nights after the fireflies quit their flashing I'd take a blanket into the backyard and lie down to star watch. Whenever a falling star shot a powdery white streak through the sky, I made a wish. Sometimes I wished something horrible would happen to Ma for all the hurt she'd brought us through, but mostly I wished we'd just all be together again and as happy as I'd always thought we'd one day be.

I felt the worst for Brother because I imagined he'd be scared in a strange place all alone with Ma and whenever he was scared he coped by hitting himself. I pictured his pink Kewpie-doll mouth swollen red and his peachy cheeks yellow with bruises and didn't know how Ma could bear to make him suffer so.

Often I tried to do what Auntie had called "Mind Mail," sending someone a happy memory or thought by imagining it into their brain. I'd picture Brother and then I'd think hard on the times we all picnicked at Culver Lake with Auntie or on all the quiet times me and Brother spent frog hunting up in East Woods, but of course I had no idea if my thoughts ever reached him.

Now when Gram lashed out at Ma I didn't care. Maybe it was because Gram was so caught up in working on the paperwork for her Great Idea that even her attacks on Ma lacked their usual bite. She'd say something like, "Lots of people have worse lives than she got and they stick around for them." But she'd say it almost offhand and I'd just shrug or agree. Maybe it was Gram's progress with the Great Idea that had taken the edge off our anger toward Ma and made us less snippy in general. Gram had tracked down a company in Albany, New York, that specialized in moving houses and she'd made arrangements with the Redevelopment Authority that entailed them buying the house from her—which they were required to do now that our neighborhood had been declared a slum—but instead of simply wrecking the place, they'd sell it back to her. Then she'd be able to move the house.

As simple as this sounded, it wasn't. There were heaps of paperwork and permits and this or that signature or stamp required and Gram would sit there at the table with the black gas gauge meter in the corner ticking like a loud and persistent clock and say, "I tell you, all them authorities is workin' in collision to make sure I can't get this done." Or "I bet they're hopin' the house gets wrecked 'fore you can get the permit to get the permit to get the darned thing moved!"

Once Edna Schwackhammer found out about Gram's Great Idea she wanted to try and get her house moved too. Gram never said so but I could tell she regretted ever telling Mrs. Schwackhammer about her plans. Some nights a dazed Mrs. Schwackhammer would sit with Gram at the kitchen table so confused by all the legal issues that she'd cry, "I don't know how to do any of this, Rowena. Otto did everything. Everything! You've got to help me. I don't know how."

"Well, ain't that what you said about writin' a check?" Gram would say. Or "Didn't you say the same thing about nailin' a dawggone nail in the wall? Yet you done both, Edna Jane. And now you done them so many times I bet you can't even imagine not knowin' how!" Then cagily Gram would suggest that it might be better to see what happened with Gram's applications for getting the house moved before doing anything with Edna's. Every now and then she'd add for good measure, "I'm the one who had the idea after all, Edna, sose if they only goin' to let one of us go, it should be me."

Then Mrs. Schwackhammer would cry that her house was slated for demolition sooner than Gram's, so if anyone should get to move their house first, it should be her. Sometimes she'd even plead her case further by claiming her Otto's spirit still rested within her house's walls.

"Well, it's both my spirit and my livin' body that rests within *these* walls!" Gram would declare. "And I ain't got no place else to go. You got three children could take you, Edna, and don't you forget it!"

And then Gram would make a pot of tea and push aside the paperwork until Mrs. Schwackhammer left for the night.

Gram had quit holding prayer meetings because she said they got her "too danged depressed," but she still said a prayer to Saint Jude each time she tackled some part of the Great Idea and she lovingly dusted her Saint Joseph statues every day. No matter how much filth managed to seep in from the dig out those statues stared cleanly out at you from every corner of the room.

"Out of your mind," Daddy said when he first heard about the Great Idea from one of the men who worked for the Redevelopment Authority. "Once they buy it, you've got nothing but their word that they'll sell it back. Even if they put it in writing, what good will that be? You think you can take the entire Redevelopment Authority to court?"

"Maybe I can," Gram snapped. "Anyhows you got any better ideas? What you think is goin' to happen once this house gets wrecked? You think some tramp's goin' to let you stay at her place? What about this girl here?" Gram stuck her arm straight out and pointed at me where I sat on the plastic-covered couch trying both to listen to them and read *A Tree Grows in Brooklyn*.

"Christ," Daddy said, rolling his eyes toward me and the mantel that still displayed all of Gramp's mass cards.

"No takin' the Lord!" Gram shouted, slamming her hand against the wall and knocking a Saint Brigid cross crooked from where it hung above the window.

Daddy took a deep breath and leveled his stare at Gram. "Tramps, Mother? Really? Now isn't that the pot calling the kettle . . ."

He didn't finish the saying but Gram's eyes went as black with pain as if he had. And from that point on she not only hardly talked to Daddy, but she stopped doing any of his cooking, mending, or washing too.

For the most part Daddy ignored the fact that she ignored him and I started doing all of his washing and ironing and mending and cooking. I couldn't turn my heart cold to him, no matter what he'd done to us. Ma and Gram could do that, but not me, and I was proud not to be like them in that way.

Sometimes when I looked at him his cheeks and eyes had a hollowness to them as if they'd caved in. Sometimes he didn't even feel like he was my daddy, just someone who'd been sick a long time who slept in Daddy's old room and drank the hot bitter coffee that he liked to brew two or three times a day. And as mad as I was at him for letting things get to where they were, my heart went out to him when I saw him like that and I'd make him his sunny-side up eggs and toast the way I used to do for him every day in Centrereach. I even started making him Auntie's remedy for what she called the liquid devil for when he drank too much. It was black tea with skullcap and sage and in a way it was a remedy for me too because just in the making of it I felt near to Auntie, which made me think of Marisol saying that Auntie's spirit was around me. Maybe I was no longer closed to her spirit the way Marisol had said I was. Maybe something in me had opened.

Twenty-five

The mail used to come at exactly a quarter after ten every morning but the dig out had made the postman Mr. Grodnik's job so difficult that sometimes he didn't get to us until half past noon. It was my job to check the mail the second it was delivered and if there was anything from the Redevelopment Authority or the moving company to run it—in Gram's words "fast as feet can fly"—to the mill so Gram could know immediately "the no good them folk is up to."

On the day we got something with the return address stamped straight from the Redevelopment Authority I took it immediately to the mill, veering onto Stone Lane at a jog. Even in my hurry my sight roved over the beautiful stone of the mill with its castlelike crenulated ridges, a word I remembered by first thinking of the word *crinoline,* and when I reached the side stairs out of breath I took a moment to appreciate the little bits of sparkle in the chunk of bluestone nearest me.

At the top of the stairs I waved at Big Berta who waved me

through to Gram but my pace slowed as I walked across the big room. The noise was grating but not as steady or deafening as usual. There were any number of sewer's chairs left empty and too many sewers gone to count. Gram had told me they'd lost dozens of gals due to the dig out, but it hadn't hit me until then how many Barrendalers had left and how much we'd eventually feel the loss of them being gone.

Gram's eyes widened as she looked at the envelope in my hand. Gripping me by the elbow, she steered me back across the room and out onto the top landing of the stairs. The noise from inside the mill made it feel like there wasn't a soul who could hear us as we stood out there looking down at the river snaking its way below the cliff.

Gram stared at the ducks and weedy grasses clustered far below us, all of it a blur I imagined since she hadn't bothered to remove the reading glasses she used to sew. "Open it," she said and then I read out loud two sentences stating that the Redevelopment Authority was in the process of finalizing the purchase of her house but had no record of any agreement to sell it back to her. It ended by thanking her for her numerous inquiries into the matter and was signed with a man's name neither of us had heard before.

Gram sucked air through the space where she had a missing tooth. "Goddamn it," she said, and I nearly dropped the letter I was so surprised by Gram not only cussing but taking the Lord's name.

Before I knew what was happening, the river and everything around it went screwy. I gripped the railing to steady myself. "It's just like Daddy said," I cried, dizzy with the upset I felt. "All we had is their word that they'd sell it back and now they won't. And what will we do, Gram? Where will we go?"

"I'll tell you where we'll go. You stay right there and grip that rail." Gram did an about-face and returned several minutes later. "Get ready, girl. We're goin' to Scranton, straight to that Revelopment office and we'll find this man what's-his-name"—Gram pointed at the letter crumpled in my hand—"and we'll find that record of agreement if we have to look through all his files ourself!"

But when we got to the office the only person there was a lady clerk who said she'd be sure to let Mr. Forsythe know we'd stopped by.

"It's a matter of urgent concern," Gram kept saying as she tilted her hat first one direction, then another. "You tell him that, little miss. You tell him he better find that record and fast."

At home me and Gram looked so out of sorts that Daddy actually noticed and asked what was wrong. His voice was so full of concern that it made me go all soft to him.

Gram smoothed the creases in her skirt. "Let's just say you better keep that job of yours, Adrian Howley. We're goin' to need it!" Then she plotted ways that the mill could pay me to do some sewing. "Those child labor laws," she said with the same disgust she used to talk about welfare or scab strikebreakers. "Gramp was workin' a lot younger than you and doin' a lot harder work than side seamin' some underdrawers, you can bet you that!" And she turned on me a stare as full of blame as if I'd made the child labor laws myself.

"I could drop out of school and lie about my age," I said to Daddy once Gram had put on her best dress and left to go talk to the mayor and every government official she could get her hands on.

"Princess!" Daddy said and his mouth opened and his face

went white as if I'd physically hurt him. "Never," he said, placing his hand over mine. "It will never come to that."

And his words made me feel so good that later I went to visit him at the mill, wanting him to put his arm around me and tell me tall tales about the fairies who lived in the nooks of the river—or for him to sing me some Irish tunes, letting me know in just the lilting of his voice that everything was going to be all right. But when I got down there I found Mr. Dober, the boss janitor, emptying the boxes of sewing waste into the big bin in the side yard.

Mr. Dober had a large vein popping out on his forehead. "You tell that daddy of yours to sober up and get here fast if he wants this job!"

"Yes, sir," I said and bolted. First I went home to pick up Auntie's remedy for the liquid devil. I kept a brew of it in an old jam jar and I grabbed it from where I'd hidden it behind some other jars of homemade teas. Then I ran as fast as I could to The Shaft, but the East Side Pit had grown to the point that it must have cost me an extra fifteen minutes to get around it.

By then the dig out had gotten so close to The Shaft that the building was only one short block away from the pit. All the shops and houses along Essex Street weren't more than twenty feet from the ledge. Dirt and coal and ash laid an inch thick on the pavement and quickly coated my skin, making me feel like I needed a bath by the time I pushed open the bar's front door.

It had been a cloudy day and it didn't take my eyes long to adjust to the dimness inside the room. Two of the old men from the disaster were at one end of the bar. Star and Bear were at the other. Joe the bartender was behind it, drying glasses. Daddy wasn't there. He must have already left for work.

I gasped in relief but then I heard a moan and noticed a heap of something by a table. It was Daddy sprawled on the floor, his head up against a chair leg.

I rushed forward and slid to my knees. I watched to make sure his chest rose and fell, I touched his cheek.

"Your daddy's just sleeping it off, honey," Joe said. "He'll wake up soon. He always does."

I swept Daddy's hair back from his face and he jolted like I'd struck him. The skin at his temple was a slick shiny purple.

"No," he moaned. "Please." He put his arms up to his head like he expected to be pummeled with fists. "Won't tell anyone. Never tell anyone."

"You hit him," I said to Bear.

"Nuh-uh, little miss," Bear said. "The table hit him. Not me."

Star laughed the same throaty laugh I'd heard when she was in the shower with Daddy and I narrowed my eyes at her. She had her arm around Bear's waist and she whispered something in his ear that made him grunt in pleasure.

"Ah, God!" Daddy shouted and his eyes opened wide in terror.

"What, Daddy? Does it hurt?" I opened the jar and held it to his mouth but he wouldn't drink. He stared beyond the table like there was something there to get him. But all that was there was some dried-up peanut shells and a mushroom-shaped stain on the floor. Then he started mumbling something I couldn't understand.

I leaned so that my body blocked him from Star's and Bear's view but I could feel their stares all prickly on my back. It took me a while to figure out he was saying, "Didn't mean it, didn't mean it," over and over.

"Didn't mean what, Daddy?" I said, but he just kept mumbling and staring out at nothing as if in fear for his life. The smell of him was of beer sweat and pee and reminded me of Gramp's sick smell. "Daddy? Can you get up? If you lean on me, can you walk?"

He stopped mumbling and shook his head but I wasn't sure he'd understood what I'd asked. Then he said something so low it was like a whisper's whisper.

"What, Daddy?" I asked. "What are you trying to say?"

He again spoke and again it was so low I almost couldn't catch it. "I killed him," he said.

"What?" I said, figuring I must have misheard but my heart pounded as if my body knew better than my mind did what was true.

"I killed him," he said.

I stared at the table leg and the faint shadow it cast from the light behind the bar and all at once I felt the shame of who we were. We weren't the proud descendants of the heroic Mollies. We were cursed white trash, liars, thieves, ruffians. We were people whose own parents left us or sent us away or wish we'd never been born. We were killers, the lowest of the low.

I bent so that my mouth was right against his ear. "Marisol's daddy, you mean? William Sullivan?"

"I killed him," Daddy said again.

And then I sat him up and smacked at his face to rouse him. When his eyes met mine and focused I whispered, "I wish you'd died in that disaster. I wish you weren't my daddy. I wish I never see you again."

I stood and glared at everyone in the bar. The look on Star's face reminded me of Aunt Janice's when she was holding Ma's business letter and laughing about it on the phone.

Stepping toward me Star said loud enough for everyone to

hear, "You're just a little bitch like your mother, ain't you? You think I don't know it was you who broke my necklace?"

"Yeah, it was me," I said. "And I'd do it again."

Then I swung at her so hard it knocked us both to the ground. Blindly I fought, shutting my eyes against Star's fake nails and for the first time I understood what Ma meant when she said, "Ain't nothing better than slapping the bitch out of someone."

Twenty-six

A hair-pulling hussy was what Gram called me over breakfast the next morning.

"Better than just being a hussy," I mumbled into the oatmeal I'd made too runny.

Gram snatched the spoon from my hand and shook it at me. "What did you say?"

I said nothing. I already regretted my words. I'd just wanted everyone to be as miserable as me.

"Sorry? Say again." Gram dropped the spoon onto the table with a clatter.

"Nothing," I said. Our eyes met and then immediately flicked off each other.

"Don't go thinkin' who you are or talkin' 'bout things you know nothin' about!" Gram declared with a stomp of her foot. Still, she wanted to know what hits and bruises I'd managed to get in on Star, and as I described them, her eyes lit with pleasure.

I didn't know if Daddy remembered anything about what had

happened at the bar. The next day he had a vacant, troubled look to him and we carefully avoided each other's eyes, skulking past each other in the kitchen or hall. He'd lost his job at the mill and for days afterward he'd sleep long stretches at a time on Ma's old mattress, often screaming out in one of the nightmares he got from time to time about the disaster. Sometimes I'd go in the room and openly stare at him sprawled out on the mattress the way he'd been sprawled out on the floor of the bar. I'd do it just to make myself face the truth of who he was—a liar, a cheater, a murderer. Worse than all those things was the fact that my whole life I'd thought he was someone else, someone wonderful. Maybe I'd never been his princess. Maybe he'd never loved me, as he'd always said, with the best of his heart. And the thought of that would leave me lying on the porch sofa for hours, staring up at the ceiling, mourning the loss of the daddy I'd loved so much, who'd never really existed at all.

"Curse or flu," Gram said, referring to the fact that by the following week all three of us were ill.

"Since Smythe has the flu," Daddy said, "I think it's safe to say flu."

"Someone speakin'?" Gram said to the air next to my face.

I turned away; I didn't want to play their no-speaking game anymore.

Daddy, ignoring, as usual, the fact that he was being ignored, said, "I heard the Redevelopment office can't find your request, Mother."

We were all at the kitchen table slurping a supper of Campbell's chicken soup that I'd heated, all of us listless and clammy with aching stomachs and heads. I bent low over my bowl but Gram rapped my head with her knuckles as if she was knocking on a door. "You tell him they just misfiled it, but if I have to I'll file 'nother one. And if I got to, I'll just file 'nother one after that."

"But those requests might be dated too late," Daddy explained. "In three months our entire street is slated for demolition. If you file a second request too late, they may be able to disregard the first request that was filed on time."

I lifted my eyes and swerved them from Daddy to Gram, trying to detect in Gram's reaction if Daddy could be right.

Gram wiped the feverish sweat from her forehead with a napkin and forgot herself enough to speak directly to Daddy. "I got the mayor and most of the town council on my side. They know I filed it on time."

"What they know and what they can prove are two different things," Daddy said with a gentleness that I could tell surprised even Gram. She tenderly stroked the napkin on her lap but only for a moment. Then she looked off to a crack that had recently appeared in the window as if Daddy had disappeared into the air.

I felt so sick I didn't even wash the soup bowls and Gram felt so sick she didn't rag me about it. She didn't even pack away her breakables when we'd been warned a dozen times that they were going to blast tomorrow. I nestled some of the Depression glass in the linen drawer and then I lay down on the porch sofa and gave in to feeling miserable. Even when I heard Daddy leave through the front door, all I did was raise my head enough to see him cut across the front lawn, a blistering orange sun sinking low behind the trees toward West Mountain.

I didn't know how many hours later it was that I woke. A fat rising moon lit the air a chalky blue. I sat up and my head fell forward. Dizzy and nauseous, I lay back down, patting my clothes, surprised Gram had let me fall asleep fully dressed on the porch, but then I remembered that Gram had gone to sleep even before I had and that Daddy had left to The Shaft or O'Malley's—or Star's.

I leaned over the sofa to retch but nothing came up. Resting my head against the pillow I dozed and dreamt that I was in Old Man Hudson's shack and Ma, Brother, and Daddy were trapped down in the bootlegging hole but I couldn't figure out how to get to them.

"John?" I heard Gram yell from the bedroom. "That you?" She called "John" again, then again. By the fourth time she called, I was fully awake.

"Gram?" I shouted. "You all right?"

There was no answer. Sometimes she talked in her sleep. Slowly I sat up and waited for the room to steady itself. The wooden figures standing at the base of the lamp swayed like they were dancing, then gradually went still. Through the trees I could see part of the newly abandoned Williamson's house and beyond that, West Mountain smoking an eerie purple. The gas gauge meter ticked, out of sync as usual with the grandfather clock. I shivered, feeling like I was being watched and I wondered if crazy old Mrs. Novak was out in the yard somewhere plotting against us. I locked the door. The only other occupied house on the street was the Kazinskis and they were far enough away we'd have to scream bloody murder before they'd hear us.

Light-headed, I walked to the living room and checked the clock. Nearly 2:00 A.M., which meant it would be at least an hour before Mr. Smythe came, *if* he came. I looked to see if Daddy was asleep in his room but not only were both mattresses empty but they were unmade. The fact that the entire day had passed without Gram yelling at me for that made me more nervous than anything at how sick we might be. Thoughts of the various plagues I'd read about in my historical romances went through my head. Maybe me and Gram were going to die that very night and no one would know till Daddy came home, *if* he came home. I sat down in Gramp's Barcalounger to rest and heard Gram shout, "No, John. You got to go. I don't like this!" Then I heard the front door open. "Hello?" I called. "Inspector?"

I stood and again shivered, feeling icy cold even though I was coated in sweat. When I peered into the kitchen, the front door was closed and no one was there. Quickly I crossed the room and locked the door. But then I unlocked it, realizing I must have been mistaken about hearing the door open and knowing that if an inspector came he wouldn't have a key.

The shuffling sounds of Gram walking to the bathroom followed by the toilet flushing drew me down the hall, but instead of finding Gram in the bathroom, I found her in her bedroom. She was lying on top of the bedspread, still in her housedress and ratty pink slippers, so deeply asleep that her snores caused her cheeks to shake. But if Gram was lying here so deeply asleep, then who had I just heard in the bathroom?

At a trot, I crossed back into the kitchen, flicking on lights along the way. I locked the front door, then dodged onto the porch to make sure that door was locked as well. It was then that my neck prickled. Someone was in the room. I could feel myself being watched.

I let go of the knob and turned. There, in the entrance to the living room, stood a man. He nodded as if in greeting and I said, "I guess you're Mr. Smythe's replacement? The new inspector?"

He didn't reply but merely narrowed his eyes to stare beyond me out the window. His hair was dark and longer than most men kept it and though the porch was lit only by the moon and the light from the living room, I could see his eyes were a pale icy blue.

"I'm sick," I said, thinking maybe he was confused as to why I was up in the middle of the night.

He still said nothing and only tilted his head as if straining to hear something far away. He was dressed all in black except for a white collar that stuck up from beneath his vest. From his neck hung a large silver cross. In my feverish stupor, all I thought of was how that was the kind of cross used in the movies to ward off vampires.

He raised a finger to his lips as if someone might be eavesdropping on us.

"Did you see an old lady outside?" I said. "That's crazy Mrs. Novak. I'm pretty sure she's harmless."

He lowered his finger but still didn't say anything. Fleetingly I thought of Gram warning me about the perverts who hung out by the railroad. "They smell fear like dogs," Marisol used to advise me about those dirty leering men. "Act like you're not afraid of them."

"Is it about the fire?" I said, even though a part of me already knew this man was no inspector.

Sharply he quirked his head and I saw that his cheek was badly bruised. With his fingertips he lightly touched the wound as if he'd only just noticed it and it was then I saw that the clothing and flesh of his arm was mauled. His fingers moved from his cheek to the cross around his neck and then his lips curved into a scythelike smile. He first took one step, then another, and then he walked through the couch as if its metal frame and cushions didn't exist, as if they were made of air.

A sound like a dog's yelp escaped my throat. "You're Father Capedonico," I accused, pointing my finger at him.

He stepped into a patch of moonlight by the window and his image clouded. He seemed too handsome and young a priest to have put such a hateful curse on us and the fact that he looked nothing like I'd always imagined made him seem all at once more and less real.

Bitterly I said, "I knew you really existed. I knew Auntie was wrong. The curse isn't inside of us. It's inside *you*." I again pointed my finger at him, my body quaking with hatred and fear. "Why don't you leave us alone? Haven't you hurt us enough?"

From down the hall Gram shouted, "Go away, John! Please. I don't like this. I don't like it at all."

"Who's in there with Gram?" I said. Even my bones tingled. I had to grip the hard back of the wicker chair to keep myself standing.

With his finger he beckoned me to follow him as he stepped through the porch wall to the yard. Through the window I shouted, "I hate you! I hate my daddy too! I know what he did. I know he killed Marisol's daddy."

The priest shook his head, then held his hands up and looked at the blood that was on them in disbelief.

"Is that my daddy's blood?" I cried.

The priest gazed up at the moon and squinted as if the light hurt him. His image was quickly turning see-through and I could make out the shadows and shapes of the lilac bushes behind him. I yanked at the door to open it. The lock snagged and my fingers quivered so badly it took me two tries to push it open. Shaking, I stumbled down the steps, nearly falling to the ground. When I looked up, the priest was gone, but I heard his voice speaking to me as if it was somewhere inside my head: "It all comes back to what happened down there." Then all I heard after that was a shrill screaming.

"Father Capedonico?" I called, turning round and round, but the priest was nowhere in sight. It was only then I realized the screaming sound was the gas gauge meter shrieking its alarm. The gases had gone too high in the house!

I fled up the steps and through the porch, not even thinking to hold my breath. I understood all at once that the priest had lured me outside so he could poison Gram in her sleep. But I wouldn't let that happen. Auntie had died while I'd stood there doing nothing. I wasn't going to let that happen to Gram.

"Gram?" I cried. She still lay on top of the bedcovers but she was no longer snoring and she appeared as still as death. I slipped my arms beneath her and lifted but I could barely budge her. "Gram?" I shouted. "Please, Gram, wake up!" Nausea struck me and I nearly wept thinking again of Auntie. Yanking at Gram's arms I pulled her into a seated position. Then, hunched over, I hauled her onto my back the way I'd seen miners in photos carry their wounded and dead.

Gram was nearly as tall and heavy as me, her feet dragged on the floor. It felt like forever before I even managed to get her into the hall. Worse, waves of dizziness forced me too many times to count to pause and steady myself. When I finally reached the porch, the sight of the door gave me the burst of strength I needed to fling us down the steps. I hit the ground hard, Gram on top of me, and that was the last I remembered until I woke on a bed in the hospital with Gram in a bed beside me.

Gram kept calling for Gramp.

"He's gone, Gram," I said gently to remind her.

"No, he ain't. I seen him plain as day." She turned toward me, her glazed eyes weepy. "I saw him sittin' in the wing chair in the corner of the room, like he always done. He was coughin'. That's what woke me to his presence."

Our eyes combed over each other's faces. Then, slowly, I sat up, expecting the room to shift and slide but everything stayed put. I crossed to Gram's bed and sat down on the edge and told her how Father Capedonico had appeared to me and how he'd lured me outside to poison her.

I put a hand to my chest, winded. It got me out of breath just to talk.

Gram blinked. "You coulda died," she said, her voice hushed with amazement. She gripped my hand so hard the bones of my fingers pressed painfully together and she repeated, "You coulda died comin' for me."

When she met my eyes, she looked deeply into them as if she wanted to see as much of me as she could.

"Glory be, you two gals were lucky," the nurse proclaimed as she entered the room pushing a tray displaying two apples and two sandwiches. She had a red face made redder by the white of her uniform and she cheerily informed us that we'd been given oxygen and had our blood tested and we'd be fine. "But we want to keep an eye on you a little longer just the same." She winked and left the room.

I got Gram to sip some water but she refused to eat a bite until

I described what Father Capedonico looked like. When I did she grunted, "He ain't nothin' like I expected." I agreed and then she had me repeat what he'd done as exactly as I could remember it. I paused when I reached the part about Daddy. I studied Gram's face as if everything I wanted to know could be read there. "When I told him that Daddy killed William Sullivan, he shook his head no. I thought Daddy did kill him. I can't believe I thought that." With the heels of my palms I jabbed at my eyes like I wanted to put them out for picturing such a thing.

"Quit that, girl," Gram said, and she yanked at my hands and clasped them. "What else he say?"

"He said it all comes back to what happened down there. I heard him say it clear as anything. What could that mean?"

Gram said nothing. Her eyes moved from one spot on the wall to another as if hunting for clues and the tip of her tongue traced the creases on her bottom lip. "Gramp must have come to warn me about the priest. And maybe about the house. All he kept sayin' was 'Don't, don't.' Maybe he thinks I shouldn't have no dealings with the Revelopment Authority."

We were interrupted by Detective Kanelous knocking on the open door. "I heard you ladies were here." In each of his hands was a steaming paper cup.

"So you came to the hospital at four in the mornin' to bring us tea?" Gram said as if he were offering us poison.

"No, ma'am. I was already here. Unfortunately my job brings me to the hospital at this hour of night more often than I'd like. Certainly more often than my wife likes." His big teeth shone faintly yellow as he smiled at his quip.

Gram rolled her eyes and Detective Kanelous took that as an invitation to enter. He placed the two cups on the nightstand beside the bed and then he dragged a chair over from the window, raising his shoulders and wincing in apology for the noise. When he sat, he leaned back and crossed his legs. Gram and I raised eyebrows at each other. Where we came from only women crossed their legs. "The nurse tells me you'll both be fine," he said.

Gram turned her face toward the opened doorway and I shrugged in apology. I figured the longer we kept quiet, the faster he'd go away. He bent and picked up a gum wrapper from the floor. He crumpled it between his fingers as he said, "Of course I was concerned when I heard there was an intruder."

Gram's head swiveled toward him and she snapped, "Intruder? What nonsense! There was no intruder." Gram raised her eyebrows at me and I shook my head vigorously in agreement.

"Really?" Detective Kanelous said, tilting his head as if listening for something up by the ceiling. Then he leaned forward and bore his orangey rimmed cat eyes into me. "But you told the orderly a man got in the house. Who did you mean? Who got in? Who couldn't you lock out?"

"I didn't say anything like that," I said, shifting to sit closer to Gram.

Gram's face flushed. "The girl was sick from the fumes. Who knows what she said."

Detective Kanelous pursed his lips and stared deeply at me, the same way he had when he'd dropped me off at the house and told me I could tell him anything. "Maybe it was someone you knew?" he offered.

"No," I said. I squinted, looking at him through the narrow of my eye like Ma did when she was issuing a dare. "I saw a ghost," I said as matter-of-factly as if I'd said, "the room is warm."

Gram leaned forward trying to wedge the pillow against her

hump. "Poor thing don't know what she's sayin'. The fumes got her in the head." Gram pointed her finger at her head like a gun and cocked her thumb.

"Yes," Detective Kanelous said agreeably. "It's not uncommon for carbon monoxide fumes to cause people to see apparitions. There's a famous case of it actually in the *American Journal of Ophthalmology*—"

Gram cut him off. "Apparitions? My left foot! We know what we saw."

"Ah," he said, leaning forward, "so you both saw it. Tell me what happened."

Before I could stop myself I blathered, "He tried to trick me *outside* so Gram would die from the fumes *inside*. But the gas gauge screamed so I knew something was wrong and I ran back in." My mouth opened as if trying to get the words to fly back in as fast as they'd flown out.

Detective Kanelous didn't say anything at first. Then he uncrossed his legs and leaned forward with his elbows on his knees. A wave of thick black hair fell forward across his brow. "Sounds to me like your ghost saved you both."

"Not in a million years," I said.

"A hundred," Gram corrected and I wondered what Detective Kanelous would say if I told him about our century-old curse.

From his shirt pocket he pulled out a small notepad and pencil. "Well, on the off chance it really was an intruder, I'll take a statement." He tapped the pencil tip against the paper and looking in our general direction said, "How would you describe him? Did you get a look at his face?"

Gram and I slid eyes sideways at each other and Gram's rubbed off with a warning to watch my words. I described the priest's somewhat longish dark hair and pale blue eyes. I mentioned his height and the lankiness of his limbs.

Detective Kanelous wrote this all down without comment. Then he again tapped his pencil against the pad. "You sure it wasn't your father? Sounds a bit like his description. Maybe the gases just made you—" He stopped talking when he saw my face. "Anyway, I'd like to talk to him too." Then he offered to drive us anywhere we needed and added that he'd heard we were trying to get the house moved.

"Tryin' is right," Gram said. "'Parently there's a problem with the paperwork."

"Well, maybe I can check into that for you," Detective Kanelous said, beaming on us both a broad smile.

"Maybe," Gram said without a lick of thanks. Her nod good-bye told the detective just how much she thought of cops and the government.

Gram waited until the sounds of Detective Kanelous's shoes hitting the hall floor disappeared and then she asked me to again describe everything the priest had done and said. This time I could see her bafflement turn to fear when I repeated the words "It all comes back to what happened down there," and I was reminded of Ma's words to Daddy just before we left Centrereach: "We both know you been dying to go back there ever since we left. To the place where it all happened, where it all went wrong."

For a while me and Gram sat in silence. Gram reassuringly patted my leg, but her expression remained as grave as if she'd seen the exact way death would eventually come for the both of us.

Twenty-seven

An inspector from the Redevelopment Authority came to the hospital to request that we stay away from the house for several days until they were sure the gases had cleared, but it took me a full hour to get Gram to call Mrs. Schwackhammer to ask if we could stay with her. "It's quite an impishisition," Gram said yet again as we stood by the pay phone with the dime the nurse gave us to place the call.

"She's got plenty of room, Gram," I insisted, adding, "Where else can we go?"

We locked eyes and it seemed to me we were both thinking the same thing—not only did we have no place else to go, but the only people in the whole world we could depend upon was each other. We both opened our mouths but didn't say anything and then we turned to look down the empty hall as if to make certain we were still in the same place with no other options.

Eventually Gram said, "Gonna scare the woman half to death callin' at this hour." But we didn't scare Mrs. Schwackhammer. If anything, she was glad to come get us, even though it was only 5:00 A.M. She picked us up in her old Ford sedan, a kerchief tied over her head, and immediately wanted to know all the details of what had happened.

"Can't it wait for mornin', Edna?" Gram said, leaning her head against the passenger side window as if trying to get as far away from Mrs. Schwackhammer as possible.

"Well, it *is* morning," Mrs. Schwackhammer said. She patted Gram's knee. "But sure, it can wait."

Mrs. Schwackhammer set us each up in our own bedroom and seemed to thoroughly enjoy tending to us with tea and soup and hot or cold washcloths. She'd hobble around with her crooked hip, her face all aglow as she talked about the ways she used to care for her Otto. As a thank-you, Gram and I told her all about the gas poisoning and the hospital care, exaggerating our fear and illness as much as possible, but neither one of us mentioned the curse or Father Capedonico.

"For heaven's sake, Edna, I can take care of myself," Gram snapped more than once. Her bedroom was across from mine and the way the beds were positioned we wound up staring at each other if the doors were left open.

"I know, I know. I just thought maybe once you felt better—"

Gram didn't give her a chance to finish. "Edna, I can't even get my own house moved, forget about yours."

"No. I meant . . . It's just that . . . ." Mrs. Schwackhammer's cane clicked on the floor as she approached Gram's bed and sat down.

"What for goodness sake? What?!"

"Maybe you could call to my Otto. You know the way you did to your John. Maybe you could get Otto to come and talk to me?"

Mrs. Schwackhammer looked over to where I sat propped up with pillows on the bed across the hall. "Or maybe the girl could call to him? Did he only come to you, Ro, or did the girl see him too?"

"Good Lord, Edna! You think I wanted him to come? I asked him to leave is what I done." Gram crossed her arms and dramatically shivered. "A ghost ain't nothin' anyone *wants* to see. Still, I got to wonder what he come for is all."

The next day Gram insisted we visit Gramp's grave to ask him if he was trying to warn her about moving the house. "What we got to lose, John?" Gram asked Gramp's headstone. "They're gonna wreck the place anyways. At least I might have some money in hand even if they don't let me buy the place back." Then Gram whispered to make sure Mrs. Schwackhammer couldn't hear her from where she stood several yards away by Otto Schwackhammer's grave, "Or did you come to tell me about the priest?"

Gram stood there waiting as if she expected Gramp to give an answer. It was a pleasant day, the end of August, that time of year when you first start feeling the yearning that comes with fall. We were up past Saint Barbara's church, well out of the fire zone, and there were tons of purple and white asters blooming and lots of finches and sparrows flitting around. Maybe it was that feeling of goodness, of nature being as it should, of death and loss all rolled together that made Mrs. Schwackhammer bring up past regrets.

Carefully she made her way over from her husband's grave to suggest we all rest for a bit on a nearby bench. She cleared her throat and smoothed the pleats of her dress across her lap. "Rowena, there's something I got to tell you." She shifted her eyes to Gram and Gram stiffened.

Mrs. Schwackhammer continued, "For a long time now, I've wanted to explain why I treated you the way I did when you first came to Barrendale."

"You told me you was sorry, Edna. That's enough said!"

"I'd like to clear my conscience, Rowena. Will you allow that?"

"Somethin' tells me I got no choice."

Mrs. Schwackhammer nodded in agreement. "I'm sorry to say I was jealous of you. There you were, brand-new to the mill and telling Boss Betty we needed better lights and an extra fan. I was jealous that you'd have the nerve to come to a town where you didn't know a soul and to speak your mind like that. You know something, in all these years we've known each other you never told me what brought you here—why you left Centrereach."

Gram shot me such a look that my mouth clamped shut even though I had no intention of speaking. "We was lookin' for a brand-new start," Gram said. "Wasn't nothin' much left for us in Centrereach." And from the way Gram's eyes lowered I imagined she was thinking about her ma and all the mean things she must have said when Gram got pregnant with Daddy. And I realized right then that that was why they'd left Centrereach—to escape the shame, and not the curse as Gram had always said. Maybe Gram even worried when Daddy and Ma moved back to Centrereach that they'd find out about Gram's shame. Maybe they had.

"And I'm so glad you did come," Mrs. Schwackhammer proclaimed, pounding her cane on the ground for emphasis. "I'll tell you, it sounds awful to say it and I don't mean it the way it sounds, but I'm glad in a way your John got sick. Once he did, I got to thinking of when my Otto took sick and I could see on your face all I'd been going through and all I wanted to do was help you out as much as I could."

Mrs. Schwackhammer dropped her cane and pressed her face into her hands. "And when I got the call from you in the hospital. To think you almost died. If not for this girl here carrying you out, why we'd be here today burying you!"

Gram then pressed her hands to her ears and Mrs. Schwackhammer again pressed her hands to her eyes and all I could think was if I pressed my hands to my mouth, we'd be the spitting image of hear no evil, see no evil, speak no evil.

Mrs. Schwackhammer's voice came muffled through her fingers, "I knew I'd been jealous of you back then and I'm jealous now that your John came to you. I know my Otto and the only place he'd ever come back to, if he'd ever come back, is the house. Once it's gone—"

Gram raised her eyes to heaven. "Lord Almighty, Edna, enough! You win. Tomorrow you and me will go down to that Revelopment office and you're going to speak to the clerk yourself. You don't *need* me to go with you, Edna Jane. You *want* it. Big difference twixt the two."

I didn't see Daddy until the following day when Gram sent me over to get the mail. I'd been wanting to see him since Father Capedonico told me that Daddy didn't kill William Sullivan and that want had been building in me almost to the point where I couldn't stand it anymore. He was taking his chances staying at the house and I found him at the kitchen table clasping one of Gram's yellow china cups in both his hands. He looked thin, his clothes were stained and wrinkled. He needed a shower and a shave.

"Oh, Daddy, you look so sick." I wrapped my arms around his

shoulders. His coppery scent filled an empty part of me and made me aware of all the other parts that still had nothing inside.

He let me make him sunny-side up eggs and toast and when I served him I was reminded of when he'd let the egg drip down his face, a game that would be silly now because I didn't think we could laugh like that at anything ever again. I told him that the Redevelopment Authority was in the process of buying the house but, just as Daddy had predicted, Gram's first application to buy back the house still couldn't be found and her second one had been filed too late.

Daddy said nothing. He bit into the toast and pushed the plate away. Then he reached for the stack of mail on the table and from the bottom of it slid out a postcard. The front of the postcard showed a picture of a diner. Beneath the picture in little print it said, THE CORNER DINER, ONE OF BALD KNOB KENTUCKY'S FINEST DESTINATIONS SINCE 1921. On the back of the card Ma had written, *Were fine. Dont wory.*

"I hate her," I said.

"You can't hate your ma," Daddy said, not looking up from his cup.

"But you hate Gram," I said. "Don't you?"

"I hate how she feels about me. That's different." Daddy took a sip of his coffee. "I'm proud of you, Brigid. I heard how you saved Gram. You're a brave girl. You didn't get that from me. That comes from your ma."

I tossed the postcard across the table. "Ma ran away and left us. You're the one who survived the disaster. You're the brave one, Daddy."

"It should have been me here that night with the gases. You two shouldn't have been alone."

I didn't say anything because I didn't want to think about where he'd been instead of being with us. I didn't want to think about him being with Star and not wanting to think about Star reminded me of what else I didn't want to think about—like what Daddy meant when he said, "I killed him."

"Detective Kanelous said he wanted to see you," I said. "He came by when we were in the hospital."

Daddy put the cup to his mouth but then hesitated and didn't drink. "Yes, he wanted to ask me some questions." He put the cup down. "He told me that you said a ghost saved you." Daddy's gaze slid off to the living-room entryway as if the ghost might be there by Gramp's altar on the mantel.

Before I knew it I was telling Daddy how Father Capedonico appeared and how he'd lured me outside. "And then he told me things, Daddy." I stopped talking. It felt like what people said about the devil—that if you talked about him, you brought him near.

Daddy's blue eyes had paled and looked as liquidy as water. "It's okay," he said. "You can tell me. I know he came for me. That's who he meant to find here, not you or Gram. It's me he's after. I feel it."

In a rush I said, "No, Daddy. When I said that you killed Marisol's daddy he shook his head no." My mouth opened almost in wonder, I was so relieved to have this be true.

Daddy shut his eyes and then pressed a hand to his mouth. He sobbed. I didn't speak. I'd never seen Daddy cry before and it unsettled a deep place inside me. I looked away and waited for him to stop, even though there was another part of me, almost but not quite separate from me, who already knew I'd be sorry I hadn't at least patted his hand—that I hadn't in some way let him know I hurt for him.

Finally, Daddy nodded. "What else?"

"He said it all comes back to what happened down there."

Daddy wiped his nose on one of Gram's embroidered dish towels and then stared at the crack in the wall. He nodded for me to continue.

"That's all he said. What does that mean? What comes back? What happened down there?"

Daddy opened his hands and looked at them like they could tell him something. Slowly his eyes turned inward to that other place, the dark place he disappeared to more and more. "Don't ever ask me that again," he said and then he walked off and left me staring at his uneaten eggs and Ma's postcard.

I brought the postcard with the mail to Gram. I guess I wanted to start something with her. Gram was seated in the chair by the window of the room she was staying in at Mrs. Schwackhammer's. She sorted the pile I handed her, barely glancing at Ma's postcard, but surprising me by asking how Daddy took seeing it. She hadn't asked anything about Daddy in so long it had felt like she never would again.

"I don't know how he took it. Not well. He's sick, Gram. Really sick." And in my voice was an accusation I didn't try to hide. My life was so screwed up because my parents were so screwed up because of what *their* parents had done to them. Gram must have understood the feeling in my words because she said, "I'm sorry your daddy is the way he is. And I'm to blame for that to some degree, that's true. But comes a point when a person's got to take 'sponsibility for who they is no matter what their parents done to them. That's somethin' your ma could learn. She acts like all her problems go back to her bein' dumped in an orphanage. But some things you got to get past, no matter how bad."

As Gram spoke, she twisted the ring on her finger, her daddy's ma's ring, the one she'd promised to Ma on Ma's wedding day. Sometime after Ma left, Gram took to wearing it. "Now listen," Gram continued. "There's somethin' I want to say to you. I saw that look you give me when Edna mention me and Gramp leavin' Centrereach. But we made that wrong situation right by gettin' married and movin' to a new town. So don't go thinkin' you're all high and mighty. Believe me you could just as easy make a mistake and ruin your life too." Gram shook her head. "That's not what I mean to say. You ain't gonna ruin your life and I didn't ruin mine neither. I fixed it."

Gram put a finger to her mouth as we heard a creak on the hall stair. Gram motioned for me to shut the door and then we waited in silence until we heard the thud of Mrs. Schwackhammer's cane on the kitchen floor beneath us.

"There's somethin' else I want you to know," Gram said. I sat on the bed facing her, but I didn't look at her. I looked at the window that framed part of a sassafras tree that had gotten so hot from the fire that it had shed its bark like it was shedding a coat. Gram continued, "I took my 'sponsibilities and did the best I could with them. I hope your daddy can see that one day. A mother's mistake ain't the child's and if I had to do it over I'd have treated your daddy different." Gram tilted her head back and massaged the base of her hump. "After all, it wasn't his fault he was the kind of baby he was, all squirmy and never wanting to eat. You be surprised the kind of bad you feel when your own child don't want to feed from you."

I said nothing, merely fixed my stare on the ring on Gram's hand.

"This ring was my grandma's," Gram explained. "My daddy's mama. My daddy's parents lived not ten miles from where Mama's parents lived. They knew each other's people. I think for Mama that kind of made them like family, even before she married into them. She must have needed that, to feel like there was at least some connection with where she came from."

"Don't you think that was the same for Ma? Don't you think she needed that too?"

Gram narrowed her eyes. "What the heck you talkin' 'bout?"

"Daddy had to take that money from Uncle Jerry to buy that ring. And that's something he'd never have done if you'd just given Ma your grandma's ring, like you'd promised. If you had, Daddy wouldn't be like he is now and Ma and Brother wouldn't be living in some nowheresville in Kentucky!" A sob caught in my throat and I coughed to cover it.

"That's just what a little girl would think. A ring ain't gonna change a whole lot one way or 'nother. A ring is the absolute least of a marriage, I can tell you that."

"The ring wasn't about the marriage, Gram," I said, blindly following my instinct, not quite understanding what I meant but from the look on Gram's face I knew I was onto something. "*You* shouldn't have kept it from her."

"Mama gave me this ring because I was Daddy's favorite. I ain't got nothin' else from him but one of his old shirts that got all moths holes in it now."

"Then you shouldn't have promised it to Ma."

"I suppose that's true, but I felt for your ma so. I don't know why she could never see that. As soon as we met at the mill, I felt for her comin' from an orphanage. It reminded me of Mama havin' to leave the orphanage and then havin' her own aunt turn her away. I was tryin' to do for your ma what somebody should have done for my own."

"Well, then you should have done it because she needed somebody to do that for her. She needed it bad!" I stood and swiped Ma's postcard from the pile of mail and then I ripped it and crushed the pieces in my hands.

Gram squinted. "What's got into you, girl? What are you all hot about? Somethin' goin' on I don't know about?"

I opened my hands and let the pieces of postcard drop from them. Gram stood and looked into my eyes with as much concern and kindness as Auntie used to.

"Ma's daddy touched her," I said, the words falling heavy off my tongue, they were so difficult to say. "He touched her the way a daddy's not supposed to touch. That's why her stepma sent her away. To save Ma from him. To keep her from getting touched." I crossed my arms and squeezed as if I could cradle the place in my heart that had been hurting all these months since I'd found out what had happened to Ma.

I met Gram's eyes and saw in them some of my own pain. For several moments we stood there frozen until all of the tears and rage I'd been holding on to for so long came out of me in bawling wails.

Gram grabbed me to her and rocked me. "That ain't your fault, girl. You hear me? It ain't your ma's neither. Let's just pray one day she knows that. Let's pray one day she can let it go."

"I think somehow she blames me for what's happened to her," I cried.

"Nah. Your ma's just got so much hurt inside her she don't know who she is without it. That's all you're feelin'. That hurt pushin' out from her." Gram gripped my chin, forcing me to look right at her. "You listen to me, love is like anythin' else in this world. People do it the best they can. Took me a lifetime to figure that out. Your ma loves you best she's able, you can be sure of that. You hear? Hear?"

Mrs. Schwackhammer pounded at the door demanding to know what awful thing had happened but Gram ignored her, repeating, "Hear? Hear?" until I nodded.

Twenty-eight

We were all home the day Ma pulled into the drive. Gram immediately went to her room and shut the door. Daddy charged outside and I hid behind the aspidistra plant on the porch and watched and listened to them through the row of open windows.

Daddy didn't even give Ma a chance to get out of the car. He swung open the door, yanked her out, and kissed her while she leaned up against the car.

"That don't change nothin'," Ma said when they parted.

"That changes everything," Daddy said.

"Nah, it don't. Anyways alls I come back for is some of my things."

"If you wanted to hurt me, Dolores, you did. If that's what all this was about, you got what you wanted."

"Not everything is about you, Adrian. You might as well know I got me someone. He says he'll take care of me the rest of my life.

I'll never want for nothing he says. You couldn't do that, Adrian. You couldn't even if you tried."

Ma finished her speech and stepped around the car so that the trunk was between her and Daddy. Even from the distance I was at I could tell she was breathing hard and I knew without even being able to see them that her eyes were as bright and as hard as river rocks. Her chin was raised in challenge. It was obvious to me that she'd been hot to get to this moment for a long time.

It must have been obvious to Daddy too and he set his jaw the way that sometimes worked on her. "No one knows you better than I do, Dolores. No one understands better what it's like to have memories you can't live with."

"That don't matter no more. You was right, Adrian, when you told me all those years ago not to marry you. That you had something broke inside that nothing in this whole world could fix. I don't know what happened to you that day down there in the mine and that don't matter anymore neither."

Slowly Daddy made his way around the car and as he moved he spoke: "No one's ever going to make you happy, Dolores. Can't you see that? Not this guy. Not someone else."

With each step that Daddy took forward, Ma took a step back. "Maybe so. But I got to try."

"I loved you more than anything else in the world," Daddy said. "But I don't think you ever believed it, did you? What else do you want from me, Dolores? What?" Daddy stopped when he reached the spot where Ma had been standing when he started moving toward her. Ma had back-stepped all the way around to the front of the car and was now in the backyard, near the catalpa tree.

"Nothing, Adrian," she said. "That's my point."

"Then I guess this is so long, Dolores," Daddy said, and you could just hear the plea and hurt in his words.

"Then I guess it is."

"I'm going to leave now, Dolores. And I'm not going to chase after you and I'm not going to beg you to come back. But you'll always have a home here with us. We'll always be your family, no matter where you go or what you do. You know that, don't you? There's nothing that could ever happen that could change that."

Ma scratched at her eye like a gnat had flown into it, but I suspected she was swatting away tears. Daddy always knew how to reach the soft places inside her no matter how hard she tried to pretend that he didn't.

Daddy turned and started walking toward the street and I suppose he must have wanted Ma to call him back, but he also must have known her well enough to know she wouldn't. Maybe he even knew those would be the last words they'd ever say to each other. From the way he stopped when he reached the curb and looked back I think he must have sensed that he needed to see Ma one more time and from the way he cradled his bad arm, I think he must have been feeling how close the curse was to us at that moment, closer than it had ever been before. I felt it too and shivered where I stood behind the plant. But there was only so long Daddy could stand at the curb looking back. Then there was nothing left for him to do, but to do what he'd said. He had to go and not ask her to stay and so he walked forward into the cracked and dipping street and didn't look back again.

As soon as he was out of sight I pressed my face to the screen. I could see Ma walking alongside the house peering in windows and I was reminded of Ma in Stepma's kitchen plucking spoons off the spoon rack and dropping them into her bag. All at once I felt a rush of hate for her, having all of Daddy's love and not wanting it. When she turned the corner to the back of the house, I darted out the front and crept to the car, expecting to find Brother asleep on the backseat but instead I found only a couple of crayons and a coloring book.

"Ain't you gonna say hello?" I heard.

I turned and there was Ma. We were the same height, five feet four and a half, and we stood maybe a foot apart, eyes locked on each other.

"Huh?" she said again with the teasing smile she used as a cover for whenever she was feeling uncomfortable.

"Where's Brother?" I said.

Ma didn't answer. She broke stare and turned to the house with a kind of stunned look on her face.

"Ma." I gripped her arm. "Where is he? What did you do with him?"

"Jesus Christ, Brigid!" Ma shook off my hand. "What do you think? I'd dump him in some orphanage somewheres? Chrissakes, I'd rather leave him on the street!"

Ma swung open the car door, grabbed some leftover sandwich that was heating up on the dashboard, and threw it into the drive for the birds to peck. A starling immediately flew to the ground and in moments a whole flock of them was there, pulling at the bread, ripping it away from one another.

Ma shook out a cigarette from the pack she'd left on the passenger seat. "I left him with Louie. He's got a room upstairs from us, him and his little boy do." She lit the cigarette and then with her sharp little pinky nail picked at something stuck to her lip. "Quit lookin' at me like that. Alls we're doing is helping each other out. I have a right to some help. Ain't nothin' wrong with that."

Ma swerved her head to take in the abandoned houses across the street. Her hushed voice came off awestruck. "Driving in I couldn't believe how bad it all looks. Makes you think of Revelations. I wouldn't be surprised to see the four horseguys come riding out of them clouds up there." Ma gazed up at the three puffy white clouds hanging low in the creamy blue September sky.

"That's right, Ma. It *is* bad. Where are you living? Is Brother all right? Is there room for me?"

"Now I just told you about Louie. You're getting to be a young lady now. Louie's a stranger to you. Wouldn't be proper for him to stop by for a visit if you was there. A man's a man, after all. Can't blame him for what he is."

"But you blame Daddy."

"You're too young to understand. Your daddy's just your daddy to you. You don't know what it's like. A husband needs to be"—Ma inhaled and slowly exhaled—"much more. You know, you was always so close to your daddy, wondering what he went through down in that mine. But you never thought about me like that, what I went through that day they sent me to the orphanage, did you?"

I looked away. I didn't want Ma to see the place inside me that was as stark as the woodlands in the fire zone. It was the place where I'd failed her as a daughter and a friend. Truth was I'd never wanted to get that close to Ma.

Ma tossed her cigarette onto the drive and left it there burning. "Anyways, I got some things I need to get." Then she swung open the porch door, letting it slam shut, which I guessed meant she thought Gram wasn't home. She walked through the living room picking up this or that statue or vase and I kept fast on her heels. When she went to fondle some of the objects on Gramp's altar on the mantel, I stepped right up behind her.

"Good God, Brigid!" she shouted. "I ain't gonna steal nothing. You don't got to keep following me around."

I stepped back and gave her some space as she went into Daddy's childhood bedroom. She stood there, looking around the room dazed, as if everything about it had changed, when all that was different was that it was a mess. Then she opened the closet and started picking out clothes of hers that she wanted to take. She made me think of the starlings pecking the bread outside. She made me think of "The Great Forgetting" and the child who got chained to a mountainside for giving the people what they'd asked for but didn't want.

"Maybe you should take Stepma's offer to go live with her, Ma," I said. "Maybe it would be the best thing for Brother. Maybe she was trying to do right by you all along."

"What do you know about right from wrong? The world's a screwed up place, Brigid. Sometimes right ain't possible to do."

"But that doesn't mean you have to do wrong."

"Well, what in the heck do it mean then?" Ma sat down on the little wooden chair and rubbed at her forehead with the heel of her palm. "Is this the way things is going to be between us? I was hoping for better."

"So was I."

"You got some mouth. But I guess I can see where you'd get that from." Ma did her playful smile and I looked away. This was how Ma always turned me to her when she'd hurt me in the past and I wasn't going to let her do it this time.

Ma pointed at the mattress. "Just sit down for chrissakes, Brigid. You're making me nervous standing there staring at me." Ma's glance sliced into me, then out. Her gaze softened. "Remember when you used to ask how my heart got broke?"

My eyes widened, wanting to take in as much of Ma as possible. I had asked Ma that question too many times to count, but I hadn't asked it since before Auntie died and never once had Ma brought up talking about it on her own.

"Do you remember?" Ma asked as if I could have possibly forgotten that long-ago moment when Brother took his first steps and something within Ma changed for the worse.

"Every time you asked about it," Ma continued, "I'd tell you the same thing—that my heart had forgot it was broke but then it remembered. But I never told you *what* it remembered."

Ma met my gaze straight on and I sat down on the mattress. She continued, "We was sitting in the trailer, you remember?"

I nodded. "We were playing tiddlywinks," I said. "And Daddy was lying on the cot in the living room telling stories about the tiddlywinks queen and princess."

Ma smiled, surprised I had remembered it that keenly. "That's right," she said. "We was just playing a game but for some reason I remember being struck by the fact that you was the same age I was when I got sent off to the orphanage. I was just sitting there thinking that when all of a sudden John Patrick stood up and took his first step. Then he took another, then another, and right then I saw it. I saw it as if I was reliving it all over again. There I was outside the house in Loppsville. I was in the car with Stepma. I had my stuffed bunny rabbit and cloth doll Abigail on my lap. We was going on a trip, that's what Stepma had told me, but I was nervous because there was only one suitcase. 'Are Daddy and Bropey going?' I said. 'They'll join us later,' she said and I believed her, even though I wondered how they'd do that when we had the car. Daddy and Bropey stood on the porch waving and then as we started driving away Bropey ran down the steps toward us, crying and screaming for me. Somehow he knew better than I did what was about to happen."

Ma's eyes blinked with dryness. "I guess seeing John Patrick stumbling toward me, crying, brought me back to my little Bropey running toward me. It wasn't long after that I started remembering other stuff. Just pieces here and there. But before I had that memory of Stepma taking me away, I didn't remember much at all. Before that I used to figure my stepma must have snuck me out of the house 'cause how else would my daddy have let her take me away?"

Ma tilted her head and gazed up at the ceiling in recollection. "There was this nice nun there in the orphanage. Sister Joseph Thomas was her name. I asked her once why God had let my stepma dump me in an orphanage and she said that God's will was mysterious and we must not question it but must do the best with what we were given. And it was right then I decided I didn't want another thing to do with a god like that. I mean, who in the heck is he to decide I should get sent off to an orphanage? Why do I got to make the best out of *that*?"

My eyes shifted off Ma's face. "Do you think of your daddy when you look at me?"

"Sometimes. You got this way of looking at things that makes your face resemble his. But you ain't nothin' like him, Brigid. You got a heart so big, I bet we could all live inside it. I bet you'd let us live in it too. I'll tell you there ain't many people who'd do that. You're"—Ma paused and slowly pronounced—"extraordinary. And don't you ever forget it."

"How could I, Ma? You already live in my heart."

Ma leaned forward and brushed a strand of hair from where it lingered near my eye. "From the time you was born I could tell you was what gets called a wise soul and I got afraid for you. I got afraid as soon as I saw that wiseness in your eyes. I got afraid for all you'd wind up having to see and know to earn the wiseness you already had inside you."

There was the sound of clinking china from the kitchen. "Shit," Ma whispered, looking at her watch. "Shouldn't she be at the mill?"

"She had her shift switched to the early one," I said.

And as Ma stuffed her clothes into one of the boxes we'd taken from Auntie's I considered telling her why Gram had had her shift switched, but I didn't. I didn't want to hear Ma dismiss the Great Idea as stupid or impossible and I didn't want to give her any additional ammunition against Gram. I watched Ma awkwardly clutch the box to her chest and I thought she'd head straight through the living room and out the porch, to avoid Gram. But she didn't. She turned into the kitchen.

"Ain't you hurt the girl enough?" Gram said from where she sat at the kitchen table.

"If I was you, Rowena, I wouldn't go sitting in no judgment lest you want to start getting judged."

"Believe it or not, I was hopin' you'd come back," Gram said.

"Don't take it the wrong way, Rowena, but I don't believe it."

Gram's reading glasses were hanging from a beaded string around her neck. There were papers for the Great Idea in front of her. She pointed at the other end of the table. "Put the box down. I have somethin' for you."

Ma gave me a look like, You believe *this*? But she plunked the box down and said, "Hope you're not planning on hitting me 'cause I'd have to sock you back."

Gram slid her grandma's ring off her finger and offered it to Ma. "If I gave you this now, would it change nothin'?"

Ma eyes glittered as brightly as the ring. "I ain't coming back, if that's what you mean."

Gram stood and walked toward Ma. "I ain't tryin' to bribe you to come back. You listen here. This ring was my daddy's mama's. I treasure it. But you can have it, if it'd mean somethin' to you, Dolores. If my givin' it might change somethin' about how you feel"— Gram tapped between Ma's breasts—"in here."

Ma swallowed and she leaned closer to the ring that Gram held pinched between two fingers, but she still didn't touch it. It almost seemed like Ma was afraid to touch it.

"Nah," Ma said. "You keep it, old lady, and every time you look at it you remember how mean you was to me." But Ma's voice didn't deliver the way she wanted. She lowered her eyes and you could just see her whole body go limp. Ma added, "When Brigid's old enough you let her have the ring, you hear? That'll be like a gift from both of us, Brigid. You remember that."

Then Ma clasped the box to her chest and nodded at me to open the door. She stepped out and headed down the path to the drive and as I moved to follow, Gram gripped my arm. "You remember what I said. All she can do is love the best she can. That's all you can 'spect from her, girl. For the rest of her life, for the rest of yours."

At the car me and Ma hugged. She got into the driver's seat and shut the door. The window was partway open and I placed my hands on the edge of the glass, gripping it like it was a ledge.

"You got to let me go now, Brigid. I'll be late. I got to get back. When I get a phone, I'll call. That's all I can do right now." Ma started the car and shifted it into reverse. "That's all I can do," she repeated.

"I'm afraid of what's going to happen, Ma. To Daddy and to me. To all of us."

"We all are, Brigid. That's what life is. Now come on." She put her arm behind the empty passenger seat and looked behind her, preparing to back down the drive. "Come on now, Brigid. You're making me late. I got to get moving."

She waited to press the accelerator, sensing the moment when I lifted my hands and let go.

Twenty-nine

Within hours of Ma's leaving I got a bad feeling, the worst I'd ever had, and in my mind flashed a vision of Daddy on the uppermost ledge of the East Side Pit. I saw him in a swirl of steam standing with the dead deer and dogs and coons and cats that had fallen in and died there. The more I tried to dismiss the image, the stronger it got until there was nothing left for me to do but go and find him.

I took a flashlight because dusk had begun its slow creep up the hill and as I swung the beam back and forth, looking for fissures and sinkholes along the path, I was surprised by how many asters and everlastings sprung out from the silty cracks. Dozens of beetles and spiders skittered away from my light and made me guess that even if Russia did drop the bomb on us, little bits of nature would still cling on.

When I reached the pit, I took my time scanning the various shelves and ledges that had been created by the men as they dug it deeper and deeper. The topmost ledge was only maybe ten yards or so down the slope of the pit, but at times the steam and smoke was so thick I could barely see. Worse, occasionally flames shot out from caverns farther below and momentarily blinded me, spotting the back of my eyelids with shooting stars of light. Still, I didn't find any trace of Daddy, only the heated carcasses of whatever animals had had the misfortune to fall in.

Looking down into that pit got me feeling unsteady on my feet. There was a pinkish glow to the air from all the heaps of burning coal and it started to feel like even the pink air was on fire—it was so hot and seemed to flicker before my very eyes. I started to feel like I was on fire; there was a feverish heat to my skin. Every now and then I thought I saw Father Capedonico, hovering just on the edge of my sight. His image wavered like he was made of steam and I didn't know if he was the curse out to get us or my mind playing tricks on me. Then I recalled what Marisol had said about curses coming from ignorant spirits who could be banished by a stronger spirit. I shouted, "I'm not afraid of you! You need to go back where you belong. We've paid our price. You've had more than your just revenge."

I wiped my forehead and waited. I shined my flashlight in every direction but the priest didn't appear and I wondered if that was what Auntie had meant about the curse being inside us. Maybe she'd meant that the power to get rid of it was inside us, not the curse itself.

I'd completed my walk around the pit and as I meandered further into the zone I saw old Mrs. Novak on a stoop that wasn't attached to a house. Her greasy skin and hair caught the pinkish light and gave her an eerie kind of halo.

As I passed she said, "Rowena liked to think that Frank of

hers was God's gift, but he was a little bastard. I saw that the first time I laid eyes on him. He'd a done anything to save his own skin."

There was a glaze to her stare that told me she knew something I didn't and it was right then I understood that it hadn't been my mind tricking me into seeing the priest, but the priest tricking me into believing the curse was going to strike in the pit. It was then I ran, cutting through yard after abandoned yard, side-stepping boreholes and sinkholes like I had an instinct for them, like I had the magical quality Daddy used to say we had. Like I *could* actually walk on fire or air.

As I reached the front walk, Detective Kanelous came out the door. He stood in the yellow light cast from the kitchen window and pressed his lips together. His big orangey cat eyes were tinged with sorrow and made me dread what lay in wait for me behind the shut front door.

"If you ever need something, you remember you can come to me," he said. Then we both turned because we heard Daddy and Gram yelling at each other from inside the house. "Maybe you should wait before you go in," he said. "Give them a few minutes."

Still breathless from the run, I shook my head.

He touched my arm. "Good luck, Brigid," he said and it seemed such a strange thing to say and so full of its own kind of bleakness that it made the feeling of dread go all hollow inside me. I opened the door as quietly as possible and crossed through the kitchen, avoiding the spots that creaked.

"Least I now know it was Frank, not Dad, who killed Sully," Daddy said from where he and Gram faced each other by Gramp's altar on the mantel. "Least I know there were some things Dad wasn't willing to do for him."

They hadn't noticed me come in. And I stayed, hardly daring to breathe, a few feet back from the living-room entryway.

"Well, he must a had a good reason to do what he done," Gram said. "We can't know what was in his heart."

"Good reason?" Daddy said. "Kanelous just told you the reason. *I* told you the reason. When Sully found out Frank took bribes to say the mines were safe, he tried to blackmail Frank so Frank killed him. Joe at The Shaft heard them. He *heard* Sully tell Frank he wanted a thousand dollars. He *heard* Frank say he'd kill him before he'd give him a dime. That was the same night Sully disappeared. *That* was Frank's good reason. Keeping all his bribe money to himself!"

"You're like a scratched record, Adrian, playin' the same words over and over. I don't care 'bout no bribes or blackmail."

"I know you don't. But what *do* you care about, Mother? Do you care to know that your sweet, wonderful Frank, the apple of your eye, tried to kill his own brother?"

I must have made a sound and they both turned. Daddy's eyes were as crazy as old Mrs. Novak and he looked as wild as the werewolf poster that used to hang beside his bed.

Daddy cradled his head with his hands. "And I loved him so, but he never believed it. And I tried not to do it, I tried." Daddy lowered his hands and stared at them as if he didn't recognize them as his own. Then he gripped his bad arm and held it like he was in the worst pain I'd ever seen.

Gram pressed her hands to her ears and wildly shook her head.

Daddy squeezed his arm. "I went down there to help him. To tell him it wasn't too late. He could still do right by the men. He could still get them out. But then he did *this* to me." Daddy let go

of his arm and looked down at it like it was as mauled and bloodied as Father Capedonico's arm had been. "He would have killed
me if I hadn't—"

"Don't tell me!" Gram shouted, pulling at her ears as if she
could pull them from her head. "Alls I got is my memory of him.
Don't take that away too!" She lunged toward Daddy but Daddy
sidestepped and bolted past her and out the porch door.

Dazed, Gram walked off into her room and I walked onto the
porch to stare at West Mountain that had an odd almost greenish
tint to its smoke, similar to the color the sky turned when a tornado was brewing. Staring at that greenish glow put me in mind
of crazy old Mrs. Novak's words and in a sort of senseless rush I
replayed all the various things I'd heard Daddy say about Uncle
Frank and the mines and the day of the disaster. It felt like I was
coming toward an understanding that had been waiting for me to
come to it, practically all my life. It felt like I was dropping down
into the endless blackness of the bootlegging hole all over again,
but this time what I'd discover would be worse than finding my
best friend's dead daddy. It would be the worst thing I'd ever in
my heart hope to find.

Flashlight in hand, I rushed out onto the lawn and into the
cracked and splintered street. I wasted no time getting to The Shaft.
The entire sidewalk was roped off though, so I was forced to enter
through its back door. As soon as I stepped through, I saw Star.
Her gaze slowly went down the length of my body before mean-
dering its way back up. Bear was standing next to her and when
he leaned to whisper in her ear, she pushed him away, saying, "I
told you, I ain't talking to you till you apologize."

Joe stepped out from behind the bar and steered me right back
out the door. We stood in the side lot and Joe told me that Daddy

had just been in and had left. Joe gripped my shoulder and lowered his head to talk against my ear. "I should never have told the cops what I heard that day. I just figured Sully's wife and girl had a right to know. That's all I was thinking." Joe's breath was hot and felt sticky on my skin. "Frank and Sully had been dead so long, you understand? That's all I was thinking. The girl and the wife should know. But your daddy came in here talking crazy. He said *he* killed Frank. You need to get him home before he does something he'll—" But Joe didn't finish the statement. He just stared down at the dirt beneath our feet.

Fast I circled round the building and slipped underneath the rope that blocked off the sidewalk. In just a few steps I was at the lip of the pit. The air was an even brighter pink now that the night was darker and I saw Daddy right away. He was there on one of the upper ledges, just like I'd seen in my vision. Steam and smoke whirled around him and there was what looked like a dead German shepherd at his feet.

"Daddy?" I called, but he didn't seem to hear me. The slope down to the ledge was rocky, jagged with tree roots that in the eerie pink light seemed to shift and move. I searched for the best place to make my way down, but since no one spot looked better than any other, I sat where I stood, my legs dangling over the edge.

"Girl! You crazy?" I heard Joe shout. "Get back up here!"

Quick, I turned around and started backing down the slope the way I would down a ladder, but I lost footing and slid several yards, jarring my hip against a boulder. Dirt and gravel rained down, pelting my eyes and making it impossible to see if Joe was coming after me.

"Daddy?" I shouted, glancing to where he'd been on the ledge and not finding him there. I reached for a tree trunk that stuck out from the slope like a gigantic battered limb and found sure footing. Still in a crawl position, I kept backing down. The slope gradually began leveling out and it wasn't long before I finally reached the ledge.

The heat was fierce. "Daddy?" I called as I walked in the direction he'd been. Ahead of me something appeared to be rising up out of the mist but as I stared at it, I saw that it was only an old icebox that someone had chucked down the slope.

I wiped my face on my sleeve, not sure if it was raining or if my skin was soaked from the damp of the steam.

"Brigid!" I heard, and there was Daddy, only a few feet from me, as if he'd just formed out of the smoky air. Daddy looked sicker than I'd ever seen him. The skin on his face sagged like it was melting. Littered at our feet were some broken brown bottles and part of a cat.

"My God, you shouldn't have come down here," he said, and for the first time in my life I saw fear blacken his eyes.

An explosion from farther down below shook us and a roar of hot air blasted up from the mouth of the pit. "I think it wants us," I cried and Daddy nodded. We held each other and I squeezed his waist as if I could find what I needed to say somewhere within his bones. When I finally spoke I didn't know where the words came from or how I knew the truth they held. "Daddy, you didn't mean to kill your brother and hide him in that monkey shaft. You did it to save your life."

"So what?" he said and stepped away from me. "That doesn't make it right." He turned toward the pit and gazed down at the smoke-filled abyss as if he were looking for something within it.

I searched his face for clues of what to say next. I knew I

needed to speak from the place his love had formed inside me, but that place was aching and silent. In desperation I repeated Ma's words to me, "Sometimes right ain't possible." But soon as I said it my mouth went stiff. "I love you, Daddy," I said. "No matter what you've done. No matter what you'll ever do."

Daddy's eyes nearly squinted shut from the smoke. My own eyes teared uncontrollably.

"You're meant for better than this world can give, princess," he said. "Don't ever forget that." Daddy pressed me hard to him and it took us a few moments to realize someone was calling down. We stared up through the clouds of steam that were flecked with coal ash and cinders and for a moment could make out a blurred face and a waving hand.

"Joe saw me—" I said but couldn't finish the sentence because of a coughing fit.

"Pull your shirt up over your mouth," Daddy instructed, turning his head and pulling his collar up to the bridge of his nose so he could breathe through the cloth. I did the same, telling myself that none of this was real, that me and Daddy were outlaws, like the type we saw in TV Western shows, bandits with handkerchiefs tied across our faces, but my eyes and throat stung so bad that pretending got me nowhere. Through a sliver of opened eyelid I watched a fireman climb down to us by holding on to a rope. As soon as the man reached the ledge Daddy pushed me toward him. "Take my girl," he pleaded as if the man had come down for some other reason than to rescue us.

The fireman crouched and told me to ride him piggyback with my arms looped round his neck. "Hold on tight," he said and before I could say anything else to Daddy, me and the man started up the gentlest part of the slope. "Daddy?" I called, looking back over my shoulder.

He waved to me. "Hold on, princess. Hold on with all your might!"

The fireman grunted and snorted and snuffled like a wild, angry animal. "You're doing good," he'd call out to me each time he had to heave us up and over a particularly dangerous crag. My arms grew so tired that more than once I pictured myself letting go and tumbling backwards into the abyss. My brain must have gone sick from the smoke and the fumes because I started to imagine that the pit was merely the pothole in Pothole Park. Sometimes I pictured it as the sinkhole that swallowed Auntie. By the time someone pulled me off the fireman's back and stood me on solid ground, I was confused as to where I was and what had happened. It took a few minutes of listening to sirens and staring at fire truck lights to snap me back into the moment.

Someone had wrapped a blanket round me and was trying to guide me to an ambulance, but I refused to budge. "Daddy," I said.

"The fireman went right back down to get your daddy, sweetheart," the person said.

But it took so long for Daddy and the fireman to come back up that two more firemen went down. I could hear the shouts of the firemen calling back and forth to each other but no one would tell me what was going on.

"Daddy?" I yelled. "Daddy!" But my throat was so coated with ash and soot that I don't think anyone could hear me.

Night turned into morning and morning into afternoon. I'd been to the hospital and back, and by the time the sun sank behind

West Mountain, me and Gram had been sitting on the front stoop of The Shaft for hours, watching firemen and volunteers make their way down to the ledge of the pit to search for Daddy.

Mr. Gilpin, the fire chief, had been over to talk to us twice already but there was something in the tense, hunched way he approached us this time that told me he wouldn't be coming over to speak to us again.

"I'm sorry to report, Mrs. Howley, that our search into the pit is through."

Gram's expression hadn't changed since she'd arrived. All her features had gone slack with the shock of everything that had happened in the last twenty-four hours and she looked older than the hills surrounding us. "You found him?" she said.

"No, ma'am. Sorry to report." And his eyes cut apologetically toward me, then lowered to the ground.

"So then what?" Gram said. Her gaze stuck to the same spot of ground the fire chief stared at. "He fell in?"

"It's a possibility, Mrs. Howley."

"Jumped then?" Gram's voice jumped slightly as she said it.

The fire chief made the sign of the cross. "God willing, he did not."

Slowly Gram's eyes moved from the ground to the fire chief's face. "What are you sayin', Mr. Gilpin? And remember I known you since you was a boy and sprinkled dirt on both your mama's and daddy's coffins. I 'spect you to be straight with me, with me *and* the girl, and tell us the truth."

"Yes, ma'am. What I mean to say is, it's a long ledge. It goes clear across to the other side of the pit. He might have climbed up somewhere along the way and with all the steam and smoke—" Mr. Gilpin shrugged.

"I don't get what you're sayin'," Gram said. "That he just done walked off and left us?"

Mr. Gilpin sucked his teeth in a sort of whistle. "That's just what I'm saying, Mrs. Howley. We don't know."

And then he tried again to explain what might have happened, but I'd stopped listening. In my mind I was tall tale-telling with Daddy. We were back in Centrereach at Culver Lake, like we used to do so many summers ago, drifting into the water lilies, telling stories about the lake ladies who swam below us, trying to catch us up in the duckweed and turn our souls into liquid amber. Dripping, we walked up onto the shore and waved to Auntie who sat knitting in the shade of the willow trees. Daddy and me collapsed on the beach blanket as I told him about all the things I used to tell him about before we moved to Barrendale, before our lives got eaten away by fire, by the past, by our hate and love.

In my mind, I kept talking to him even after all the firemen and ambulance workers left and me and Gram were driven home in the back of a police car. I kept talking because I wanted to believe that wherever Daddy was, he was back to the way he used to be, to the Daddy he was when I was little—when the dark part of him was the smallest part and nothing made him happier than hearing what I had to say.

EPILOGUE

For nearly five years we've been living up on what's called the East Mountain Plateau but what everyone around here just calls The Ridge. The house sits high on the foundation Gram had built for it. We've got a view of most of Barrendale and face West Mountain, which still steams and smokes like it might one day turn into the volcano we all suspect it once upon a time was. I don't think anyone from around here would be shocked to see it erupt coal chunks and sulfur fumes.

Up on The Ridge we got a little creek and any number of apple and pear trees that bloom and fruit and shed their leaves all when they're supposed to. The street has never cracked or shifted once. The birdcalls deafen us and each winter we're amazed by how long snow lingers. That's what living in the fire zone does to you. Makes the mundane marvelous and the extraordinary humdrum. I guess in a way you could say that was its gift. We'll always see the world different from most. As Gram and me have come to understand, you learn a different kind of instinct when your feet tread on hollow ground.

It's been more than five years now since we lost Daddy. That's how me and Gram refer to it since we never found out anything additional about what happened to him. We hammered a wooden cross into the ground beneath one of the apple trees to mark his final resting place because, though we don't speak of it, we both know in our hearts he's dead. I reckon Gram also knows, just as I do, that it was facing up to what he'd done to Uncle Frank that struck the mortal blow. Gram's got some of that facing-up going on herself. Detective Kanelous had to close the investigation into William Sullivan's murder, but he said he had "probable cause to believe" Uncle Frank had done it. Gram said that meant she had "probable cause to believe" he hadn't, but I think those were just empty words because not a Sunday in Lent passes without her voicing regrets over how she'd treated Daddy and Uncle Frank as boys. Every now and then she ends those regrets with: "If I'd felt different 'bout each of them maybe . . ." But she always leaves that "maybe" dangling, wanting, I guess, to leave all of its possibilities open.

Marisol and me are friends again. She felt bad for the way Daddy disappeared and she came to the house with the prayer cards and holy oils her grandfather had sent for me to get rid of the curse. So far, ever since, only good luck has followed. Due to Detective Kanelous's help, Gram saw her Great Idea come to pass and was able to pay for the move and all the house repairs because the government finally came through with the money they owed us for Auntie's house in Centrereach.

Often Gram likes to talk about seeing what she calls "the Great Idea come to life." She likes to describe the house gliding down the hill on the back of a flatbed truck, just as she'd seen it in her vision. She especially likes to comment on how smooth the ride was, noting that the aspidistra plant remained in exactly the same position on the porch during the entire trip. That plant remains in that spot on the porch to this day, only a stone's throw from Mrs. Schwackhammer's house, which was moved on that same truck the following morning, trailing ivy vines behind it. Mrs. Schwack-hammer has since rooted those vines and her house is once again wrapped around with the ivy she'd planted more than half a century ago from her bridal bouquet. We were especially lucky that both houses got moved because soon after the Redevelopment Authority refused anyone else's applications, claiming the paperwork involved was slowing the demolition process. But we all knew they just didn't want to be bothered with the hassle.

The fire beneath the west side of Barrendale still burns and the dig out continues. Some say it will take another five years to dig it out. Some say ten. It's already forced more than a thousand people out of their homes and destroyed more than a hundred and twenty acres of houses and streets and landmarks that will now only exist in photos and memory. After they finish digging the fire out and fill in all the trenches, the west side will be just one huge flat piece of land in an otherwise jagged landscape because even its telltale slopes and dips and hills will be gone.

Though it's only been five years since we lost Daddy, Ma's been with three different guys. If this one doesn't stick she says she's off men altogether. It doesn't matter to me really either way. I just want what's best for Brother, who Ma keeps switching from school to school to avoid him getting left back or suspended. Slow and subtle I'm working on Gram to let Brother come live with us. Soon I think she'll give in, even though she's worried we can't handle whatever problems he's probably now got worse than he had before. But deep down Gram's got a good heart. She's actually encouraging me to save enough money to move to New York City's Greenwich Village, even though she calls it Hedonland. "Still," she says, "it's your dream and dreams is best lived than remembered."

It's both my and Marisol's dream and we're pulling extra shifts after school and on the weekends working the cash registers at the Hi-Lo to make it happen. We've turned into what people call hippies. We read Ginsberg and Kerouac and sport peasant skirts and love beads. We do yoga and wear peace signs and work hard on acceptance. Marisol is working hard to accept that her daddy might have loved her if he'd had the chance, and I'm close to accepting that I couldn't have done anything to make Ma love me better or to put peace into Daddy's heart. We all walk our own path, as people say. And we walk it alone. All I can do now is wish Ma and Daddy the best life and death can offer. And I do wish them that. I especially wish Daddy that, wherever he is now.

Gram says she feels like she's a hundred and one. "And I'm nowhere near that!" But she looks it. She and Mrs. Schwackhammer resemble dried-up scarecrows sitting out on one or the other's porch, wrapped in blankets, staring off at West Mountain while they shell peas or crack nuts or crochet or braid rugs. Or they just sit there rocking hard as if the rocking itself has got a purpose. They inevitably complain about this or that person who's moved on to The Ridge or gossip about ladies from the mill or bicker about the best way to clean a chicken or cook a pot roast.

Today we're all sitting out on Gram's closed-in side porch to celebrate my eighteenth birthday. Marisol gave me a fringed vest, the color of which is the same green as her eyes as we sit beside the aspidistra plant. Mrs. Schwackhammer gave me an empty book to use, she said, as a diary or what-have-you. And Gram presented me with two gifts, both ones I'll cherish the rest of my life. One is the clay pipe that was Gramp's granddaddy's, the Molly. And the other is Gram's grandma's ring, the one Ma had wanted for so long that when she finally got it, she couldn't bear its sight. That's what wanting does, I guess. It takes away everything, even the pleasure of getting the thing you wanted in the first place.

Gram and Mrs. Schwackhammer are sitting in rockers, stringing the last of the garden's beans and dropping them whole into bowls by their feet. I've got my clay pipe lit and clenched between my teeth, my ring shooting bits of rainbow onto the wall. It's Indian summer. The trees up on this end of The Ridge have all turned gold and umber, ginger and crimson. The porch is warm but Gram and Mrs. Schwackhammer are bundled. Marisol and I are in our favorite skirts and sandals. Holding back our nearly waist-length hair are flower headbands made of aster and yarrow that we wove ourselves. The headbands have launched Gram onto one of her favorite tirades about flower children and what she calls "this godforsaken generation."

Gram holds a bean string up in the air as if it's something worth pondering and then she offers all sorts of condemnations against pot and girls crazy enough not to wear bras. She's just getting up steam. The floorboards creak under the rhythmic weight of her rocker. Shading her eyes is a large-brimmed straw hat and when she lifts her head the afternoon sun cuts half her face in shadow. She's on to the evils of communes and the pill now. She's rocking hard like she intends to lift off into outer space. She's talking loud enough for her voice to echo back and forth off East and West mountains. "Free love?" she declares. "My left foot! Why, love ain't free. It costs and costs. . . ."

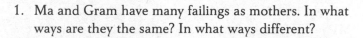

1. Ma and Gram have many failings as mothers. In what ways are they the same? In what ways different?

2. Daddy tells Brigid that Gram and Ma fight so much not because they hate each other, but because they love each other. He says that one of them has got to give the love first and they're each too stubborn to do it. "So they hold on to the love for each other and it turns all ugly inside them." How accurate is Daddy's assessment of Gram and Ma's relationship? Is there any truth to his words?

3. Ma and Daddy are greatly influenced by their pasts. Memories and repressed memories—what they remember, what they don't remember, as well as what they misremember—shape who they are. Discuss how all these different types of memories contribute to how they perceive themselves and others.

4. In many ways *The Hollow Ground* is a story of survival. How well would you say Brigid survives? Do you think she has a chance at being happy in her adult life? Do you think this is also a story of survival for Ma?

5. In some ways Gram is a champion of women's rights. In other ways she subverts them. Discuss how she does both.

6. How does the author use the fire to help tell the story of this family?

7. Discuss the ways the novel explores the nature of love between a parent and child. Are there any limitations to that love?

8. *The Hollow Ground* could be viewed as a cautionary tale about what happens when we delve underground. Do you think mine fires such as the one that took place in Barrendale could serve as an argument against other environmental issues of concern such as fracking or oil drilling?

Discussion Questions

St. Martin's Griffin

9. Do you think Stepma did the right thing by sending Ma away? Do you think Ma is capable of forgiving her? Why or why not?

10. How is Auntie's story "The Great Forgetting" meaningful to the novel as a whole?

Pre-Reading Activity

The Hollow Ground is inspired by real-life events in Centralia and Carbondale, Pennsylvania, where devastating coal mine fires irrevocably changed the lives of residents. Before reading *The Hollow Ground*, have students explore textbooks and the Internet to get some historical perspective on:

- Pennsylvania coal mining
- Northern Appalachian coal mine fires
- The Molly Maguires

Group Discussion Questions & Writing Assignments

1. In *The Hollow Ground* Brigid's story takes place in what's called a fire zone. How does this setting contribute to the story? Imagine a different setting. In what ways would this different setting change the story?

2. When Gram was young, Barrendale was a thriving city, a place Daddy described as a "little Philadelphia." What are the historical events that led to Barrendale's prosperity and what were the events that led to its demise? Using library resources and the Internet, research one of these events and discuss its effect on the American economy.

3. Daddy tells Brother that you can't judge a man for trying to "make a wrong situation right." Name some of the "wrong situations" to which Daddy could be referring. Choose one and create an argument defending whether or not this "wrong situation" could in fact be "made right." Based on your argument what would you say is your definition of "wrong"? What is your definition of "right"?

4. What is the message in Auntie's story "The Great Forgetting"? What details in the story convey this message? Write a story of your own that conveys a message. Be sure to use at least one of the techniques discussed in class such as description, dialogue, symbolism, irony, etc.

5. List some of the significant moments in Brigid's life. Choose one and, imagining that you are Brigid, write a journal entry describing your feelings.

6. Write a short newspaper article about Brigid's and her friends' discovery in the abandoned mine shaft. (Remember the journalistic formula of who, what, when, and where that we discussed in class.) Keep in mind that after making the discovery Brigid says that the community reacted with scorn or fear.

7. *The Hollow Ground* is a coming-of-age story. Describe the significant events that contribute to Brigid's "growing up." Why do you think they caused her to mature at such a young age?

8. What do you think happens to Daddy at the end of the book? Write a different ending to the last chapter of the novel. In what ways does this new ending change the story or the meaning of the novel as a whole?

Multimedia Activities

1. *The Hollow Ground* could be read as a cautionary tale of what happens when we delve underground. Using library resources and the Internet, research fracking or offshore oil drilling. Make sure you consider definition, purpose, and potential consequences. Once you've completed your research, use PowerPoint or Prezi to create a slideshow.

2. Using drawing materials or computer graphics, create 2 to 3 illustrations of the fire zone.

Additional Resources

- DeKok, David. *Fire Underground: The Ongoing Tragedy of the Centralia Mine Fire.* Globe Pequot Press, 2009.

- Munley, Kathleen Purcell. *The West Side Carbondale Pennsylvania Mine Fire.* University of Scranton Press, 2011.

- Dublin, Thomas. *When the Mines Closed: Stories of Struggles in Hard Times.* Cornell University, 1998.